Dark Destiny

For Arenadd, the journey through the shadows with Skandar was like using his own newly discovered gift—but a hundred times more powerful. This wasn't mere shielding. He clung on to his partner's back, feeling the massive strength beneath him; and despite the icy cold, despite the fact that he couldn't see anything around them but black void, he had never felt so powerful in his life.

But it was humbling, too. For the first time he was beginning to see the full extent of Skandar's power. It had brought him back from death, and now it was taking them all to freedom.

Unseen in the darkness, Arenadd began to smile. They had the power, and soon they would have a plan. The Night God's will would be done, and he and Skandar would take everything the world had denied them for so long.

Anyone who stood in their way would die.

D0963512

Ace Books by K. J. Taylor

The Fallen Moon

THE DARK GRIFFIN
THE GRIFFIN'S FLIGHT
THE GRIFFIN'S WAR

The Griffin's War

THE FALLEN MOON
BOOK THREE

K. J. TAYLOR

ACE BOOKS, NEW YORK

THE BERKLEY PUBLISHING GROUP
Published by the Penguin Group
Penguin Group (USA) Inc.
375 Hudson Street, New York, New York 10014, USA
Penguin Group (Canada), 90 Eglinton Avenue East, Suite 700, Toronto, Ontario M4P 2Y3, Canada
(a division of Pearson Penguin Canada Inc.)
Penguin Books Ltd., 80 Strand, London WC2R 0RL, England
Penguin Group Ireland, 25 St. Stephen's Green, Dublin 2, Ireland (a division of Penguin Books Ltd.)
Penguin Group (Australia), 250 Camberwell Road, Camberwell, Victoria 3124, Australia
(a division of Pearson Australia Group Pty. Ltd.)
Penguin Books India Pvt. Ltd., 11 Community Centre, Panchsheel Park, New Delhi—110 017, India
Penguin Group (NZ), 67 Apollo Drive, Rosedale, North Shore 0632, New Zealand
(a division of Pearson New Zealand Ltd.)
Penguin Books (South Africa) (Pty.) Ltd., 24 Sturdee Avenue, Rosebank, Johannesburg 2196,
South Africa

Penguin Books Ltd., Registered Offices: 80 Strand, London WC2R 0RL, England

This is a work of fiction. Names, characters, places, and incidents either are the product of the author's imagination or are used fictitiously, and any resemblance to actual persons, living or dead, business establishments, events, or locales is entirely coincidental. The publisher does not have any control over and does not assume any responsibility for author or third-party websites or their content.

THE GRIFFIN'S WAR

An Ace Book / published by arrangement with the author

PRINTING HISTORY
HarperCollins Australia mass-market edition / January 2010
Ace mass-market edition / March 2011

Copyright © 2010 by K. J. Taylor.
Maps by Allison Jones.
Welsh translation on page 166 by Janice Jones.
Cover art by Steve Stone.
Cover design by Judith Lagerman.
Interior text design by Kristin del Rosario.

All rights reserved.
No part of this book may be reproduced, scanned, or distributed in any printed or electronic form without permission. Please do not participate in or encourage piracy of copyrighted materials in violation of the author's rights. Purchase only authorized editions.
For information, address: The Berkley Publishing Group,
a division of Penguin Group (USA) Inc.,
375 Hudson Street, New York, New York 10014.

ISBN: 978-0-441-02010-2

ACE
Ace Books are published by The Berkley Publishing Group,
a division of Penguin Group (USA) Inc.,
375 Hudson Street, New York, New York 10014.
ACE and the "A" design are trademarks of Penguin Group (USA) Inc.

PRINTED IN THE UNITED STATES OF AMERICA

10 9 8 7 6 5 4 3 2 1

If you purchased this book without a cover, you should be aware that this book is stolen property. It was reported as "unsold and destroyed" to the publisher, and neither the author nor the publisher has received any payment for this "stripped book."

Dedicated to Jackie French.
This book doesn't have any wise mentors,
but I do.

Acknowledgments

Thanks to all my friends. Allison, my friend and brilliant illustrator; Stephanie, my friend and publisher; Jackie, my friend and mentor; Anne, my friend and mother; Rod, my friend and father; and Claire, my friend and sister. And thank you as always to all the awesome people at the Eyrie, because without readers a book is a sad thing.

And final thanks to Nightwish, whose album *Dark Passion Play* was the soundtrack to all my work here.

Author's Note

The language of the Northerners is Welsh, a very ancient and beautiful language.

Accordingly, in line with the rules of Welsh pronunciation, "dd" sounds like "th."

Hence our protagonist's name, Arenadd, is pronounced as "Arrenath." Likewise, Saeddryn is pronounced as "Saythrin," and Arddryn is pronounced as "Arthrin."

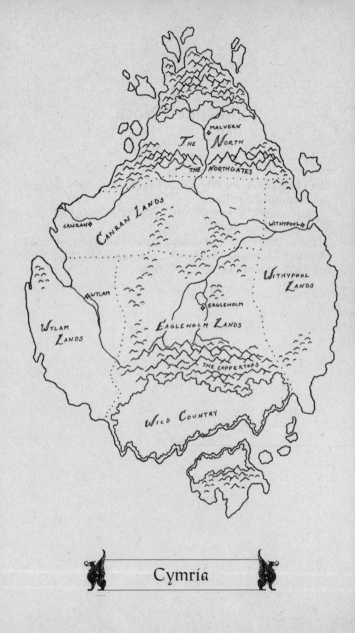

Cymria

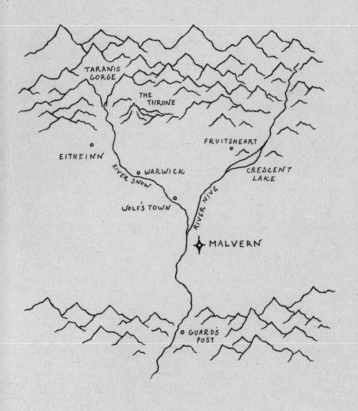

TARANIS GORGE

THE THRONE

FRUITSHEART

EITHEINN

RIVER SNOW

WARWICK

CRESCENT LAKE

WOLF'S TOWN

RIVER NIVE

MALVERN

GUARD'S POST

 The North

1

Whispers

Huddled alone in a cell deep below the city of Malvern, Arenadd Taranisäii sang.

He wasn't sure of the words or the tune. In fact, he couldn't quite remember what he was trying to sing. That didn't matter. Keeping his bandaged hand tucked in against his chest, he opened his mouth wide and sang as loudly as he could. His voice came out cracked and raucous.

". . . danced around the tree when you came to look for me, round and round the . . . tree we went . . . back again . . . take my hand and we'll . . . something something . . . dance around the—" He broke off in a fit of coughing.

He had lost track of how long he'd been here. Time had no meaning when there was no light, and even less when you couldn't sleep. And pain made every moment drag out and stretch. He hadn't eaten anything in a while, but that didn't seem to matter much. His mouth hurt where one of his teeth had been knocked out. The swelling on the side of his head had claimed one eye, so seeing wasn't easy, either. But none of it hurt as much as his hand.

He sang anyway. It was all he could think of to do, the only thing that seemed to block out the whisperings in his head.

He thought he must be going mad. His mind was a jumble.

Sometimes he would think that someone else was there with him in the cell, until he blinked and they disappeared.

Arenadd, the voice whispered again.

He waved his good hand around wildly. "Go away!"

The voice kept on calling, and he sang again until it went away. After that he dozed for a short while.

When he woke up, there was someone else there. A blurry person, standing in a doorway made of light. He blinked and rubbed his good eye, but the intruder didn't leave. The figure came into focus.

Eventually, he realised the person was talking to him. He jerked his head toward him. "Eh? Eh? Who's that? Rannagon? Is that you? Have you come back for me?"

The reply came: "It's me. Remember me?"

Arenadd blinked some more, until he finally took in the person in front of him. A stocky, blond young man with a boyish freckled face and blue eyes. Familiar eyes. Eyes full of disgust and hatred—and fear.

Arenadd grinned horribly. "Erian Rannagonson. Malvern's favourite bastard. Why are you here? Want me to bite *your* ear off next?" he said, and cackled.

Erian retreated slightly. "I wanted to see you one last time. Ask you something."

Arenadd dragged himself forward, pulling on the chains that held his wrists to the wall. "The last time before what? Eh, Bastard? What's poor Arenadd got coming next?"

Erian's eyes spat hate at him. "They're going to hang you in the morning, murderer."

Arenadd rubbed his head with his good hand. "Finally. Lazy Southern bastards took forever."

Erian glanced over his shoulder. "Listen to me. *Listen!*"

Arenadd just stared at him, through a red-rimmed black eye.

"I want to know something," said Erian. "Why did you do it? Why did you kill my father?"

"It seemed like a good idea at the time."

Erian stared blankly at him for a moment, and then gave a strangled shout of frustration. *"Answer me!* Why did you do it? Why did you *really* do it?"

The voice had begun to whisper again. It was growing louder. Tired anger coursed through the muddle in Arenadd's mind. Pushing at the floor with his feet, he tried to get up—and fell back against the wall when his chains caught. "What do you want from me, you sun-worshipping nitwit?" he yelled. "I killed him because he killed me. That's why." He slumped, chest heaving. "Now bugger off and leave me alone."

Erian tried to question him more, but Arenadd started to sing again and didn't stop until he went away.

Once he was alone, he stopped singing and tried to think. So, they were going to hang him. At last, he was going to leave this cell. Tomorrow he would be given death . . . or his chance to escape. Only time would tell which. And by now he would welcome either one.

Erian let himself be escorted out of the dungeon. His heart pounded sickeningly the entire time. In his head, the vision stayed with him. The bony, wild-eyed wreck of a man, crouched in the corner with one bandaged hand cradled against his body, long black hair matted into ropes around his swollen face. The pointed chin beard crusted with blood, the black robe and leggings all torn and filthy. And that voice, harsh and crazed . . . mad.

He wished he knew why he had gone to visit him at all. He had been there when Arenadd had been captured, the murdering blackrobe raving all the while. He had seen Malvern's council sentence him to death without a trial, after the Master of Law had claimed that Arenadd was insane and couldn't be tried. Even the guards Erian had bribed to let him in had warned him. Violent and deranged, they said. But Erian had gone anyway.

He was glad when he emerged from the narrow dungeon corridors and back into the more spacious lower level of the Eyrie tower.

Senneck was there, idly grooming a wing. She came to meet him. "Are you satisfied now, Erian?"

He shook his head vaguely. "I don't know."

"Did he tell you what you wanted him to?"

"No. He won't say anything except nonsense. He didn't even look afraid when I told him he was going to be hanged."

"So be it, then," said Senneck. "Let us go and meet with the Mighty Kraal now. He will be waiting."

Erian walked obediently beside her, up the ramps toward

the upper levels of the tower. She moved unhurriedly, with the graceful loping gait of all griffins, her tail waving gently behind her. Erian kept pace easily, though his mind was elsewhere.

"I just don't understand it!" he burst out at last.

Senneck didn't look back at him. "Understand what?"

"Any of it! He did all those terrible things, killed all those people—murdered my father—and he didn't even have a reason! *That's* why I went down there," he added, realising it just at that moment. "I wanted him to give me a *reason*. But he didn't. I just don't understand why something like that could just . . . happen."

Senneck's back paws padded on the carpeted floor. "There does not have to be a reason, Erian."

"Yes there does! The gods wouldn't—"

She stopped and turned her head sharply toward him. "There are no gods. Do not delude yourself. Nothing happens but what is made to happen by us and by nature."

Erian gaped at her, before hastily backing down. "I suppose you're right," he mumbled, as she turned away and walked on. "It'd just be *easier* that way."

"Nothing is easy."

"I know." Erian adjusted the sling holding his right arm. The shoulder still ached.

"Besides," Senneck added more kindly, "the murderer is done with now. We have played our part, and all that is left for us is to claim our reward!"

Erian cheered up a little at that. But a moment later his heart quailed when he remembered that seeing the Mighty Kraal would also mean seeing his human partner. Beautiful Lady Elkin. The woman he now knew he loved but who did not love him in return. But, he told himself quickly, now maybe it would be different. He had caught Arenadd Taranisäii, the notorious destroyer of Eagleholm, the man who had stolen a gang of slaves and led them to overrun the mountain fort called Guard's Post and kill everyone inside it. Arenadd had been one of the most wanted men in Cymria, and Erian had been the one to finally capture him. Now he and Senneck were due to be rewarded, but that didn't matter so much to Erian as the idea that maybe Elkin would be grateful to him. Maybe she would even respect him now for what he had done.

He held on to that hope all the way up to the very top of

the tower, where Lady Elkin's audience chamber was. But the moment he stepped into the big marble-lined room, that hope died.

The middle of the audience chamber featured a stepped platform made from slabs of white marble. It may have been large, but it was dwarfed by the massive griffin that crouched at its top. The Mighty Kraal, his white feathers glossy in the lamplight, golden eyes half-closed. There was nobody else with him.

Erian, feeling as if a lead weight had replaced his stomach, knelt in front of the platform. Beside him Senneck bowed her head to the superior griffin, saying nothing.

The Mighty Kraal regarded them both. Finally, he lifted his head and spoke. "You have come to ask me for your reward, Senneck?"

"I have," she said.

"And that is all?"

Senneck's tail flicked uncertainly. "All, Mighty Kraal?"

He looked at her, then at Erian. "You have nothing to tell me?"

"I have not," said Senneck.

Erian felt the giant griffin's gaze burning through him. Feeling he should say something, he finally came up with: "I heard they're going to execute the murderer tomorrow."

"That is true," said Kraal. "But you and I were both there to hear it. Do you have any other thing to tell me about this man you call your enemy?"

Erian squirmed under that golden stare. "He's mad."

Kraal kept his gaze on him a moment longer, before finally looking away with a dismissive huff. "I will give you your reward now."

He used his beak to hook something from under his wing and dropped it in front of Senneck. It was a leather bag, heavy with gold oblong. Erian picked it up happily; he could buy new clothes with this, and a new bow, and better food and nesting material for Senneck.

"You may go now," Kraal told them both, and without waiting for a response he settled down and closed his eyes.

Erian left the audience chamber very gladly, clutching the bag of oblong. "He's a very odd griffin, isn't he?"

"He is old," said Senneck. "And I think he has been idle here too long. A griffin that grows bored can become lazy and foolish—inclined to mystical thoughts."

"He doesn't look that old to me," said Erian.

"I do not know his true age," Senneck admitted. "But he is at least as old as your father was, and probably older. Stories of him go back many, many years. My mother told me about him when I was a hatchling, and said her own mother had once told *her*."

Erian rubbed his head. "Good gods. Do griffins live that long?"

"Some of them do, it would seem," said Senneck. "Now, let us go back to our nest. I am ready to eat."

On his platform in the audience chamber, the Mighty Kraal shifted and scratched his flank. Yet another meeting with Senneck and her human, and something still nagged at him. Senneck was simple enough. Young and ambitious, as arrogant as every young griffin who had only just chosen a human. But her human was another question. He looked very much like his father, but there was something else about him. Whatever it was, it wasn't anything particularly special. He wasn't important as humans went, just a lowly newcomer to the Eyrie. He wasn't a great fighter or particularly intelligent for a human. But despite all that, Kraal couldn't shake off that feeling. That feeling that was almost . . . *familiarity*.

The sound of a door opening behind him brought him back to the present. He didn't need to look to know who the intruder was.

Lady Elkin, Eyrie Mistress, white blonde and fragile. She appeared at Kraal's left side as if by magic. But next to his enormous bulk her tiny frame was easy to miss.

Kraal wordlessly shifted back to make room for her. She sat down between his forepaws, almost lost among his thick chest feathers. "Did you talk to Erian?" she asked.

"He is gone now," Kraal said by way of an answer. "With his reward."

Elkin tucked her hands into the wide sleeves of her gown. "That's good."

"He looked for you," Kraal added. "I think he was unhappy that you were not here."

Elkin said nothing.

"You do not want to see him," said Kraal. "Why have you

been hiding? Are you afraid of him?" He sounded genuinely curious.

"I don't have time to deal with him," Elkin said, more sharply than she needed to. "I have other things to worry about. An Eyrie to run."

"He did you a great service by capturing the rogue dark-man," said Kraal. "You should have thanked him yourself."

"We gave him his reward," said Elkin, deliberately ignoring her partner's real meaning. "I don't want to talk about him any more. I have work to do."

Kraal took the hint and dropped the subject, simply getting up to follow her when she left. She had been throwing herself into her work lately, as if nothing else mattered. Maybe, for her, nothing did. But Kraal didn't believe that.

Kraal was not the only griffin worried about his human.

Out beyond the city, near the glorified village called Wolf's Town, Skandar huddled down in a thicket of wattle bushes and rested. He had been flying for days, often unable to find food, and by now his wings and his stomach ached.

Nervous and angry with fear, the big griffin pecked at a tick hiding among his wing feathers. He wanted food. He wanted to go back to his new home. But most of all, he wanted his human.

When Arenadd had disappeared, it had taken Skandar some time to start looking for him. He had been too caught up in his new territory and even more caught up with his mate, Hyrenna. After far too long forced to live a life without the things he expected and loved, finding the mountains at last had been a blessing. No more hiding like a rabbit down a hole. No more doing whatever the human said so that the human would show him to a new and better home for them both. Instead he had had freedom in the mountains and a mate to bear his eggs—and to teach him all the things he should have known all this while. And Arenadd had been there, too, living the way *he* was sup-posed to live—with other humans of his own race.

So when Arenadd had gone, Skandar had assumed that all was well and that the human would come back when he was ready. The other humans seemed to think so, too, for a little while. But when they began to worry and to look for the human, Skandar's confusion had grown. Where was Arenadd? Why was he not in the mountains any more? The other humans were leaving, and Hyrenna with them, and Skandar couldn't follow without his human.

So he didn't. He ignored Hyrenna's warnings and flew away to find Arenadd.

It went beyond mere friendship. Arenadd was *his*.

But no matter where Skandar went, he found nothing. He stayed away from human nests; Arenadd had warned him not to let other humans see him. Skandar didn't want to be seen anyway. He knew what humans that weren't Arenadd could do to him.

He searched the other places instead, where there were trees and hills and rocks. Places he had been before with Arenadd. He found nothing. No sign. No scent.

The great dark griffin rested his head on his talons and sighed. He was lost and starving, and no closer to finding his human. But how could he go back to the mountains alone? He needed Arenadd, needed him to help make sense of the world.

A rustling from nearby made him raise his head sharply. Keeping still, he listened. Something was coming.

Skandar sniffed, and the tip of his tail began to twitch. *Human*.

He peered through the branches and eventually spotted them, two humans walking together and making noises—that ugly soft-sounding language they used, which made no sense to him. They were coming straight toward him.

Watching them cautiously, Skandar noticed the brown fur on their heads. Not dark humans, like Arenadd. *Those* humans were good humans that would help him and Arenadd. But these were the other humans, the pale-furred ones, the same ones who had hurt him and tried to take his human away.

Arenadd had explained why Skandar should leave dark humans alone, and he had decided that his human knew best.

But there was no reason to stop *these* humans from being food.

His mind made up, Skandar slowly rose to his paws. Huge black talons extended. His wings rose.

The humans wandered closer, oblivious.

Skandar leapt. Crashing through the bushes as if they were nothing, he pounced on both humans. One went flying; the other caught the full force of his front paws and was crushed into the ground, its body tearing open. Leaving it dying, Skandar went after the other. The surviving human managed to get up and run, but even with his massive bulk Skandar was faster. He chased it down and killed it with a blow of his beak, before dragging its limp corpse back to where the other one lay.

Humans were far too easy to hunt.

They were delicious, too. Skandar ripped the bodies apart and swallowed them, clothes and all. Nothing was left but a few blood stains.

Once he had eaten, he lay on his belly for a short time and rested. He gulped a little. The food felt good in his stomach.

Having his hunger satisfied made him feel much better, and more optimistic. Newly determined, he got up and walked away south. It was better not to stay near a kill outside of your own territory; the smell attracted danger.

He was near the edge of the trees and preparing to take off when the wind, blowing toward him, brought him a scent.

Human!

Skandar drew back under the trees and lifted his head, sniffing. Humans, further away this time. But these weren't food. These were familiar. The unaccustomed word rose up in his head: *friends*.

But not his friends.

2

Condemned

Skade sat with her back to a tree and watched the Northerners argue. It seemed they had done nothing else since Arenadd had helped them escape by giving himself up to his enemies. Saeddryn Taranisäii, ragged but wiry, faced off against Davyn and Cai, two of her friends. Davyn was arguing the loudest.

". . . sayin' we should just do nothin', then? Is that it?"

"I'm sayin' there's nothin' we *can* do, and ye know it," Saeddryn snapped back.

"Yer talking about yer own mother here," said Cai. "How can ye be so cold?"

Saeddryn shook her head. "Don't ye get it, Cai? They've got Arenadd. He must've been in their cages for a week now. More than long enough. He'll have told them everythin' they wanted t'know."

Skade spoke up for the first time. "He will tell them nothing," she growled.

Saeddryn rounded on her. "He'll tell them everythin'," she said. "I know what they do. By now they know about the others. Where they are, who they are. It's too late."

"But we've gotta try an' do *somethin'*," Rhodri interrupted. "Are we just gonna sit here on our backsides while our friends get killed?"

Saeddryn gave him a look so full of tired resignation that

it made her seem as old as her withered mother. "Can ye fly, Rhodri? Do ye have a griffin? Because they do. They'll send griffiners. Probably have already. Even if we weren't months away on foot, we'd never stand a chance. By now the others must be dead already."

Grim silence fell over the little camp.

"So we're all that's left," Cai muttered.

No-one else spoke.

"Damn ye, Arenadd," said Rhodri. "Ye've destroyed everything."

At that, the only Northerner there who hadn't taken part in the argument stood up—Annir, robed and collared like the slave she had been, made older than her years by suffering and grief. "Don't you dare say that about my son," she said quietly. "If it weren't for him, *you* would be the one locked up in that cell."

"She's right," said Saeddryn, in the same tired voice as before. "If he hadn't saved us, they would've tortured us instead. The story would've turned out the same in the end."

"They'd never make me crack," Davyn spat. "Never."

Saeddryn laughed bitterly. "So ye say. So everyone says, until the Southerners get their fingers in a vice and keep turnin' the handle until—"

"Stop it!" Annir's cry twisted into a sob. She slumped back beside Skade, holding her ears. "Stop it, Saeddryn."

Saeddryn's expression softened. "I'm sorry." She looked into the fire, and her shoulders hunched. "I know what they do. They did it to my father. He killed himself in his cell rather than take any more of it."

"Yer father was a great man," Davyn said. "But Arenadd . . . hah. He ain't one of us. He's one of *them*. He might look like a Northerner, even a Taranisäii, but he's a griffiner just like the rest of them. Talks like one, walks like one. He can *read*, for shadow's sakes."

"He killed Lord Rannagon," Cai pointed out.

"Yeah, not knowin' why we wanted him dead," said Davyn. "He killed him for some stupid griffiner squabble. I know the type. Spoilt brats what think murder's the best answer to all their problems."

"It wasn't like that," Annir snapped.

Davyn broke off, glaring at her.

Annir stared at her hands, her greying black hair stirring in the breeze. Curly, just like her lost son's. "He trusted Lord Rannagon. They were friends. Until Rannagon betrayed him. He tried to have Arenadd killed. Arenadd survived, but his griffin didn't. He lost everything. Do you understand that?" She looked up, hollow eyed. "That griffin was his life. I think—I *know* he loved her more than us. He ran away from home when he was ten rather than be separated from her. When she died, he had nothing. That's why he killed Rannagon."

"She is right," Skade added quietly. "Rannagon did to him what he did to you: took everything away. Even dignity."

Silence followed. Davyn looked embarrassed. "Fine," he said eventually. "I believe ye. But that doesn't help us any." He turned to Saeddryn. "If Arddryn's dead and Arenadd's gone, then it's down to ye, Saeddryn. What do ye say we do now?"

She looked utterly miserable. "There's really not much we can do now, not that I can see. But there's no goin' back to Eitheinn or the Throne. We'll have t'find a new place t'hide. Somewhere we can start again."

The others seemed to have caught her mood, and their suggestions were half-hearted.

Skade, for her part, openly growled her disgust and walked off. These humans weren't worth her attention any more; they were weak and indecisive and stood no chance against their enemies. At least they seemed to be realising that themselves, but she wouldn't wait for them.

Once she was out of sight—but not completely out of earshot, just in case—she leant against a tree and stared restlessly at her own hands. Thin and delicate and weak, they gripped the bark. What set them apart from ordinary human hands were the nails. She had none; instead a small, curving black claw tipped each finger. She was grateful for them, the last remnants of her old strength. Even her eyes had become more human, but her claws were there to stay.

She dug them into the tree, relishing the way they cut into the bark. They could do the same to flesh, and had done. She dearly wished they were doing it now.

She had already decided not to stay with the humans. They were no friends of hers, and staying with them would only bring her more danger. Only two humans had ever meant a thing to Skade, and both of them were dead.

The only other gift left from her time as a griffin brought her out of her reverie. She froze, sniffing the air. Sure enough, there it was. A scent. A griffish scent.

Skade tensed, holding up her clawed hands instinctively. The scent was fresh. Male. Coming this way.

Very cautiously, she crept toward the source. Best to see what this was coming from.

Moving quietly, like the hunter she had been, she reached a stand of spice-trees and peered around a pale trunk.

Moments later the griffin came into view.

Skade's breath caught.

The griffin was monstrous, massive, bigger than any other male she had known. The feathers on his front half were silver, his wings mottled with black and white. The rest of him was black. Black fur, black forepaws, and a huge, pitted black beak.

The eyes were silver, watching suspiciously for any sign of movement.

Skade stepped out into the open. "Skandar."

The dark griffin halted, one forepaw raised. His head tilted. Then he relaxed and came toward her. "You silver human, Are-nadd mate."

"Yes." Skade didn't try to touch him. "How did you find me?"

"Not looking," said Skandar, with an irritable shake of his head, "Where Arenadd?"

"He is not with you?"

"No, Arenadd leave. I come look."

Skade wrapped her arms around herself. "I know where he is."

Skandar rose up instantly, full of angry threat. "You tell! Tell now! Where Arenadd?"

"He is in Malvern," said Skade. "The enemy has him."

Skandar blinked. "Enemy?"

"Yes. He is in a cage, Skandar, as he was in Eagleholm. As you were." Skade shuddered. "They will not set him free. They will hurt him. And then they will kill him."

Skandar's tail lashed. "Not kill! Not kill human!"

"I am sorry."

Skandar wasn't listening. "Where Mal-verk?"

"It is that way," said Skade, pointing. "A great human nest, with many towers and walls. Arenadd will be underground, under the towers."

Skandar huffed. "I go. Find human."

"You will die," Skade told him flatly.

"Not die!" Skandar said at once. "Kill."

Skade hadn't really expected him to listen. She watched the big griffin huffing his offence, and to her surprise, her heart went out to him. He was wild and always would be, but for all that he had made Arenadd his human, and nothing would stand in his way.

And what of yourself? she thought. *You are human now, but Arenadd is yours as well. You lost the last human you cared for—would you allow it to happen again?*

Deep down, Skade knew that without Arenadd she was lost. Without him, her life as a human would be the same torment it had been before.

She huffed back at Skandar. "So be it. You will not abandon him, and neither should I. If you will let me, I will come with you to Malvern, and we will find him together."

She half-expected Skandar to be offended by the suggestion that he might need help, but the dark griffin only flicked his tail in a satisfied kind of way and said, "You good human to help. Come now!"

He offered her his back.

Even though she had been carried by him in the past, Skade still hesitated. Before, she had always ridden with Arenadd. She had never flown on griffinback alone.

Skandar quickly grew impatient. He shoved her with his head. "Come! We fly now. *Now!*"

She climbed onto his back, settling into the hollow between wings and neck. On most griffins this spot was only just big enough for a single human to sit, but Skandar was large enough for two.

The moment Skade had sat down and put her arms around his neck, the dark griffin made a shambling and messy take-off, bursting through the branches overhead without a pause. Skade barely managed to hold on. Leaves smacked her in the face, and only a last-minute grab saved her.

Once Skandar levelled out, she relaxed a little. She could do this.

As the dark griffin began to fly south toward Malvern, Skade wondered briefly whether she should have told the others where she was going. She dismissed the thought almost instantly.

They didn't matter. Only Arenadd mattered, and she vowed to herself now that she would have him back or die in the attempt.

On the night before his execution, Arenadd tried to rest. He was too tired to sing any more, so he stayed huddled up in his corner and did some counting.

How many meals had he eaten here? Ten? Twelve? They usually brought in soup for every other meal—if salty water with uncooked vegetables in it counted as soup. Maybe the soup was breakfast. How many bowls of the stuff had he choked down so far?

He spent far too much time trying to work this out. Anything was better to think of than tomorrow.

Eventually, he decided that there had been about seven bowls, maybe six. That meant six or seven days here at most. A week in prison.

Not the first time he'd been locked up but definitely the longest. He growled to himself. Prisons, prisons, always prisons! Was he going to spend the rest of eternity running from one kind of captivity to another?

Still, he supposed he didn't have much right to complain about it. He had committed enough crimes in his life to earn this cell a hundred times over.

Trying to ignore the throbbing agony in his hand, he made a mental list of all his bad deeds over the years. It was longer than he had expected. Theft. Bribery. Poisoning his old master—but that didn't count, he added hastily. It had been the old man's life or his own. What else had he done? Abducted a griffin chick, broken out of gaol.

Murdering Lord Rannagon and his partner Shoa, burning down the Eyrie at Eagleholm and going on the run with a man-eating griffin were probably a lot worse.

Arenadd counted off on his remaining fingers, muttering to himself. "Then there was stealing all those slaves and using them to massacre everyone in Guard's Post, along with two griffins and two griffiners. Oh, and that man I killed up at Taranis' Throne. And then I tried to kill Rannagon's bastard . . . hah." He spat. The arrogant bone-headed Southerner had got away from him once, and that was one time too many. Arenadd had a score to settle with him.

Still, he looked back over his list of misdeeds with a kind of wonder. He had to admit that hanging was probably too good for him by now.

The thought of his impending execution rose up horribly in his mind. Without thinking, he wrapped his good hand around his throat. The same throat that had been cool and lifeless for months now, the same one he had touched obsessively every day ever since that night.

Once again, he asked himself the one question that had yet to be answered. The question whose answer would change everything.

Can I be killed?

Erian woke up early on the day of the execution. He had slept badly the night before, but anticipation woke him up like a slap to the face.

He rolled over in bed, feeling as if his stomach was being wrung out. It wasn't excitement, and it wasn't fear; he probed for both emotions while he got dressed.

He smoothed down his new blue velvet tunic and tried to flatten his hair, doing his best to ignore the fluttering in his chest. He could hear Senneck moving around in her nesting chamber and hurried to get her some food before she came to complain.

Half a carcass had been hung up the night before in a cupboard used for just that purpose. He lifted it out one-handed, holding it away from his body, and carried it through the archway.

Senneck crouched in her big untidy nest, busy grooming her chest feathers. She didn't look up when Erian came in and only moved when the meat was in front of her, hooking it toward herself with her beak.

Erian left her to eat. He felt too queasy to bother with his own breakfast. How soon would it be? When would they bring the murderer up out of his cell to face the noose?

To distract himself, he looked up at the sword that hung over the fireplace. His father's sword, lost for all those months but now back with its rightful owner.

Erian lifted it down, admiring it yet again. A two-handed weapon, meant for battle, its bronze hilt decorated with griffin

designs. On the blade just below that, the name had been etched.
Rannagon Raegonson.

The blade itself was a little rusted now, from when it had
fallen into *his* hands. Who knew what it had been used for in
that time?

Erian grimaced and clutched the hilt more tightly. It made
him furious to think that his own father's sword, the sword of
the great hero Lord Rannagon, must have been used at the massacre at Guard's Post. A beautiful sword meant for a mighty
griffiner lord, turned into a murder weapon.

Not for the first time, Erian wished he had used the sword
to cut Arenadd to pieces the moment his father's murderer had
given it back. And he probably would have if he'd had the chance.

Still, he would go and watch the filthy blackrobe hang,
and that would be enough. Lord Rannagon's murder would be
avenged.

Senneck entered to interrupt him. "I have eaten, and now I
am ready to leave. I do not want to miss this day."

Erian clumsily put the sword back onto its hooks. "Let's go,
then."

Senneck had brought her harness; she dropped it at his feet.
"Put this on me, and we will fly."

Erian strapped it on over her head and neck, where it would
provide handholds for him. She walked back through her nest
and onto the balcony beyond, and he climbed onto her back,
holding on awkwardly thanks to his wounded shoulder.

She must have been in a daring mood that morning, because
once he was safely on she moved forward to the edge, which
had no railing, and stepped off into space. For one long, screaming moment they were falling, headfirst. Erian wrenched at the
harness, yelling something completely incoherent, but Senneck
ignored him. Her wings opened, and with one quick blow she
lifted herself out of the dive and flew leisurely down toward the
open space outside the Eyrie gates.

There were other griffins already there. She landed a short
distance away from them and allowed Erian to get off. He
hit the ground and nearly fell over, but managed to recover
himself—more for fear of looking stupid in front of the other
griffiners than anything else.

Senneck didn't seem to notice. "Come now, let us find a
good place to stand," she said, already walking off.

Erian followed, light-headed.

There were more griffiners here than he would have expected, and even more griffins. He wondered why. They couldn't know the murderer as well as he did, and there was no way they could hate him half as much. Griffins were almost indifferent to this sort of thing.

Senneck had chosen a place near the edge, keeping her distance from the larger griffins nearby. Erian came to stand just in front of her, beneath her beak—the traditional place for a griffiner to stand, under his partner's protection.

Ahead of them, downhill from the Eyrie gates, the platform stood. It had a clear space in front of it, where the common people of the city had gathered. Most of them were Northerners, all black-haired and black-eyed. For some reason Erian's tension increased at the sight of them.

Foreboding, he thought. *That's it.*

The platform itself was almost featureless. A lever stuck up at the centre, below a wooden beam.

The noose dangled in between.

Erian's foreboding increased. He stared at the noose, unable to stop himself wondering what it would feel like around his neck. He wondered how long it would take the murderer to die and how painful it would be.

He thought of his father's death and hoped it would be as painful as possible.

His bravado dribbled away when Arenadd finally came into sight. Two guards appeared, having emerged from the Eyrie somewhere behind the crowd of griffiners. Two more walked behind them, weapons drawn.

The first two were on either side of Arenadd, whose hands were tied behind his back, and they held on to his elbows and pushed him along. Both of them had their own weapons close to hand.

When Erian saw them, a queasy jolt in his stomach brought him back to reality. He tried to fight down his fear, struggling to replace it with something braver, such as hatred. He shouldn't be afraid of this man, not any more, not now when he was helpless.

Arenadd's head turned toward Erian, and his heart froze.

In daylight, the murderer's face looked even worse. Pale, like any Northerner's, but the features that had once been angular were now swollen and ugly. One eye had disappeared under an eyelid that had turned purple, and the cheek below it bulged as if he had something in his mouth.

The other eye stared straight at Erian. An unreadable Northern eye, fixed on his face.

For an instant Erian was paralysed, but in the brief moment that stare lasted, his fear finally swung around into rage. This man, this wretched, broken *blackrobe*, had taken his father and destroyed hundreds of lives. He had no right to make Erian afraid, not now.

Without so much as a thought, Erian broke away from the crowd. He ran past the guards and headed them off. They halted, instantly pointing their weapons at him.

Erian ignored them. He faced Arenadd, breathing hard through his nose. "I swore I'd see you brought to justice, blackrobe. Now I have."

Arenadd gave a lopsided sneer. "If you say so," he said, slurring a little.

The guards tried to move around Erian, but he sidestepped. "This is for my father," he said, and punched Arenadd in the stomach as hard as he could.

Arenadd lurched backward and would have fallen if the guards hadn't pulled him back. They shoved Erian out of the way and hauled their prisoner toward the platform. He struggled along between them, wheezing.

Erian let the little group pass and fell into step behind them. They didn't stop him; they all knew who he was. This was his right.

As Erian reached the top of the stairs, he heard someone coming up behind him. He hopped up the last few steps and turned, backing off to get out of the way.

"Elkin!" he blurted.

She offered him a faint smile. "Good morning, Lord Erian."

He could feel himself blushing. "I, uh, I . . ." He coughed. "I want to see this properly. If you don't mind."

"Of course you may," she said briefly, and walked toward the front of the platform.

Erian stayed where he was and watched her. He had never felt so awkward in his life.

The Mighty Kraal hadn't come up onto the platform; there was no room for him there. He had stayed where he was at the forefront of the assembled griffiners, watching in silence.

Erian couldn't see Senneck from here.

Arenadd had been taken to stand just below the noose. Two guards kept hold of him, while one of the others took up his station by the lever.

Elkin stood at the front of the platform, to one side so the crowd could see the condemned man. "Arenadd Taranisäii," she began, "also known as Arren Cardockson of Eagleholm, you have been found guilty of the following crimes." She began to list them all, patiently reciting each one from memory.

". . . treason, sedition and consorting with rebels," she finished eventually, her quiet, clear voice carrying over the crowd quite well. "For these crimes, the Master of Law for the territory of Malvern, acting under authority from myself as Mistress of Malvern's Eyrie, has laid down the sentence of death by hanging." She glanced at Arenadd. "Under our laws, as a former griffiner you have the right to speak before the sentence is carried out. Speak now, or I will assume that you have waived that right."

Arenadd's pale face had turned even paler, but his open eye was alight. "I swear," he said. And then again, much louder: "I swear. I swear on my dead heart that no Southerner will ever have power over me again."

The crowd was staring at him. Nobody spoke.

"And the same goes for the rest of you!" Arenadd yelled. "You cowards! Will you let the Southerners grind you into the mud forever? Or will you do something about it?"

The eerie silence broke, and the crowd of Northerners began to shout. In anger or agreement—who knew?

Elkin had already nodded to the guards. One of them took the noose and put it over Arenadd's head, pulling it tight. He fought back then, hurling himself bodily at them and head-butting one in the face. He kicked the other one in the kneecap before both men retreated out of his reach. There was no need to hold him any more.

Elkin didn't wait for things to calm down. "Sentence will now be carried out," she said, her voice lost in the uproar.

The crowd had not stopped shouting. Erian thought he could make out one thing, repeated by many voices. *Dark Lord, Dark Lord, Dark Lord*.

Arenadd spat at the guard by the lever. "Pull the damn thing and be done with it."

"Gryphus will burn you forever!" Erian shouted as the guard obeyed.

The trapdoor opened, and Arenadd fell. The noose pulled him up short with a hideous crack and a jerk, and after a brief struggle he hung there, swinging gently back and forth.

3

The Night God's Promise

Death, for Arenadd, was darkness.

He felt the brief lurch of his stomach as the trapdoor gave way beneath him. Felt his neck break. *Heard* it—that sick, muffled crack. There was no time for pain.

He felt his body convulse as utter blackness swallowed him, and after that he couldn't feel anything. His body and all his senses were gone, and the world around him became an icy void.

He floated through it in silence, drifting away from life and into absolute nothingness. But one thing had stayed with him.

The voice.

Arenadd. Arenadd. Listen to me, Arenadd. Speak to me.

No sign of anyone. Only a voice that seemed to come from everywhere at once.

Arenadd. You cannot run from me. You cannot hide from me.

And, at last, he replied. "Go away."

As if his words were a signal, the void changed, and he found himself standing—standing on a surface he couldn't see, no different from the blackness all about.

And *she* was there.

She looked like a woman, a Northerner like himself. She didn't seem to have an age. Her only clothing was a silver mantle that covered her shoulders and nothing else. In one hand she held a sickle. She held the other hand out, palm up, and there was the full moon, somehow floating between her fingers.

The Night God.

Arenadd tried to back away from her, but there was no space to do it. "I told you to leave me alone."

I do not abandon my people, the Night God said. *Even if you have done so.*

"You know I only wound up like this to save Skade and Saeddryn. And her friends." Arenadd remembered something, and wrapped his fingers around his throat. "And now they've killed me. Again."

You tried to kill the Bastard, the Night God admitted. *I am pleased that you tried.*

"Tried, failed. Who cares? It's not going to do me any good now."

Faithless darkman! She pointed the sickle at him. *I could have helped you, but you did not listen! Your mind was full of cowardice and doubt. You did not intend to obey me but to try and hide from me, as you have tried since boyhood to hide your own true self.*

"I'm sure I don't know what you're talking about," Arenadd said sourly.

You have lied to yourself long enough, said the Night God. *You are a Northerner. The world would not let you forget, and neither shall I. Accept it.*

"I have." Arenadd pulled up the sleeve of his robe, showing the spiralling tattoos. "I accepted it when I got these."

Then accept me!

"Why should I? What did you ever do for me? I only ever prayed to you once, and you ignored me."

I heard you.

"And did nothing!" Arenadd raged. "I prayed to you; I asked you to save me! *And you let me die.* You let me fall hundreds of feet, break every bone in my body and then drown in my own blood! So forgive me if I don't look overly impressed!"

The Night God's expression did not change. She lifted the glowing white orb in her hand and placed it into the black hole where her right eye should have been. *Your death was inevitable.*

"You could have stopped it!"

No. There was nothing I could do. The Night God's other

eye, her black Northern eye, stayed fixed on Arenadd's face. *I am not a part of the solid world. All of my powers are wielded through my people. And that is why I chose you.* Her expression grew distant. *Many years ago, a man called Padrig was kept in the cell where you suffered. He was tortured until he was near madness, but he would not speak. Rather than betray his people, he ended his own life. In his final moments, he cried out to me. "Help us, Night God. Save us." I hear every true prayer. I heard his. And I heard another voice. A young man called to me on the final night of his life. When he did so, I knew that a part of him had begun to long for me. And so I chose to give him my greatest blessing. My greatest trust.*

"I was scared witless," Arenadd mumbled. "Of course I prayed. I couldn't think of anything else by that point."

And so, in your desperation, you came to me. And when I appeared to you at last, you swore to do my bidding.

"What else was I supposed to do? I thought you would kill me if I didn't."

But you want to obey, said the Night God. *You long to obey. I feel it in you.*

Arenadd said nothing.

The Night God smiled very slightly. *You still have a chance. Give yourself to me completely, and I will send you back. Commit to my cause, and I will give you all you desire. Love me, and I shall love you.*

"You mean I can go back? I can wake up?"

Yes. I will send you back, and your true powers will be unlocked. You will have another chance to kill your enemy and to destroy all those that have stood in your way.

"And then?"

When you were a boy, you dreamt of becoming the greatest and most powerful griffiner ever to live. Fight in my name, and you shall have your desire.

Arenadd began to smile. "My own Eyrie? A proper home for me and Skandar?"

And freedom for your people. The Night God's expression softened. *They suffer, Arenadd. Their lives are far harder than yours. You had power and privilege once; they have never had either.*

"I know that—"

The time has passed for you to think as a griffiner does, Arenadd. Fight for them . . . and so fight for me.

Arenadd shook his head slowly. "You're right. My life ended a long time ago. If I have to be this—this *thing* I am now, then I should use it. Try to make a difference again. What choice do I have, anyway? There's nowhere else for me to go." He looked up at her. "I'll do it."

Then swear yourself to me.

He knelt. "I'll do it. I hate the Southerners as much as you do. I'll make them suffer for what they did to us. I'll kill Rannagon's bastard. I'll set the North free and make it ours . . . master."

Rise.

He obeyed. "Now what?"

The Night God said nothing more. She reached out, pulled him toward her and took him in her arms. Then she kissed him.

Her lips were icy against his, and for a moment he tried to pull away—until he felt the power flowing into his body. Her lips were cold, but her power was colder. It filled him from end to end, rushing through his veins like blood, but it was dark and lifeless—and familiar.

As it moved in him, he felt his senses come back. Light touched his eyes, and he began to breathe. Before the void left altogether, he heard the voice of the Night God one final time. *Use the shadows, Dark Lord.*

W hen Arenadd woke up, he felt wonderful. All the pain in his body had gone, and new strength had replaced it.

His eye opened, and the first thing he saw was the hated face of Erian looking down at him. The instant he saw it, rage gripped him. Erian the Bastard, who had become a griffiner in front of him and mocked his own disgrace. Erian, who had sold Arenadd's parents into slavery. Erian, who had hunted him across Cymria and finally dragged him to Malvern and handed him over to be tortured and killed. Erian, the one his new master wanted dead.

All those thoughts flew through his mind in a moment. Then Erian saw him move.

His scream shattered the stillness as he reeled away, one arm flailing for a sword that wasn't there.

Arenadd sat up—his hands were untied!—and was on his
feet in an instant. He didn't even bother to look around and see
where he was. He ran straight at Erian, eye fixed on his throat.

Erian had turned sickly white. He stood and stared at Arenadd for one terrified moment before he pulled himself together
and ran away.

Arenadd felt hands grabbing for him, but he dodged them
and sped up. He found himself running into a familiar place:
the same open space where the people had gathered to see him
hanged. He had woken up underneath the platform before they
could drag him away, and most of the crowd were still there.
Erian plunged into their midst, pushing people out of the way
in blind panic.

Arenadd followed, completely ignoring the guards on his
tail. "Stop him!" he yelled at the bewildered people in his path.
"Stop him in the Night God's name!"

They moved out of his way very quickly, but if any of them
tried to stop Erian they failed. He reached the shelter of the
buildings and ran on, into the city.

But Arenadd's fellow Northerners did help him. The guards,
following close behind him, suddenly found that what had been
a clear path wasn't a path any more, and a moment later they
were being tripped up and shoved from all sides.

By the time they had extricated themselves, Erian and Arenadd had disappeared.

Erian had never been so terrified in his life. Unable to think,
heedless of direction, he dived through a gap between two
houses and sprinted down the street beyond, his mind full of
nothing but the need to escape.

No matter how far or how fast he ran, it never seemed to be
enough. All the while, along every street and around every corner, his enemy followed. Every time Erian glanced back, there
he was, bounding over the cobbles like a hunting animal, never
seeming to tire or to slow.

He made no sound. That was what made it worse. No grunts
or gasps for breath. No footsteps.

Erian sprinted on, not even noticing the pain from his bandaged arm as it bounced against his chest. He searched desperately for a hiding place, but there was nothing. No place to

go that wouldn't mean being cornered. And Senneck was not there to help.

Arenadd was gaining on him. "Isn't it fun, Bastard?" he called. "Running through the city, running for your life?"

Sobbing with fear, Erian ducked into an alley and hid behind a stack of boxes.

It did no good. He had barely begun to catch his breath when he heard the voice again, coming closer and closer.

"It's a terrible thing, isn't it? To be hunted. Running from place to place, knowing there's no escape. Knowing what will happen when you're caught. Because you can run from fear . . . but you can't run from blood. Not your own blood."

Erian listened, scarcely breathing. The voice was coming from the other side of the stacked boxes. He braced himself against the wall and pushed them over.

He heard a yelp of surprise as he ran out of the alley and away.

The boxes bought him some time—time to think. *Don't try to hide,* he told himself. *Head for open spaces!* Senneck must be looking for him, and if she could see him, then she could help. It was his only hope now.

With that in mind, he went out into the street and ran straight down the middle, dodging oxcarts and people. Arenadd was quick to follow.

Shortly afterward, something strange began to happen.

Oxen, hitched to wagons or carrying loads, suddenly panicked and ran, trampling several people in the process. A herd of goats being driven along the street broke and scattered, fleeing in all directions. Everywhere in that part of the city, other animals reacted in the same way.

Birds flew up from the buildings in a cloud of whirring wings. Rats left their holes and skittered away. Dogs, trapped in houses and yards, lifted their heads and howled.

Erian hesitated very briefly, half-turning in mid-stride to see the chaos. But he saw Arenadd, still running toward him without seeming to notice, and quickly forgot about it. He tried to call for Senneck, but he had no breath left for it.

Ahead, a large building loomed. Its huge front doors were open, and to Erian they looked inviting. Safe.

He reached them and dived inside. Sheltering in the entrance, he turned and sent out his call as well as he could. *"Erian!*

Erian! Erian!" His voice seemed weak to him, but he kept trying, even when he saw Arenadd coming and it began to waver.

Arenadd's pace slowed. The expression on his swollen face was steady, calm. He charged.

Erian stumbled backward, raising his good hand to shield himself. "No!"

And then, the impossible happened. Arenadd ran through the doorway, and stopped. He staggered forward a few more steps, but came no further. Erian, staring in terror, saw him double over in pain. A soft groan came from him.

Erian backed off further, searching for a weapon, but he kept watching.

Arenadd looked up. His face had turned grey, the mouth stretched into a grimace. The one eye narrowed and he came on again, but there was no strength in him. He took every step as if it was a massive struggle.

Erian snatched an unlit torch off the wall and held it up like a club. "Don't come near me!" His voice sounded high-pitched and strangled.

Arenadd didn't look like a rampaging predator any more. His back was hunched, as if some huge weight pressed down on him. He looked like an old, sick man. "Come—back—here, you little rat," he gritted out.

Erian's courage rose. "Come and get me yourself, black-robe!"

Arenadd let out a yell of frustration. Abruptly, he turned away and ran out, leaving Erian to collapse against the wall, overwhelmed by exhaustion and fright, thanking Gryphus for his strange salvation.

A renadd stumbled out into the open, swearing. The pain still burned in him; he retched a few times, but there was nothing in his stomach to bring up. He leant on a post to try to catch his breath, looking back now at the building his enemy had escaped into. He didn't really need to look. Only one thing could do this to him.

A shout made him turn back sharply.

The guards had found him. At least ten of them stood there in a line, armoured in leather. They carried swords and spears. And chains.

Arenadd straightened up. "Oh no."

"Get him!" a voice yelled from behind him. "Kill him!"

Arenadd glanced back and saw the Bastard watching him from the doorway that had saved him.

The guards advanced. "Hold up yer hands," one said. "Come quietly."

Arenadd could feel the sweat running down his back. "No," he said. "You won't take me. Never again."

He searched for a way to escape. But there was nothing. They had him surrounded. His new strength had gone. The chains . . .

An awful calm came over him. *Use the shadows,* the Night God's voice whispered. *Use the shadows, Dark Lord.*

He stood tall, snarling defiance. "You'll never catch me. Nobody will ever catch Arenadd Taranisäii again." He turned quickly, edging along the wall. He could feel the shadows at its base, could almost smell them. They beckoned to him, promising safety. They were his now. Before he let them take him, he saw Erian one last time, appearing through the door to see him go. "Remember my face, Bastard!" Arenadd shouted to him. "It's the last thing you'll ever see."

Then the shadows swallowed him.

4

Reunion

At first, it seemed ridiculous to think that the shadows could possibly hide him. But they did. Acting on instinct, he flattened himself to the ground, tucking himself into the dark patch by the base of the wall. The moment he did, a wonderful sense of strength and calm came over him. He looked up at the guards and saw them through a dark veil. They didn't seem to be able to see him at all. He saw several of them staring straight at him, blank faced with confusion.

Snickering softly, he wriggled along through the shadow, turned a corner and ran silently off into the city.

After that, his escape was easy. Wall to wall, shadow to shadow, slipping past people, both Northerner and Southerner alike, unseen. Dark and terrible joy went with him. At last! He was free, and he was safe. They would never catch him now.

Mentally, he gave thanks and praise to the Night God. She had told him the truth. Accepting her had been so simple, and the rewards were already so great. If only he had seen it before. If only he had let her into his heart all those long months ago when his troubles had begun. But now he knew what her blessing could do, he vowed that he would never doubt her again. And he would never disobey. She was his master now, and he was glad.

As he passed through the market district, he took the opportunity to steal a knife from a butcher's belt. The weapon felt good in his uninjured hand.

He reached the city's outer wall and followed it, searching for a way out. The huge main gates were no use: they were closed and guarded. He paused by them, hidden in a shadow, and considered his options. There had to be other entrances, smaller side doors for emergencies. No doubt they would be guarded as well. But he could handle a few guards, surely. If they never saw him coming, they wouldn't stand a chance.

Only one way to be sure. He continued on, all senses alert. Once a roaming guard wandered too close to his hiding spot. Without even thinking, Arenadd grabbed him from behind and slit his throat. The man fell with scarcely a sound.

Arenadd moved on before anybody even noticed the death. A short while later he found what he was after: a door set into the outer wall, watched by two alert guards.

He killed them both. The first one he struck from behind, reaching out of a shadow to slash his throat. When the other ran over to help his comrade, Arenadd pounced on him and finished him with a quick stab.

He stepped over the bodies and went to the door. It was locked, but he hadn't spent years mixing with the seedier side of Eagleholm's city life for nothing. He picked the lock with the point of the knife, lifted away the bar that held the door in place, kicked it open and ran through to freedom.

At the moment Erian saw Arenadd vanish, his terror finally bubbled over. He ran back and forth along the wall, searching in vain, and when he found nothing, he started to shout. "Where are you? *Where are you?* Come back here, you coward! Come back!"

The guards who had cornered Arenadd—or thought they had—were just as bewildered. They searched the wall in disarray, the most senior of them trying to give orders and failing because he didn't have any more idea what to do than the others.

"Spread out!" he yelled eventually. "Search the area! Don't let him get out of the city!"

Erian heard him through a kind of mist. The back of his neck prickled. The murderer could be anywhere. *Watching.*

Panicking, he darted back into the building that had seemed

to protect him. Once inside he felt safer, and it finally occurred to him to wonder exactly what this place was.

Just beyond the entrance hall, the space opened up into a huge round room—a room full of pure sunlight. The air glittered golden, and threads of incense smoke twisted and glowed between vases full of fresh flowers.

A temple! Of course!

Erian stepped into the main room, and a new feeling of peace soothed his fears. Ahead he could see the stone altar, decorated with gold-inlaid griffins grouped around a sunwheel. At the centre of the wheel stood a carved man, bearded and crowned, with a long sword in his hand. That was how Gryphus was usually portrayed, but to Erian the great sun god had always looked like his father.

He knelt to the altar. "Thank you, Gryphus. Thank you for your protection."

Sounds from behind him made him turn, groping for a sword that wasn't there. But there was no danger. Senneck came charging into the temple, all flailing wings and lashing tail. "Erian!"

He ran to her. "Senneck!"

She covered him with her wing. "You are not hurt?"

"No, but listen, something awful's happened! It's—"

Shouts interrupted him. Shouts, and running feet. He pulled away from Senneck, and there she was. Lady Elkin herself, coming into the temple with the Mighty Kraal close behind.

"Elkin!" Erian exclaimed.

The Eyrie Mistress' reserve and control were utterly gone. She ran straight to him and grabbed him by the shoulders. "Erian, for Gryphus' sake, are you hurt? Where did he go? What happened?"

Not caring about the consequences any more, he put his good arm around her and gave her a hug. "I'm all right. I—are you *crying*?"

Elkin pulled away from him and rubbed her eyes. "Never mind about that," she said, with just the slightest quaver to her voice. "What happened?"

The Mighty Kraal appeared at that moment, looming over them both. "You must tell us at once," he said.

All of Erian's fear returned. "He came back."

"What is this?" Senneck demanded. "Who came back?"

"*He* did," Erian exclaimed. "The—the—*Arenadd*. He came back from the dead!"

"Don't be ridiculous," said Elkin. "The execution was obviously botched." She didn't sound very certain.

"His heart," Kraal interrupted. "Tell me at once, human, if he had a heartbeat."

"No," said Erian. "They checked. After the hanging was done they checked for a pulse. They checked *everything*. He was dead. I came to see, and . . . *and he got up.*"

"I don't understand this," said Elkin. "It makes no sense! Even if he survived the hanging, there is no way he could have—his neck should have been broken!"

"It *was* broken," said Erian. "I heard it myself. I'm telling you, he was dead."

"Then how?" said Elkin, turning to look at Kraal. "How could this happen?"

Kraal's golden eyes looked dim. "Then I was right. *Kraeai kran ae* has come."

"What foolery is this?" Senneck demanded. "*Kraeai kran ae* cannot be real."

"What *is* that?" said Elkin. "What does it mean, Kraal?"

The massive white griffin regarded her for a moment, and walked away. He went to stand behind the altar, rising to rest his forepaws on the golden inlay. A shaft of sunlight shone across his face, making the pale feathers turn bright. "*Kraeai kran ae* is the living dead. A human whose life has run its course but who is brought back by magic."

"Like a ghost?" said Erian.

"A ghost of flesh," said Kraal. "Dark magic drives the blood through his veins. He has no soul. Ordinary weapons cannot kill him."

"How could this happen?" said Senneck. "A human cannot have magic."

"He is not human any more," said Kraal. "And the magic is not his. Only one griffin could create it. A dark griffin."

"*Darkheart!*" Erian exclaimed. "Of course!"

"Tell me," said Kraal, looking at him now. "How did this human come to meet this one—this dark heart?"

"Darkheart's a wild griffin," said Erian. "A man-eater from the Coppertops down south. The—the *blackrobe* caught him and brought him to Eagleholm and sold him to the Arena. After the blackrobe was locked up for his crimes, he escaped. Before he ran away, he set Darkheart free. Nobody knows why, but they became partners after that."

Kraal made a booming noise deep in his chest. "There is no way to know when the human died. But Darkheart must have chosen him. In gratitude for his freedom, maybe. What did the human do once he had awoken?"

"He tried to kill me," said Erian. "He chased me here. He kept saying horrible things about how he was going to catch me and kill me. He was so fast."

"But he did not catch you," said Senneck.

"He nearly did," said Erian. "He caught me here. But when I went inside, somehow he couldn't come in after me. It was strange—it looked like it was *hurting* him somehow. He kept trying, but he couldn't do it. He gave up and ran out again. And then he just disappeared."

"Disappeared?" said Elkin. "You mean hid somewhere?"

"No, I mean he *disappeared*," said Erian. "Vanished. I saw it happen. He stepped into a shadow, and then he was just . . . gone."

"Then that is all I need to know," said Kraal, with finality. "He fears holy places and uses the shadows to hide. He is *Kraeai kran ae*."

Silence fell. Even Senneck looked as if she didn't know what to say.

"What do we do?" said Erian. "How can we stop him?"

"It is simple," said Senneck. "If he is driven by magic, then magic is what we will need."

"But what kind?" said Elkin. "Kraal, do you know?"

The massive griffin looked away for a time, apparently thinking. "There is only one thing I know that we can do. Erian, listen closely to me."

Erian glanced at the others. "I'm listening, Mighty Kraal."

Kraal brought his head down close to his three listeners, but his eyes were on Erian's face and nothing else. "Out to sea off the eastern coast of Cymria, there is an island. No human or griffin lives there. It is called the Island of the Sun. Many long years ago, one of your race found enlightenment on that island. It is where our civilisation truly began. You must go to that island. If there is an answer, it waits for you there."

"What's there?" said Erian. "A weapon? Something that can kill him?"

"Perhaps," said Kraal. Abruptly he straightened up, casting a dispassionate glance at Senneck. "Senneck, you must take your human there. I command it."

"I will do this thing, Mighty Kraal," she said at once.

Erian couldn't believe what he was hearing. "Why us?" he said. "Why me?"

"Because you are *Kraeai kran ae*'s enemy," said Kraal. "He wishes to kill you before any other human, and you long to see him dead in return. I understood that when we first spoke. I know that your determination will give you what is needed to do as I have decided. Are you willing, Erian?"

"Yes." Erian lifted his chin. "I trust you, Mighty Kraal. And I'd do anything to stop him. He's evil." He tried to fold his arms boldly, but he had forgotten his injured shoulder. Screaming pain shot up to his neck, and he gave a strangled cry.

Kraal sighed. "Do not move."

Erian held still, wincing. "I don't know if I can travel like this."

The Mighty Kraal opened his beak wide and breathed out. Soft, pure white light came from his beak. It touched Erian's shoulder, and a moment later his entire arm felt warm as sunlight. He sighed with pleasure, and as the light vanished he realised the pain had gone.

He flexed his arm experimentally. Still no pain. "What the—"

Elkin smiled at his bewilderment. "Don't worry. He's healed you. Take the bandage off and see."

Erian ripped it away. Sure enough, the wound had gone. A fresh pink scar remained to tell the tale. "Gryphus' talons!"

"You should be very grateful," said Elkin. "He doesn't do that for most people."

Kraal regarded him serenely. "Now you have nothing to hinder you. Senneck, take your human back to the Eyrie and rest. You must leave tomorrow."

"I shall," said Senneck. "Erian, come."

He left the temple with her, unable to find anything more to say. Once they were outside he got onto Senneck's back and held on as she flew away. His mind was so crowded that he missed most of the short trip, and he was glad to be back in his own room.

Light-headed with shock, he stumbled over to the little desk.
There was a note on it.

He picked it up and squinted at the words.

Lord Erian,

Your sister has arrived and is waiting for you in the
audience chamber.

Skade and Skandar hid together in a little copse not too far
from Malvern's walls, and rested. Skandar seemed content
to lie on his belly and doze, leaving Skade to do the worrying.
She climbed up a tree in a few easy bounds, her claw-like nails
gripping the bark, and perched high in its branches to watch for
danger. Everything seemed quiet.

Now she was in sight of the hated city, she found herself
confused. What should she do next? How could she get in?

She tried to think, struggling to use a part of her mind that
had never been important before. Despite her human shape and
the emotions that had come with it, she was still a griffin at
heart, and griffins did not plan. That was what humans were for.
They were the ones who plotted and schemed; griffins acted.

The trouble was that she had no-one to help her decide *how*
to act. If Arenadd was here . . .

But he wasn't here, she reminded herself. He was in danger,
and it was up to her to plan.

She looked down at Skandar. There was no way *he* could go
in there. Even if no-one in the city knew what he looked like—
and they surely would—the other griffins there would recognise
him as an outsider immediately. And if he couldn't give a good
reason for invading their territory, he would be torn to pieces.

Maybe *she* could go in. Nobody knew about her, did they?
She could pretend to be another human. Humans didn't use
scent to tell where you were from, did they?

She shredded bark with her claws, trying desperately to
decide. How did humans know? They didn't seem to use smell
to recognise things, and they didn't have plumage. Most of
them looked the same to her. How did they work among themselves; what were their rules?

She wrestled with these mysteries a while longer and finally gave up with a hiss of frustration. It was no good; she couldn't work it out at all. If she was going to do this, she would have to take the risk of making a mistake and hope for the best. If she needed to, she knew she could fight.

But once she got into the city, what would she do next?

Growling with frustration, she jumped down out of the tree and went to see Skandar. The big griffin hadn't moved. As she got closer to him, her skin prickled. Something was wrong.

"Skandar," she said. "Are you well?"

No reply. Skade walked around him, looking for some clue. His eyes were closed and he sat very still, head drawn in close to his body. She could hear his slow, rumbling breaths. He didn't look to be in any distress, but something about him made her uneasy.

She sniffed the air, feeling her body tense instinctively. Only one thing could make her feel this way. *Magic*. She began to back away within an instant of realising it. Once she was at a safe distance, she turned and ran up another tree.

Her actions took no thought at all; a human would have stayed to watch or tried to ask questions. But Skade knew magic as only a griffin could; that knowledge was written into her very being. One did not stay near a griffin when he or she was using magic, especially when that magic was unknown. Anything could happen.

Safe in the treetop, she looked down at Skandar, who was just visible through the leaves. He didn't look to have moved at all. What could he be doing? Did he even know? He had never struck her as very intelligent, or as knowing much about his own powers.

She looked out over the plain that lay between her hiding place and Malvern's walls.

And saw something moving.

She slid back down the tree at top speed and ran out onto the plain, stopping to squint at the shape. It came on, straight toward her—it was human! A lone human, sprinting for the trees. A moment later she saw why, when an arrow shot past it and stuck in the ground.

The human didn't stop running. He put his head down and sped up, zigzagging to avoid the arrows coming at him. They couldn't all miss him, and as Skade watched he jerked and stumbled, crying out.

She knew that voice.

"Arenadd!" She ran toward him, but she was overtaken by something huge.

Skandar charged past her, massive paws thudding. Arenadd went straight to him, taking shelter under his partner's wings. Turning back, Skandar herded him to the trees, with Skade close behind.

Arenadd didn't slow down, even with the arrow sticking out of his back. He ran into the copse, tripped and fell headfirst, landing with a thump and an unearthly scream.

Skade ran to him. "No!"

He rolled over and curled into a ball, swearing incoherently. His right hand spasmed, trying to cover his left, which he held close to his body.

Skade knelt by him and tried to comfort him with touch. "Arenadd, I am here. Please be still. You are safe."

He relaxed, panting. "G-gods . . . help me, someone is going to *burn* for this."

Skade glanced over her shoulder; Skandar was there, huffing aggressively and looking for pursuit. "You must get up," she said. "We are not safe here."

Arenadd pulled himself into a sitting position. "Skade! Thank the—what are you doing here?"

"I came to find you, of course," she said.

He frowned at her. "I gave myself up to get you out of there, you daft woman. What were you thinking, coming back again?"

She hissed. "You are mine and I will not live without you. You know that."

He softened. "Are you all right?"

"I am not hurt. But you—" Skade caught his left arm, trying to see the hand. "What have they done to you?"

"I'll be all right," he said. "I just landed on it, that's all. No, look, just leave it alone, all right? Can you pull that thing out of me?"

She inspected the arrow. It was embedded in his upper back, but it didn't look like it had gone in too deeply. "How do I remove it?"

"It's easy," he said, wincing. "Just pull, and wiggle it from side to side. Don't worry about me; just do it quickly, or we'll both end up looking like pincushions."

She gripped the shaft and pulled hard. Arenadd cried out but twisted his shoulder forward to help. She moved the shaft around as she pulled, and it worked: the point came free, and she hurled the bloodstained thing away.

"Thanks." Arenadd got up. "Argh." He looked down. "You know what?" he said. "I really hate arrows."

Skandar lumbered over and shoved him roughly with his beak. "Human come back now," he said. "Come find you."

Arenadd gave the griffin an awkward one-armed hug. "I couldn't have made it here without you, Skandar."

Skandar did not look pleased. "Human leave!" he said, his black tail swishing angrily from side to side. "Leave mountain. Human run away."

"Yes, I did," said Arenadd, unsmiling. "To rescue Skade."

Skandar shoved him again, even more roughly. "Not go without me. *Never* go without me. Human never go alone, never! You my human, you stay with me."

"I had to do it alone," said Arenadd. "If you'd been there, they would have killed you."

"Not kill!" Skandar screeched. "*I* kill! No human kill dark griffin, no griffin kill dark griffin. Am dark griffin. Am one who kill. Not *be* killed."

"You didn't want to go," said Arenadd. "You wouldn't let me leave. That's why I ran away, Skandar. *That's* why I left you behind."

Skade snarled at Skandar. "Your choice was right, Arenadd. I did not think that your partner would care for me."

"Listen," Arenadd said sharply, cutting through the argument that looked about to start. "I'm not going to say I know what's right or that I made the right decision. All I know is this: whatever we do, we do together. Always."

"Together!" Skandar agreed.

"All of us," Arenadd growled. "All *three* of us."

Skandar huffed disgustedly. "Human need mate for eggs. Keep her until egg come. *I* not need such long time!"

Arenadd's mouth twisted as he suppressed a laugh. "Exactly. A male's not a male unless he fertilises a few eggs, is he?"

Skade didn't smile. "We have no time to waste here. They will be coming."

"That shouldn't be a problem," said Arenadd.

They were indeed coming, and Skandar had spotted them. He drew himself up, preparing for a fight. "You, no problem," he snapped. "Enemy come now, and I *fiiiight*!" The last word was a screeching cry, hurled out over the plain at the oncoming men.

There were only a handful of them, and they were disorganised and apparently leaderless. When they saw the monstrous dark griffin step out of the trees, screaming a challenge, they stumbled to a halt and backed away. Skandar came on, rasping threats and taunts. None of them looked likely to fight back, and the dark griffin probably would have attacked and killed them all anyway, if a sound from overhead hadn't made him look up.

Arenadd and Skade, staying safely among the trees, heard the screech from the sky. "Griffins coming," Arenadd muttered. "Damn it! We could have handled humans without much trouble, but—"

Skandar loped back toward them. "Come, now," he said. "Not fight here. Too many."

"You're right," said Arenadd. "Shall we fly?"

Skandar crouched low. "You, come," he said. "We fly in shadow."

Arenadd climbed onto his back at once, and Skade leapt up behind him. Skandar didn't complain. He stood up and walked off.

Behind them Skade could hear their pursuers catching up. "Skandar, we must fly quickly," she called. "If you are struck in the air, Arenadd and I shall fall!"

Skandar ignored her. He sped up into a lope, then a run and then a charge. Skade held on to Arenadd for dear life as they were both bounced up and down.

"I'm slipping!" Arenadd yelled. "Skan—"

Skandar leapt, straight forward and into darkness.

For Arenadd, the journey through the shadows with Skandar was like using his own newly discovered gift—but a hundred times more powerful. This wasn't mere shielding. He clung on to his partner's back, feeling the massive strength beneath him; and despite the icy cold, despite the fact that he couldn't see anything around them but black void, he had never felt so powerful in his life.

But it was humbling, too. For the first time he was beginning to see the full extent of Skandar's power. It had brought him back from death, and now it was taking them all to freedom.

Unseen in the darkness, Arenadd began to smile. They had the power, and soon they would have a plan. The Night God's will would be done, and he and Skandar would take everything the world had denied them for so long.

Anyone who stood in their way would die.

5

The Half-Breed

Erian and Senneck arrived at Elkin's marble audience chamber and found not one but two people waiting. Two people, and two griffins.

The woman who came forward to meet him looked older than he remembered, and worn. She wore her light brown hair in a braid, and her eyes were as blue as his own. A young grey griffin followed by her side, clicking its beak nervously.

The woman held out a hand to Erian and smiled. "Erian. For a moment I thought you were our father!"

Once Erian might have smiled back at her, but all he saw in that moment was the bundle in her arms. "Flell. Why did you come here?"

There were lines around her eyes now; they deepened as she looked at him. "There was nowhere else to go. Eagleholm's a ruin. I had to come and join you."

Erian looked past her to the other person in the room. "You! What are *you* doing here?"

A burly, bearded young man gave him a grin that, to Erian, looked insufferably smug. "Nice t'see yeh again, Erian."

Erian drew himself up. "That's *Lord* Erian, you lowborn thug."

"An' that's *Lord* Branton Redguard to you, Bastard," the man said, taking a step closer toward the red griffin that sat beside him.

Erian stared in outright horror. "*You*, a griffiner?"

The red griffin gave a yawn calculated to cause as much offence as possible. "This man is my human," she said lazily. "I have brought him here, with Thrain and her own human, who is his mate."

"His—" Erian turned to Flell. "You, with *him*?"

Flell looked steadily at him. "Bran is my husband."

"Yeah, that's right," said Bran. He put his arm around her. "After all, a man's gotta look after his own blood."

Erian's eyes flicked to the bundle. "I see."

Flell held up the infant inside for him to see. "Our daughter. She was born on the journey."

Erian saw the tiny face, the eyes milky blue, looking myopically up at him. He could have been looking at any baby in its mother's arms, but he knew he wasn't—even before he saw the wispy hair on the head, already as black as sin.

If his disgust showed on his face, Flell pretended not to notice. "Your niece," she said, cradling the child to her chest. "Her name's Laela. Laela Redguard."

Erian had never been more furious in his life. "What are you *doing* here?" he almost shouted. "What are you doing here in this room, pushing that *thing* in my face? Have you gone completely mad? Do you have any idea what'll happen when people find out—"

"That's enough, Erian." Flell spoke quietly, but her voice cut across his. "No-one is going to find out. Laela is Bran's daughter, and that's all there is to it. All we want is a new home, and we need your help."

"Why should I help you?" said Erian.

"Because you're my brother," said Flell. "You're the only family I have left, apart from Laela. And why would you turn your own sister away?"

Erian opened his mouth to retort, and shut it again when he saw the trap he was in. *Damn her!* "Fine," he growled. "I'll try and persuade Elkin to give you a place here."

"Thanks a lot," Bran's rough voice interrupted. "Glad t'have yeh as my brother-in-law." The grin returned, full of insolence.

Erian resisted the urge to punch it. "But you're going to stay out of my way, understand?" he said. "And you're going to keep that—that half-breed brat out of my face. If the truth about this *ever* gets out, to anyone at all, I'll disown you."

If Flell was finally going to shout back at him after that, none of them ever found out. The griffins started up suddenly, and everyone there turned as Kraal and Elkin arrived.

The red griffin and the until-now-silent Senneck instantly bowed their heads to their massive elder. He stood over them, focusing his attention on the red griffin. "I do not know you. What griffin are you?"

"I am Kraeya, hatched at Eagleholm," she said, without looking up. "And this is my human, Branton Redguard."

Kraal had seen Thrain as well. "And who are you, little one?"

Thrain looked up at him. "I am Thrain," she chirped. "My human is Flell."

"More newcomers," Kraal summarised. "Elkin, speak with them."

She waited to receive them, hands folded into the wide sleeves of her gown. Flell and Bran both stood in front of her and bowed respectfully as they introduced themselves.

"Ah!" she said on hearing Flell's name again. "I remember that name now. You're Erian's sister, aren't you?"

Flell, who was a head taller than the Eyrie Mistress, nodded. "It's an honour to meet you, Lady Elkin."

"And who's this?" Elkin added, looking at the child. "Erian never told me he had a nephew!"

"Niece." Flell smiled. "This is Laela."

Elkin glanced at Erian. "You must be very proud."

"Of course." Smiling at that moment was sheer agony, but he forced himself to keep going. "Lady Elkin, my sister and her husband are looking for a home. After the disaster at Eagleholm, they have nothing left. They came here to ask me for help."

"Oh, I would never turn away the daughter of Lord Rannagon," Elkin said at once. "Or a child without a home, for that matter. Of course you can stay. Perhaps they can use your rooms while you're away, Lord Erian."

"They're welcome to them," said Erian, through gritted teeth.

"Wonderful! Go on, then, why don't you, and get yourselves settled. You must be tired after your journey."

Bran bowed to her again. "We won't forget this, milady. Me an' Kraeya never had an Eyrie, so we'll swear ourselves to yeh. I'm sure yeh can find a use for us."

"We shall be honoured," Kraeya said gravely.

"Thank you," said Elkin. "I'll have a message sent when the proper arrangements have been made." She nodded, dismissing them all, including Erian. "I will see you later," she said, every bit the gracious lady. "Oh, Erian?"

He stopped on his way out. "Yes, Eyrie Mistress?"

Elkin smiled at him. "I would be honoured if you would join me for dinner this evening. The dining hall two levels down, at sunset."

It would be some time before Erian could recover from his rage and his fear, but those words helped to carry him for the rest of that day.

Midday, and in Saeddryn's little camp near Wolf's Town another argument had broken out.

"We can't go without her," Annir said yet again.

"She's left us," said Saeddryn. "She wants t'be left behind. If she didn't, she wouldn't've run off."

"How do you know she didn't get into trouble?" Annir persisted.

"Then that's her lookout," said Cai. "She didn't want t'stay, an' we didn't want her along, either."

"She ain't one of us," Rhodri agreed.

Annir tried a different tack. "What if she gets caught? She could tell them things you don't want them to know. Have you thought of that?"

They glanced at each other.

"She doesn't know nothin'," Saeddryn said at last. "Nobody told her."

"I still say we should look for her," said Annir. "Just in case."

"Well, I don't," said Rhodri. "What I say is, the longer we stay here, the more people can find us. We've waited for her long enough."

"You're right," a voice interrupted. "There's no time to waste at all."

Everyone around the fire froze.

"Who's that?" Cai exclaimed.

Saeddryn stood up. "I know that voice!"

As if by magic, Arenadd appeared. He walked out from among the trees, looking ragged and exhausted, but there was a smile on his face. Skade was on one side of him and Skandar the other.

Annir ran to him. *"Arren!"*

He opened his arms to receive her, and held her tightly without saying a word. She sobbed softly, holding on to him as if she would never let go.

The others were quick to crowd around, all of them talking at once. "How did ye get here?" "What happened?" "Are ye hurt?"

Arenadd let go of his mother and reached out to pat Saeddryn rather awkwardly on the shoulder. "Hello, cousin. It's good to see you again."

She grinned disbelievingly at him. "It's a miracle! I thought we'd lost ye for good!"

Arenadd shrugged. "I'm like a bad cold: impossible to shake off. Come on, let's all sit down for a bit. We've got time for a rest before we go."

"Go where?" said Saeddryn, as she led the way back to the fire.

"Back to the mountains, of course." Arenadd sat down. "We've got important things to do. But . . ." He looked down at his bandaged hand. "First things first. Saeddryn, do you know anything about healing?"

"I can help," Cai piped up.

Arenadd's mouth tightened. "I need some help. Mum, you should look away."

She was already moving closer, reaching out. "Let me see. What happened?"

He pulled away gently. "It's not pretty. Cai—"

Cai took his hand and very carefully peeled off the bandages. Arenadd sat very still, tensing in anticipation. He groaned softly when the last layer came off.

Cai gave a strangled cry of disgust. "Sweet Night God!"

Every single one of Arenadd's long, slender fingers had been broken—horribly broken. The flesh had turned purple and blue, bulging over crushed bones and mangled joints. They barely looked like fingers any more.

Saeddryn cringed. Skade hissed to herself. Annir cried out and clutched her son's arm. "My poor sweet boy, what have they done to you?"

Arenadd's face looked tired and old with pain, and his voice sounded thin. "Every finger was a question. 'Where are they?' Snap. 'How many are there?' Snap. 'Who is their leader?' Snap. 'Where is Darkheart?' Snap."

Saeddryn's look toward him was full of pity. "I knew they'd do that to ye, Arenadd. I'm sorry."

"It could have been worse," he said, with forced good cheer. "Cai, can you do anything?"

Cai was still examining the ruined fingers. "I can splint them, but I don't have any equipment. It'll have t'be just sticks an' string. But even if I had everythin' I needed, it wouldn't change much." She looked steadily at him. "Ye know ye won't be able t'use them fingers again, don't ye?"

Arenadd nodded. "I suppose I should thank them, really."

"For *what*?" Saeddryn exclaimed.

"For letting me keep my right hand." Arenadd nodded to Cai. "Do it, then, for what it's worth."

Cai turned to the others. "Rhodri, could ye go an' find some sticks? An' if anyone's got somethin' we could use for strings, pass 'em over."

Arenadd clenched and unclenched his good hand, and sighed. "I'll never use a long sword again, that's obvious. Besides, I lost mine. I need a new weapon. Something I can use one-handed."

"Worry about that later," said Saeddryn. "Tell me now, Arenadd"—she leant in close—"what did ye tell them?"

Everyone watched him closely, waiting for the reply.

He sighed. "They broke my fingers—"

"I know," said Saeddryn. "We won't blame ye. Just tell us the truth. What do they know?"

"They broke my fingers," Arenadd repeated. "They broke *all* my fingers on that hand before I even started lying."

Cautious hope showed on Saeddryn's face. "Lies?"

"You saw me," said Arenadd. "When they caught me."

"Ravin' like a lunatic," said Davyn. "I thought—"

"So did they," said Arenadd. "I thought, they all think I'm mad. Why not let them go on thinking it? So I kept pretending. Did everything I could think of. Sang all night, talked to walls. I did everything short of wearing my pants on my head. And then I bit half the captain's ear off, but that was just me losing my temper."

Rhodri and Davyn both sniggered, but Saeddryn didn't even smile. "So they know nothin'? Ye didn't give anythin' away?"

"Not a thing," said Arenadd. "They decided I was too deranged to be any help, so after the fingers they stopped torturing me."

Saeddryn rubbed a hand over her face. "What about the others, then? Up at the Throne? Ye were the last t'see them."

"Don't worry about them," said Arenadd. "I saw what had happened at Eitheinn and gave your—gave *her* a warning. They'll all be long gone by now."

Saeddryn relaxed. "Thank the Night God. I was so worried."

Arenadd smiled. "No need to worry any more. Not unless you're me, anyway."

Rhodri and Davyn had helped Cai to gather the sticks she needed, and some strips of cloth would serve to hold them in place.

"I can start now," she told her patient. "But I'm warnin' ye, it's goin' t'be painful."

Arenadd nodded stiffly. "Do it."

Cai began her work. Arenadd made no sound; he clenched his jaw, and sweat beaded on his face. Annir sat close by him and held his other hand, and he leant on her for comfort. None of the others wanted to watch the gruesome process of straightening each bone before the splints were strapped in place, and Saeddryn quietly motioned them away with her to search for food. Skade went with them, and Skandar lay down by a tree and slept, apparently unconcerned.

By the time Saeddryn returned, the splinting was done and Cai was wrapping the bandages back over Arenadd's hand. He looked even more haggard than before.

"Are ye all right?" Saeddryn asked.

Arenadd winced as Cai tied the end of the bandage down. "Gods, I would kill for a drink. But I suppose I'll just have to wait." He stood up. "Saeddryn, I need to talk to you. Alone."

"Ye should rest," she said gently. "Ye look about t'fall down."

"Later. This is more important." He walked out of the campsite, waving to her to follow. Skandar glanced up and rose to go with them.

Skade watched them go, narrow-eyed with suspicion, but stayed where she was.

* * *

The moment they were out of sight and earshot, Arenadd stopped. "Saeddryn," he said. "There's something I have to tell you."

She stopped, too, standing close and facing him. "I know," she said softly.

Arenadd looked away for a moment, his good hand rising compulsively to fiddle with his beard. "I'm going to be honest with you now," he said. "Completely honest. And I know this is going to be hard to accept, but I promise you that it's the truth."

"I believe ye," she said. Nearby, Skandar looked on with vague interest.

"I know you want a war with the Southerners," said Arenadd. "A war with Malvern. That's what your mother wants."

Saeddryn nodded. "Ye know it all, Arenadd. T'fight is all we've wanted all these years. My whole life I've been raised to it. But we knew we couldn't begin until the time was right. We needed more followers—needed *griffins*." Her hands curled into fists. "That's why we lost before."

Arenadd nodded. "You wanted a war, and a war is what you're going to have."

"When we've got the right—"

"Now," he interrupted. "It starts now. Here. Today. All I wanted to know was whether I had your support." Arenadd turned to Skandar. "And yours," he added, using griffish now. "Skandar?"

The massive griffin looked up. "What have?"

"War," said Arenadd. "To fight the other griffins, and the pale humans. Do you want to do that, Skandar?"

Skandar opened his beak and made a low, ugly rasping sound. "Want fight! I kill, kill many, kill enemy! Kill human and griffin who hurt us. Take all territory, all for us! Fight!" He slammed one huge forepaw into the ground, talons ripping through the dirt.

Arenadd smiled darkly. "That's what I thought. And that's what I want, too." He moved away, turning to look at both Saeddryn and Skandar. "War," he said again, in a low voice. "I've made my mind up. No more running. No more hiding. I was a lost soul my whole life, and I didn't even know it. But now

I know the truth. Now I *know* who I am, and I won't ever try to hide from it again. I'm going to start a war, Saeddryn, and I need you with me."

She came closer. "To the death, Arenadd."

"Then it's decided," said Arenadd, as if that settled it.

"Wait," said Saeddryn. "I still need t'know how this is goin' to go. Ye know we can't just march out there. We need support—an' not just a few hundred, we need thousands. We need good fighters, we need *griffins*. That's the only reason we hadn't started already. We failed before, Arenadd. Hundreds of us died. Our people haven't forgotten that yet. I believe in ye, I do, but ye must tell me—what are ye goin' t'do? What's goin' t'make it different this time?"

Arenadd stood tall, black eyes glinting. "This time you'll have us."

"We had a griffiner before," Saeddryn pointed out, not unkindly.

"I'm not your mother, and Skandar isn't Hyrenna. We have . . . a different power on our side now. The greatest power in the North."

Saeddryn stared. "What?"

"We have the Night God," Arenadd said softly. "She's come, Saeddryn. She's answered your prayers. She sent us. Both of us."

She looked uncertain. "It's good t'have faith, but . . ."

Arenadd braced himself. "No. It's not faith; it's reality. Touch my neck."

"What? Why?"

"Just do it. Here." He lifted his chin, exposing his throat, and indicated a spot just below the angle of his jaw. "Put your fingers there, and tell me what you feel."

She had already seen the ugly purple mark on his neck. "Sweet Night God, what's that?"

"A rope mark. Just touch it, would you?"

Saeddryn did. "What am I meant t'feel for?"

"A pulse."

She kept her fingers on the spot for a few moments, frowned and tried again on the other side. "That's odd . . ."

Arenadd reached up and gently grasped her hand. "Don't bother. There's nothing there."

Saeddryn looked bewildered. "What are ye talkin' about?"

He looked tired, but steady. "There's nothing there. Try all you like, but you won't find anything. I tried every day for months. There's no pulse."

Silence.

"No heartbeat," Arenadd said softly.

"But that's—that's . . . that doesn't make sense. Everyone's got a—"

"Not me." Arenadd straightened up. "I'm not human, Saeddryn. I'm not alive."

Saeddryn only looked at him.

Arenadd couldn't take the tension any more; he began to pace back and forth, shoulders hunched. "I died the day after my twentieth birthday. Fell to my death. I shouldn't be here at all. But Skandar was there. He found me; he was the only one there when I died. He used his magic on me. Brought me back. I look the same, I talk the same, but I'm not the same." He stopped and looked at her. "I don't have a heart. I don't have a soul. They're gone forever."

He had been speaking griffish for Skandar's benefit, and the griffin had been listening "Is true!" he said unexpectedly. "True, truth. Use magic, first time that day. Black magic, like black scream."

"Magic the Night God gave him," said Arenadd. "I didn't know it at first, not until I came here—neither did Skandar. But on the night of the Blood Moon, when I killed that man—"

"She came," Saeddryn rasped. "The Night God came."

"Yes. I summoned her without even meaning to. She told me the truth then. Told me what I am. What Skandar is." Arenadd seemed to age as he said the words. "I am the man without a heart. I am the Master of Death. I am *Kraeai kran ae*, the Cursed One. I am the Night God's creature. I don't have a life any more; the purpose she gave me is all I have left."

"What purpose?" said Saeddryn, though she looked as if she already knew.

"To destroy her enemies. To free the North." *To kill Rannagon's children.*

"And I see," said Skandar. "See too. Have dream. White griffin with one eye. She say, never leave dark human. Say, fight by side. Kill all enemy. Fight, and have all you want."

"She said the same thing to me," Arenadd told him. He smiled very slightly. "I never was happy except when I had power. So we're going to take it now. All of it." He looked at Saeddryn. "I thought I was cursed, but now I know the truth. It's not a curse; it's a blessing. I'm immortal, cousin. Unkillable. They hanged me today at Malvern—I *heard* my neck break. But here I am."

Saeddryn said nothing. She had become very still.

"So you'll get your war," said Arenadd. "And when our people know what I am, they'll come to us. *All* of them, every true Northerner in Tara will come. Skandar and I will crush the Southern scum like insects. Anyone who tries to stop me— *anyone*, even another Northerner—will join me in death."

He fell silent, and at last Saeddryn moved. She took a stumbling step back, stopped and knelt at Arenadd's feet. "Master," she whispered. "Holy warrior. I'm sorry I didn't recognise ye, I'm sorry."

She looked up to see Arenadd reaching down to her. "Get up." He pulled her to her feet. "You don't kneel to anyone, Saeddryn," he said sternly. "You're a Northerner. We stand on our own two feet, or we die."

She smiled hesitantly. "I always knew the Night God would help us one day. I knew she'd answer our prayers. I should never have doubted."

"Everyone doubts," said Arenadd. "Especially me." He glanced at Skandar and translated the gist of what had been said. "So, we're agreed?" he finished.

"Agree!" Skandar snorted. "I take humans back to mountain. Where Hyrenna is. Know where they nest."

Saeddryn nodded. "We'll go back t'my mother an' the rest. They'll have good advice, an' we can't abandon them."

"Go now." Skandar walked off, back toward the camp.

Saeddryn had one more question. "The others—should I tell them? About . . . what ye are?"

"Not now," said Arenadd. "They'll have enough on their minds. And we'd better get back to them now. There's work to be done."

6

The Chosen One

Erian and Elkin ate together that night, alone but for Senneck and the Mighty Kraal. The two griffins crouched together by a wall in the massive dining hall and shared a huge ox carcass that nevertheless didn't look big enough to feed Kraal.

As for the two humans, they sat at the long table. Elkin ignored the impressively carved chair at the head of the table and sat opposite her guest instead, watching him with those pale green eyes while servants laid out the food.

Erian's mouth had gone dry. He drank some cider to calm himself down and tried to think of something to say. All his words seemed to disappear when Elkin was there.

"Try some of the venison," she said. "It's roasted in cymran juice and honey."

He obeyed. "It's delicious." Any possible follow-up escaped him.

They ate in awkward silence, while behind them Senneck and Kraal huffed at each other. Senneck seemed intimidated by the massive white griffin and kept her distance from him. Erian saw her, and felt more empathy for her than he had in ages.

As the uncomfortable meal drew on, he started to panic. He'd barely said anything since he'd arrived, and if he didn't speak soon his last chance would be gone.

He was so caught up in his own embarrassment that he

utterly failed to notice that Elkin was just as quiet and fumbling as himself. But in the end, it was she who spoke.

"What do you think about all this, Erian?" she asked.

He started, nearly upsetting his cup in the process. "What— I mean, uh . . . what do I think about what?"

"All this," she said. "Everything that happened today. After all, you were mixed up in it."

Erian glanced at Kraal. "I don't really know what to think. I'm . . . scared."

Elkin half-laughed. "Of course you are! *I'm* afraid. If you said you weren't, I would know you were lying."

Erian blushed, but his old desire to impress her made him square his shoulders. "I'm afraid of him, but I'm going to fight back. I swore to see him dead, and I'll keep my word. I'll *always* keep my word, the way a griffiner should."

Elkin smiled. "I knew you would. But I wonder . . . what does Kraal think you're going to find on this island?"

"A weapon," Erian said instantly. "Something that can kill him. I'm sure of it."

She put her head on one side. "Why so certain, Erian?"

He could feel his blush deepening, but he pushed on regardless. "What else could it be? If I'm the one to find it—I'm not much, but I know I'm a warrior. I was trained in swordplay since I was seven years old. If I'm going to be given something to defeat him, it has to be a weapon."

"I suppose so," said Elkin.

The cider had already gone to Erian's head. "And—and— I've been thinking. If *he's* been sent to fight us, then maybe I'm meant to fight *him*. Maybe it's destiny. Maybe—maybe it's Gryphus' will."

Elkin watched him. "May—be," she said, very slowly. "You could ask Kraal that, but now isn't the time. He never talks when he's eating."

Erian's look toward her didn't waver. "I think it's Gryphus. I think he sent me. Made me. To stop the darkness."

"You sound very certain," said Elkin, in the same cautious manner as before.

"I have a reason," Erian told her hastily. "There's a reason I think that."

"Yes? What reason?"

He looked at the tabletop. "I've . . . I've never really told anyone this before, but . . ."

"Yes?"

Erian gathered his wits, and ploughed on. "I was born in a village called Carrick. They farmed cows there. And bees. It's where Eagleholm got most of its honey. There were orchards there, too. I remember them . . . they smelled wonderful in the spring. I used to practise there, with my wooden sword." He looked wistful. "My mother was a tavern maid. Belara. Bell, they called her. My father stayed at the tavern on his way back home from the war, and he and my mother—well, they spent the night together. He left after that and never came back to her. But when the tavern owner found out she was pregnant, he threw her out. She went to the temple instead. There was a small one there, with just one priest. No griffin, just a bell. The priest let her stay and help him gather flowers and bring new candles." Erian took a deep breath. "I was born in that temple. My mother went into labour one day while she was working. There was no time to take her anywhere, so she lay on the altar. That's where I was born. At the stroke of noon, just as the sun touched her. I came out into sunlight. That's what my grandmother used to say. Came into life, into sunlight. A gift from Gryphus."

Elkin's eyes had widened. "Great sun. Is all that true?"

"That's what my grandparents told me. My mother—she didn't survive. She died as I was born. But when I found out where I was born, and how, I thought it meant something special. I started going to the temple more, to pray. I believed it was all a message—a sign. That's why I never gave up, why I went all the way to Eagleholm to become a griffiner. I knew it was what Gryphus had always meant to happen. And now—now this. A Dark Lord. A special weapon. It's destiny, Elkin, I know it is." Erian smiled beatifically.

Elkin smiled back, uncertainly. "That's . . . an amazing story. And maybe it will be better for all of us if you're right. But you know that isn't why I asked you to come here."

Erian looked at her properly for the first time in a while. "I'm sorry. I shouldn't have talked so much . . . I suppose I got carried away."

Elkin coughed. Her hands, resting on the table in front of

her, played compulsively with her spoon. "I asked you to come here mostly because I felt I owed you an apology."

"An apology? For what?"

"Just a few days ago, you confessed something to me and I ignored it. I was cruel, and I haven't stopped regretting it since."

Erian's heart paused its beating. "I don't understand," he lied.

For almost the first time since they had met, Lady Elkin, Eyrie Mistress, looked utterly lost—even afraid. "You said you loved me," she said. "And I pretended not to hear. I made you think I didn't care, but the truth is that I didn't know what to say." She gave him a weak smile. "I am very clever. I know three languages, I've memorised the names of every town and village in my territory, I can tell you who invented the woodcut—but *feelings* are something that have always been a puzzle to me. I can analyse your emotions like they were a book, but my own are confusing sometimes, a riddle I can't solve."

To Erian, nothing that had happened that day could be as terrifying or as magical as this. For once, he didn't try to say anything.

"I have had more marriage proposals than years on this earth," Elkin went on matter-of-factly. "But I turned them down, every last one. Some people think it's because I don't want to risk sharing my power with a husband, but the truth is simpler. All those men who wanted me didn't want me at all—they wanted other things. My money, my power, my beautiful Eyrie. Even access to my magnificent partner. But you're different. I know you well enough now. You don't want power or money or status. You only want my love. Don't you?" she added, suddenly forceful. "Isn't that the truth, Lord Erian Rannagonson?"

A great weight seemed to press down on him at that moment, heavy as the hand of Gryphus himself. When he opened his mouth to reply, the words nearly stuck in his throat; he all but choked them out. "Yes. I don't want you because you're an Eyrie Mistress; I want you because you're you. I always have."

"Why?" she demanded. "*Why?* Why me?" Her face was almost angry.

"Because—because—because you're beautiful and clever and kind and graceful and everything I'm not, and when I'm with you I—" Erian's babble spluttered to a halt as suddenly as it had begun. "I feel . . . *alive*. When you're there. But"—he bowed his head—"I shouldn't have said anything. I'm just a stupid bastard peasant, and I'll never be good enough for you. I should have left it alone."

"We both should," Elkin said softly. She glanced toward Kraal. "Chaos is coming. War, most likely. I can feel it. Who knows what could happen? When a man can come back from the dead, nothing is certain any more. In times like these, perhaps an Eyrie Mistress can love a bastard."

Erian felt close to tears. "Maybe. But it's happened already, hasn't it? I love you, Elkin, and not even Gryphus himself could change that. And if you love me, too, then . . . then so be it."

Her eyes shone. "Then so be it. Kiss me."

He did.

Over by the wall, Senneck nervously allowed Kraal to groom her. But she soon relaxed and began to purr. Neither griffin seemed to have noticed Erian and Elkin.

That day at Malvern, everything changed. A man came back from the dead, and an Eyrie Mistress loved a bastard.

It made no difference to Erian. He leant over the table, feeling Elkin's lips pressed against his, and his heart, his living heart, pounded as it had never done before. He already knew that this was the happiest moment of his life, and he grasped it with both hands, determined to remember it forever. He knew, too, really knew, that what his grandmother had always told him was the truth: that love was the greatest power in the world, and nothing—not magic, not even death itself—could ever destroy it. Love was life.

To him, Elkin was life. His Elkin.

Arenadd and Saeddryn returned to the camp together, and were greeted by some slightly suspicious looks.

Arenadd, however, was businesslike. "All right, everyone, get yourselves together. We're leaving."

They seemed happy enough with that. Rhodri complained, though. "Why should we be takin' orders from ye?"

In response, Arenadd unfastened the front of his robe and freed his right arm from its sleeve. Spiralling blue patterns stood out all over the grimy skin as he held the limb out for them all to see.

Rhodri and his friends all went very still. "Are those—" Cai began.

Arenadd stuffed his arm back into its sleeve. "Yes. Arddryn Taranisäii has retired. I am the chief now, and I have the tattoos to prove it."

Rhodri and his fellows sprang into action at once, with muttered apologies. Only Annir still looked confused as they put out the fire and set about hiding it.

"Arren, what's going on?"

"It's Arenadd now," he told her gently. "I'll never be Arren again. Come here."

She obeyed. "Where are we going?"

"To the mountains," said Arenadd. "We have friends there." He reached out to touch her neck, where the collar of a slave gleamed dully. "Does it hurt?"

Annir nodded. "They're made to hurt."

"I know," he said grimly. "But don't worry, I know how to take it off. I should do it now, before we leave."

"You know how to remove them?" she said. "How?"

Arenadd looked around the campsite. "I wish I had a hammer . . . a rock should do the job, though. Help me find a big one."

They wandered around for a short while until Annir picked up one about the size of an orange. "Is this big enough?"

Arenadd took it and weighed it in his hand. "It should do. Now listen. I've done this before plenty of times. All you have to do is lift your chin and hold very still, and I'll give it a good hard whack in the right spot. If I do it properly, it'll break the locking mechanism and the collar will spring open."

"Is that all?"

"Yes. But I should warn you: it *will* hurt, and if I don't do it right the first time, I'll have to try again."

Annir smiled wanly. "It's a small price to pay for freedom." She lifted her head to expose the collar. "Do it."

"Saeddryn!" Arenadd waved to her. "I need your help. Hold on to her, or she'll fall over."

Saeddryn took Annir by the shoulders. "Don't worry. I've got yer. Go on, Arenadd."

The others had noticed what was going on and came over to watch.

"Look closely," Arenadd advised. "One day you might have

to do this, too." He pulled the rock back and bashed it against the collar with all his strength.

The impact threw Annir back against Saeddryn with a cry of shock and pain, but she had barely recovered herself before she began scrabbling at the collar, wrenching it open. It swung apart on its hinge, the ruined lock mechanism protruding. She hurled it away into a tree, where it got hooked on a branch and stayed there, swinging back and forth.

Rhodri had already torn a strip of cloth into a bandage. "Here, use this."

The collar had left dozens of small bleeding puncture marks on Annir's neck. She dabbed at them, breathing hard. "It's not so bad."

"Bandage it up anyway." Arenadd rubbed his face. "Gods, how did it come to this? If I'd known what I was sending you into . . . and Dad as well . . ."

Annir finished wrapping the makeshift bandage in place, and she looked up sadly. "I know what happened to him. Skade told me."

"He died bravely," Saeddryn said stoically.

"He was always brave," said Arenadd. "I can't bring him back or undo what happened to you. But I promise you, the Bastard will pay. They'll all pay."

"All of them," said Skade.

"Aye, they'll pay in blood," said Saeddryn. "Rhodri— c'mon, hurry up an' finish buryin' them ashes."

Arenadd was looking at the sky. "We'll head north, obviously. That way." He pointed. "Don't bring anything you don't need. Skandar?"

The dark griffin listened. "I fly," he said. "Watch from sky."

"Good idea," said Arenadd. "I'll stay down here and keep everyone together. Skade, you and Saeddryn stay close by me. Rhodri, you and Davyn bring up the rear. Everyone has to stay alert." He squared his shoulders and smiled to himself. "Time to go home."

Erian's departure from Malvern was a quiet affair. On the morning after Flell's arrival he and Senneck went to meet Elkin and Kraal in the audience chamber, and found them both waiting there. To Erian's dismay, Bran and Flell were there, too, the former watching him with barely concealed contempt.

Erian ignored the former guard captain and embraced Elkin.

She returned the gesture, a little awkwardly. "Good morning. Did you sleep well?"

"Not really," Erian confessed.

"I know that," said Senneck. "You did not stop pacing until the Day Eye was near to opening. The noise kept me awake."

"Sorry," said Erian.

"Are you prepared?" Kraal interrupted.

"I think so," said Erian. He already knew Senneck wouldn't be able to carry anything beyond himself and his sword, and had chosen the single warmest and toughest set of clothes he owned. A bag of oblong hung from his hip, and he had filled his pockets with travel rations.

"But are you *ready*?" said Kraal.

The question caught Erian off guard. "Uh, I . . ." He caught a glimpse of Flell and straightened up. "Yes."

"Well then, that's good," Elkin said brightly. She held out a hand. "Here. A gift for you."

It was a golden sunwheel: three curling lines connected at the centre like the petals of a flower. The place where the lines intersected was set with a large blue stone.

"It's very nice," said Erian.

"It belonged to my father," said Elkin. "My mother told me it was passed down to him by his grandfather, and he wore it when he fought in the war."

Erian smiled and tied it around his neck. "I won't lose it."

Bran pushed forward. "Excuse us," he said.

Erian glared at him. "What do you want?"

Bran glanced quickly at Kraeya, who was busy grooming her feathers. She flicked her tail but said nothing.

Bran turned his attention back to Erian. "Yer sister an' I came up 'ere to see yeh off, as yeh might've noticed. Trouble is, no-one's told us where yer goin' or why. Lady Elkin said we oughta wait for yeh an' yeh'd tell us yerself, like."

"I didn't think it would be fair for us to tell them," Elkin put in. "This is for you to tell, Erian."

Erian gaped at her. "But I . . . Elkin, should we really be telling people?"

"I think your sister has a right to know," said Elkin. "Kraal agrees."

"Tell her," Kraal rumbled.

Erian tried not to look at the child in Flell's arms. "Senneck and I have to go east," he said eventually. "To find something."

"All the way t'Amoran?" said Bran.

"No, not that far," said Erian.

"So, what is this thing?" said Flell. "And why do you have to go after it?"

"Well . . ." Erian glanced desperately at Kraal, who stared back, calm and still. "Well," he said again. "It's something magical. A weapon."

"Magic weapon?" said Bran suspiciously. "What sorta magical weapon? What for?"

Erian felt cold hatred rise up inside him at the sound of the man's voice. "You know about what happened yesterday," he said, trying to keep his own voice level. "In the city."

"When Arren escaped," Flell said coldly.

Erian turned away. "You don't understand, Flell. You don't know what he did. He didn't escape. He came back from the dead."

"What?" said Bran.

Erian found himself savouring the disbelief in their faces. "Yesterday morning, Arenadd Tanrisäii was executed for murder and sedition. He was hanged, in public. I was there. I saw it. I saw him come back to life. He has magic; I saw him use it. He disappeared . . . like a shadow."

Erian watched the horror etch itself into Bran's and Flell's faces as he spoke, and felt his embarrassment vanish as well.

"Your *friend*," he said. "Your dear, misunderstood pet blackrobe—he's not human any more. He's become something else."

Flell gripped her husband's arm. "Become what?"

"Kraeai kran ae," Senneck hissed.

Every griffin in the room stilled. Thrain whimpered and pressed herself against Flell's leg, and Kraeya stood up sharply.

"What is this?" the red griffin demanded. "Senneck, what are you speaking of? *Kraeai kran ae* is not possible; it cannot be real."

"It is real, and if you do not accept it then you are a bigger fool than I thought," Senneck snapped back. "The blackrobe is

Kraeai kran ae. He has the powers of death and the shadows; he is chosen by the dark griffin. The dark griffin has shared his magic with him, and soon they will both return to bring down the same fate to Malvern as they did to Eagleholm."

"And that's why we're leaving," Erian interrupted. "Senneck and I are going to find a special weapon that can kill him. He has to be stopped, and I'm the one who's going to do it."

"Why you?" said Flell.

Erian drew himself up. "Because I'm his enemy. Gryphus chose me."

"You think that this bastard is *Aeai ran kai*?" said Kraeya to Senneck.

Senneck snapped her beak at her. "I do not know."

"But I do," said Kraal, silencing them both with a glare. "Save your petty bickering for another time; we do not have any to waste. This human is *Kraeai kran ae*'s enemy, and that makes him *Aeai ran kai*, and that is all. I have spoken, and my word is final. Senneck, I have entrusted you to help him reach the Island of the Sun. Once you are there, you will know what must be done. Protect and guide your human."

Senneck arched her neck and puffed out her chest proudly. "I shall, Mighty Kraal."

"We shall have our own work to do while they are gone," Kraal added. "Return quickly, Senneck, and we shall fight *Kraeai kran ae* as well as we can until then."

"I shall not fail," said Senneck.

Kraal drew himself up to look at them all. "It is time," he said. "Come."

They followed him through an archway and out onto an oversized balcony, where a cold wind ruffled hair and feathers. Erian looked out over the city and the lands beyond. They looked enormous. To the east were farmlands and, beyond that, the darkness of wild forests. Somewhere on the other side of them was the sea.

Senneck nudged him. "Come. We do not have time for dreaming. Say your farewells."

Erian gave Flell a quick hug, knowing it was expected of him, and forced himself to kiss the infant on the forehead. "Goodbye, Flell. Look after yourself, and my niece."

Flell smiled at him. "Don't worry. Bran can protect us, and Kraeya can protect all three of us."

"I can, and I shall," Kraeya rasped, her tail lashing.

Erian embraced Elkin far more warmly. "Stay safe," he murmured in her ear. "I want you here waiting for me when we get back, understand?"

Elkin turned her head and kissed him on the cheek. "Of course I'll be here, silly. Where else would I go? And of course I'll be safe. I have Kraal to protect me, you know."

Erian kissed her on the mouth. "I just want to know you'll be all right," he mumbled.

"And I will be," said Elkin, letting go of him. "If anything, it's you who should be careful." She gave him a playful nudge. "So stay close to Senneck and follow her advice, and don't rush into things without thinking, the way you're prone to do. We need you alive, too, you know."

Erian clasped her hands. "I'll be back," he promised. "I swear I'll be back, and I'll bring the weapon. I won't fail you, or the North. I won't."

"I trust you," Elkin said softly. "Now go and be blessed, Erian Rannagonson."

Erian let go of her hands, though the action made his heart hurt, and climbed onto Senneck's back. She dipped her head to Kraal one last time, glanced briefly at Thrain and Kraeya, and loped away toward the edge of the balcony. She sped up as she went, wings opening, and as Erian braced himself she launched herself into the sky.

Erian could feel his heart thudding as Senneck flew higher, and not just from the instinctive fear he had every time they flew together. He wished he could turn and look back at the others, but didn't dare: if he didn't keep still he could make Senneck lose her balance or be torn off her back. But he could still feel Elkin's presence behind him, as if she were standing there, and when Senneck finally steadied and he could risk a glance back, his stomach lurched when he saw how far away she was already.

That feeling of sickness built and then settled into a dull ache inside him as the Eyrie began to fall away behind them and Malvern passed below. For one wild moment he wanted to wrench at Senneck's halter to try to make her turn around, or to yell out to her and plead with her to turn back.

Erian's face remained calm, and his body still. But the ache in his chest did not fade away.

* * *

Bran and Flell flew back to Erian's home without having exchanged a word, and when they landed and Bran slid off Kraeya's back, Flell was too afraid to say anything. He helped her down and hung up Kraeya's harness without a word.

Flell cradled Laela against her chest to soothe her, and watched her husband as he paced back and forth, shoulders hunched.

"What are we going to do?" she said at last, a little nervously.

Bran stopped abruptly. "This is bilge," he said. "That's what it is. It's a load of steaming shit."

"Bran, you know I don't like it when you talk like that," said Flell.

Bran ignored her. "I ain't gonna believe it. I ain't gonna believe a *word* of it. What's wrong with that lot? They're out of their godsdamned minds! Arren, usin' evil magic? It's shit. All of it. An' they reckon *he's* mad?" He spat.

"But why would they be making that sort of thing up?" said Flell.

"I dunno," said Bran. "But—"

Kraeya started up. "I do not believe this story either, Bran. Nor do I trust Senneck."

"What about Kraal, though?" said Flell. "He seemed awfully certain."

"The Mighty Kraal," said Kraeya, and hissed to herself. "He is very old, and by all accounts too caught up in his own mysticism for his own good. And in either case we have nothing but the Bastard's word that your friend has these supposed dark powers."

"So yeh don't believe this 'kray kran ee' nonsense?" said Bran.

"I do not." Kraeya's tail lashed. "*Kraeai kran ae* is a myth— pure legend, a story old hens tell to frighten chicks. Humans do not possess magic—they cannot—and the gods are nothing but human arrogance made into imaginary friends. They cannot control us."

"But there's still somethin' goin' on here I don't like the smell of," said Bran. "How did Arren survive back at Eagleholm if it wasn't by magic? He fell off the edge of the damned city—no-one could live after that!"

"How do you know Darkheart didn't catch him?" said Flell.

Bran paused. "It was *dark*. Griffins don't fly in the dark, Flell."

"That is not true for all of us," said Kraeya. "Some griffins can see in the dark; perhaps this Darkheart is one of them."

"Well, what are we going to do?" said Flell. "We can't just stay here and do nothing."

"I know what I'm gonna do," said Bran. "I'm gonna go out there an' look for him, an' I ain't givin' up until I find him."

"But why?" said Flell. "And how are you going to find him? After all the things he's supposed to have done . . ."

"I don't care about that," said Bran. "I'm gonna find him, an' damn the difficulty. I owe him, Flell. He trusted me, an' I let him down. He was my best mate, an' I let all those things happen to him—an' I can't let it happen again. I've gotta find him an' help him get away, or at least warn him about what's goin' on."

Flell looked at Kraeya. The red griffin had sat on her haunches and was grooming her chest feathers, apparently uninterested in the conversation. Now, though, she looked up and said, "I agree."

Bran paused. "Yeh do?"

"Yes," said Kraeya. "You and I should look for your friend."

"But why do yeh care, Kraeya?" said Bran. "Yeh never knew him."

"I know Senneck," said Kraeya. "And I do not trust her. I believe I see more than lies and foolish superstition at work here. Senneck is ambitious and arrogant. Of all the griffins living in the hatchery, she was the most self-centred and had the loftiest goals. Nothing would be enough for her; no human was good enough, no station high enough. She would have nothing but the best, and I believe that she would go to any lengths to take it. She has chosen this human—this fool of a boy—and already she has manipulated them both into an official position. Her human is still a bastard, and that will always stand in his way—but if they were both to convince Kraal that your friend was *Kraeai kran ae* and that the Bastard was *Aeai ran kai*, they could do much more. All the Bastard must do is murder your friend, and he will be a hero."

Bran gaped at her. "Wh— y'think . . ."

Flell was more composed. "Kraeya, do you honestly think

they could do something like that? I mean . . . it sounds very outlandish to me."

"More outlandish than the idea that your bastard half-brother is *Aeai ran kai*?" Kraeya shot back. "No. To me this sounds like the work of a cunning liar and schemer—Senneck's work from beginning to end. I doubt the Bastard could have imagined it himself."

"Yeah . . ." Bran said slowly. "Yer right, Kraeya. It's gotta be a lie—a stupid one." He straightened up. "Well, I ain't lettin' my best mate be murdered just so the Bastard an' his bird can get a fat reward. I'm gonna put a stop to it."

"We shall *both* put a stop to it," said Kraeya. She stood up. "You and I shall find your friend and do what we can to help him, and I shall enjoy seeing Senneck's plot fail. If there is any griffin who needs to be humbled, it is her."

"Yeah," Bran growled. "An' if there's any human who needs t'be brought down a peg, it's the Bastard. *Chosen One*," he added contemptuously.

7

Night Travels

The journey back to the mountains began slowly. All of them were exhausted and underfed; even Arenadd felt weaker than he would admit. He gave nothing away, determined to keep up a facade of invulnerability. Now that he had confessed to being the Night God's avatar, he had burdened himself with a role to play. Saeddryn believed he was infallible and unstoppable, and he couldn't let her know that he could still get tired and hungry, and feel pain. The others couldn't know it, either. Everything hinged on his new persona and their belief in it. He hoped he could go on believing it himself.

Unfortunately, it wasn't just tiredness that made the travelling slow. Food was scarce, and made scarcer by the fact that they had to find it in complete secrecy. They could allow nobody to see them; the risk was too great. The moment anyone knew where they were, half the country would come running. Arenadd and Skade had to draw on everything they had learnt during the time they had come this way before. The trouble was that back then, there had been only two of them and Skandar, and they had been able to fly most of the way. Hiding seven people and one enormous griffin was next to impossible.

Arenadd and Skandar took to flying ahead to scout out the path and gather food, Skandar by stealing livestock and Arenadd by using his newfound power to sneak into homes and help himself to whatever he could find. For some odd reason, the first things he stole were a hairbrush, a razor and a bottle of hair lotion. Nobody had the spine to make any remarks about this, but Cai tittered when he went off by himself one evening and came back so well groomed he might have been on his way to a dance.

Arenadd studiously ignored the woman's giggle. "I've found some water. Skade, could you come with me and help carry some back?"

She stood up at once and silently walked with him back the way he had come. He led her to a small stream, where a scatter of black stubble had been left on the banks. Arenadd glanced at his reflection in the water. "*Much* better. I tell you, Skade, I'll take another hanging before I let myself get so grubby again."

She rolled her eyes—a new trick she had learnt from watching humans. "I see that nothing you have suffered in all this time has managed to change you, Arenadd Taranisäii."

He gave her a mischievous sideways look. "And you're very glad, aren't you?"

"Yes," she said softly. Tentatively, she reached out to touch him. "I had given up any hope of seeing you again. When you went into those mountains and did not return, I thought you had broken your promise. I thought . . ."

Arenadd's expression darkened. "I knew what you must be thinking, but believe me, it wasn't my fault. I honestly thought I'd be back in a day or so, but I should have suspected . . . The way Saeddryn was acting, it was obvious she wasn't telling me something."

"Then what was there?"

"Her mother," said Arenadd. "Arddryn. And her partner, Hyrenna. They're both supposed to be dead, although not in the same way as me. Saeddryn took us to them, and after that they wouldn't let us leave. Skandar went off with Hyrenna, and I had to stay with Arddryn."

"A prisoner?" said Skade.

"Not really. More like an apprentice." Arenadd gave a short laugh. "Finally, an apprenticeship I got to finish."

"I do not understand," she said, in the stiff voice she used in moments of uncertainty.

Arenadd shrugged. "She wanted me to be her successor, and she trained me for it—whether I wanted her to or not. When we were finished, she gave me the tattoos of manhood. See?" He rolled up his sleeve to show her. "I'm a proper Northerner now."

Skade clicked her teeth. "You told me you did not want to be a Northerner. You were ashamed of it."

"Yes. I was. But now I know why." Arenadd's eyes narrowed. "It was because of *them*. The Southerners. I gave myself to them when I was only ten; I let them raise me. They tried to turn me into one of them; they taught me to hate what I was. I turned on my own people—my own parents. But now I know the truth. Caedmon helped to teach me that, and Arddryn and the Night God finished it."

"But there is no such thing—" Skade began.

Arenadd wasn't listening. "I didn't know who I was," he muttered. "Now I do, and I've made peace with it at last." He smiled very slightly. "A darkman, and a griffiner. A Dark Lord."

Silence, and stillness, just for a moment.

Then Skade smiled. "And do Dark Lords have time for poor ugly creatures like me?"

Arenadd hesitated. "You're not ugly."

She moved closer, resting her head against his. "You have found your pride at last, and I am glad. I do not care that it kept you away for so long, not now that I see what it has done to make you stronger. I am proud of you, and . . . I love you, Arenadd."

"Still?"

"Yes. I had already forgiven you for leaving me alone. When you gave yourself up to save me, I knew that you still cared. It was enough, many times enough. I only asked to be certain."

Arenadd took her hands, clumsily with his bandaged fingers. "You remember the last thing I said to you, when they caught me."

"Yes . . . I did not understand it. You have no heart."

"But I do. I do, Skade. I have a heart. Yours." Arenadd gripped her hands more tightly. "I realised it just in that moment. You're all I have left; you're the only thing that keeps the last human part of me alive. Without you, there'd be nothing left inside me but darkness."

She managed a smile. "A great responsibility for one human to carry."

Arenadd let go. "You know you only have to take it if you want to."

"Do not speak nonsense," Skade rasped. "You know this is

a question that found an answer long ago. You need me, and I need you; and if we both know it, then there is no more to say."

Arenadd smiled—a sweet young smile, the kind of smile he would never give to anyone else but her. "You're right, Skade, as always."

"I have seen how your cousin looks at you," she said abruptly.

"Oh, that. Don't worry about it, Skade. I'm not interested in her. She expected to marry me the way her mother wanted, but I won't. She's a good woman, but she'll never be anything more than my second-in-command. Try to be nice to her; she doesn't deserve your jealousy."

Skade kissed him. "I will leave her be. You are the only human that matters to me."

They kissed again, harder this time. Arenadd began to pull closer to her, his excitement mounting as their breath mingled and her warmth soaked into his cool skin. He'd been away from her far too long, and what did it matter if—

"Human!"

The voice lashed out like a whip. Arenadd and Skade pulled apart instantly, shock on both their faces.

Skandar stood over them, his tail swinging from side to side. "Am thirsty. Humans move now." Without waiting for an answer, he stepped over the pair of them and thrust his beak into the water.

Arenadd cringed and got out from under the griffin's belly. "Good gods, Skandar, you're welcome to a drink, but you didn't have to go and shove your balls in my face."

Skade hissed. "You have no respect at all, dark griffin."

Skandar finished his drink. "Not need respect; am very big," he said arrogantly. He turned to face Arenadd. "Come to find you. Want talk."

Arenadd got up, dusting himself down. "Of course. What is it?"

Skandar lifted a forepaw, displaying knife-sized black talons. "Moving too slow. Need to reach mountain faster."

"We all want to get there quickly," said Arenadd. "I'm afraid it just can't be helped."

Skandar put his head on one side. "'Be help'? What mean?"

"I mean we can't really do anything about it. If we want to all get there—"

"Can do!" said Skandar. "*I* help."

"How? Do you have an idea?"

"Know what to do," said Skandar. He spread his wings. "I carry human there, like before."

"We can't just leave the others behind," said Arenadd.

"Carry *all* human," Skandar snapped. "Carry you, mate, mother, daughter of Hyrenna's human, other humans who follow you. I carry all to mountain."

"You can't carry seven humans at once," Arenadd said. "I know you're strong, but no griffin can do something like that."

"Can!" said Skandar. "And will."

"How?" said Skade.

Skandar huffed at her. "Use magic. Like before."

Arenadd stared. "You mean—with the—through the shadows? Like you did before, with us?"

"Yes," said Skandar. "Am strong now, but even stronger in shadow. Come. I show you."

A short time later, the dark griffin stood in the remains of the campsite and shuffled about irritably while Rhodri tried to find a seat on his back. Arenadd, Skade and Annir were already sitting squashed up on his shoulders; Saeddryn was perched precariously between his wings along with Cai; and Davyn was just managing to balance on his rump. Unfortunately this left no room for Rhodri, and Skandar was getting impatient.

"This is mad anyway," Rhodin growled, sliding off onto the ground for the third time. "No way he's carryin' us anywhere. What are we even doin'?"

Skandar's feathery tail smacked him in the face. "If not fit, then hold tail," he hissed. "Or stay!"

"Hold on to his tail," Arenadd translated. "He says to."

Rhodri grabbed it obligingly. "This is even stupi*deeeeeer*—"

The last word stretched out into a yell as Skandar leapt forward and into utter blackness.

Arenadd could hear the others screaming, but he couldn't see them. He couldn't see Skandar, either, but he felt him—felt the dark griffin's massive body go hurtling through the void, incredibly fast. It was just like their last strange journey together, but this time it went on much longer. Skandar showed no sign of slowing down, but it was impossible to judge how far they had travelled. Arenadd turned his head, trying to see, but still found nothing. He could feel Skade clinging to him, her claws digging into his skin.

"Hold on!" he yelled to the others. "Don't panic! Hold on! Whatever you do, *hold on*!"

The wind snatched the sound away the instant it was out of his mouth, and he could only hope that they had heard it. If anyone fell off or let go . . . then there was no telling what would happen to them. Even Arenadd felt uncertain of his own safety.

Arenadd began to panic. Something this extreme must be taking a lot of magic. Maybe too much.

He knew what could happen to a griffin who used too much magic in one go. It was rare, but griffiners everywhere told stories about it. Some would be weak for a few days. Those were the lucky ones. But if their magic was allowed to drain out of them much longer than that, unconsciousness and death would follow.

Arenadd pulled on Skandar's neck feathers. "Skandar! Skandar, stop, now! You'll hurt yourself! Stop, before—"

Skandar ignored him. In fact, he sped up. The darkness rushed by, and at last Arenadd heard the others. They were shouting, panicking, scared out of their minds.

And then, at last, Skandar slowed. Arenadd felt the griffin's muscles bunch, and he leapt—up and out of the shadows, back into the bright light of the living world.

Skandar landed with a thump on solid earth, and Arenadd was the only one who kept his seat. Skade tumbled off sideways, nearly dragging him with her, and he let go and slid after her rather than risk pulling out any of Skandar's feathers. The others had landed much less gracefully. He turned quickly, and relaxed when he saw they were all there, groaning and picking themselves up out of the dirt.

Once he was free of his burden, Skandar lay down on his belly and groaned softly. "Here now," he muttered. "Safe."

Arenadd went to him. "Skandar, are you all right?"

The dark griffin yawned and blinked. "Tired. Not hurt. Journey over now; can all rest."

The others grouped around Arenadd, staring at their new surroundings with bewilderment and, for all of them except Skade, fear.

"What happened?" Davyn exclaimed. "How'd we get here? What *was* that?"

Arenadd did his best to look confident. "That was the

shadows. That's part of Skandar's power—he can use them to travel." He didn't add that this was only the second time he had seen him do it.

"I know this place!" Saeddryn said suddenly. She turned, looking up at the mountains that loomed over them. The ground where they stood looked like a small plateau, damp with melted snow. The air around them felt icy and thin. "We're in the mountains!"

Arenadd nodded. "I told you Skandar would bring us here. The others must be hiding somewhere nearby."

Skandar lifted his head, sniffing the air. He stirred and stood up, and after what looked like a moment's thought he pointed his beak skyward and screeched. *"Skandar!"* He followed the call up with several more, repeating his name again and again until the sound of it echoed off the mountains all around. The humans there cringed and covered their ears, and Arenadd was tempted to do the same, but he didn't. Instead he moved to stand by Skandar's side, and added his own voice and his own name to the call. *"Arenadd!"*

His throat hurt, but he kept on going regardless. To his surprise he found himself enjoying it. A savage energy rushed through his body, and Skandar's presence made it stronger, fiercer and more exhilarating. In that moment, realisation flashed into his mind—or rather, memory did. *My power comes from him. Not from myself, not from the earth, not even from the Night God. Skandar is the key. My partner. My friend. This began with him, and it'll end that way, too.*

Eventually he ran out of breath. Skandar relaxed as well and sat back on his haunches to groom himself.

"Doesn't look like anyone heard that," Saeddryn said eventually.

"They heard," said Arenadd, a little hoarsely. "Sound carries a long way in these mountains."

"Better hope the right people heard, then," Rhodri muttered.

"I'm sure—" Arenadd broke off. He stood very still, frowning, and turned his head slowly. He sniffed. Then he smiled and pointed at a nearby heap of rocks. "I know you're there, Hafwen," he called.

Silence followed for a moment. But then a scrawny tattooed woman stepped out from her hiding place, scowling. "So here ye are, Southerner."

Arenadd's smile disappeared instantly. "I'm happy to see you, too, Hafwen. As I'm sure my friends are."

Hafwen's gaze shifted to Saeddryn and her friends. Her expression did not change. "Ye brought them back, at least," she said, as if it was that easy, and then turned and walked off. "C'mon back to camp," she called over her shoulder.

Arenadd grimaced. "I was hoping they'd be happier to see me. Oh well." He followed Hafwen, with the others close behind. Skandar came, too, choosing to walk for now.

The new camp made by Arddryn's followers was closer than Arenadd had expected. Hafwen led them down the side of the plateau and around into a small valley, and there it was waiting for them. Fires had been lit here and there, in sheltered spots where the smoke wouldn't spread too far, and when Hafwen appeared with Arenadd in tow people appeared as well. Men and women, all tough and scarred, wearing ragged furs and spiral tattoos as their tribal ancestors had done, most of them holding spears or bows. They eyed the newcomers warily.

Arenadd, however, was in no mood for ceremony. He went straight to the centre of the camp, ignoring Hafwen, and said loudly: "Where's Arddryn? I need to talk to her, right now."

No-one replied. Finally a man jumped down from a rock and landed in front of him. "What are ye doin' here?" he asked in a harsh voice.

Arenadd bared his teeth. "I went to rescue Saeddryn and her friends from the enemy, and now I've brought them back."

The man sneered at him. "Liar. Ye ran off on us. Turned yer back on Arddryn. Soft Southern bastard—"

Arenadd's punch sent him sprawling. He lay on his back, staring in shock.

Arenadd turned around to address the others. "I said, go and get Arddryn. Bring her here, *now*."

The man who'd spoken before got up, clutching his jaw. "She ain't comin'," he said sourly.

"Why not?" said Arenadd. His voice had gone hard and sharp, full of command.

"She's dead."

The words were enough to rob Arenadd of his new authority. "What? When? How?"

"Two days ago," said Hafwen. She glared at Arenadd. "Travellin' here was too much for her. She died of cold an' exhaustion."

Arenadd looked at Saeddryn. She had gone very pale, but she said nothing. "I came back here as fast as I could . . . what about Hyrenna?"

"Left," said Hafwen. "Went off by herself t'lay her eggs. With Arddryn gone, there was no reason for her t'stay, was there?"

Saeddryn came to Arenadd's side. "It wasn't his fault, Hafwen. Ye know that. He saved our lives."

"So ye say," said the man with the bruised jaw.

"Shut up." Arenadd drew himself up and raised his voice. "I know I disturbed your quiet little mountain retreat, and I'm sorry for that. But Arddryn trained me to be her successor, and she believed in me. Now, so do I. I left to rescue Saeddryn and the others, and I have. Now I'm back, and this time I won't leave again. I wish I could have said goodbye to Arddryn, but I can't. All I can do is make her dream come true."

"Her dream?" Others had come over, leaving their hiding places. Most of them looked angry. One man jabbed a spear into the ground. "Ye ain't worthy to do anythin' like that, Southerner."

Arenadd rounded on him. "Call me that again and I'll break your jaw, Nerth. Now you listen to me. I *will* do what Arddryn trusted me to do. You saw the tattoos; you know the plan. It hasn't changed." He glanced down at his bandaged hand and looked thoughtful. He touched it, feeling it experimentally. Then he ripped off the bandages, splints and all. The fingers underneath were twisted and ugly, but they were healed—or as healed as they ever would be. Arenadd curled them into his right palm, and rubbed them back and forth until they made a ghastly cracking noise. He smiled grimly. Then, apparently remembering what he had been doing, he looked up and showed his hand to the onlookers, letting them see the crippled fingers. "The Southerners are our enemies. *My* enemies. Every last one of them. I am the Dark Lord Arenadd, and *I* say that I will leave these mountains tomorrow and I will make a war like the North has never seen. The Southerners will leave our lands forever, I swear it. They can try to fight me if they want, but I'm not afraid of them any more. Skandar and I will take the North from them, and anyone—*anyone*—who tries to stop us is dead. If you want to come with me, you're welcome. If not, you can stay here and freeze to death. It's your choice." With that, he slammed his left hand into his right, making a loud *crack*.

The Northerners looked a little surprised, even embarrassed.

"But how are ye goin' to do this?" Nerth asked. "There's so many of 'em, they're so strong . . ."

Arenadd smiled horribly. "Not as strong as us, Nerth." With that, he stepped sideways into Skandar's shadow, and disappeared.

Several people there screamed.

Arenadd reappeared, still grinning. It was a wolf's grin; there was no trace of humour in it. "You'll win this time," he said. "Because you have us. The Night God gave her power to Skandar, and Skandar shared it with me. *That's* why we're going to win."

During the stunned silence that followed, Saeddryn spoke up from Arenadd's side. "He's right!" she yelled. "Our time's now, damn it; there's never been a better time! The Night God has answered our prayers. She sent him an' Skandar. Come with us, come an' fight! Everyone'll join us once they know the truth. We're gonna win, I know it."

"Thank you, Saeddryn," said Arenadd. "We *are* going to win. They can't kill me—none of them can. I promise you." He flexed his twisted hand, and smiled grimly.

Nerth glanced at Hafwen, then at the others. "Where should we start . . . sir?" he said at last. Around him the rest of Arddryn's former followers had begun to gather close, all listening intently.

Arenadd nodded to himself and fingered his beard. "I've already been thinking about that . . ."

8

Gwernyfed

Erian and Senneck made good progress on the first day; Senneck flew for decent periods of time before stopping to rest, rather than attempting to stay in the air for as long as she could, and this proved efficient. Toward evening they came across a village, and Senneck landed, touching down in the open space at its centre.

Erian dismounted and stretched. "I suppose one of these peasants will give us somewhere to stop for the night," he remarked, rubbing his sore backside as he looked around.

The inhabitants had seen them coming. He saw a few pale faces peering at him through windows and from behind doorways, but nobody came out to greet them. A door slammed shut, and somewhere a dog started to yap.

"That was a warm welcome," Erian muttered.

"This is a small village, and isolated," Senneck reminded him. "They are probably not used to seeing griffins. Wait until they gather their wits."

Erian was tired and in no mood for dealing with ignorant darkmen, and he stood and glared at nothing in particular. Beside him Senneck settled down and began to groom her wings, as calm as always.

Eventually there was movement from a nearby building, and

three Northerners appeared, walking slowly toward them. They were simply clad, and all looked highly apprehensive.

"Finally!" said Erian, turning to face them.

They stopped, and two of them pushed the third forward, muttering encouragement. The man ventured closer, ducking his head and keeping his eyes averted. "My lord," he mumbled.

Erian straightened up. "Look at me."

The man did. His eyes were black and unreadable. "Yes, my lord?"

"I'm in no mood for your nonsense, blackrobe," Erian snapped. "What village is this?"

The man flinched. "This is Gwernyfed, lord. I'm Rhys. We're honest men, lord, an' we have nothin' to—"

"Shut up. My partner and I need somewhere to stay for the night, and we need food."

Rhys looked slightly panicked. "Ye—yes, lord. Anythin' ye need. If ye can wait a little while, lord, I can ask my friends an' see if anyone has a room spare an' a stable, lord."

Erian sighed. "Fine. Get on with it."

Rhys bowed and scurried away. Other darkmen had ventured out now, and Erian watched as they conferred among themselves, speaking quickly and with much gesticulation.

"Look at those idiots," he muttered in griffish. "I mean, look at them."

"I am looking," said Senneck. "And I think your view of them has been tainted by the murderer."

Erian started. "What? No it hasn't! I mean, everyone knows . . ." He pulled himself together and tried to think of a counter-argument, but at that moment Rhys returned.

"We have a place for ye, lord," he said. "Come this way, an' we'll see ye in comfort for the night."

Erian nodded curtly and followed him to one of the houses. This one was a little larger, adjoined to the village's mill house, which had a small stable with accommodation for a single horse at the back. The stable proved to be empty, and looked to have been for some time.

"Here," said Rhys, showing them inside. "The . . . yer partner can stay here"—he cast a frightened look at Senneck—"an' there's a room for ye inside, lord."

"Thank you," said Erian.

Senneck went into the stable, looking disdainfully at the dusty straw. "I shall need food."

"She needs food," Erian told Rhys.

"Yes, lord. The finest meat, lord. The miller can feed ye inside, lord. Come, I'll show ye to the house so ye can rest an' clean yerself."

Erian sighed. "Fine." He turned to Senneck. "Will you be all right here?"

"Well enough, if the spiders do not kill me," said Senneck. "I shall call if I need you. And you do the same." She looked at Rhys, her ice-blue eyes narrow. "Be careful. I do not trust these people, and neither should you."

"I know. I won't. I'll come and visit you later."

"Go, then," said Senneck.

Erian allowed himself to be shown to the mill house, where he was greeted by the miller, a middle-aged man who let him into the house after casting several veiled looks at Rhys, who hastily excused himself and disappeared. Inside the house there was a single room with a stone-flagged floor, where the miller's wife was preparing dinner and a row of small faces stared inscrutably from behind the table.

Erian ignored them all and followed the miller into the adjoining room, where there was a single large bed and several cots on the floor for the children.

"My bed is yers, lord," said the miller. "My wife an' I will sleep on t'floor."

Erian gritted his teeth. "Thank you. That will be fine."

The miller did not smile. "Ye can leave yer sword here, lord, an' come for dinner."

"Thank you, but I'll keep it with me," said Erian.

"As ye wish, lord."

They returned to the next room, where Erian accepted a seat at the head of the table and waited in silence while the miller's wife added more vegetables to the pot over the fire.

The two adults kept away from him and made no attempt at conversation, but the children were openly staring at him. There were four of them—three boys and a girl—and eventually the girl came up to him, standing only an arm's length away.

Erian ignored her for as long as he could, but the intrusion quickly became irritating.

"What are you looking at?" he said.

The girl's eyes widened, but she said nothing.

"Well?" said Erian.

Apparently plucking up some courage, she reached toward him. "Yer sword," she said.

Her mother hurried over. "Adyna! Stay away from him!" She scooped the girl up in her arms. "I'm sorry, lord," she said to Erian. "She's never seen a Southern . . . one of yer people before, lord," she corrected hastily.

"She seems to be more interested in my sword," Erian said sourly.

The woman eyed it. "She's . . . never seen one of them b'fore either, lord."

On an impulse, Erian drew it. The other children darted away, and their mother gasped and half-fled before she restrained herself.

Erian laid the sword down on the table. "There. Look at it if you want to, girl."

The woman relaxed slightly. "Can . . . can she?"

"Yes," said Erian. "They all can."

The girl started to wriggle in her mother's grasp. "I wanna see!"

"Well, if his lordship says ye can, then take a look," said the mother, putting her down.

The girl instantly made for the table and climbed onto one of the stools so she could look more closely at the sword. She turned her head, watching the light play over the blade, and cooed excitedly. Her brothers emerged from their hiding places and came to join her.

"It's like ice!" the eldest one said. "See how it glitters there on the edge?"

"It's so big!" said another. "How d'ye lift it, sir?"

"He lifts it 'cause he's big an' strong," the third said instantly. "See how thick his arms are? I bet he's stronger'n Da!"

Despite himself, Erian swelled a little with pride. "This sword is very old," he said. "It belonged to my father. You can see his name engraved there, just below the hilt."

They looked respectfully at the engraving.

"Can ye read, sir?" said the eldest, in awed tones.

Erian started. "What? Of course I can! Can't you?"

"I met a man who could read once," said the boy. "He come over here for the fair. He was very clever."

"It says 'Rannagon Raegonson,'" said Erian. "He was my father. Before him his father, Raegon, had it, and all the way back to our ancestor Baragher the Blessed." In fact he had no idea if this was even close to the truth, but he told himself it didn't matter. What would they know anyway?

"What's *your* name, sir?" said the girl. She reached out to touch the blade.

Erian batted her hand away. "Don't touch it! *Never* touch it, understand?"

The girl stared blankly at him for a second and then burst into tears. Erian gaped at her and then looked away, embarrassed, as she ran to her mother for comfort.

The eldest boy glared at him. "Why can't we touch it?"

Erian picked up the sword. "My name is Erian Rannagonson. And you can't touch it because it's against the law. None of your people are allowed to own weapons or even touch them. On pain of death."

"Why?" said the boy.

The mother rushed to intervene. "Yorath! Stop that now! Don't ye dare speak that way to the—"

"Because your people already proved that you can't be trusted with them," Erian snapped, ignoring her. "The last time you handled weapons, you did terrible things to other people. That's why we made a law to stop it from ever happening again."

The boy, who looked about thirteen, thrust out his chin. "Well, ye can't make us be like that forever. Lord Arenadd is gonna stop ye. He's gonna drive ye out of Tara, an' then we can do whatever we want."

Erian reached down and slapped him across the face, so hard he threw the boy to the floor. "*Never* say that name. Do you understand? Never say it in front of me, or any other time. If I ever hear you say it again, I'll kill you. Understand?"

The boy struggled to his feet and ran out of the room as fast as he could. His sister cried harder than ever.

The mother struggled to keep her self-control. "Go on," she said, pushing the girl toward the door. "All of ye, go outside an' play. Ye can eat later. Go on, go! The griffiner needs t'be left alone now."

The children needed no further encouragement; they all but ran out of the house.

Erian sheathed his sword and turned to look at the parents. Part of him was horrified, but he was too angry to care.

"My lord, I'm so sorry," the miller babbled. "I never knew he could say anythin' like that, I swear. He must've bin—there was these traders in here last week; they was—"

"I'll make sure he's punished, l—" the wife began.

"Shut up," said Erian. They did. "Now," he said, glaring at them. "I don't know where that boy heard that, and if I ever found out who told him that, I'd see them executed on the spot. Fortunately for that person, I'm in too much of a hurry. But I intend to make sure that the Eyrie finds out about this very soon."

The miller blanched. "My lord, there's no need to—we're only farmers; we can't do no harm t'ye, lord—"

Erian almost hit him, too. "I've seen all the harm in the world done by the son of a leather worker. Now be quiet and give me my food."

They looked slightly relieved as he sat down again, and scurried to bring him a bowl of stew. It was overcooked and had dirt in it and mostly consisted of vegetables, but he took it anyway and ate it. It was almost certainly the most unpleasant meal of his life; the miller and his wife ate nothing and stayed at the edges of the room, saying nothing and only watching him.

It seemed to take an eternity to get to the bottom of the bowl, but in the end he finished and put it down. "No thank you," he said in reply to an offer of another helping. "I'm going to go and visit my griffin now."

He left the house without another word, and the instant the door shut behind him he felt relief wash over him like a bucket of cold water.

In the stable, Senneck was busy tearing her way through what looked like a side of salted pork. The bones made an unpleasant crunching noise under her beak.

"These fools would not know good meat if it bit them," she muttered. "Ah. Erian. Back so quickly?" She paused to rip the spine in half and rubbed her beak against the wall to dislodge a piece of bone that had caught in it. "Did you find a better meal than I did?"

Erian picked up a stray piece of meat and toyed with it. "Not really. It wasn't very . . ."

She raised her head. "Yes? What is it?"

"There was a boy in there. The miller's son. He said something about . . . Arenadd."

Senneck became instantly alert. "What did he say?"

"He said that the . . . that Arenadd was going to drive us out. He said he would set them free."

She hissed to herself. "Already, the message is spreading. Yet it seems odd—"

"Well, yes!" Erian burst forth. "How could they be talking about him like that now? The story of what happened at Malvern couldn't possibly have reached here yet. Even if a griffiner could have carried it, it's obvious none have been here for a long time."

Senneck nibbled at her toe. "There must be another explanation behind this. I only wish we had the time to discover more. As it is, I suggest that you avoid mentioning this again. We cannot afford to risk any trouble for ourselves, and I wish to leave here as soon as possible."

Erian tried to calm down. "Yes. I suppose you're right." He thought of the frightened faces of the miller and his wife. "I should probably go back. I need to ask if I can have some supplies for tomorrow anyway."

"Go," said Senneck. "I am tired and need to rest; I must regain my strength for tomorrow."

Erian nodded gloomily. "See you in the morning."

He left her to her food and wandered back to the house, absent-mindedly chewing on the piece of meat.

He was reaching out to open the door when he heard the argument on the other side. He froze for a moment and then crept closer, flattening himself against the wall and placing his ear close to the wood to listen.

". . . can't do anythin', understand? It's too late!"

"Well, he's got t'be warned. Does Caerwys know about this?"

"Of course he bloody does! It's all right, understand? There's no way the Bastard could know about him. He's bin warned by now, sure as fate; he'll be miles away before the moon even rises."

"An' just as well." This was the woman's voice, laced with bitterness. "If the gods're kind, he won't be comin' back. All this nonsense about raisin' the stones—it's Arddryn's talk, all over again, an' it'll come to t'same end, ye can be sure of that. Bloody blackrobes, they're nothin' but trouble. An' trouble for *us*. If those whore's sons at Malvern find out about—"

"Well, they won't, see? It was just a threat, an' what's he gonna tell 'em? It was nothin' but a boy's talk—when would Malvern take that seriously?"

"It's nothin' we want anythin' t'do with anyway," said the woman, more calmly. "An' if Garnoc thinks . . ."

Erian listened further, until the argument wound down, and then quietly turned and left, making for the stable at a fast walk.

The boy, Yorath, darted behind a patch of thorn-bushes and hid there, panting. His heart was pattering frantically, like a rabbit's, and he breathed deeply. Almost immediately, though, his breath became a shudder, and he struggled to stop himself from crying. His face throbbed, and he could feel a bruise starting to rise on his cheek. The griffiner's threat still rang in his ears; the thought of it, and that huge sword, made him tremble.

Tears started to leak from his eyes, but he gritted his teeth and forced the rest to stay back. He peeked out from behind the thorn-bushes, and once he was sure there was no-one else around he ran into the trees and away from the village as fast as he could go.

He hadn't been this way on his own before, and once or twice he thought he was lost, but he found a familiar tree or stump and sped up.

It was further than he remembered. He slowed down after a while, gasping for breath and suddenly aware that it was getting dark. He looked upward and was alarmed to see the first stars had come out.

He looked forward again. Light had drained out of the trees with frightening speed, and he realised that if he didn't find the place quickly he would be lost.

He screwed up his courage and moved on, biting his lip.

A twig snapped behind him. He froze and then turned, raising his hands to defend himself.

There was no-one there. Yorath resisted the temptation to call out and stayed where he was, watching for any sign of movement. Nothing. He snatched up a stick and ran away, heart pounding, expecting something to grab him from behind at any moment, but nothing did, and he ran on blindly, branches lashing at his face.

Something caught around his ankle, and he pitched forward with a yell of alarm, landing hard on his face. For a moment he lay there, winded and gasping, before fear galvanised him back into action.

He got up, swearing to himself, and stopped dead when he saw a light up ahead. Relief flared in his chest, and he picked up his stick and ran toward the light as fast as he could.

The light was coming from a clearing hidden among some birch trees. Yorath burst into it, shouting. "Garnoc!"

A fire was burning in the middle of the clearing, and the man who had been sitting by it leapt to his feet; grabbing a long spear. "What?"

Yorath skidded to a halt and threw his stick down. "Garnoc, it's me, Yorath! The miller's son!"

Garnoc stared at him, and then relaxed. "Dear sweet holy gods, boy, yer scared the skin off'f me. What are y'doin' here?"

Yorath bent almost double. "There's a griffiner," he gasped. "In the village."

"I know," said Garnoc.

Yorath looked blankly at him. "You do? How?"

Garnoc, a big, heavy man whose black hair was cropped close to his head, growled to himself and ran his thumb over the blade of his spear. "D'yer think the villagers are stupid, boy? They sent a runner down 'ere to tell me what was happenin' before the Southern filth had even touched ground."

Yorath nearly gaped at him. "But . . . well, he's staying at our house," he said lamely.

"Lucky you," said Garnoc. "He didn't see yer come out here, did he?"

"No. He was inside when I left, an' the griffin was in the stable." Yorath paused. "He hit me."

"The son of a bitch," Garnoc growled. "Why, did yer say somethin' to him?"

Yorath hesitated. "He said his name was Erian Rannagonson."

Garnoc started. "What? Rannagonson? Did yer say his name was Rannagonson?"

"Yes," said Yorath.

"What's he doin' here?" said Garnoc.

"I dunno," said Yorath. "He said as he was on his way somewhere."

"But where? For gods' sakes, you didn't tell the Bastard anythin', did yer? What did yer do t'make him hit yer?"

"He said we couldn't touch weapons," said Yorath. "I said Lord Arenadd was gonna drive the Southerners out, an' then we could—"

Garnoc swore violently. "You damned idiot!" he said. "What did yer go an' do that for? D'you realise what y've done?"

"He never knew nothin' about it," Yorath said belligerently. "He's too stupid t'know anythin', idiot Southern—"

As he spoke, he heard something behind him and saw Garnoc's eyes widen suddenly. As he turned to look, it was as if the entire wood exploded.

Something huge and horrible came bursting through the birch trees and rushed into the clearing. He saw it hit Garnoc full in the chest, throwing him violently to the ground, but as he opened his mouth to shout, a pair of hands closed around his neck and shoulder, dragging him sideways.

Yorath struggled. "Let me go! Garnoc!"

The great brown griffin had pinned Garnoc to the ground and was holding him there, snarling and hissing. The big Northerner moaned and tried to pull himself out from under her, but she wrapped her talons around him and trapped him.

The griffiner hit Yorath as he tried to escape. "Hold still, boy, or I'll snap your neck."

Garnoc managed to raise his head. "Let him go!" he yelled. "He's only a boy, he's done nothin' wrong. I'm the one yer want, see?"

Erian stalked toward him, dragging Yorath. "Garnoc, is it?"

Garnoc glared up at him. "That's me name, you sun-worshippin' son of a bitch. What's the matter? Are yer too much of a coward t'fight me on yer own, if yer need this overgrown pigeon t'help yer?" He cried out as Senneck tightened her grip, her talons driving cruelly into his skin.

"I'm not interested in fighting," Erian snapped. "I want answers. How did you get here?"

Garnoc said nothing.

Instantly Senneck closed her talons, squeezing until Garnoc's ribs cracked and he screamed.

"How—did—you—get here?" Erian repeated. "Answer me!"

Garnoc spat blood. "Sod off, Bastard."

Senneck squeezed again, and this time she did not loosen her grip. She lifted him from the ground, crushing him mercilessly, her talons tearing through his clothes and into his flesh, until blood began to run down her paw and drip onto the ground and Garnoc thrashed and screamed, howling in agony.

Yorath began to cry. "Stop it! Stop it! Please, stop it, leave him alone!"

Erian spoke quickly to Senneck in griffish, and she opened her talons and let Garnoc drop. He fell limply and lay on his back, shaking violently with shock.

Erian placed a boot on his chest and drew his knife. "I can see you're brave enough for a blackrobe." He looked down at Garnoc, examining him. "Hmm. Scars on your neck and a brand on your hand. You're a runaway slave. And I think I know who set you free. But I want to know for sure." He pressed the knife into Yorath's neck. "So I'm going to ask you one more time. Tell me the truth, or your little friend dies."

Garnoc's eyes spat hate. "Kill me if yer want to, Bastard. But yer gonna get yours."

"Is that so?" said Erian. "Well"—he pressed the knife down harder—"if that's all you have to say . . ."

"Let him go, you son of a whore," said Garnoc. "I'll tell yer this, an' much good it'll do yer. I was a slave at Herbstitt. Me an' my mates was buildin' a wall there while the governor was away. One day a new man joined the gang. His name was Arenadd Taranisäii, an' he set us free. Him an' Skandar."

Erian breathed deeply. "And then he led you all to Guard's Post, where you slaughtered nearly sixty innocent men and two griffins."

"He set us free," Garnoc rasped. "All of us. He led us to victory, an' as a reward he took off our collars and let us go free. We scattered. I dunno where the others are, an' I wouldn't tell yer if I did. But they're spreadin' the word now. They're tellin' every Northerner about what he did an' who he is. You can't stop it, Southerner. He's comin' back. He's gonna lead us."

Erian waited, still holding Yorath with the knife to his throat. But Garnoc said nothing more, and Erian took the knife

away and let the boy go. Yorath stumbled off and then ran from
the clearing.

Garnoc did not move. "That's all I know. Kill me now. I'm
done."

Erian sheathed his knife and lifted his boot from the man's
chest. His breathing was ragged and unsteady with suppressed
fury. "I would love to kill you," he said.

"And so would I," said Senneck. She glanced at her human.
"He has nothing more to say, that is clear. We should make an
end to it; we must go."

Erian ignored her. "I want to kill you," he said. "But I'm not
going to. I want you to stay alive."

Garnoc looked warily at him. "It's to be Malvern, is it? An' a
hangin'? Or maybe back to the slavers—that it, Bastard?"

"No. You can keep your life. I want you to go, Garnoc.
Leave here. Go and find your master, and give him this message
from me. Tell him I said . . ." Erian closed his eyes and breathed
deeply. "Tell him I said 'I know what you are, *Kraeai kran ae*,
and I know what you're planning. The Night God can't protect
you, and neither can your evil magic. I am *Aeai ran kai*, and I
am coming.'" He paused. "'Remember my face, murderer. It's
the last one you'll ever see.'"

9

Starting a War

Yorath almost fled the forest altogether after Erian let him go, but he didn't. Later on he tried to convince himself that it was because of his own courage and his refusal to leave Garnoc alone, but the truth was that he didn't know the way back. It was pitch-black by now, and the moon was hiding behind a cloud, so he could barely see an arm's length in front of his face. He ran blindly out of the clearing and immediately collided with a bush, bounced off it, and landed hard on his back.

The landing winded him badly, and he lay there, gasping and sobbing.

Moments later, he heard loud crunching and snapping from somewhere to his left, mingled with the thud of footsteps—large ones. He lay very still, not daring to move, and as the moon emerged from the clouds he saw the outline of the griffin, so close, walking almost straight toward him.

His heart beat fast. She was coming for him; she was going to crush him in her talons just as she had done to Garnoc. As this idea spread hot panic through his body, he almost got up and ran, but instinct kept him still, lying half-hidden under the bush like a hare.

And then the griffin was no longer coming; she was *there*, nearly standing over him, so close he could hear her low, rumbling breaths and smell the musty scent of her feathers. She paused to look over her shoulder at something, and said some harsh griffish word. Then she turned back, toward him, and walked away, turning to one side to avoid the bush, with her human trailing behind her.

And then they were gone.

Yorath waited for a long time before he moved. His back felt broken, and his chest ached. Eventually it was the thought of Garnoc, still back there in the clearing, that made him get up. He rolled over and levered himself upright, and limped slowly back the way he had come, toward the light.

The clearing looked very big now. Garnoc's camp had been destroyed, and the fire had burned low. Garnoc was lying beside it, on his side, motionless.

Yorath ran to him and crouched, all his fear forgotten. "Garnoc!"

Garnoc's face was red, and there was blood on his lip from where he had bitten it. His clothes were torn and stained with more blood, but for some reason Yorath noticed his hands more than anything else. They were resting against his chest, and the fingers, all rigid like claws, were entangled in the torn cloth of his tunic.

Very hesitantly, Yorath reached out and touched him. "Garnoc? Are ye dead?"

Garnoc groaned softly, and Yorath's heart leapt.

"Garnoc!" he said again. "Please, get up. It's Yorath. They've gone, ye're safe."

The big man did not respond at first, but Yorath kept talking to him, and eventually his eyes opened. He looked up blankly at him. "Yorath. Are yer all right?"

"He cut me neck a bit," said Yorath. "But it's fine. Garnoc, I think . . . ye're hurt bad."

Garnoc shuddered, and his hands curled inward; and then, quite unexpectedly, he rolled himself onto his back. There were deep bruises on his chest, already turning blue and purple, but he kept his eyes open and began to look more aware. "That . . . son of a gods . . . cursed . . . whore." He groaned. "If he'd . . . fought me himself, he'd have . . . my spear through his gullet."

Yorath clutched at his hand. "Can ye get up, sir?"

Garnoc laughed painfully. "I ain't no sir, boy. I was born a slave."

"But ye're not one now," said Yorath. "Ye're a warrior now, sir. Brave Crow-tribe warrior."

"Just like . . . yerself, eh, boy?" Garnoc grinned.

"I want t'be," Yorath said, almost shyly. "An' that's why ye've got t'live," he added. "I want ye t'teach me fightin', sir."

Garnoc breathed deeply. "Yer right. Got to . . . get up. Help me, Yorath."

Yorath pulled him by the arm to help him sit up, and then hooked an arm behind his shoulders to lift him to his feet. Garnoc was heavy, but he managed to stand without knocking his helper over, though it obviously caused him pain.

"Are ye okay?" said Yorath.

Garnoc stood hunched, his eyes crinkled. "Back seems fine. I think I can walk."

"Well, come on then!" said Yorath. "I'll help ye. We got t'get back to the village so the healer can help ye."

"Straight to where the griffiner went?" said Garnoc. "No."

"But ye need help, sir," said Yorath.

"Bring me my spear," said Garnoc.

Yorath did, and Garnoc took it and leant on it.

"That's better," he said. "This'll keep me standin' upright. Think I can walk, if I take it slowly."

"But where are ye goin', sir?"

Garnoc took a few slow, hobbling steps. "That's . . . yeah, that's good enough. Yorath, can yer do me another favour?"

"Sure, sir," said Yorath.

"Good. Gather up . . . there's some supplies an' whatnot scattered around . . . could yer gather 'em for me?"

Yorath nodded and darted around the camp's remains, picking up bags of food and a leather waterskin, and wrapping them up in a blanket.

Garnoc tucked the bundle under his arm. "Thanks, lad. Ye've been a great help."

"But it's my fault," said Yorath. "I led the griffiner here."

"I know, but it can't be helped," said Garnoc. "Yer didn't mean t'do it, an' I know yer meant well. I ain't angry with yer. Now, get back home, Yorath. Yer parents'll be worried somethin' terrible."

"But where are ye goin'?" said Yorath.

"I'm doin' what that bastard told me t'do," said Garnoc. "Should've done it a long time ago. I'm goin' t'find him."

Yorath's eyes widened. "Lord Arenadd?"

Garnoc nodded. "He's got t'be warned. An' if he's going t'fight Malvern, then he could use my help."

"I want t'come with ye," said Yorath.

"Well, yer can't," said Garnoc.

"But how am I gonna learn about fightin' if ye leave an' I never see ye again?"

"There's other people y'can ask," said Garnoc. "I ain't a master warrior anyway. Most of my life, the closest thing to a weapon I used was a pickaxe."

"But I can help ye," said Yorath. "Ye need someone t'look after ye an' help ye travel. I could do it; I know how t'—"

Garnoc shook his head once and walked away, heading northward.

Yorath watched him go, a lump of misery growing in his stomach. He couldn't bear the thought of going home—home, where there would be chores and arguments and his father's discipline. Home, where the griffiner was waiting.

Garnoc didn't look back. He walked out of the clearing, moving slowly but with surprising strength. Soon he would be out of sight.

Yorath thought of calling out to him but didn't. He watched him for a few moments longer, his fists clenching. Then, as Garnoc left the clearing, Yorath went after him and didn't look back.

10

Warwick

The journey out of the mountains, which began only a day later, was a long and difficult one, but less eventful than Arenadd had expected. He let Saeddryn take the lead, along with Nerth and Hafwen.

Skandar, of course, flew overhead, ranging here and there, but he never quite went out of sight.

Saeddryn helped them navigate their way out of the mountains, and they eventually emerged into the warmer country of the plains further south. There Arenadd ordered them to make a new camp in a small dell, where there was running water and game.

Nerth and his hunters were able to catch a pair of deer, and Cai, foraging for edible plants, found a ground-bear's burrow.

They spent a good length of time in the dell, gathering food and building up their strength. During that time Arenadd felt more of his own strength return; his chest and throat stopped hurting at last, and his fingers improved as well, though he didn't delude himself that they would ever be anything but deformed. His eye, too, finally returned to normal, the swelling going down until it opened again. He was relieved to find that he hadn't lost any vision.

One evening nearly two weeks after their arrival, he called the others together.

"Now," he said, once they were ready. "We've had time to rest and eat, and I think we're about ready to get moving."

"We are, sir," said Saeddryn.

"I've been thinking," Arenadd went on. "Thanks to Saeddryn, and some of the rest of you, I've built a good enough picture of this country in my head to decide where we should go next." He absent-mindedly rubbed his twisted fingers. "If we're going to fight, then we need a stronghold, and we need followers. And if we want followers, then we have to attract them to us. Namely, by sending out a message and making it loud enough for the entire country to hear. Now"—he unrolled a small map and laid it out by the fire—"this is my plan."

It had been a trying day for Lord Tynan, governor of the little walled town known as Warwick. He climbed the steps to his private quarters in a foul mood, vowing that the next person who came to him with bad news would be in deep trouble.

Not for the first time, he reflected bitterly on how he hadn't even wanted this position in the first place. Warwick was one of the larger towns this close to the mountains, but it was absurdly remote—weeks of travel away from Malvern on the ground and several days in the air. Most of the land around it had been converted into pasture land for flocks of black Northern sheep, and the cloth made from their wool was its main source of commerce.

Virtually everyone living in the city was a Northerner. Tynan disliked Northerners. They were a cunning, silent lot, full of lies and trickery and always ready to make things more difficult for his officials—and, by extension, himself. But the last few days had been aggravating even by those low standards. There had been dozens of thefts all over the city, including one in the Governor's Tower itself. Several criminals had escaped from the local prison and so far had evaded all efforts to recapture them, and there had been a nasty riot in a tavern the night before. All of which he had to deal with in some way, and the truth was that he didn't know much about law and order. Let the guard deal with it.

This day, though, had managed to cap it all. There had been an accident in the weaving house: the pair of oxen driving the weaving device had panicked and broken free of their harness, causing enough damage to the thing that it would be useless for days. And so far nobody seemed to have any idea what had set them off or why they had continued their frenzy for so long afterward.

Now, of course, he was going to have to pay for the repairs from out of the treasury, which was already drained after the outbreak of disease in the flocks last year, and Retha was no help at all, spending all her time in her nest and complaining she was "tired."

With all this on his mind as he entered his chamber, he was so preoccupied that he had taken his boots off and was about to sit in his chair by the fire before he noticed there was already someone sitting in it.

"What in the love of Gryphus!" He recovered his senses. "*What* are you doing in here?"

The man sat back and rested one long leg on the other. "You seem awfully distracted, my lord. I thought you were going to sit on top of me for a moment there."

Tynan took in the sight of him with considerable puzzlement. He was a young Northerner wearing the black robe of a slave, but he looked very refined: his beard was neatly trimmed into a point, and his hair, which was long and curly, fell in a glossy, well-groomed mane down over his shoulders. There was a long scar under his eye and more on his neck, but he looked for all the world like an aristocrat relaxing after a feast.

Tynan advanced on him. "I said, who are you?"

"Actually, you asked me what I was doing in here," said the man. He didn't sound like a Northerner; in fact, his accent was distinctly Southern. He stood up. "Please do relax, my lord."

Tynan pulled his dagger out of his belt. "What are you doing in here? Who are you?"

"I didn't want to bother you," he said, "but I've just been down in the city for the last few days. You know, looking around, taking it all in. In fact, you won't believe this, but I actually met a couple of old friends down there. And made a few more. One of them was kind enough to make me a new robe—nice, isn't it? Much more comfortable than the last one."

Tynan gaped at him. He was too bewildered to call the guards. "I'm sorry, but what are you talking about?" he said. "Who *are* you?"

"Just a sightseer," said the man. "Well, all right, I'm after a few things." He gave him a bright smile. "You're the governor of this city, aren't you?"

"I am," said Tynan. "And you—"

"Wonderful!" said the man. "I'm very impressed by what you've done with it. It's a beautiful city." He scratched his beard. "I like it. I think I'll take it."

Tynan finally pulled himself together, and shouted for the guards.

"Oh, I'm sorry," said the man. "But I'm afraid they can't come just at the moment. They've been taken sick."

"What d'you mean, sick?" Tynan demanded.

"A rather bad case of being dead," said the man, quite calmly. "That was probably my fault. I suspect I'm contagious. Now, then . . ."

Tynan glanced quickly at the archway that led to Retha's nest. There was no sign of her, or of the guards.

"Your partner isn't available," the man said, still speaking in light, genial tones. "She's feeling very, very tired. That, and she's tied up."

Tynan darted toward the archway, but the man placed himself in the way.

"Please, stay calm," he said, holding up his hands.

Tynan ignored him and ran for the door instead. But before he was halfway there the man was in front of him, as if he had appeared out of nowhere.

"I told you to stay calm," he said. "It really would be better—"

Tynan drew his dagger and attacked, still shouting for the guards.

The man neatly sidestepped his attack, evading the dagger. His own hand shot out, catching Lord Tynan by the wrist. Tynan twisted, agonising pain blasting up his arm to his shoulder. He screamed and dropped the dagger, and the man let go of him and sent him sprawling with a swift kick to the stomach.

"So," he said, standing over him, "perhaps you're ready to listen."

"*Kri a-o ei!*" Tynan screeched, clutching his wrist.

The man blinked. "That was rather uncalled for, my lord. I didn't think your sort even *knew* that kind of language." He wasn't even out of breath. "Now, I have an offer for you."

Pain was clouding Tynan's senses. "What?"

"I want this city," said the man. "I need a good home for my friends. Surrender it to me, and I won't kill you. I won't even take any of your belongings. You can keep them all."

Tynan managed to laugh. "You think you can *steal* a city, you lunatic?"

The man lost his smile. "I'm not crazy, just a little unwell. And yes, I do think I can steal a city, as a matter of fact."

"You're . . . dead," Tynan spat.

"Correct. But you don't have to join me." The man scratched his beard. "You're a man who knows about numbers. Perhaps you'd prefer to hear it in these terms: there are six hundred and twenty-five people living in this city. Out of those, there are one hundred and five guards—wait, sorry, ninety-eight guards now—fourteen officials, and you. I make that out to be a hundred and thirteen Southerners, against five hundred and thirteen of my people."

"That doesn't mean a cursed *thing*, blackrobe," said Tynan.

The man kicked him, hard. Tynan doubled up.

"Never use that word in my presence again, or next time I'll aim lower than your stomach," the man said.

Tynan threw another griffish curse at him. "You're insane! You can't do anything!"

"So they tell me. But I'm afraid I can." The man sighed. "You asked for my name. It's Arenadd Taranisäii."

Tynan went pale. "What? Not—"

"Yes, *that* Arenadd Taranisäii," said Arenadd, with a touch of impatience. "I'm afraid Malvern didn't manage to deal with me as well as they thought. And I intend to make them pay for trying."

Tynan slumped. "Oh . . . gods."

Arenadd crouched beside him. "I'm tired of killing," he said. "I want to do this as bloodlessly as I can. Just give me the damned city and go away. If you don't, I will . . . you'll regret it."

"You're bluffing," Tynan whispered. "You can't do it. You're on your own."

"Not any more." Arenadd stood up. "The people of this city have accepted me as their leader. They're on my side now. One word from me, and they will tear this tower apart. And as for you . . . well, I could show you what they did to me at Malvern, if you like. A practical demonstration." He took the glove off his left hand and flexed the fingers. "You hear the bones breaking, you know. It sounds like someone crushing a piece of wood."

Tynan retched. "No! For the love of gods . . ."

Arenadd watched him dispassionately for a moment, and then put the glove back on. "I didn't think you'd be interested, somehow. But my offer still stands. Get out of here, my lord. Just go."

Tynan felt new strength come into him then, and certainty. "Never," he snarled.

"If you insist," said Arenadd, and struck.

He watched Tynan's last, bloody struggle on the floor until the griffiner was still.

"I suppose I shouldn't have expected anything less," he muttered. He threw the dagger away, at the wall, where it stuck, point-first in the wood. "And perhaps it's better this way," he added, and left the room.

The capture of Warwick, which would become the subject of dozens of poems, songs and legends, was, in the event, almost ridiculously simple. While Arenadd had not actually won the allegiance of every person in the city, the band of followers he did have on his side—including Saeddryn's warriors—was enough to storm and then occupy the Governor's Tower, which was lightly guarded and occupied mostly by Tynan's officials and their families. By the time the city guard arrived in force, they had barricaded themselves in and armed themselves. A brief siege ensued, but the guards weren't accustomed to out-and-out warfare, and though they outnumbered the rebels they came off worse. Eventually Arenadd himself led a group out of the tower, and a short but bloody fight took place in the streets surrounding it. Many of the locals fled, but others, having found out who was in the city and why, joined in on Arenadd's side.

The guards were quickly scattered, and many surrendered or were killed.

Arenadd, fighting at the front of a group that included most of Saeddryn's band, had armed himself with Tynan's sword. As a knot of guards they were trying to back into an alley broke and ran, he cut one down from behind, shouting, "After them!"

He sprinted down the main street, narrow-eyed, every sense intent on his prey, his followers close behind him.

The guards stayed together as a group, following the commands of their captain. Arenadd kept at their heels, determined not to let them get out of his sight, but they managed to evade him and finally took refuge in a building at the end of the street.

Arenadd ran straight after them, reaching out to shove open the pair of solid wooden doors before they could be shut. But moments before he touched them, he felt a terrible weakness go rushing through him, all cold and smothering, and panic sparked in his brain. He stumbled to a halt, nearly falling against the doors.

Panting, he glared at the gold sunwheel set into the wood.

One of his followers, a local man, caught up with him. "Hah! They're done now!" he yelled. "There's no other way out of there!"

Arenadd turned to the others as they arrived. "They're trapped," he told them. "If they think Gryphus can protect them, they're mistaken." He nodded at the doors. "Go in after them. Kill them all. I don't care if they surrender."

"Yes, sir," said Saeddryn.

Arenadd paused before he turned away. "After they're dead, burn it to the ground."

He left them there and walked back toward the tower, feeling a strange, dark pleasure burning inside him like a flame. *Not just the pleasure of killing,* he thought, *or the thrill of victory.* This was something else. The Night God, telling him she was pleased.

You want me to destroy Gryphus' temples, he thought. He smiled grimly. *Consider it done, my lady.*

He returned to the Governor's Tower, to find it ransacked. His new allies—many of them criminals he had freed from the local prison—had gone through the storerooms and the treasury, helping themselves to whatever they liked. Arenadd had to pick his way through the ruins of some shattered furniture to get through the dining hall, and nearly slipped over on a squashed wheel of cheese. A pair of women were lounging on the table, busy drinking their way through a barrel of wine.

One of them waved cheerily at him. "Welcome back, lord! Have a drink!"

Arenadd opened his mouth to snap at her, but suddenly

found himself shrugging and reaching out for the proffered cup. It had been a long time since he had tasted wine, and he downed the contents in a few swallows, much to the delight of the two women. It was fine wine, rich and sweet, with plenty of kick to it. He grinned. "Very nice. Save some for the rest of us, all right?"

The woman giggled. "There ain't no worries over that, lord; the cellar here's full of it. The whole city could drown 'emselves in it an' die happy."

"Sounds good to me," said Arenadd, and gave the cup back to her before he left the room. Elsewhere he found similar sights of greed and misbehaviour, and privately marvelled at how little time it had taken for them to start indulging themselves. The last of the guards hadn't even been defeated yet, and they were already drinking and looting. His first response had been anger and disgust, but now he found that he didn't particularly mind. *What does it matter that they're having a little fun? I want devotion; I want them to like me. And I want to send a message. The more chaos I create here, the louder it will be and the more Malvern will fear me. I can worry about discipline later.*

Besides, he had more important things on his mind. He climbed the stairs to Lord Tynan's chamber. He had given everyone very clear instructions to stay away and was pleased to see he'd been obeyed. Or at least no-one had come this far yet. He unlocked the door and went in.

Tynan's body was still lying on the floor where it had fallen. Arenadd barely spared it a glance before he passed through the archway and into Retha's nest. Retha, a slim white and grey griffin, was lying on her side in her bedding. She looked as if she was still asleep, just as he'd left her, but he could see the blood on her neck and side. Skandar stood over by the trough, panting and bloodied. "My nest now," was all he said.

Arenadd didn't argue with him about that; the big griffin obviously resented the fact that he had been asked to stay away from the fighting in the streets and instead hide here. Killing Retha must have helped him deal with some of his frustration.

"It's over now," Arenadd said. "Let's go and see what's happening in the city."

Skandar came at once, all aggression and excitement. "Come, we fly," he said.

Arenadd got on his back willingly enough, and the dark griffin ran out and nearly hurled himself into the sky, circling over the buildings several times before coming down to land.

Outside, the fight was more or less over; Arenadd couldn't see any of the enemy left alive, and things looked fairly calm. He hoped the looting hadn't spread out into the rest of the city; the situation could become extremely ugly if it had. He would worry about that later.

As he approached the temple, he could already see a thick plume of smoke rising over the rooftops, Saeddryn and her friends had worked quickly.

The fighting had reached this far; he saw several bodies lying here and there in the street. A couple of Northerners were busy looting them, but they stood up and bowed reverentially when they saw Arenadd and Skandar coming.

He nodded curtly. "Carry on."

"Yes, lord."

In the open space in front of the temple, Arenadd found Saeddryn and her friends just emerging through the shattered front doors. Nerth and some others were dragging several bodies out with them.

"Saeddryn, what happened?"

She stopped and wiped the sweat off her forehead, leaving a smear of blood. "Sir. There ye are."

Arenadd made a quick count of the dead. "Seven of the poor bastards. What happened? You had them outnumbered, didn't you?"

"There was more inside, sir," said Saeddryn. "An' some others showed up. They must've all had the idea t'come here an' hide. Lucky for us, some of ours came t'help." She gestured at them.

Arenadd gripped the hilt of his stolen sword. "*Skade!* What are you doing—are you all right?"

Skade was breathing heavily, and her clothes were torn and stained red. "This blood is not mine," she said. "I am not badly injured."

Arenadd strode toward her. "I *told* you to stay with Skandar. You were supposed to wait until I gave the all clear—for gods' sakes, Skade—"

"I am not one of your followers," she snapped back. "I do what I choose, and I chose to enter the city and fight."

"You should've seen her, sir," Nerth put in. "She bit one bastard t'death, I swear. She fights like a wolf. I offered her a sword, an' she wouldn't take it!"

Arenadd grabbed her arm. "You could have been killed! Skade, it wasn't necessary—you have to stay safe. What if something happened to you?"

She pulled free. "I can care for myself. I am not a hatchling, Arenadd, or a coward."

"It's not a question of . . ." Arenadd realised people were staring at him. "Fine," he muttered sourly. "Do what you want to do. I've got other things to deal with right now."

"I assume it was a victory?" Skade asked coldly.

"Yes. Skandar and I came to see how things were going— care to join us?"

Skandar had already wandered off, sniffing here and there and huffing irritably to himself. Arenadd grinned and ran after him, waving at Skade to follow.

In the streets of Warwick, people stopped to watch them. Many of them bowed to Arenadd; some even cheered, and some darted over to touch his robe then backed away, wide-eyed and mouthing his name.

Arenadd did his best to acknowledge them, though awkwardly, and tried not to shy away when they came too close; he had always disliked being touched, and it had become even worse lately. They didn't seem to notice, or to mind.

He soon forgot his irritation in the joy of the moment. They had won their first victory, and nothing mattered more than that.

11

Rebirth

They celebrated that night in the dining hall with dozens of friends and followers. Arenadd had managed to round up the kitchen staff and had ordered them to cook everything they could lay their hands on. The centrepiece was half a dozen mutton carcasses stuffed with expensive yellow cymran fruit—something only griffiners and the wealthy usually enjoyed. Arenadd had more of them sent out into the city for the general population to enjoy, and opened the cellars and distributed all the alcohol. There had been some looting out in the city, but not as much as he had feared, and now the atmosphere had relaxed somewhat.

In the hall, Arenadd passed a chunk of mutton to Skade. "Here, try it."

Skade tasted it. "It is strange. Unlike anything I have tasted before . . . but not unpleasant."

Arenadd chewed his own portion, and sighed beatifically. "Gods. There's nothing like mutton cooked with cymran juice. I've only ever had it three times before, on special occasions."

Skade tried another mouthful. "Tangy," she commented. "I like it."

Arenadd poured himself some more wine. "D'you know Cymria is actually named after the cymran fruit?"

"Of course I do," said Skade.

"Ah, but do you know *why*?"

She hesitated. "No."

"Not many people do. Well . . ." He paused to gulp down some wine, and sighed again. "Oh gods, I needed that so badly . . . all right. So, you know the Southerners originally came from Eire and a few of its neighbouring countries. After the first of them found this place—that was hundreds of years ago, of course—they wanted to encourage more Eireans to come here so they could conquer it before anyone else did. No-one was interested at first, so they told all sorts of lies about what a rich country it was." Arenadd took another throatful of wine. "Including the little tidbit that it was stuffed full of cymran trees. They said, 'There are so many cymrans there that everyone will be able to eat them, no matter how rich or poor they are!' Back in Eire, you see, cymrans were so rare they were practically sacred. So, people started believing the lies, and they actually named the country Cymria—Land of the Cymran fruit, see?" He sniggered. "I love how people work. They're so easily fooled sometimes, aren't they? So the people came in droves, to feast on cymrans. And after that they realised this place was dry and rocky and full of these strange giant creatures they called *gryphans*."

Skade laughed. "Ah, but humans are so clever. Perhaps you do not have magic or wings or talons, but you have a cunning that griffins do not, and a resourcefulness. That is why you have survived and the wild griffins are all but gone. It was a great sacrifice of my—of Skandar's race to do what they did, choosing to live alongside humans. They put aside their pride."

Arenadd drained his cup. "Well, they didn't have much choice, did they? Humans cut down the trees, drove away the animals . . . we changed everything. No amount of strength or power could undo that. Not even magic could."

"No." Skade sighed. "Griffins may be intelligent, but they are still animals at heart, as humans are. In the end, their only instinct is to survive. And if survival meant changing their way of life, then they did what they had to."

"Yes, well . . . they make use of us as much as we make use of them."

Skade nodded and helped herself to some more mutton. Arenadd, meanwhile, downed several more cups of wine while he talked to the people around him, growing more relaxed and expansive as the evening went on. He was on his fifth cup and looking rather woozy by the time Saeddryn came over to talk to him.

"How long are we stayin' here?" she asked, raising her voice over the hubbub.

Arenadd refilled his cup yet again. "Not too long. A few days, maybe. Once we're ready we can leave, before the griffiners get here. Tomorrow you can help me decide where to attack next."

"Is that yer strategy, then?" said Saeddryn. "Keep attackin' cities an' gatherin' followers until we're ready t'go after Malvern?"

Arenadd finished filling the cup and took a healthy swig from it. "No. Can't keep that many people on the move long enough for that. We're heading for Malvern before the next full moon."

Saeddryn looked bewildered, and then irritated. "Yer drunk. I'll wait until tomorrow to discuss this."

Arenadd grinned and toasted her. "Relax. Have a drink. You've earnt it."

Saeddryn rolled her eyes and left.

Skade watched her go. "She is far too serious."

Arenadd laughed. "And coming from you, that means a lot, Skade."

"What do you mean?" said Skade, quite innocently.

"Oh, come on now," said Arenadd, nudging her. "Do you *know* how many times I've seen you actually smile?"

"Griffins do not smile," she said primly.

"But humans do," said Arenadd, and polished off another cup.

Skade eyed him. "But perhaps Saeddryn was correct—you are drinking a lot, Arenadd."

He reached for the jug. "I know. I have a lot of catching up to do."

"Be careful you do not make yourself ill," said Skade.

Arenadd filled the cup and gulped some down. "I'm drinking to forget," he said impulsively. "If you must know."

"Forget?" Skade looked puzzled. "I do not understand."

Arenadd squinted at her; she was starting to look a little blurry. "People drink," he said. "I mean, when they want to forgot . . . forget things." He took another mouthful. "And I have a lot of things I'd rather . . . not remember." Another mouthful. "Everything, for a start. And at the very least"—he made a grab for the jug, but missed—"I'd like to sleep tonight."

"You sleep every night," Skade pointed out, as she moved the jug out of his reach.

Thwarted, Arenadd sat back. "Yes, but I'd like it if it felt, you know, *restful*," he said bitterly. "Instead of being full of nightmares. Give me the damn jug, will you?"

When Skade didn't, he stood up and grabbed it himself, and refilled his cup yet again.

"Being tortured once was bad enough," he said, holding on to the table to steady himself and staring into the red depths of the wine. "Now I have to relive it every time I go to sleep. I'm tired of it, Skade. Tired, tired, tired. I want it out of my head, all of it. Instead of everything else that's gone."

Skade touched his arm. "Arenadd—"

He ignored her and downed the cup, too quickly for his own good. He retched. "Oh, yuck. I think I'm going to throw up."

"Come," said Skade. "We should go and check on Skandar now."

Arenadd nodded vaguely and yawned. "All right."

She helped him out of the hall as discreetly as she could, hoping he wouldn't stumble too obviously. A few people waved or called out, and Arenadd grinned and waved back, which turned out to be a mistake; he promptly tottered sideways into the doorway, and Skade had to help him recover his balance. There were a few laughs, but fortunately most of the people in the hall were too busy eating or talking to notice.

Skade helped him out before anything else happened, and they headed upstairs.

Arenadd weaved slightly on the steps but managed to keep his balance. "Oooh, I'm going to regret this tomorrow," he mumbled. "Didn't realise how strong that stuff was."

By the time they reached the door to Tynan's chamber, he looked to have sobered up a little and managed to open it himself. It was dark inside, but there were still a few flames flickering in the fireplace.

"I'll sort it out," Arenadd said confidently. "I've got good night vision."

He staggered over to a table and found a candlestick with a

candle in it. He lit that from the fireplace and then went around the room, lighting the lamps.

"That's better. Now . . ."

He stumbled off toward the archway, still carrying the candle. Skade, fearing he would set the straw on fire, hurried after him.

"Arenadd—"

He had stopped in the archway, and as she approached he turned to look at her with a wide smile. "Come and see this," he said. "Be quiet, though."

Skade came to his side, and he wordlessly held the candle out in front of him, casting light over the nest.

There was blood on the bedding. Retha's body had been ripped limb from limb, and the entire chest and part of the haunches had been stripped to the bone. Tynan's remains were nowhere to be seen. But neither of the two humans were particularly bothered by the carnage.

Skandar was curled up in the middle of it, close to Retha's carcass. He was lying on his stomach now, with his legs folded beneath him and his head tucked under his wing. He had eaten so much that his flanks were bulging.

Arenadd grinned, his face ghostly in the gloom. "You old glutton," he murmured.

Skade couldn't help but smile, too. "He must have been hungry. It was kind of you to leave food for him."

"Come on," said Arenadd. "We'll leave him to sleep."

They returned to the bedchamber, and Arenadd put the candle down and took Skade in a crushing embrace.

"Yes, yes, *yes!*" he exalted. "We did it! We bloody did it! We won!"

Skade, returning the hug, couldn't help but be the voice of caution. "You were lucky this time. Next time may be more difficult."

Arenadd was too elated—and drunk—to care. "Let's hope so. Skandar wants to fight next time. And he will. We'll fight side by side at last, and *that'll* be something to remember! I just wish I could still use a sword." He kissed her on the lips. "Never had the training back at Eagleholm. I was meant to be an administrator, not a warrior. But"—he kissed her again—"I have other skills, don't I?"

She kissed him back. "No sword can kill you, Arenadd."

"No arrows, either," he agreed. "But magic, maybe."

They kissed again. This time, it lasted longer.

"Magic cannot kill you, either," Skade said afterward. "You have come through every kind of danger and lived."

Arenadd laughed and nuzzled the nape of her neck. "No. Not lived, Skade. Not *lived*."

She pressed herself against him, tangling her fingers in his hair the way he liked her to. "Well, it is living to me," she murmured. "You do not look dead, or feel dead."

He didn't hear her, but kissed her again and ran his hands down her body. "Gods," he almost whispered. "I need you, Skade. I need you so badly. I need to be loved. I feel so empty sometimes, but you make it go away. You make me feel like I still have a heart, somewhere . . ."

She unfastened the front of his robe and reached inside, touching the bare skin of his back, feeling the marks of the lash there. "You have a heart," she said.

Arenadd could feel himself trembling. "Yes. And it's all yours, Skade. Protect it, and I'll protect you."

"I shall."

He kissed her, harder this time. "If I can't stop you from fighting, then promise me this."

She drew back and looked him in the eyes. "Yes?"

He put his arms around her, holding her close. "Stay by me," he said fiercely. "Stay behind me. Let me protect you; keep me between you and danger. Let me be a shield."

"A shield does not feel pain," said Skade.

"I don't care. I don't care. Stay behind me. Promise me you'll do that, Skade."

"I . . ."

"Promise," he said fiercely.

"I shall," she said.

Locked together, they staggered and fell onto the bed. They lay there, still clinging to each other, and laughed.

Arenadd found Skade's arm. "Is this mine?" He tugged it. "Wait . . . no, that one's yours."

Skade grabbed on to one of his. "This one is yours, silly."

"Ow. Yes, definitely . . . whose leg is this? Wait, that one's mine, too. The boot's a dead giveaway . . . the sole's coming off." He pulled the boot off and tossed it aside.

"I think this leg is yours as well," said Skade, tapping the other one on the knee.

"Yes, definitely." He took the other boot off and turned it upside down, tipping out a handful of dirt. "Urgh, I had no idea that was in there." He threw it away. "Now then . . ." He pretended to notice Skade's own footwear for the first time, and did an exaggerated double take. "Hey! Take those off—d'you want to get dirt on the sheets?"

Skade pulled them off and put them aside. "Oh, I am sure someone will clean them for us."

Arenadd tickled her toes. "Now, these toes are definitely yours."

She giggled. "How can you tell?"

"Well . . ." He tapped them one after the other, as if counting them. "For one thing, mine are longer. And for another, they're hairier. And they're more flexible, too. See?" He flexed his own toes. "They match my fingers. And for *another* thing, *my* toes don't have nails like *these* on them." He tugged at one of Skade's toenails, which were in fact not toenails at all but curved black claws. "By gods, I'd hate to be kicked by *you* with your shoes off."

"Why, because of the scratches?" she said.

"No, the smell."

She kicked him. "Smell! If you had *my* sense of smell, you would know how terrible *you* smell."

Arenadd put on an exaggeratedly sinister leer and waggled his fingers at her. "Why, do I smell like *blood*?"

"No, like sweat," she said, and pushed him off the bed.

He hit the floor with a thud, and waved an arm over the edge of the bed. "All right! I surrender!"

Skade leant over and pulled him back up. "Fine, come back up, then, but if you insult my toes again . . ."

Arenadd climbed up beside her. "No, the toes are safe. Trust me. But this ugly dress, on the other hand . . ."

Skade prodded him. "Indeed, I cannot for the life of me understand why you are still wearing it."

Arenadd pouted. "Well, fine. I'll let you see the ugly skin underneath, then."

She helped him struggle out of the robe, and he dropped it on the floor.

"See?" he said. "Now I bet you're sorry."

She leant forward and touched his chest, smooth and white with a scattering of coarse black hair where it wasn't broken up by scars and the tattoos that covered his shoulder.

"I would like you better if you had more feathers there," she said.

"I'll try to grow some. Promise."

"What colour?" she asked seriously.

Arenadd grinned. "Black, to match my eyes."

She fingered the little patch of hair around his belly button. "Ah, but you already have fur. Although not much of it."

"I bet I have more than *you* do," said Arenadd.

He helped her struggle out of her dress. Once she was naked, he examined her chest.

"Nope, no fur here," he said. He felt her breast. "None here, either. Wait . . ." He reached into her armpit and found the patch of hair there. "Ah-ha! There we go. So that's where you were hiding it!"

Skade laughed. "You talk far too much," she said, and pounced on him.

Arenadd let her pin him down. "Actually—"

She silenced him with her lips.

12

The War Begins

Erian and Senneck left Gwernyfed so early the sun had barely begun to rise. It meant they avoided the villagers, but doing so created a lump of unease in Erian's stomach that stayed there for much of that day's travelling. He tried to ignore it, but it wouldn't leave him alone. He felt like a thief stealing away in the dead of night.

I didn't do anything wrong, he told himself dozens of times, but the feeling refused to be convinced and continued to nag at him until later that morning, when Senneck stopped to rest, touching down in a snowy field.

She curled up, apparently unbothered by the snow, yawned and rested her head on her talons. "Loosen up your legs," she advised briefly. "I will not stop again soon."

Erian drew his sword and walked back and forth, making experimental slashes at the air while he limbered up. "D'you think we'll get to another village tonight?"

Senneck yawned again. "Unlikely. We shall probably have to camp."

Erian stabbed the sword at nothing. "Good," he said, almost angrily. "I'd rather freeze than entrust myself to those people again."

"I doubt we will encounter the same people in the next village," Senneck said acidly.

"You know what I mean." Erian paced back and forth more rapidly. "By Gryphus, they harbour a criminal and then treat us as if *we* were the ones who'd committed a crime." He put on a high-pitched whine. "'What've ye done with our son, ye bastard, ye've killed him, haven't ye?' Hah!" He made another slash with the sword. "I'd have liked to take the brat's head off. If that sister of his hadn't seen us follow him . . ." The memory of the distraught faces of the miller and his wife rose up, and Erian struck at the air again, more violently. "It wasn't my cursed fault," he muttered. "I didn't kill him, just scared him a bit . . . if he couldn't find his way back, then that's his fault. Anyway, they'll find him on their own—how far could he have gone? The stupid little—"

Senneck sighed. "Erian, stop that at once."

Erian glared at her. "I'm just tired, all right?"

"*Rest*, then," said Senneck. "Or at the very least allow me to."

"Fine." He stalked off.

Erian found a half-rotted stump at the edge of the field and spent a good while hacking pieces off it, which helped to soothe his temper. When he had calmed down he wandered back to Senneck and found her busy grooming her wings.

"I am nearly ready," she said.

Erian nodded and stood by until she crouched low to let him get on her back.

They travelled on for the rest of that day without incident, stopping a few more times to rest, before making camp shortly before sundown. Erian built a crude lean-to and got a fire going while Senneck flew off to hunt. She returned after dark with the carcass of a wild goat and allowed him to take one of the animal's hind legs to cook while she ate the rest herself.

Erian cut up the meat and spitted it over the fire. While he waited for it to cook, he sat back and ate a dried apple.

"Senneck," he said, once she had finished eating and settled down to gnaw on the bones.

She flicked her tail briefly to acknowledge him, and he plunged on. "I was thinking . . . well, wondering . . . could you tell me more about this place we're going to? I mean, is it dangerous?"

Senneck paused and then spat out a bone. "I do not know much. It is said to be the place where a band of your ancestors stopped as they entered this land for the first time."

"Yes, I know that part," said Erian. "And Baragher the Blessed was with them, as their leader."

"How much do you know of your ancestor, Erian?"

Erian shrugged. "He brought Gryphus to Cymria, they say. He built the first temples to him, and created the rituals and the chants. They say Gryphus appeared to him in a dream and gave him this symbol." He touched the sunwheel around his neck.

"Some even say he became the first griffiner, because Gryphus willed it," said Senneck. "I do not believe in your gods, but if Baragher discovered a powerful object of some kind . . ."

"What do you mean?" said Erian.

"Simply that the Island of the Sun is said to be where Baragher concealed an item with great powers; therefore, if it is real, it must have magic inside it."

"I don't understand," said Erian. "How can magic be *inside* something? I thought only griffins—"

"Magic comes from the world, from nature," Senneck told him in clipped tones. "We are part of nature. Some believe that our kind was created by magic, when—"

"Oh yes, I know about that," said Erian. "That old children's story about how Lion and Eagle fought each other until they fell into a bottomless pit, and while they were in there a great light appeared and changed them into one being called Griffin."

Senneck glared at him. "Magic is in us, and we wield it, but nature wields it also. That is what makes the sun rise and the seasons change. And magic can be in certain objects— sometimes placed inside them by griffins, perhaps by accident. I have heard of an object becoming infused with magic accidentally, simply by being close to a griffin using magic."

"Oh!" said Erian. "So . . . so you think that whatever Baragher hid on this island must be something like that."

"That is the only logical explanation," said Senneck.

"I wonder what it could be, though?" said Erian. "If it's a weapon . . . maybe it's a dagger . . . or a sword!" His eyes gleamed. "By gods, a magic sword . . . when I was a boy, I used to pretend I had a magic sword, and I called it . . ."

"Erian."

". . . and I used to pick up a stick and pretend that was it, and—"

"Erian," Senneck repeated patiently. "Your food is burning."

Erian jerked back to reality and retrieved the charred meat, swearing colourfully.

Senneck chirped and cracked a bone into splinters with her

beak, while her human gloomily settled down to his blackened meal. "That'll teach me to daydream," he muttered. "Magic swords—hah."

"I doubt it could be a sword," Senneck said unexpectedly.

"Hmm?" said Erian.

"I said, I doubt it could be a sword."

Erian deflated slightly. "Why?"

She struck the goat's skull with the point of her beak, cracking it open in order to get at the brain. "Think carefully. Whatever it is, it has been there for hundreds of years. Any sword would have rusted away to nothing by now. No matter how magical."

"Oh." Erian couldn't help but be disappointed. "But . . . how can it be a weapon, then? If a sword would rust away, so would a dagger or a spear or anything else."

"As I said before, I do not know," said Senneck. "But we shall find out, you and I."

Erian chewed at a piece of burned meat for a moment, and then gave up and threw it into the fire. "There's something else I was wondering about," he said.

Senneck made a rasping noise in the back of her throat but said nothing. She pulled the goat's brain out of the skull in chunks and swallowed them.

Erian tried not to let his revulsion show. "I'll wait," he muttered.

Senneck finished eating and rubbed her beak on the ground to clean it before she settled down to groom her chest feathers. Erian didn't try to interrupt, and she proceeded to reorder feathers and fur, even nibbling the length of her tail and combing the fan of feathers she used to steady herself in the air. After that she cleaned her talons, nipping away a few dead scales from her toes and forelegs. That done, she shook herself vigorously, sending up a small cloud of dust. She scratched her flank, dislodging a few loose feathers, and then lay down again with a contented sigh.

"Always questions with you!" she said abruptly, as if there had been no interruption to their talk.

"Well, what do you expect?" said Erian, a touch irritably. "One moment everything's normal and I think we're done with . . . with *him* at last, and now people are telling me I'm some sort of Chosen One or something."

"I suggest you accept it," Senneck said brusquely. "I believe Kraal's word—do you?"

"Of course I do. But I was wondering . . ." Erian sat back. "If I'm *Aeai ran kai*, shouldn't I have powers? *He* does—why not me?"

"For a human to use magic is not as simple as you think," Senneck snapped. "You are not born to it. If you were to use it, you would have to become something other than what you are now. It would change you in ways that would make you unrecognisable. You would not be Erian Rannagonson any more, or even human—you would be something else, something as warped and hideous as *Kraeai kran ae*. Would you, too, choose to be heartless; would you give up your very soul simply to have what only griffins were supposed to have?"

Erian gaped at her for a moment, and then looked away and shuddered. "No. I didn't mean . . ."

"I do not know all there is to know about this," said Senneck. "Only what Kraal has told me, and the things I knew already. But I know this: if *Kraeai kran ae* uses magic, then he is no longer human. And the more he uses it, the further from human he will become. It will corrupt him in ways you cannot imagine."

Erian felt cold inside. "I understand, Senneck. But—" He couldn't stop himself from persisting. "But isn't there something—some sign—something I'd be aware of myself?"

Senneck clicked her beak. "It is said that *Aeai ran kai* sees Gryphus—the god—in his dreams, or that some voice comes to him with advice and warnings, which humans believe is Gryphus."

Erian tried to think. Had he ever dreamt of the Day God, or something that could have been him? He trawled through his memories, looking for something—some message or symbol—but he had always been bad at remembering his dreams, and nothing struck him.

"I don't know," he said. "I don't remember ever seeing him."

"Then perhaps you will one day," said Senneck, though she didn't sound as if she believed it.

Erian returned to his ruined meal, deep in thought. He wondered if *Kraeai kran ae* had had dreams, if Scathach, the Night God, had come to him in his sleep. Had she appeared to whisper her dark messages and commands in his ear? Was she truly the one commanding him to do the things he had done? Erian felt his stomach twist. If she had, what did that mean? Did *Kraeai kran ae* have any control over himself; could he refuse to obey the Night God? She was said to be powerful and seductive, and full of deception, just like her chosen people. What would she do if her creature disobeyed her? What would Gryphus do to him, Erian, if *he* became defiant?

But I won't, he promised himself, thinking that perhaps the Day God could hear. *I don't want to disobey you. I* want *to kill him; I want to protect Malvern. You won't have to punish me. And I won't fail you.*

He thought back to his boyhood, back at the little farm where he had grown up. His grandparents had raised him, and his grandmother had been the one who liked to tell stories and teach him the history of the world.

Long ago, she had said, long ago, there was a giant egg, floating in the void. One day it hatched, and two great lights came out. One was gold, one was silver; the first was male, the second female. They were called Gryphus and Scathach, the two gods. In the beginning, Gryphus and Scathach were in harmony. They loved each other dearly, and together they conceived a second egg, which hatched into the world. Then they created humans, to live on this world and be their children. Scathach, who was clever as well as beautiful, said that she and Gryphus could not rule the world together. And so they agreed that they would share, taking turns. Those times became day and night, and Gryphus ruled the first and Scathach the second. Gryphus created the griffins to be the guardians of day, and he gave them magic and wings so that they could fly to him. But Scathach was jealous of what he had made. She did not have the power to create new life, only to end it, and one night she gathered a group of humans together. They were outcasts: liars and thieves and rapists. Scathach gathered them to herself and said that they would be her own people; they would live in darkness and worship her alone. And as they bowed down to her and turned their back on the sun, their skin became pale like the moon and their hair and eyes turned black as night.

When Gryphus saw Scathach's people, he became angry and said that if she could have her own people then he would, too. He gathered the rest of the people—the strong, the brave, the kind and the honest—and he gave them yellow hair like the sun and blue eyes like the daylight sky.

But the people of the night, seeing Gryphus' chosen, became angry and jealous and began to attack them. They would steal

into their villages at night and kidnap their women and take
their children to sacrifice to Scathach. When Gryphus saw
this, he was angry, and he commanded the griffins to help his
people. So the first griffiners were born when the griffins chose
humans worthy to ride them, and they attacked the night people
and massacred them and drove them into the cold North.

Scathach had no griffins, but she chose to protect her people
by her own power. She found Gryphus at night, when he was
asleep, and she took the sickle moon from the sky and stabbed
it into his back. But Gryphus did not die. He woke up and they
fought, and he took his sword and cut out Scathach's eye. Her
blood created the colours at sundown, and his created the sunrise. Scathach was defeated and fled north with her people. She
took the full moon from the sky and put it into her eye socket to
replace the eye she had lost, and forever after she and Gryphus
were bitter enemies, and so were their people.

"And that is why the griffiners have always hated the Northerners and fought them," his grandmother had said. "And why the
Northerners have always tried to attack us and take our lands."

Erian sighed. He had loved that story then and had often
asked the old woman to elaborate on the battle scenes and the
creation of the griffiners. Now though . . .

Could it be true? he thought.

Maybe it was. After all, the world and its people couldn't
have come into being all by themselves. Something must have
been there, some magic . . . and perhaps Senneck was wrong.
Perhaps magic, too, had an origin and a creator. Perhaps everything did.

*He killed my father like a coward, the way Scathach stabbed
Gryphus in the back. Now she wants to destroy us, just as she
did back then. It's happening all over again, all of it. History
repeating, like a giant wheel turning.*

He retired to his shelter with thoughts like these still churning around in his head. Senneck curled up in the entrance and
went to sleep before he did, protecting him from the wind.

Skade woke up with a bad taste in her mouth, and skin that
felt as if it had been soaked in hot water. She sat up, pulling
the sheets away from herself, and then slumped back to rest.
Her head ached.

Beside her, Arenadd rolled over in bed, mumbling, "Come near me and I'll bite your nose off."

The lamps had burned themselves out, and the room was full of daylight. Skade prodded him in the back. "Arenadd, wake up."

He stirred briefly and flopped onto his front, with his face buried in the pillow. Skade sighed and climbed out of bed. She found her gown and pulled it back on, and splashed her face with water from the jug on the table. That helped to wake her up, and she wandered into the nest to check on Skandar.

Moments later, she came hurrying back. "Arenadd!"

It took some coaxing, but eventually he rolled out of bed. Naked, and looking very unhappy, he tottered over to the jug and stood there for a long time, staring at it. Then he picked it up and poured the contents over his head before returning to the bed and slumping face-first onto it.

Skade growled to herself and gathered his clothes up off the floor. "Arenadd, this is no time to be feeling sorry for yourself. You have work to do."

He managed to grasp his robe and drag it toward him, but didn't put it on. "By gods, I am one hung-over Dark Lord," he mumbled into the pillow. "Remind me to kill myself after I've sobered up."

Skade sighed. "Put your clothes on."

Arenadd levered himself upright and dragged the robe on over his shoulders. "Ugh. I'd say I wish I was dead, but on second thought there wouldn't be much point."

He struggled back into his trousers and boots, and fastened his robe, then took a comb out of his pocket and set to work on his hair. "Curse everything, I knew I should have washed it."

Skade, knowing how long his grooming usually took, said, "I shall go and find some food."

"Good idea. Could you please find Saeddryn and give her a message from me while you're down there?"

"I could do that."

"Thanks. Tell her to find Rhodri, Hafwen, Nerth, Cai and Davyn—the old guard. And tell her to find Caedmon as well; he should be there. Tell her I want the hall cleared out and everyone I mentioned to gather there. We have work to do."

"If I can find her, I shall pass it on," said Skade and left.

Once she had gone, Arenadd searched a cupboard and unearthed a razor and some soap. "Thank gods," he muttered. He went over to a mirror hanging on the wall.

As he busied himself with the normal concerns of shaving, washing and neatening his cherished hair, his mind was free. His head still felt as if it was full of straw, and he felt sick and dizzy, but he almost didn't notice it once his mind began working again.

The war had begun now, regardless of whether he wanted it to or not. From this point, there was no turning back. A hard and dangerous road lay ahead, and he knew he was facing challenges that would test him more harshly than ever before. He couldn't pretend to be an ordinary person any more; from now on he had a very daunting pair of boots to fill—not just Arddryn's but *Kraeai kran ae*'s. He had to be more than a leader and more than a fighter. If he was going to be *Kraeai kran ae* and let his people come to his side, then he would have to live up to that at every turn or risk losing them for good. Darkmen were independent by nature; they didn't look kindly on incompetence or cowardice.

But just now, none of that worried him much. And why should it? He knew the truth now, knew what he had truly become.

Why should an immortal fear anything; I don't have to fear death any more, do I?

And, more importantly than that, he had Skandar. With the big savage griffin by his side, nothing looked daunting. Arenadd might have doubts, but Skandar had none and never had. And, so far as Arenadd knew, he had never been frightened of anything in his life.

Arenadd scraped away the layer of soap on his upper lip. *And I have a god on my side,* he reminded himself. *Who could stop me?*

He looked into the mirror and found himself wondering how he could possibly have changed so much. His face looked older and much thinner; the skin was unhealthily pale, the eyes hollow. He looked ill and drawn, but that was probably partly due to the hangover. The scar under his eye looked even more pronounced than he remembered; it nearly reached to the corner of his mouth.

Remember my face, Bastard . . .

The face smiled grimly back at its owner. "Erian the Bastard. What a joke."

13

The Council

When Arenadd arrived at the dining hall, it was to find Saeddryn and her friends waiting for him. But they weren't the only ones who had come. Annir was there, too, sitting next to Caedmon, and Skade, and—

A skinny shape rushed across the room and hugged him around the middle. "Taranis!"

Arenadd smiled and clapped the boy on the shoulder. "It's Arenadd, Torc."

Torc let go. "Sorry, sir. I'm just used t'you being Taranis."

Arenadd looked him up and down. "By gods, you've grown tall. How old are you now?"

"Nearly fourteen, sir," said Torc, with a shy grin.

Arenadd regarded him. The boy had spent most of his life as a slave, and had the collar scars and the callused hands to prove it, but there was still a certain innocence about his face and eyes. Arenadd couldn't help but think of him as a boy, though he was a man now by Northern law. *He's only six years younger than I am,* he thought suddenly.

"Torc." Caedmon's stern voice came from the table. "Get over here an' leave him be."

Torc looked suddenly embarrassed. "Uh . . . sorry, sir . . . I'll go."

"It's all right." Arenadd followed him to the table and sat down. "Well . . . good morning, everyone."

"It's lunchtime," said Caedmon.

Arenadd chuckled and then winced. "Yes, well, considering what went on last night, that's close enough for me. Anyway . . . since everyone is here, we may as well get started."

"Saeddryn says ye've got somethin' planned," said Caedmon.

"And so I do." Arenadd nodded toward Annir. "I assume you've met my mother?"

Caedmon, who looked much older than he actually was, directed a brief smile toward her. "So I have, an' to my enjoyment."

Annir unconsciously touched the bandage on her throat as she smiled back. "You didn't tell me you'd found another Taranisäii, Arren."

"I didn't realise I had at first," said Arenadd. "And Caedmon, I'm sorry about what happened to Arddryn. I know she was your sister."

He nodded slowly. "I never expected to see her again anyway. But I'm happy t'have met my niece. A worthy woman, aye."

Saeddryn smiled. "Ye look like her, ye know. Like my mother. Same eyes."

"So all the surviving Taranisäiis are back together," Arenadd resumed. "And we may only be three, but—"

"Four," said Caedmon.

"I'm sorry?"

The old man patted Torc on the shoulder. "I've adopted the lad. Now we're four."

Arenadd paused and then smiled. "Four, then. Well, I was going to ask Torc to leave, but if he's a Taranisäii then he should stay. Unless he'd rather go?"

"I'll stay, sir," Torc said instantly. "I want t'hear."

"So be it, then. Mother, do you want to be a part of this?"

Annir nodded silently.

"Then we'll begin." Arenadd reached into his robe and pulled out a scroll of paper, which he opened on the table. "As you can see here, this is a map of the Nor— sorry, Tara. Just let me weight it down." He picked up a few stray cups and a jug and used them to stop the corners from curling. "That's better." He sat down again. "Now that we've captured Warwick, we have a good stronghold. I'm tempted to stay here, but obviously we can't do that."

"Why?" said Rhodri.

"Because we're not strong enough," said Arenadd. "Yes, we have walls, and I'm fairly sure a good portion of the locals here would agree to fight for us, but the instant Malvern hears about this Elkin will send her best fighters against us—in other words, griffins. We wouldn't stand a chance."

"I've thought of that," Saeddryn interrupted. "There's ways of fightin' griffins, sir. Mother taught me how t'make weapons—spear launchers an' things of that nature. They can take a griffin out of the air."

"Yes, I know. But there's still no point. Even if we managed to hold on here for a few months, what would that achieve? They'd overwhelm us eventually, and that would be the end of it. No. We're not strong enough to go into open war."

"I know," said Saeddryn. "What, then?"

"Easy," said Arenadd. "We become shadows. Invisible. We make ourselves impossible to find, and we force them to fight in the dark. We can disappear, reappear, cause some damage and then vanish again."

"Ah!" Davyn grinned. "Covert fightin', eh? We can do that, sir. That'd work."

"Of course it would," said Saeddryn. "We'd have the advantage. This is our land, not theirs; we could make it work for us."

"Indeed," said Arenadd. "But that on its own won't win us the war. We need followers. And not just whoever we can pull in off the streets or recruit from villages in the middle of gods-know-where. We need a force that will stay with us, and a large one. We need people who'll do what they're told, ones who are used to hard work."

"That's nice, sir, but we can't expect 'em t'show up just because we need 'em to," said Saeddryn. "We'll take what we can get."

"An' our people can fight just fine," Rhodri added hotly. "We ain't no Southerners with their fancy armour an' their marchin' an' whatnot. We're *warriors*. We know about courage an' honour, an' we can—"

"I say we go westward," Hafwen interrupted. "There's places out there no Southerner's ever been—all wild. There's villages out there that still live by the old ways, an' they'd help us. It's said there's shamans can turn 'emselves into wolves an' make blood potions that'll give any man a—"

"We can't go chasin' after legends, Hafwen!" said Saeddryn.

"In case ye didn't notice, we're tryin' t'fight a war here, an' we ain't got time for fairytales, see?"

"They ain't fairytales, Saeddryn. If ye knew anythin' about—"

"No. Just shut up. I mean it, Hafwen." Saeddryn glared at her. "Listen. What we need are real followers, an' we'll get those by seekin' out real people. If we take everyone who'll come with us from Warwick, we can move on to another city, take that, recruit more an' then move on. Sooner or later—"

"It's too obvious!" said Rhodri. "Ye heard what Arenadd said! If we go 'round with a damned great army draggin' after us, how long d'ye think it'll take for Malvern t'find us, eh? It'll be Tor Plain all over again. We've got t'—"

Arenadd watched them arguing, first with resignation but then with a look of amusement. And then, quite suddenly, he started to laugh.

The others around the table fell silent and glared at him.

"Sir, with respect, this ain't the time t'be laughin'," Saeddryn said stiffly.

Arenadd leant forward, resting his hands on the table. "Thank you, everybody. You just provided exactly the right demonstration."

"What demonstration, sir?" said Hafwen. "I don't see why—"

"That's my point!" Arenadd burst forth. "Look at yourselves! For the love of gods, is it any wonder you lost the last war? Saeddryn, I don't want to insult you, but this is not what wins wars." He started to pace back and forth. "We're darkmen, oh yes. And we know how to fight, and we know about courage. But there's a difference between warriors and soldiers, and I'm sorry to say that it's soldiers that win wars." He stopped pacing and faced them. "I can't lead that kind of follower into battle. The loss of life would be horrific."

Saeddryn stood up. "Sir, if ye're suggestin' that we don't know how t'fight—"

"You argue too much!" Arenadd said. "Saeddryn, Hafwen—all of you—I don't need this. I don't need an army that has to argue about everything. You're too undisciplined. And what I need in my followers is *discipline*. I need people who'll do what I tell them without wasting an entire morning debating about it."

Saeddryn bristled. "Well, I'm sorry, sir, but ye can't change people. That's how we are, an' if we weren't that way then we wouldn't be darkmen. We're free, sir. Free in the mind. We ain't scared t'say what we think." Several of the others nodded and muttered their agreement.

"Yes, I understand—" Arenadd began.

"If ye don't respect us," said Saeddryn, "then we don't want ye leadin' us, sir. Ye can leave if that's what ye want. I'll lead my friends if they ain't good enough for ye."

Arenadd waved his hands in the air. "That's not what I was trying to say, Saeddryn. I'm sorry. No, listen. Yes, I understand all that. Warriors have their uses as well, and I'm sure that will help us. We can do what the enemy won't expect; they don't know what we can do. We have imagination and bravery that they don't. But I need something else—something to *complement* that, understand?"

"Well, what would that be?" said Saeddryn, not looking very placated.

Arenadd paused and rubbed his hands together. The damaged knuckles on his left hand made a horrible cracking noise as they flexed. "I don't pretend to be an experienced general; in fact I've only ever read about warfare in books. But what I do know is that the best armies have balance—a mix of qualities. A thousand screaming darkman warriors will be very good to have, but we need a more conventional kind of fighter to form the core of our army. And I think I know where to find that."

"Not mercenaries?" said Saeddryn. "Tell me ye ain't thinkin' of that, sir?"

"What? No, definitely not. They'd be Southerners. Why would they fight for us? Even if we could find enough of them, I'm damned if . . . no. No, I was thinking of other darkmen. They understand discipline, they'll follow orders without question—it's bred in them to do as they're told—most of them are tough and hardened and used to hard work, and they're quick to learn, as I've discovered in the past."

Saeddryn went white. "*Slaves?* Ye're jokin'. Tell me ye're jokin'."

"Yes!" Arenadd grinned triumphantly. "That's exactly what I'm talking about: slaves."

Rhodri stood up. "Bloody blackrobes! Sir, for the love of the Night God—"

Arenadd leant over the table and hit him, hard, in the face.

Rhodri yelped and toppled backward, and everyone else there stood up sharply, many with yells of outrage.

Arenadd rubbed his knuckles while Saeddryn helped her friend up. "*Never* use that word in my presence again," he said.

Rhodri, his face bright red on one side, stared at him in shock. "Sir—"

"I don't want to hear anyone say that word, Rhodri," said Arenadd. "Not you, not anybody. Is that understood?"

"Sir, I didn't—"

"I said, is that understood?"

Rhodri sat down again. "Yes, sir," he muttered.

"Good." Arenadd slapped his hand down on the map. "Listen to me. I captured Guard's Post with an army of slaves. They'd had a week or so's training at most. *At most.* They overran that fort in a single afternoon. Why? *Because they were disciplined.* I stole them from Herbstitt. As far as they were concerned, I was their new master; they did what I told them. I told them to capture that fort, and they did. Isn't that so, Caedmon?"

Caedmon nodded grimly. "What he says is true. The lads from Herbstitt followed him there on foot an' fought because he told 'em to. An' afterward—"

"Yes, afterward I set them free. That was their reward. And listen to me." Arenadd took a deep breath. "One of the biggest reasons I even decided to do this is the slaves. And maybe *you* don't care about them any more, now they've become somebody's property, but I do. I've been a slave. I know what it's like to be nothing, to be sold for money as if you were an animal. I know what it's like to be branded and flogged and work all day for nothing but a bowl of slop. Uh"—he glanced at Torc—"I know you made that stuff, Torc. I don't mean to insult you."

Torc nodded gravely. "It's all right, sir. I know it was rubbish."

Arenadd glared at the other Northerners. "And I see my so-called people have short memories as well. Because, in case you didn't notice, we're all slaves. Maybe we don't all wear robes and collars, maybe we aren't all bought and sold, but we aren't free, and we'll never be free until Malvern has been destroyed. We haven't ruled ourselves in centuries. We can't own weapons, we can't worship our own god or speak our own language. They've *destroyed us.* Don't you see that? They're taking away the things that make us who we are—turning us into nothing. We've got nothing left to be proud of, nothing to believe in, nothing to bind us together. And that's what they want. They took all that away so we'd forget. If we stopped believing we were our own people any more, then we'd never be able to fight again. We're second-class citizens in our own home. And those of us who rebel have to hide ourselves away, as if we were ashamed of ourselves. You can call me mad or stupid if you like, but that doesn't sound like freedom to me." He drew himself up. "I mean to take our freedom back, and I mean to give those slaves back their pride by letting them do what all Northerners were born to do: fight."

Silence followed. The others exchanged glances. Some looked uneasy, but Caedmon was looking at Arenadd with open pride.

Saeddryn stirred. "Sir . . . I see what ye mean, an' maybe it could work, but how are we going t'get these b— slaves? They're all in the South, ain't they? Are we gonna go there an' free them all?"

Arenadd shook his head. "Too impractical. There are hundreds of them, at the very least—taking that many slaves by force would be next to impossible. And it would bring the wrath of the other eyries down on us, which is the last thing we need. No. We're going to do this legitimately."

"What d'ye mean by that, sir?" said Davyn.

"We buy them, of course," said Arenadd. He cracked his knuckles again. "Because if there's one thing my years as Master of Trade taught me, it's that some men are open to persuasion, some will cave in to blackmail or force, but *everybody* listens to the sound of a bag full of golden oblong."

Saeddryn stifled an incredulous laugh. "*Buy* them, sir? Are ye serious?"

"Why not?" Arenadd asked mildly.

"Sir, where in the gods' names would we get the money? Buying every slave in the country would cost a fortune!"

"More than a fortune," said Arenadd. "But I've already thought of that, and I know where to get it."

"Where?" said Caedmon.

"Malvern."

"What, rob the treasury?" said Hafwen.

"Well, theft would be a part of it, yes. Now." Arenadd leant forward to point at a spot on the map. "We're here. And over here—a week or so's travel at the most, by my estimate—is

Crescent Lake. Next to that is Fruitsheart—a very large and wealthy city, thanks to the orchards and the vineyards all around it. Obviously we can't capture it yet, but my plan is for us to move there next. We'll take a few people with us—not too many—and go to ground there. We'll take money from the treasury here and buy a house or two, and we can use those as hideouts. You, Saeddryn, will hide there with the others, including Skade. It's a big city, so I'm sure you'll be able to avoid detection as long as you're careful."

"An' what will *ye* be doin', sir?" said Saeddryn.

"I haven't finished yet. You won't be idle while you're there. We'll discuss this in more depth later, but I expect you to be active in Fruitsheart. Start recruiting, spread the word. Very cautiously, of course. We'll start sending out people to other cities to do the same. I hope to have a cell in every major centre in Tara, including Malvern itself. I need eyes and ears everywhere."

"It sounds like a good plan t'me, sir," said Saeddryn. "What's t'other part?"

"Yes, the other part . . . while you're doing that, Skandar and I will be in Malvern."

Saeddryn started up. "What? On yer own, sir?"

"Yes."

Annir, who had stayed silent so far, looked horrified. "No," she said. "Arren, you can't go back there. I won't allow it."

Arenadd gave her a warning look. "I'm sorry, Mu— Mother, but this is my decision to make."

Annir realised she was embarrassing him. "I understand, but surely—"

"She has a point, sir," said Saeddryn. "We can't risk losin' ye, or Skandar."

"I agree," said Skade. "You should not go back there, Arenadd. If you were captured again . . ."

"Send someone else," said Saeddryn. "I'm sure we can find someone."

"No," Arenadd said flatly. "It has to be me who goes, and Skandar."

"Why? Sir, I know ye've only been leadin' us for a short time, so I understand that ye might want t'look brave an' so forth, but when ye're a leader ye have t'be selfish sometimes. Ye have t'look after yer own safety. If we lost ye, we'd lose everythin'."

Arenadd smiled faintly. "I'm flattered you think so. But you don't quite understand. I have to go because I'm the only one who can do what I have in mind. May I remind you, Saeddryn, that unlike you I have . . . certain talents. And the Night God didn't give them to me so I could let them go to waste."

Saeddryn withdrew. "Aye, I understand, sir. But what d'ye plan t'use 'em for?"

"Something that will get us the money we need and completely cripple the Eyrie at the same time," said Arenadd.

"An' what would that be?"

He told her.

"Are ye sure ye could do it, sir?" Saeddryn said doubtfully.

"Yes. With Skandar's help."

There was silence for a while. Rhodri, Davyn and Hafwen began to grin.

Saeddryn couldn't stop herself from doing the same. "Ooh, they're not gonna like that, sir. They're not gonna like that at *all*."

Arenadd grinned wolfishly. "I doubt they will."

Saeddryn glanced at the others and then nodded. "I think it could work, sir, provided we do it right."

"Well, I'm not going to pretend I don't need your input," said Arenadd. "So if anyone has any suggestions . . ."

They spent the next hour or so deep in conversation around the table, discussing, speculating, making plans. Everyone had suggestions, and they gradually refined the plan and added to it, building on Arenadd's original ideas until they began to agree that they had come up with something workable.

"So that's it, then," Arenadd said when they were done. "We're ready to go ahead if I'm any judge. As long as Skandar agrees, we can do it."

"When shall we leave here, sir?" said Saeddryn.

"In a few days," said Arenadd. "Once we're well rested. And for the love of gods, *don't tell everyone where we're going*. Not even our friends. Rhodri, you and Davyn will tell people we're going to Wolf's Town. Saeddryn, you tell them we're going back to the Gorge. Hafwen, Cai, Nerth . . . just make something up. We won't tell anyone where we're going until we're well away from the city. Got that?"

Saeddryn nodded. "I was goin' t'suggest the same thing myself, sir."

"Sensible as always, Saeddryn." Arenadd nodded. "All right.

I think that's enough for now. Let's get some rest and something to eat. I could probably do with some more sleep as well."

The council began to disperse, and Arenadd sat down with a sigh and drank some more water. The hangover hadn't gone yet; it had probably made him a little more snappish than usual during the meeting. Still, he was pleased with how things had gone.

"Arren?"

He looked up. "Oh, hello, Mother. How are you?"

"Fine. Arren, can I talk to you?"

Arenadd turned around in his seat to look at her properly. "Of course you can. Please, sit down—d'you want something to drink?"

She took some water and drank it. "Thank you." She glanced over her shoulder. The other councillors were all leaving, including Skade.

Arenadd stifled a yawn. "What is it, Mother? How's your neck?"

She touched the bandage. "It's healing well, Hafwen says."

"That's good. I was afraid it might get infected; it looked a bit red the last time I saw it."

"No, Hafwen's ointment kept it clean. Arren . . ."

"Please call me Arenadd. Arren is too"—he shook his head—"I don't know. I don't feel like it belongs to me any more."

She smiled very slightly. "You didn't used to think that."

Arenadd sighed. "Let's just say that I've changed a lot since then."

"Arren . . ." Annir surprised him by reaching out to touch his hand. "Arren, I know . . ."

"What is it?"

"I know you're too old to . . . I mean, I know you're old enough to make your own decisions now," said Annir. She laughed sadly. "You stopped obeying your father and me when you were ten, if I remember."

"Mother, I know I—"

"It's all right. I don't mind. Every boy grows up. But I wanted you to know that I still love you." Her grip on his hand tightened. "I love you so much, Arren. You're my only child, and you always will be. My little warrior." She gave a watery smile. "Aren't you? My little Northern warrior. You always were. Even when you were tiny."

Arenadd looked at her, taken aback. "I understand. I know I was never very close to you and Dad after I became a griffiner. I've never forgiven myself for that. But that doesn't mean I don't love you any more. I always came back to see you, didn't I? And I never stopped caring about you, or looking out for you. In fact, I . . ." He paused. "You know how . . . when that other boot maker set up shop in the village, not too far away from you?"

"Yes."

"He was taking all your business," said Arenadd. "Until I raided his shop and had him arrested for smuggling whiteleaf."

"Yes, I remember that," said Annir.

Arenadd looked slightly guilty. "I never told you this, but . . . he was innocent. I planted the whiteleaf myself."

Annir started. "What?"

"I know. It was dishonest of me, and . . . but I had to do it. You and Dad were going to go out of business. If you'd lost your shop, what would you have done then? I saw how badly things were going for you, so I decided to get rid of him."

Annir made an odd sound, half-laughing, half-sobbing. "Oh. Oh, you little . . . I always thought it was strange that that happened just a few days after your visit. I don't think your father ever suspected, though." She became serious. "But Arenadd, if you love me, then listen to me."

"I'm listening."

She took in a deep breath. "Don't do this."

Arenadd looked slightly surprised. "I understand that you don't want me to go to Malvern myself. I know it's dangerous, but that's the nature of this kind of thing. I promise I'll be careful."

"I don't mean that," said Annir. "I mean everything." She gripped his hand. "Don't do it, Arren."

"Don't do what?"

"Any of it. Don't go to Malvern. Don't start a war. *Don't do it.* Please."

Arenadd stared. "Mother, please. Try to understand—"

"No. I understand perfectly well." Annir looked him in the eye. "Arren, what's happened to you? What did they do to you?"

"I don't want to talk about it," Arenadd said stiffly.

"What's happened to you?" said Annir. "I don't understand. You're not who you used to be. You've changed. I thought . . ." She looked at the ground. "I thought I knew you. I thought I knew all of you. But this is . . ."

Arenadd leant toward her. "What is it? What are you talking about?"

She looked up. "I don't know you any more. I feel as if you've turned into a stranger. Arren . . ."

Arenadd watched her, dismayed. "I haven't changed that much. I'm still me, I—"

"You're not!" Annir exclaimed. "You're not who you used to be. Listen to yourself! Can't you hear what you sound like? I know my son, Arren. You weren't like this before. The man I knew would never have talked about war and death this way. He would never have talked about killing people as if it was nothing. He would never have *enjoyed* the idea. You used to hate it when your father talked about Arddryn's rebellion—now you're talking about restarting it. You're talking about destroying Malvern—don't you care about all the people you're going to kill?"

"They're my enemies," Arenadd said flatly. "Enemies of us all."

"They're human beings! How many people have you killed, Arren? After Rannagon—how many?"

Arenadd shifted uneasily. "Does it matter?"

"Of course it matters! They were people, Arren! People with lives, people with *families*. Have you thought of that? What about the men you killed yesterday? Don't you feel any guilt at all?"

The headache was coming back. Arenadd gritted his teeth. "This is war, Mother. People die in war. I don't like it, but it's necessary."

"If you don't like it, then don't fight!" said Annir. "Don't start it. Don't go to Malvern."

His head was pounding. "Well, what d'you suggest, then?" he said, more sharply than he had intended to. "What did you have in mind?"

She clasped his hand in both of hers. "Leave!" she urged. "Get out of here, go as far away as you can."

"What, run away like a coward? Let them win?"

"It's common sense!" said Annir. "If you leave—if *we* leave—then nothing will happen. No war, no killing. For gods' sakes, do you honestly think you can win this? Against Malvern? Against griffiners?"

"I can, and I will."

"But . . . Arren . . ." Annir calmed down a little. "What if they catch you again? What then? You've already been caught once, and next time you might not be so lucky. What if you are killed?"

"I won't be."

"But how do you know?" Her face was pleading. "I've already lost you twice. If something happened to you again, if . . . if you were lost and didn't come back, I don't know what I'd do."

Arenadd felt a faint ache in his chest, where his heart had been. "I understand. I do. My powers will protect me, Mother. They have before."

She looked away. "I don't understand this. None of it. How could the Night God have given you this—this *magic*? How could you be this . . . chosen one?"

"She's a god." Arenadd's voice was full of bitterness. "Gods can do whatever they like."

"But how could she have spoken to you? How do you know it wasn't just Skandar who gave it to you?"

He gave her a terrible look. "So, you think I'm mad, do you?"

"No!" said Annir. "I don't. That's not what I meant. I only . . ." She looked up. "So, that's it, is it?" she said abruptly. "You're doing this because you believe a god told you to do it."

"I'm doing it because I have to," said Arenadd. "These people need me; I can't turn my back on them."

"You're willing to kill people?" said Annir. "You're willing to become this . . . this *Shadow that Walks*, this Dark Lord?"

Arenadd pulled his hand out of hers. "I'm those things already, Mother. Whether I want it or not. And I don't care how many people I kill. They don't mean anything to me. They're enemies, and my enemies die—including the Bastard and anyone else who stands in my way."

Annir stared at him in silence for a few moments, and Arenadd stared back. The words had come out without any warning, without his even thinking, as if someone else was speaking for him. He watched Annir, wanting and not wanting to say something else, to try to explain himself, but nothing came to him.

Annir stood up. "You are not my son," she said quietly and left the room.

14

Treasures

Skandar circled high over the city, enjoying the feeling of the wind in his wings. His joints felt stiff and sore, which made him clumsy in the air, but he ignored the urge to return to the ground and rest. He *wanted* to feel the ache in his wing joints, wanted to exert himself as much as he could. It was an escape, one he didn't want to lose.

He had been furious when Arenadd had told him he shouldn't fight in Warwick, and it had taken a lot of persuasion to make him agree. This fight had to be a small fight, a quiet one. And besides, there would be no other griffins for him to fight. There had only been one in the city, and she hadn't put up a fight. Arenadd hadn't even dared to mention the real reason for Skandar's exclusion: that after using so much magic he was simply too weak to risk a fight. Those lingering feelings of exhaustion had been the only thing that had made him give in, and once he had taken cover in Retha's nest he had slept through most of the fighting.

In his dreams, the white griffin had come once again. She was light and slim, but though she was smaller than him there was something about her that made her look bigger. Her feathers and fur were extraordinary, so white they seemed to glow in the blackness. But she had only one eye; one was silver, and the other a black hole.

You . . . griffin, Skandar rasped. His voice sounded like an echo inside a cave.

She dipped her head to nibble at the feathers on his neck. *I am whatever I want to be.*

What you? said Skandar, not understanding.

The white griffin raised her wings, opening them toward him. They glowed silvery white, from within. *I am the night,* she said. *I am the moon, I am the stars, I am the shadows.*

Not griffin? said Skandar.

Griffin, human, spirit, magic, she said enigmatically. *I am* Kraeae ee ra ae o.

Skandar knew that when a griffin died, something would come to take away his magic and return it to nature. *I die?* he asked, almost nervously.

Not now. I protect you.

You protect?

She flicked her tail. *You are the Night Griffin, and I rule the night. I rule you. It is from me that your magic came.*

You give magic?

Yes. I chose you while you were in the egg, Skandar. If I had not touched you then, you would have been brown like your siblings, and small. You would not have the wonderful powers you have used. You have done well so far, Skandar. You found the human chosen for you and guided him to his death. You used his body to create Kraeai kran ae, *my avatar, and brought him to my land where I could reach him and you.*

You speak with human? said Skandar.

I have spoken to him, and told him the truth. He has now accepted his role to do my bidding, with your help.

Why help? Skandar's tail began to twitch. *Why do what you say do?*

She chirped and batted at his head with her forepaw. *You are a griffin, Skandar, and you and I have more in common than you think. You do nothing unless there is benefit in it for yourself, and I know this, for I am the same.*

Same?

Yes. Listen, Skandar. I know your desires, and I will give them to you. She drew herself up, terrible and regal in the blackness. *You and your human together are all but indestructible. You have the power to gather humans to you to fight on*

*your behalf, and you can destroy the griffins at Malvern and
take their land for yourselves. Would you like that, Skandar?*

Skandar's tail twitched faster. *Land? Big territory?*

*Bigger than any griffin's in the world, Skandar. Forests, riv-
ers, plains and mountains. Humans to bring food and make
the finest nests for you, and beautiful stones for you to own—
stones that shine like the moon. You will have respect, and
humans and griffins will dip their heads before you and call
you master.*

Want, Skandar said instantly. *Want that. Want all.*

*And you shall have it, Skandar. All of it. But first you must
do something for me.*

Do what? He bristled, instantly suspicious.

*Nothing that will be hard. You and Arenadd can take your
reward, but there is someone who can stop you and take all of
this away.*

I kill, said Skandar.

*That is exactly what you must do. There are three humans
who must die. They are the family of Rannagon, the man you
and Arenadd killed at Eagleholm. One of them is* Aeai ran kai.
*That human has the power to kill Arenadd and will not rest
until it is done.*

Not kill me? said Skandar.

Aeai ran kai *seeks to destroy Arenadd, not you, but you do
not need to fear for your human. Gryphus' chosen cannot win
the fight against* Kraeai kran ae; *he will die. Skandar, your task
will be to help Arenadd find and destroy these three humans;
he will know who they are and where to find them.*

Why help? Skandar asked sullenly. *I find, I kill.*

Leave your human to fight other humans, said the white
griffin. *You have your own foe.*

What foe? said Skandar.

*There is a griffin living at Malvern. His name is Kraal. Most
call him the Mighty Kraal. He is master of the North now, and
he is powerful and wise. You must kill him to win this land for
your own.*

Skandar's talons flexed. *I kill*, he said. *Where find?*

*At Malvern. Arenadd cannot hope to fight Kraal on his own;
you must do this yourself. Do this in my name, and you will be
rewarded.*

I kill, Skandar promised. *Find Kraal. Kill. Kill!*

But do not forget this, said the white griffin. Suddenly she looked much bigger, almost towering over him. *You must protect your human, Skandar. Protect him at all costs. Do not lose him; do not betray him. If he dies, you will have nothing. A griffin without a human has no status; he is nothing but a wild animal to be hunted. With Arenadd beside you, your future will be assured . . . and the rewards will be great.*

I stay, said Skandar. *Protect. Not let leave.*

That is all I ask, Skandar.

She walked away from him and lay down, her limbs suddenly stiffening. Blood ran from her beak before she became still. Skandar got up and went to inspect her, and as he stepped forward the shadows faded away and he realised he was awake again. In front of him was the dead griffin, smelling of cooling flesh and blood.

Skandar let his hunger take control and settled down to eat with barely another thought. But as he tore into the carcass, he smelled something else in the air: the lingering scent of a living human. A human he knew. Arenadd had been here recently. Watching over him.

I will eat and become strong again, he told himself. *Then I will find Kraal at his nest and kill him. Arenadd will help me.*

He recalled that thought now as he flew, and that same certainty came back. Yes. The white griffin had helped him and was a friend. Arenadd knew about her, too—he had talked about destroying Malvern. He *must* know; she had spoken to him as well.

The idea fitted comfortably into Skandar's simple thought process. He would fight his enemies again and take their land for himself, with Arenadd's help. The human was clever. He could make good plans.

Skandar sent out a screeching call and executed a fantastic swoop and twirl in midair, just for the sake of it. His wings felt stronger every moment.

Torc heard the screech from down in the city. After the meeting he had helped his adopted father find an empty room to sleep in for a while, and now that was done he was left to his own devices.

He wandered along a corridor, thinking. There should be

food in the kitchens, and even though he wasn't particularly hungry he decided to go there anyway. He had spent more than thirteen years as a slave, and the novelty of being able to eat as much as he wanted was one that hadn't worn off yet.

On his way back past the hall, he looked through the open door and was surprised to see a black-robed figure slumped over the table. He paused in the corridor, wondering whether he should go in. Arenadd, unaware of his presence, heaved a deep sigh. It sounded so tired, so miserable, and so *human* that Torc couldn't make himself leave.

He went into the hall and ventured toward him. "Um . . . sir?"

Arenadd looked up sharply. For a moment Torc saw an emotion flicker about his pale face before it abruptly vanished, leaving it cool and reserved. "Torc."

Torc bowed hastily. "I'm sorry, sir, I was just passin' by . . ."

Arenadd stood up. "That's fine. I should be getting things done now anyway. D'you want to come with me?"

"Er, all right, sir, if y'need help."

"I've got a little errand to run," said Arenadd. "I think you'll like it. Come on."

Torc followed him out of the room, feeling inexplicably frightened. He had caught the look of unutterable despair on Arenadd's face, and having seen it, he felt as if he had been caught spying on something he wasn't meant to see.

"You'll be old enough for your manhood ceremony very soon," said Arenadd. "Did Caedmon say anything about that?"

"Yes, sir."

"What did he say?"

"He said every Northerner used t'be tested when he was my age, an' when he was ready he'd be given the tattoos, an' then he'd be ready t'get a wife an' a family."

"That's right. They did that with me when I found Taranis' Throne," said Arenadd. "I was lucky. I got my tattoos from Arddryn herself."

Torc sped up to keep pace with him. "What was she like, sir?"

Arenadd slowed to accommodate him. "Old. I think she looked older than she was—a hard life will do that to you. But she was so strong as well. She could hardly walk without someone to help her, and she was blind in one eye, but you got the feeling she was made of steel—nothing could stand against her. She hit me, you know."

"She *hit* you?" said Torc.

"Yes. When I first came there, she didn't know if Skandar and I were friends or not, so she and Hyrenna attacked us on the spot. We lost very quickly. I had to convince her I was on her side, so I told her my name. When I told her I killed Lord Rannagon, she punched me in the face."

"Why?" said Torc.

"Lord Rannagon took her eye," said Arenadd. "He led the attack that destroyed her army at Tor Plain. He was her worst enemy. She was furious to find out someone else had killed him before she had the chance. Still." He chuckled. "It made her see I was a friend quickly enough."

"I wish I could've met her," said Torc.

"So do I," said Arenadd. "Almost as much as I wish Caedmon could have." They had descended into the lower levels of the tower, and by now there were no more windows and their way was lit by torches. Arenadd stopped in front of a heavy metal door. "Ah, here we are. Just wait a moment . . ." He rummaged in his pocket and brought out a large brass key. "I think this is the right one . . . ah-ha!" The key fitted and turned. Arenadd turned to Torc. "Could you just pick up one of those torches? Thank you."

He pushed the door open, and they went in.

The room beyond was small. Its stone walls were lined with shelves. They were laden with metal chests, neatly lined up. At the end of the room, sitting on the floor, was another much larger chest, also made from metal.

Arenadd walked the length of the room, examining the boxes. "Perfect. If these are full, we'll have more than enough."

Torc followed him with the torch. "This is the treasury, isn't it, sir?"

"It certainly is. There must be thousands of oblong in here. Among other things. Now, let's see . . ." Arenadd chose a box at random and opened it. It was full of money.

Torc's eyes widened. "By gods, that's a fortune!"

Arenadd picked out a gold oblong, turning it over in the light. It was decorated with an embossed griffin on one side and a line of text on the other. "You've never owned money before, have you?"

"Not really, sir."

"Well then. This is a gold oblong, worth the most. Actually

it's made from bronze; gold is too soft to last. And this . . ."
He picked up a smaller silver coin of the same rounded rect-
angular shape. This one bore a picture of a serpent. "A silver
half-oblong. Worth half as much as a gold one. And this one
here"—he picked up the smallest coin, dark grey, with an ox on
it—"made from iron. Ten of these make one oblong, five make
a half-oblong. Simple!"

"So, we're gonna take all this?" said Torc.

"A good amount of it, yes. We'll need all we can get if we're
going to buy our friends back into freedom." Arenadd closed
the chest and moved on to the large one at the end of the room.
"I've got a feeling there's something in here that isn't money."

The chest proved to have a lock on it. Arenadd tried to wrestle it open. "Damn!"

"Maybe we could break it open, sir," said Torc.

"Not easily. These things are designed to be tough. But
don't worry; I'm not beaten yet." Arenadd drew his dagger and
jabbed the point into the lock. He spent a few moments twid-
dling it this way and that, until the mechanism made a loud
clicking noise. "Got it!"

He removed the dagger and tugged at the lid. This time, it
began to come open.

"Where'd you learn how t'do that, sir?" said Torc.

Arenadd stood to heave the lid up. "When you deal with
smugglers, you pick up a few useful skills. Ye gods, look at this!"

Torc nearly dropped the torch. "Treasure!"

Gold gleamed at them from inside the chest. Gold, and jewels
as well. Unable to stop himself, Torc reached out and touched it,
burying his fingers in gold chains, rings and arm bands.

Arenadd crouched beside him. "Thank the gods we got
in here before anyone else. If I hadn't had the key, this room
would've been stripped bare in the blink of an eye." He started
to rummage through the chest's contents. "By the moon . . . I'd
love to keep some of this, if it wasn't so impractical."

Torc desperately wanted to try some of the jewellery on, but
the thought struck him that he could be accused of stealing. He
withdrew his hand and sighed miserably.

Arenadd glanced at him and grinned. "If you like the look
of anything, take it. Make sure it's something small, though,
and keep it hidden—or it'll be stolen from you before you've
finished breathing in."

Torc's face spread into a slow, disbelieving grin. "Can I really?"

"Of course. Go on."

Torc lunged forward, burying his arm to the elbow in jewellery, pulling out whatever he touched and scattering it on the floor, looking for the most beautiful or valuable thing he could find. During his search, he unearthed several very large rings—some silver, some gold, some set with precious stones.

He examined one, puzzled. "Is this a neck . . . thing, sir?"

Arenadd took it and turned it over in his hands. His face lit up. "I know what this is! This—no, they're not for humans at all. No-one's got a neck this thick. No, this is for griffins to wear. On their forelegs. See the hinge there? You snap it on, like a . . . well, like a slave collar, really."

"Griffins wear jewellery?" said Torc. "Sir?"

"Oh, yes. When a griffiner is honoured with a new official station, his or her griffin gets given rings like these to wear. The higher the station, the finer the rings. Griffins love gold and jewels. Hmm . . . I wonder if Skandar would like a pair?"

"I'm sure he would, sir," Torc said politely.

Arenadd shook himself and put the ring down. "All right, that's enough daydreaming. You choose something while I get on with this." He rummaged through the chest and pocketed a couple of rings and a necklace before finally coming up with what he was looking for; he examined it and offered it to Torc. "Here. This is for you."

It was a large precious stone, very dark blue in colour and beautifully faceted. Torc examined it, awestruck. "It's beautiful! What should I do with it, sir?"

Arenadd straightened up. "You'll be a man soon, and one day you'll need that."

"What for?" said Torc.

"One day you'll see a woman you like," said Arenadd. "One you'd like to spend your life with. If you're sure you've found that woman, then give her that stone."

"Oh!" said Torc. "Of course. Caedmon told me—I see, sir."

"Well." Arenadd rubbed his broken fingers. "Now that's done, I'm going to gather some of these chests together and leave them by the door so we can take them when we leave. Put all that back in the chest while I'm doing that, will you?"

"Yes, sir," said Torc.

Arenadd looped a couple of the griffin-rings over his arm and went to examine the moneyboxes, while Torc repacked the treasure chest, though he couldn't stop himself from secreting a few choice items away in his clothes.

Arenadd finished stacking several boxes by the door and filled a small bag with money from one of them before turning to look at Torc. "Are you done?"

Torc shovelled the last handful of gold chains back into the chest. "Yes, sir." They left the treasury together, and Torc summoned up the courage to say: "Sir, why aren't we taking *all* the money?"

"We won't be able to carry it, for one thing," said Arenadd. "And besides, we'd bankrupt the city. Everyone in it would suffer."

"Oh."

"Now, you take good care of that stone, won't you?" said Arenadd. "Don't lose it, and be careful who you give it to. Once you've given it to a woman, you can't take it back unless she gives it to you of her own free will. If she keeps it, you're betrothed."

"Yes, sir," Torc said solemnly.

Arenadd's black eyes glinted. "You saw my cousin Saeddryn at the meeting, didn't you?"

"She was the one who argued with you, sir."

"Do you like her?"

Torc looked slightly puzzled. "How d'ye mean, sir?"

"Do you think she's pretty?" said Arenadd. "Would you like to get to know her better?"

"I think so, sir," Torc said shyly.

"That's good. I think she'd like a new friend. She's a rather lonely person. Her mother made her swear never to marry anyone but another Taranisäii."

"But don't ye love Skade, sir?" said Torc.

"That's beside the point," said Arenadd. "I don't have my stone any more. Anyway," he said abruptly, "thank you for your help. I've got to go and deal with some other things."

"Yes, sir," said Torc.

Arenadd nodded and smiled briefly, and walked off, leaving him alone. Torc watched him go, and then reached into his pocket for the stone. It looked even more beautiful in daylight, and he turned it over in his fingers, examining it thoughtfully.

15

An Old Friend

Arenadd and his followers stayed at Warwick for several days, planning, resting and recruiting. The city had remained surprisingly calm after the Governor's Tower was overrun, but Arenadd knew that wouldn't last; with all its administrators killed, it would soon fall into chaos. He knew there wasn't much he could do about that, and had determined to leave before it happened. Even so, plenty of the city's occupants wanted to join his cause, and he spent most of his time mingling with them, talking to them to find out more about their backgrounds and skills. But there were many of them—over two hundred offered their services during the first two days alone—and he knew there was no way he could take them all with him to Fruitsheart. He also didn't want to reject them; every follower was valuable.

Nerth provided the solution. Arenadd ordered the tough darkman to take most of the volunteers back to the mountains and go into hiding with them there, ready to emerge when the time was right.

"While you're there, you can train them," he added. "They need to know everything you can teach them about hunting and weapons. You have to remind them of everything they've forgotten."

He was tempted to send Saeddryn as well—she still refused

to completely subordinate herself to him and argued with him during nearly every meeting—but decided against it. Partly it was because he didn't want to make her angry with him again, but also because, like it or not, he had to concede that she was a fine strategist and leader in her own right, and quite frankly he couldn't afford to send her away.

Caedmon also stayed with the party that would go to Fruits-heart, simply because Arenadd knew the harsh conditions up in the mountains could well kill him, as they had eventually killed Arddryn.

On the evening of the fifth day after the conquest, Arenadd returned to his temporary home carrying a large parcel under his arm.

Skade rose from the bed and came to meet him. "What is that?"

Arenadd dumped the parcel on the table and started to unwrap it. "I paid for these to be made a few days ago; they've just been finished."

It was a pair of boots made from thick, heavy leather dyed black. Arenadd tapped one. "Steel toecaps. Plenty of grip on the soles. These were made to last. Cost a tidy sum, too. You don't know how long I've wanted a good pair of boots like these."

Skade stifled a yawn. "I am sure they will serve you well."

Arenadd unlaced his old pair, holding one up to show the hole in the sole. "Anything's better than these old things." He threw them aside and put on the new pair, almost reverentially. "Perfect! And look at this, will you?"

Skade looked at the sole of the boot and saw that the leather had been etched with intricate spiral designs. "Surely you did not *ask* for that?"

"No, the boot maker did that himself. Still, I'll leave some interesting tracks behind, eh?"

She couldn't stop herself from smiling at his almost childish look of pride. "Now all you need is a new sword."

Arenadd shrugged. "I'll take one from the armoury before we go, but I'll probably only need a d—"

He was interrupted by a loud thud from next door, mixed with a scrabble of talons. Half a second later he got up and darted through the archway with shocking speed.

Skandar was in the nest. His tail was lashing violently from side to side, sweeping the straw like a feathered broom. "Griffin come," he rasped.

Arenadd swore. "How many? How close?"

"One, coming," said Skandar.

"Show me."

Arenadd dashed out onto the balcony beside him, and Skandar raised his head skyward, indicating the unmistakeable shape of a griffin flying toward the city.

"Godsdamnit," Arenadd muttered. "I should have known this would happen. It must be someone coming with official documents or something."

Skandar raised his wings. "Fight!" he declared. "You, me, fight!"

Arenadd tugged nervously at his beard. "Wait. I have an idea."

Skandar looked sharply at him. "What do? Fight!"

"They don't know we're here," said Arenadd. "They think the people down here are friends. If we hide and let them land on the balcony here, we can trap them inside."

Skandar hissed. "Yes. Fight close. No escape."

"Exactly. Come on, we have to get out of sight."

Arenadd ran back into the nest, where Skade was waiting uncertainly. "Arenadd, what is happening?"

"Griffin coming," Arenadd said tersely, sounding more like his partner than he had ever done. "Quick, go and round up some of the others. Tell them there's one griffin, coming to land on the balcony up here. We're going to catch them unawares."

Skade nodded and sprinted out of the room.

Arenadd had expected Skandar to be impatient, and angry over being asked to hold back, and was surprised when the griffin looked at him and said, "Where to wait?"

"In the nest, out of sight by the entrance," said Arenadd. "I'm smaller than you, so I'll go out onto the balcony and watch. When they're close enough, I'll signal for them to land here. Once I'm sure they're coming, I'll come inside, and you and I will wait until they pass us. The moment they're inside, we'll block the way out and attack."

Skandar listened carefully. "Ambush," he said.

Arenadd nodded and hurried out onto the balcony to check. The griffin was getting closer, but it would be a little while yet. He turned to look at Skandar, who had followed him, keeping well back from the entrance to the balcony. "There's just one other thing we should do."

Skandar cocked his head to listen.

"I'd like to keep the human alive," said Arenadd. "So he can tell us what he knows. Could you try not to kill him?"

Skandar shook his head briskly, ruffling the feathers. "Fight griffin," he grunted.

"I'll leave the griffin to you," Arenadd nodded. "It doesn't matter if she dies. It's just the human I want. If Skade and the others get here in time, I'll get them to help me take him prisoner. It shouldn't be too difficult, just as long as the griffin doesn't interfere."

"I kill," Skandar said instantly. "Not let hurt you, Arenadd."

"I trust you," said Arenadd.

They waited in silence while Arenadd watched the griffin draw ever closer, until they were interrupted by Skade's return. The silver-haired woman sprinted back into the bedroom, closely followed by half a dozen Northerners, including Saeddryn and Rhodri.

Arenadd ran to meet them and quickly filled them in on the situation. "I want you to get the griffiner," he finished. "Skandar will fight the griffin; the moment you get the chance, go for the human. Separate him from his partner and drag him out of the nest as fast as you can. The griffin will chase you, but Skandar will be able to stop her. Understood?"

"Yes, sir," said Saeddryn. "Don't worry, sir, I'll get 'em workin' together."

"Wait in here, out of sight," Arenadd told her, and hurried back to the balcony.

And not a moment too soon. The griffin looked to have sped up. She was close enough now that he could see that she was indeed female. Her wings beat steadily, and he could see the rusty red colour of them and the grey forelegs, folded beneath her.

Arenadd waved his arms and sent out a call in griffish. *"Aaekraee, aaekraee!"*—come here, come here!

The griffin heard him and angled herself down, flying toward him. Arenadd continued to wave, waiting as she drew closer and closer and began her descent. At the last possible moment, he bowed and waved his arms in a great beckoning motion and then ducked back inside. He had barely made it back to Skandar's side before he heard a thud and a scatter of talons on the balcony.

"Human?" a griffish voice called. "Where have you gone?"

Arenadd gritted his teeth and waited, pressing himself against Skandar's flank.

The griffin called out for him again, then hissed to herself in frustration and came through the entrance and into the nest. She was a fine, large female, and her orange-brown hindquarters neatly complemented her rusty feathers. Her human walked beside her, mostly hidden by her wings.

Skandar didn't wait for a signal from Arenadd. He stepped forward, blocking the entrance with his body, and raised his wings high, rearing up to make himself look even bigger. "Enemy!" he rasped.

The griffin turned sharply and found herself looking straight into the black griffin's outstretched talons. She reacted with impressive speed; shoving her human aside to get him out of harm's way, she lowered her head and breathed a column of red magic straight at Skandar's exposed underbelly.

Skandar howled in pain and fury. He dropped forward, landing on his forelegs, and charged.

The other griffin met him head-on. They collided with a horrid thud and a screech, and the next instant the two of them were grappling with each other, Skandar hooking his beak into the loose skin on the back of his enemy's neck while she turned her head, trying to bite at his throat, her talons reaching up to tear into his chest. Skandar let go and darted to the side, aiming for her flank, but she lashed out hard with her wing, knocking him aside. The way out was clear now, and she darted toward it. She stopped just outside the entrance, turning side-on to look back into the nest. Searching for her human.

Skandar, recovering his balance, rushed at her with a snarl and a flurry of wings. He hit her in the flank, hard, his talons cutting deep grooves in her skin and flesh. The impact bowled her over, but it had an equal effect on Skandar. While he stepped backward, shaking his head and hissing, she struggled desperately to get up. But her efforts proved to be her downfall. She found her paws and tried to stand, not realising how close she was to the edge of the balcony. Her hind paw lost its grip, kicking out into space, and she slid backward, rasping frantically and trying to get a purchase with her talons.

Skandar, quick to take advantage, ran at her again and lashed out with his beak, straight at the vulnerable spot on the back of her skull. She reacted quickly, twisting out of the way, but the motion dislodged her grip on the balcony and she fell off it, rolling sideways as she went, one wing flailing at the air.

Skandar didn't pause to see what happened next. He screeched and launched himself from the edge.

Back inside the nest, Arenadd had not been idle. He kept well back from the fight, cramming himself into a corner to avoid the two giants. The instant Skandar ran out, however, he shouted for his followers and made straight for the griffiner.

The griffiner, a heavily built man whose clothes were surprisingly simple given his status, had hit the wall hard after his partner shoved him aside. He was struggling to get up, one big hand reaching for his sword.

Arenadd got to him and kicked the weapon out of his hand. The man managed to pull himself into a kneeling position, but he was clearly in no condition to fight.

Arenadd nodded to Saeddryn and the others. "Take him."

They were on the man in an instant, pinning him face-down on the floor and binding his arms behind his back. He struggled, but Saeddryn dealt him a brutal blow to the back of the head, and he went limp—either unconscious or subdued.

"Don't kill him, will you?" Arenadd snapped.

"He's fine, sir," said Saeddryn. "Help me turn him over, Rhodri."

They grasped the man's shoulder and flipped him onto his back. He fell limply, head lolling, his eyes half-closed.

Arenadd looked down at the man's face, wet with blood on the forehead as it was, and felt as if someone had kicked him in the stomach. The captive was young, a few years older them himself. He had rough square features with a reddish beard outlining his jaw and a fringe of uncombed hair hanging over his forehead. His nose had been broken some time in the past, and his mouth, partly open, showed a missing front tooth.

Arenadd's expression did not change. *It's Bran,* he thought, quite calmly. *Bran is a griffiner. And now he's my prisoner.*

Bran was half-conscious when they turned him over, and began to recover his senses as he was being taken out of the room. His head hurt so badly his vision flashed red with every heartbeat, and all the strength had gone out of his limbs. The pain clouded his brain and stopped him from thinking clearly; he could hear perfectly well but couldn't make much sense of what he was hearing. Everything seemed distorted.

A voice said something, something that sounded like a command. Some part of Bran—the part that was still a guardsman—told him he should be up and obeying the voice, but he couldn't move. Hands grabbed him by the arms and shoulders and began to drag him away, and he hung from their grip like a broken doll.

He blacked out a short time later and dreamed strange and unconnected dreams, or perhaps they were scraps of memory. He remembered the Red Rat, his favourite tavern—saw a vision of it wavering in front of his eyes, full of light and warmth and faces, two faces, yes, there they were . . . he tried to focus on that, tried to remember. There was Gern, the daft boy, grinning and excited, his mouth moving, waving his hands about in the midst of some story. He was always telling stories, was Gern. He wanted to be a guard some day; he was always talking about that. He liked to boast about the fights he won down at the Arena every day; yes, he never shut up about that.

The other face looked on, smiling, a little bemused, but listening with mock seriousness; with those black eyes that always seemed to be looking somewhere else. He was a quiet one, Arren, and wary—had that look as if a wild animal lived deep inside. Never really trusted anyone, not easily, all the time looking for danger. But he'd always been like that, ever since Bran had first met him that day. A skinny little boy, crumpled on his side with his black hair covering his face, moaning softly in pain. Bran stopped to help him, not sure what to do. The boy was afraid but pleading for help—not with words, but in his face. *I fell*, he said. *I fell. The building . . . from the roof . . . my arm's hurt.*

As Bran had carried him back to his home, the boy, half-delirious with pain and fear, said one other thing. *I didn't fall. Someone pushed me. Someone pushed me off. It hurts . . .*

He never did cry, though. That wasn't Arren's way. Never was. *We have no tears, only ice*, he'd said once.

Only ice.

Bran woke up, shivering. He was wet and cold. *Ice* was his first, addled thought.

His senses seeped back, and he became aware of his surroundings. It was gloomy and the air was still, and the surface he was lying on was hard and rough. *Stone,* he realised. *Not ice.*

This was an atmosphere he knew, but how? Where had he felt it before?

He lay very still and tried to think. Cold and poorly lit, stone-lined, dank air. He could sense walls very close to him and knew he was in a confined space.

A cell.

He sat up sharply, or tried to. An instant later something caught around his wrists and he fell back with a gasp of shock, hitting his head on the floor. Pain exploded in his vision yet again, and he gritted his teeth to keep from crying out.

Another thought rushed into his mind. *Kraeya!*

His memory replayed a vision for him of Kraeya, blood soaking into her feathers, fighting for her life against a huge dark griffin. Kraeya falling from the edge of the balcony, bleeding and injured.

"Oh gods," he moaned aloud. "Gods no. Not Kraeya."

He tried to think. Kraeya was gone, and possibly dead or seriously hurt. He was locked up and in chains. Northerners had done it. They had been lying in wait with the black griffin, and they had taken him prisoner.

"Oh gods," Bran said again. "Oh great Gryphus . . ."

He knew that griffin; he had seen it before, over a year ago, in the Arena at Eagleholm. He remembered seeing it, down in the pit, wings chained, slaughtering criminals as if they were ants to be squashed and then turning on its fellow griffins in a fit of rage while the announcer's voice echoed over the crowd. *Darkheart, the mad wild griffin, who destroyed three entire villages all on his own without ever taking a wound! The biggest griffin ever to fight in the Arena! Captured alive and brought here for your pleasure!*

Darkheart, here, and among hostile Northerners. Bran closed his eyes while the inevitable answer came to him.

They had been right. The Bastard had been right. Arren was here, with the dark griffin; he had to be. And these Northerners had to be their followers. Had they conquered the city? Probably. And they had killed Kraeya and taken him captive.

Bran felt a slow tear work its way out of his eye and begin to trickle down his face. Kraeya was dead. Kraeya was gone. And what could they have in store for him? Were they going to kill him, too? But if Arren was their leader . . .

Bran's fists clenched. *No. Arren's my friend. He wouldn't do that. He can't kill me. He's got to help me.*

He repeated that in his head several times, trying to calm himself down while he waited for his head to recover. The pain persisted for some time, however, and he eventually slid into a shallow sleep.

When he woke up he felt a little better and was able to use his chains to haul himself into a sitting position against the nearest wall. He found a jug of water placed within reach, drank some of it and used the rest to clean the crusted blood off his face.

After that, he waited. There was nothing else to do.

Time passed. He had no idea how much time. He dozed and woke again, and the headache gradually went away, until nothing was left but a dull throbbing in the back of his skull.

Finally, the door cracked open and light came in. Bran squinted. "What's goin' on? Who are yeh?"

Four tough-looking Northerners entered and silently removed his manacles. Bran knew better than to struggle, and allowed them to chain his hands behind his back with a different set of restraints. He stood up when they indicated for him to do so, and let them lead him out of his cell.

"Where are yeh takin' me?" he asked.

They made no reply, although one of them smacked him in the side of the head. He winced and fell silent. No doubt he'd find out the answer soon enough.

The trip was a brief one. They took him along a short corridor in what was obviously an underground prison complex and led him into a room at the end of it. There was a heavy wooden table there, bolted to the floor, and a chair, which they forced him to sit in before shackling his wrists to the armrests. There were more shackles for his ankles, but to his slight relief they didn't put those on. He sat as still as he could, looking around the room with an increasing sense of dread.

The room was small, stone lined like the cell and sparsely furnished. But there was a brazier by the table, and he could see the long handles of some branding irons poking out of the cold coals inside. He had seen rooms like this before and even used one once. It was a memory he preferred to keep buried.

Two guards stationed themselves on either side of him, while another went to stand by the door. The fourth opened the door; Bran heard that but couldn't turn his head far enough to see. There was a brief murmur of voices, and then a little gust of air touched his left cheek as someone walked past him. Bran blinked, confused, as the tall shape made its way around the table, partly shrouded in darkness. There had been no sound. There was *still* no sound. No footsteps, no rustle of cloth. Just a faint swish of air.

The shape sat down in a chair opposite him, face hidden. He saw it shift, turning its head toward the guard by the door. "For the love of gods, could we get some torches in here? I can't see a cursed thing."

The guard by the door straightened up. "Yes, sir!"

Bran had stilled when he heard the voice. It had changed, but not completely. He tried to speak, but his own voice failed him.

The guard returned with an armload of torches, and proceeded to put them in the holders around the room and light them. They banished the darkness quickly enough, and Bran found himself staring straight into the face of what had once been his best friend.

It had changed, he saw—changed terribly. It looked older, thinner—almost gaunt. The terrible wound under the right eye had become a thin scar that looked like a pale tear track. The rest of the skin was pale, too, and the eyes were red rimmed. The hair had grown long, and he had a beard now—a neat pointed thing perched on his chin, which made him look sharper and more angular than ever.

But the eyes had changed the most, Bran thought—changed in a way he couldn't quite define. There was something about the light in them, or the expression. Something that, the more he saw it, the more frightened and despairing he began to feel.

Bran managed to find his voice. "Arren."

The expression flickered briefly. "Tell me your name."

Bran tried to lean forward. "Arren," he said again. "Arren, it's me. It's Bran. Don't yeh know me?"

"Bran, is it?" said Arenadd. His voice was flat and cool. "Would that be short for something?"

"Arren!" said Bran. "Arren, for gods' sakes, what's wrong with yeh? Don't yeh remember me?"

Arenadd's eyes were utterly expressionless. "I don't believe we've met. Now answer my question. What is your full name?"

Bran slumped in his chair. "Branton Redguard, son of—"

"And where are you from, Branton Redguard?"

Bran snapped. "I'm from Eagleholm!" he yelled. "Same as you! Arren—"

Arenadd held up a hand to silence him and looked at the guards. "You can go now."

They looked uncertain. "Are ye sure, sir?" said one. "He's a tough one—what if he gets free?"

Arenadd drew a dagger and stabbed it into the tabletop, where it stuck. "I said get out!" he roared.

The guards bowed hastily and left, closing the door behind them. Once they had gone, Arenadd got up and began to pace back and forth behind his chair, keeping his head turned away from Bran.

Bran tried to break free of the shackles. They wouldn't budge. "Arren," he said again, "I ain't . . . please, just *look* at me. What's wrong with yeh?" His voice softened. "Why can't yeh look at me, mate? What's the matter?"

Arenadd ignored him.

"Don't yeh remember me?" Bran said. "I'm yer friend. I'm yer best mate, remember? We used t'drink at the Rat together—us an' Gern, remember?"

Arenadd stopped pacing.

"D'yeh remember?" Bran persisted.

There was a silence. Then Arenadd heaved a deep sigh and rubbed a hand over his face.

"Arren?"

Finally, Arenadd turned to look at him. "Bran, what are you *doing* here?" he said.

In that instant, Bran felt a tide of warm, wonderful relief flow through him. *This* was his friend. This was his voice, his face. "Arren!" he said. "Yeh know me; yeh remember?"

"Of course I remember," said Arenadd, his voice irritable and wonderfully, brilliantly familiar. "Stop babbling."

"What was all that about, then?" said Bran, trying to wave a hand toward the door. "I don't . . ."

Arenadd slumped back into his chair. "Use your brain, you idiot. I couldn't say anything in front of them."

"Arren—"

Arenadd waved him into silence. "Stop that."

"Stop what?"

"Calling me Arren."

Bran blinked at him. "Why? What's wrong with it? It's yer name, ain't it?"

"Not any more. Did you come from Malvern?"

"Yeah, I did," said Bran. "I live there now."

"You saw Lady Elkin, then?"

"Yeah. Arren—"

"Did you see her audience chamber?" Arenadd continued.

"Yeah. Look, Arren—"

"Where is it? What does it look like?"

Bewildered and afraid, Bran described it as well as he could.

Arenadd listened closely. "Good. Thank you. Is that all you have to tell me?"

"No!" Bran almost shouted. "Arren, listen. I came lookin' for yeh."

Arenadd's eyes narrowed. "Why?"

"To warn yeh. It's the Bastard—Rannagon's son, remember him?"

"What about him?"

"He thinks he's some kinda . . . I dunno, some kinda chosen one. He's gone off somewhere with that griffin, Senneck. They're lookin' for something, some weapon or somethin' to kill yeh."

Arenadd stared, then snorted. "Oh good grief. What is this, a fairy story? You came all the way here to tell me *that*? Can't you tell me something a bit more useful, like what Malvern's doing? Do they know where we are?"

"No," said Bran. "Arren, don't yeh get it? They're gonna kill yeh!"

Arenadd shrugged. "Thanks for the help, but that doesn't really scare me any more. Now tell me: what are they doing in Malvern? What else do you know?"

"Nothing," said Bran. "I swear."

"So you say. But we'll see about that."

"I don't know anything!" Bran yelled. "Arren, for gods' sakes, let me go!"

Arenadd looked away. "I'm not Arren any more. And I can't be your friend any more, either. I'm a Northerner now, a proper Northerner. And that makes you my enemy." He called for the guards. They came in immediately, and Arenadd moved away from the table, ignoring Bran altogether.

"Take him back to his cell," he said. "We'll find out what he knows. One way or another."

Bran couldn't say anything. He had already said everything he had to say. He let the guards unshackle him and pull him out of the chair, but this time he didn't go where they directed him to. They had to drag him out of the room by the elbows, backward, and all the while he kept his eyes on Arenadd, staring at him in disbelief. Arenadd looked back, unflinching and silent.

16

Memories

Bran lay awake for hours that night, staring into the darkness and trying to think, but nothing seemed to make any sense to him now. He couldn't comprehend what had happened or think about it clearly. Arren was gone. Arren was . . . changed. Erian had been right, horribly right. This wasn't Arren any more. This wasn't the quiet, clever young man he had once known; this was someone else, someone with Arren's body and Arren's face and Arren's voice and knowledge, but someone who was not him.

Arren is dead.

"Gods," Bran mumbled into the shadows. "He's gone mad. He's . . . gone."

He had no illusions about his situation now. Arenadd's dispassionate face and voice stayed with him, and he knew there was no hope for him. Not now. The old Arren would have done something to help him, but this one would not. Tomorrow he would be tortured, just as Arenadd had been, and after that he would die. Assuming he survived the torture.

He forced himself not to think about that. Instead, he tried to think of Flell. He could picture her face as he had last seen it, looking at him with worry and grief. *Just come back, Bran,* she had said. *Please, just come back. Don't die.*

He imagined that he could still feel her kiss on his forehead,

and that made him smile a little. Sweet Flell. At least she was
safe. And the child.

Bran rubbed his aching forehead and sighed. Laela wasn't
his daughter, but he still felt as if he was her true father. The
poor child would be doomed, he knew. If she survived to adulthood, it would be only to face a life of loneliness and perse-
cution; nobody would ever fully accept her. Not her father's
people, or her mother's. Half-castes were rare, and that was
for a good reason. She wouldn't be able to hold down a job
or marry. And if Bran died, she and her mother would be de-
fenceless.

And even if he *did* escape with his life, he wouldn't be much
use to them now. Not if Kraeya was dead.

Tears weren't Bran's way. He felt a lump in his throat, and
he let out a hoarse bellow of rage and despair and slammed his
fist into the wall. Pain exploded in his hand, but he didn't care.
He lurched upright, yanking at the chains with all his might,
swearing violently.

The chains held fast. He struggled against them a little
longer and then slumped back, shuddering. *Got to keep my
strength up,* he thought once he had calmed down. *Got to think.
Try an' escape later, when they're not ready for it. Pretend to
be asleep, an' take the bastards unaware.*

Deep down, he knew any escape attempt would be a failure.
But he preferred to die fighting. It would be easier that way, and
faster. Yes. Maybe he could take one of them with him, too.
He'd make them sorry they'd taken Captain Branton Redguard
prisoner.

Yes . . .

Eventually, worn out by fear and exhaustion, he fell asleep.

Someone thumped him hard in the arm. Bran groaned but
didn't move.

The hand thumped him again. "Bran," a voice hissed. "*Bran!*
Wake up!"

Bran's eyes flicked open. "What?"

There was a sigh, and someone tugged at his arm. "Come
on, get up. *Move!*"

Bran stirred and tried to look up. "Arren?"

"Shut up!" the voice hissed. "I'm taking the chains off you now. Attack me and you die, understood?"

Heart pounding, Bran sat up and waited while the manacles were removed from his wrists. Arenadd, only half-visible in the darkness, dragged him to his feet.

"Can you walk?"

"Yeah," said Bran. "Arren, what's goin' on? What are yeh doin'?"

"Come on," Arenadd said briefly. "Follow me, keep silent, do what I tell you. Is that clear?"

Bran rubbed his wrists. "Why should I do what yeh tell me?" he asked sullenly.

"Because you'll die if you don't. Now move."

Every sense on the alert, Bran followed him out of the cell. The corridor outside was poorly lit and apparently deserted. Arenadd paused to look both ways and then beckoned him along it, away from the interrogation room.

Bran followed, searching the walls and floor for a weapon he could use. He found nothing, and caught up with Arenadd at the end of the corridor. "Arren, what's goin' on? What are yeh doin'?"

Arenadd gave him an impatient look. "I've forgotten—were you always this stupid?"

Bran itched to hit him. "I just wanted t'know what's happenin'. What are yeh doin', Arren?"

Arenadd took a key from his pocket. "What does it *look* like I'm doing? I'm getting you out of here."

Bran's eyes widened. "What? Yeh mean, lettin' me go?"

"Yes. Now shut up before I change my mind." Arenadd fitted the key into the barred door ahead of them and shoved it open.

Bran grinned disbelievingly. "I knew it," he said. "I knew yeh hadn't forgotten."

"Not quite. Now, are you going to do what I tell you?"

Bran nodded. "Just follow an' keep quiet?"

"Yes. If we run into anyone, make a break for it."

"Got it."

Arenadd nodded curtly and led the way out of the prison corridor and up a flight of stairs. The upper levels were dark and quiet, and Bran realised it must still be night. He followed Arenadd through several more rooms and down a corridor, which led them out into a little courtyard and through a gate into the city.

Once they were there, Bran allowed himself to let out a deep sigh of relief. "Thank gods."

Arenadd turned to him. He was wearing a black robe and leggings underneath, and there was a dagger in his belt. He looked tired and worn. "You can't stay in the city," he said briefly. "You're the only Southerner left; you'd be spotted instantly."

"How do I get out of the city?" said Bran.

Arenadd walked on, beckoning to him. "I'll show you."

They began to make their way through the streets by moonlight. It was quiet here, and Arenadd seemed to relax slightly. Once someone passed close by them, and he tensed and pulled Bran into an alley to hide until they had gone. Other than that brief encounter, they saw no-one. They reached a small gate in the outer wall. It was locked, but Arenadd picked the lock and ushered Bran out and into the sheep paddocks that surrounded the city.

Once they were well away from the walls, and the guards there who might see them, Bran fell in beside his old friend and dared to break the silence. "Why are yeh doin' this, Arren? I thought you was gonna kill me. I thought yeh'd . . . gone mad."

"I'm a Northerner," Arenadd said calmly. "We're all a little mad, you know. Especially when we're angry."

They reached the edge of the paddocks and entered a grove of trees, and Arenadd remained silent all the while. Finally, when they were under cover, he stopped and stood with his back to Bran, and sighed.

Bran approached him cautiously. "Arren? Can yeh at least tell me why yeh helped me?"

Arenadd didn't turn around. "I'm losing my memory, Bran," he said.

Bran froze. "What?"

"I don't know why," said Arenadd. "I don't even know what I'm forgetting. There's just . . . big blanks in my head. I don't remember anything about my childhood any more. I can't even remember how you and I met, or why we were friends, or whether I ever trusted you."

"Arren—"

Arenadd kept his back to his former friend. "I am . . . I've changed, Bran. I'm not what I used to be, or who. That fall, back at Eagleholm . . . killed me. I don't have any life left. I don't even have a heartbeat. And soon I'll have no past, either. It's leaving me, all of it."

"Then why did yeh help me?" said Bran. "If yeh don't remember—"

"I still remember some things." Arenadd turned around. "I owe you, Bran. You saved my life."

"But I didn't!" said Bran. "I tried to save yeh, but—"

"Not then," said Arenadd. "Before then. After Eluna died. What happened to her destroyed me. I didn't want to live any more. If you and Gern and Flell hadn't helped me, I probably would have drunk myself to death. I didn't tell you this, but"— he looked away—"that night when you came to see me, when you came to see if I was all right, I . . . there was . . . I had a rope. In Eluna's old nest. When you came, I was about to use it. If you hadn't come then, I would have been dead."

"You was gonna . . ." Bran went cold as he remembered that night and the drunken, dishevelled wreck that had greeted them, with that dead look to the eyes. "You were gonna kill yerself."

"Yes. But after you came, I changed my mind. I decided I still had something to live for, because I had friends."

Bran moved closer to him. "Yeh still do, mate. An' if yeh remember that, then . . . well, yeh ain't changed. Arren Cardockson ain't dead; he's you."

Arenadd shook his head. "Not for long, Bran. I remember it now, but I won't forever. I don't know how long it'll be gone, too, sooner or later. Arren—who I used to be—he's still alive, but only just. He's dying. Soon he'll be gone. I think, one day, I won't even remember who Arren Cardockson was at all. But I'm helping you for the sake of his memory. No other reason."

"What are yeh gonna do?" said Bran.

"I'm already doing it," said Arenadd. "Now go. Get out of here, and don't come back. Don't let me find you again, because if I do I'll probably kill you."

Bran looked pleadingly at him, but Arenadd's voice had become distant again. He was retreating. "How do I get away?" he asked. "If . . . if Kraeya's . . ." He tensed. "Kraeya. My griffin. Where is she? What happened to her? Is she . . ."

Arenadd shook his head. "Skandar is the biggest griffin I've ever seen, and the strongest. But he's not very fast or agile in the sky. Your—Kraeya, did you say her name was?—found her wings after she fell. Skandar says he chased her a very long way before he gave up and came back."

Bran's eyes lit up. "She's alive?"

"As far as I know. I don't know where she is, but I doubt she'll go far. A griffin always comes back for her human."

Bran hesitated for an instant and then took his old friend in a fierce embrace. Arenadd let out a quick "Hey!" but gave in. He was thin and light in Bran's arms; it seemed as if there was nothing left of him inside the robe.

Bran let go of him. "Thank you," he said solemnly. "I don't care what yeh say, Arren, you ain't changed as much as yeh think."

Arenadd gave a lopsided smile. "Get going, you big lump. I've got to get back to the tower before Skade wakes up and finds I'm missing."

"Who's Skade?" said Bran.

"Oh. Well . . ." Arenadd rubbed his twisted fingers. "She's someone rather special."

"Oh, right." Bran grinned. "Well . . . that's good. I'll tell Flell—"

Arenadd froze. "Flell? She's here?"

"Yeah, at Malvern."

Arenadd lurched forward and grabbed him by the shoulders. "Malvern?" he almost shouted. "She can't be at Malvern! What's she doing there?"

"She came with me," said Bran, taken aback. "We're . . . we got married."

Arenadd's face was full of horror. "She can't be in the North!" he said. "For gods' sakes, Bran . . ."

"What?" said Bran. "What's wrong with that?"

Arenadd gripped him more tightly. "Get—her—out of here," he said. "Go back to Malvern, take her and leave. Immediately."

"But why?"

"Because—it doesn't matter why. Just do it!" said Arenadd. "You've got to keep her away from me! I don't care where you take her; just don't let me find her."

"*Why?*" said Bran.

"Because if I find her, I'll kill her," said Arenadd. "Understand? If I see her, if I know where she is, she's dead, along with anyone who tries to stop me."

"But why?" said Bran. "What did she do to yeh? I know she left yeh, but that's no reason—"

"I can't tell you, you wouldn't understand," said Arenadd. "But as long as she's at Malvern, she's in danger. Promise me you'll take her away, Bran."

"I—"

"Promise me," Arenadd repeated. "I saved your life, remember? You owe me. Promise you'll take her away."

"I . . . I will," Bran stammered. "I promise."

"See you keep it," said Arenadd. "Oh, and one other thing."

"What?"

"I was never here. I had nothing to do with this. You escaped on your own. If you tell anybody, I swear I'll hunt you down. My followers can't know, and neither can my enemies. Don't even tell Kraeya. Just say you escaped by yourself. Understand?"

Bran nodded. "Lips are sealed, mate."

"Good." Arenadd pressed a sword into his hand. "Yours. Now go, and good luck."

Bran put the sword into his belt. "Thanks. Arren?"

"Yes?"

"Are yeh . . . are yeh really gonna lead those people? Are yeh gonna attack Malvern?"

Arenadd's face was shrouded in the gloom. "I have to go."

"But—"

Arenadd only shook his head and slipped away into the darkness, vanishing like a whisper in the wind.

17

The War Begins

Arenadd slept soundly that night, after he had returned to his room, unseen and unheard. The next morning he breakfasted with Skade in the hall, having given orders for the prisoner to be taken to the interrogation chamber again for further questioning. That done, he enjoyed a plate of hot bread, cheese and fruit and waited for the inevitable uproar. Sure enough, just as he was picking the last of the strayberry seeds out of his teeth, Cai came running in with the news.

Arenadd listened calmly and then sent for Saeddryn.

"I take it you've heard the news?" he said, once she had arrived.

Saeddryn looked politely confused. "Sir?"

"Don't play stupid," said Arenadd. "You know what I'm talking about."

"I'm not sure I do, sir," said Saeddryn.

"Our guest has vanished from his cell," said Arenadd.

"What? When did they find out?"

"Not too long ago," said Arenadd, privately thinking that Saeddryn's feigned shock was very impressive. If he had been a little less intelligent he could have been fooled, but he knew perfectly well that the news had been slow coming to him for a reason. "Cai and Rhodri checked his cell and found it empty."

"Do they know how he got out?" said Saeddryn.

"They found a lockpick on the floor just outside the door to the prison," said Arenadd. Beside him, Skade rolled her eyes.

"A—" Saeddryn massaged her forehead and cursed under her breath. "How did he get that in there?"

"I don't know, but I *am* moved to ask why nobody searched him well enough to find it. I'm also wondering why you didn't station any guards at the entrance after I specifically ordered you to keep watch over him."

"I did have someone there, sir," Saeddryn said stiffly. "The bastard must've escaped late at night, after they'd gone t'bed."

"Well, it's an odd thing," said Arenadd. "But I myself always thought the best time to escape was at the time when there weren't any guards about. What d'you think, Saeddryn?"

"He couldn't have known when they was leavin', sir," said Saeddryn. "It's just bad luck. Anyway, he won't get far. We'll find him."

"Unlikely. We're leaving today, remember?"

Saeddryn shifted. "I know, sir, but I don't think it's a good idea. We can't let him get away. If he gets back to Malvern an' tells 'em what he knows . . ."

"I doubt it," said Arenadd. "He can't travel that far in time. And besides, they won't listen to him even if he does get there. He won't be able to get to the Mistress without a griffin."

"The griffin's dead, then, sir? For certain?"

"Yes," Arenadd lied. "Skandar told me the whole story. He caught up with her and finished her off."

"Well then . . . I suppose if ye say so, we can let it go," said Saeddryn, though with evident reluctance.

Arenadd ignored the doubt in her voice. "Good. Tell the others to search the tower anyway; we may as well be on the safe side. But remind everyone we're going; I want everyone moving out of the city by noon."

"Yes, sir." Saeddryn left.

Once she had gone, Arenadd sat back in his chair. "Well," he said, to nobody in particular. "That's that sorted out."

"You do not seem very concerned," Skade commented.

"I'm not. I got what I wanted out of him already, and, quite honestly, we didn't have time to do anything much with him except kill him. And what would be the point? A griffiner without a griffin is worthless. I doubt he'll even bother to try and get back to Malvern."

Skade nodded. "Perhaps we will catch up with him anyway. He cannot travel far alone."

"It's possible." Arenadd stood up. "Anyway, let's get to work. Pack up anything you want, but try not to take too much. We're going to load up an oxcart with supplies down in the courtyard. Let's hope Skandar doesn't decide to eat the oxen."

"Let us hope that *I* do not do the same," said Skade.

Arenadd chuckled and left the hall.

Everything had been organised in advance, so there was little left to do except see to it that everyone carried out their orders and that there were no last-minute complications.

Supplies, including clothes, food, water and money, had been carried downstairs and were now being loaded onto the cart that would go with Nerth to Taranis Gorge. Another, smaller, cart with one ox had been similarly loaded to go to Fruitsheart with Arenadd and the others. Meanwhile, Arenadd had sought out a few of the locals who were able to read and write, and had given them the task of managing the city as well as they could. He hoped they would cope until the Eyrie found out about the conquest and, inevitably, sent griffiners to deal with Warwick.

Arenadd was well aware of what the consequences would probably be for the locals. No doubt the Eyrie would believe that he or some of his followers were still in the city, and would make every effort to find them or at least find out where they had gone. Knowing how griffiners generally behaved in these situations, they would probably resort to torture and mass executions.

But, he thought grimly, all that would be to his advantage. The worse the consequences were, the more they would enhance his reputation and the greater the impact would be on the North as a whole. And if the griffiners did indeed sink to that level, they would only help to make their vassals resent them even more deeply than before. It would win him exactly the level of support he needed.

He sighed to himself as he supervised the loading of the carts. He had come to like Warwick during his time there, and the thought of its being torn apart that way—and torn apart because of him—made a dull, miserable lump form in his stomach.

This is war, he reminded himself. *War is ugly. People die. That's the way it's always been.*

As he was busy with these thoughts, a voice behind him interrupted. "Sir?"

Arenadd turned, and saw Saeddryn. Nerth was with her, along with Cai, Rhodri and Davyn, and a man he vaguely recognised but couldn't name.

Arenadd nodded to them. "Hello. Saeddryn, what's the news? Did you find anything?"

She shook her head. "I'm sorry, sir. We did all we could, but we couldn't tell which way he went. He could be anywhere by now."

"Well, I'm sure you did your best," Arenadd said generously. "Is there anything else you have to tell me?"

Saeddryn smiled slightly. "It's just a little thing, sir. I . . . I mean we . . ." She glanced at the man whose name Arenadd didn't know. "Ye can tell him, if ye like."

The man glanced nervously at her, and then stepped forward. "Well, uh . . . sir . . . my lord . . ."

"Out with it," said Arenadd, as kindly as he could. "Come on, I'm a busy man. Do I know you, by the way? I think I've seen your face, but I don't remember your name."

"Aled, my lord," said the man. "I was one of them as ye chose t'go with Nerth, my lord."

" 'Sir' will be fine, Aled. What can I do for you?"

"I'm a smith, sir," said Aled. "We ain't allowed t'make weapons no more, sir, but my grandad taught me in secret— how t'make swords an' that, sir. That's why ye chose me."

"Oh yes, I remember. And?"

"Well, yer cousin . . . Lady Saeddryn came t'see me, sir, an' asked me t'make this for ye, sir," said Aled. "We decided t'give it to ye now, before we all left. Sir."

It was a long, thin object wrapped in cloth. Arenadd accepted it, somewhat bemused. "Is it a sword?"

"Not really a sword, sir," said Aled. "But I did make it for ye, sir; I think Saeddryn said ye know how t'use one, sir."

It was a sickle, not much different from the sort used to cut grass. But this was obviously not a farming tool. The blade was razor sharp on its inner edge, wickedly pointed and serrated near the tip. A tool, maybe—but a tool for killing. Arenadd turned it over in his hands, admiring the copper reinforcing on the handle and the stars and triple spiral symbol etched into the blade. "It's beautiful," he said.

"It's called a *llafn y lloergan*," said Saeddryn. "The blade of the moonlight. Did my mother teach ye how t'use one, sir?"

"Yes, a little," said Arenadd. He flourished the thing experimentally. It didn't handle the way a sword did, but it had a good balance, and he could tell that a well-aimed slash from it could do a lot of damage, especially aided by the curved inner edge. "So, you had this made especially for me?"

"Yes, sir," said Saeddryn. "Ye're our leader, after all, an' a leader needs a good weapon, especially now ye've lost yer sword, sir."

Arenadd didn't know what to say. "Thank you. Thank you very much. It's the finest gift I've had in a very long time." *Don't forget,* his mind added, *the last present you got was a hanging, so anything would be an improvement, wouldn't it?*

Saeddryn smiled. "I've tested it, sir. It's a fine weapon. I'm sure ye'll use it well."

Arenadd imagined using it at Malvern, in the temple, against the Bastard's sword. The curving point would be perfect at close quarters. A quick blow to the throat . . .

He smiled to himself at the image. "Yes. I'm sure I will."

"Well." Saeddryn rubbed her ear. "We're about ready t'get movin', sir. The others are gatherin' up their things an' should be out soon."

Arenadd nodded. "Good. This looks like it's all in order, so I'll head back upstairs. Skandar's expecting me."

"There's just one thing, sir," said Saeddryn.

"Yes?"

"Annir. I dunno where she is, sir," said Saeddryn, with a touch of nervousness. "I've asked around, but no-one knows where she's gone to."

Arenadd put the sickle into his belt. "My mother isn't coming with us."

Saeddryn opened her mouth to ask why, saw the look on his face and shut it again. "Yes, sir."

Arenadd took a horn off the back of the cart behind her and gave it to her. "Here; keep this close by while you're travelling."

Saeddryn took it. The horn had been carved from a long piece of bone and looked quite old. "To call for help, sir?"

"Exactly." Arenadd tapped the pitted white surface of the horn. "It was made from a griffin's leg bone. It's supposed to mimic the call of a griffin. I've tried it—it's not a perfect imitation, but it carries a long way. If you get into trouble, signal, and Skandar and I will come as fast as we can."

"Yes, sir."

"Good luck, then. I'll see you later." Arenadd went back inside.

Up in their temporary bedroom, Skade had finished packing and was dozing at the table, but woke up when Arenadd came in.

"Are we ready to go?" she asked.

Arenadd looked at the small bag sitting next to her on the floor. "Is that all you're taking?"

"What more do I need?" said Skade. "I have a spare gown, a hairbrush and the jewels you gave me—I could not think of anything else."

Arenadd paused a moment and then shrugged. "I don't think I can really argue with that. Anyway, Saeddryn's waiting for you, so if there's nothing else you want to do before you go—"

Skade stood up. "Only one thing," she said, and took him in her arms.

Arenadd smiled and gave her a quick kiss. "I knew I'd forgotten something."

"Be careful," Skade told him as she let go.

"I don't need to be careful," said Arenadd, touching the hilt of his new weapon. "I've got this. And him," he added, looking toward the archway.

Skandar emerged through it, limping slightly. "Go now," he said.

Arenadd nodded. "Yes, yes, I'm coming. Just give me a moment."

He darted over to the bed and did a quick check of the objects he'd chosen to take with him. There wasn't much: a brush and comb, a razor, a bottle of hair lotion, soap, a tiny packet of salt for cleaning his teeth, and a few other odds and ends. And nestled between the hairbrush and the salt was a tiny stone bottle, etched with a single rune. Arenadd touched it and grinned horribly to himself. He'd found it during a search of the medicine bay, though the contents didn't have much use when it came to medicine, at least as far as he knew. Anyone who drank it wouldn't need medicine. Ever again.

Skandar thumped on the floor. "Go now!" he repeated.

Arenadd snapped out of his reverie. "Just a moment." His eyes darted around the room.

He spotted what he needed, lying discarded in a corner. It was an old leather quiver, with a strap that looped around the chest. Arenadd tipped out a dead spider and some dust, and stuffed his belongings into it, plugging the opening with some cloth. He slung it on his back. "Perfect. Now, let's go."

Skandar rasped irritably but bent his forelegs to let Arenadd climb onto his back. The griffin's tail was lashing; he was full of pent-up energy, and not even his wounds could do much to slow him down.

Arenadd balanced himself on his friend's back. "It's been a while . . . all right. I'm r—"

He didn't get to finish the sentence. The instant he was in place, Skandar darted back through the archway. Skade jerked backward, out of the way, and chuckled to herself as she watched him make a clumsy, stumbling run through the nest, Arenadd clinging on desperately. Skandar passed out onto the balcony and launched himself into the air with scarcely a pause.

Skade shook her head. "The time is come, all speeches done, and now to war they fly. There is no mercy now inside, and so to battle they must ride." It was a fragment of an old griffish war poem, and she smiled grimly and left the room, ready to begin her own journey at last.

L ady Elkin, Mistress of the Eyrie, was sick.
    She woke up one morning, after several days of tiredness and aching joints, to a searing pain in her head and a weakness so profound it felt as if her arms and legs were made of lead. She lay in bed, having rolled onto her back with a mighty effort, and tried to yawn. The instant she opened her mouth, the yawn turned into a cough, which turned into a coughing fit, which she instantly regretted. Every cough felt like a blow to her chest, and when it was finally over she couldn't breathe for several moments. When she *did* manage to breathe in, her lungs burned. She groaned weakly and lifted a hand to her forehead. It felt burning hot.

Part of her wanted to get up. It was morning; she should be out of bed. A million things were crying out for her attention. So much to plan, so much to organise . . .

She made a mighty effort to sit up, but the instant her head lifted from the pillow a horrible wave of dizziness hit her in the forehead and knocked her back.

"Kraal." Her voice felt useless, barely louder than a whisper. "Kraal!"

It seemed to take forever for the griffin to come, but he did. He always seemed to know when she needed him. His great white head loomed down toward her out of the gloom, seeming almost to glow. "Elkin." His voice was deep and reassuring. "Elkin. You are sick."

She coughed again. "Need . . ."

"Elkin, I cannot do this forever," he said. "You are ill because you have pushed yourself too hard."

Elkin squinted; her eyesight was poor at the best of times, but now the griffin was fading in and out of focus as she watched. It made her feel nauseated. "Had . . . work to do," she managed. "Prepare the . . . important . . ." She slumped. "Please."

Kraal sighed, his warm breath ruffling her hair. "I will, but you must promise that you will rest more after this."

Elkin managed a nod.

Above her, the big blurry shape that was Kraal breathed a white mist toward her. She lay still and let it touch her and vanish into her, cooling her and soothing her aching limbs. After that she dozed briefly, and when she woke up she was clear-headed.

She sat up, and this time there was no dizziness or nausea. The strength had come back into her limbs, and she could breathe without pain.

She sighed. "Thank you, Kraal."

The white griffin regarded her solemnly. "You will be fine for now, but do not strain yourself. The sickness will return, and if it does you must recover from it yourself. The more I heal you, the worse the sickness will be when it strikes you down again. Sooner or later, it will return so powerfully that you will die before I can help you."

Elkin climbed out of bed. "I know. I promise I'll be more careful."

"See that you are. Now prepare yourself." Kraal turned and loped back into his nest, tail swishing.

Elkin hastily began to dress herself, her mind already abuzz with other, more urgent thoughts. First there were those

documents to read, after that she had a consultation with the
Master of Building, and then at noon there was a meeting of the
entire council at which they would choose a Master of War for
the first time in decades. And if she didn't keep a clear head, if
she made the wrong choice . . .

They couldn't fight against *Kraeai kran ae* without a Master
of War. All Elkin knew about warfare came from books. She
still had her father's sword but had never had the strength to
wield it. The Master of War had to be someone who could fight.

She felt another cough rise up in her throat and stifled it
behind her hand.

I can't get sick, she thought, almost panicky. *Not now!
There's no* time.

Fortunately the cough turned out to be an isolated one, and
she finished dressing and left her chamber. Kraal met her in the
audience chamber, and they went to begin the day's work.

The sickness might have been fended off for the time being,
but it left a lingering weakness behind. By the time Elkin had
finished her meeting with the Master of Building she was
already exhausted, and there was still half a day left to go.

She ate a small lunch, with only Kraal for company. Even
chewing felt like hard work.

"I wish Erian was here," she murmured aloud. "I miss him."

Kraal shifted. "I am glad that he is not."

Elkin looked up in her surprise. "Why?"

"Because he must reach the Island of the Sun as quickly as
he can and find what he needs to fight *Kraeai kran ae*," Kraal
rumbled. "And because you cannot afford to have him here to
distract you."

Elkin reddened. "You know I wouldn't let that happen."

He pressed his head against hers. "I am glad that you found
a mate, Elkin. Every creature needs one. But humans allow
mating to override all else and interfere even with matters of
life and death."

Elkin stared at her plate. "Yes . . . I suppose you're right."

He was, she thought as she finished eating. Humans were
notorious for letting their hearts rule their heads. Once she had
laughed at stories of ancient heroes killing themselves over the
death of their beloved and wars being fought over the posses-
sion of one woman. But now . . . She sighed. Poor Erian. He
was just an overgrown boy, really—with that freckled face and

snub nose and the awkward way he carried himself, as if he was unaware of his wide shoulders and big hands. Still content to walk around with his head in the clouds, in spite of the heavy responsibility that had been placed on him. But that was just his way, and despite herself she knew she loved him for it.

A servant opened the door at that moment, and she shook herself. No time for dreaming.

The councillors' chamber wasn't far away, and she and Kraal reached it in plenty of time for the meeting. The other members of the council were still arriving, and Elkin took her place on the dais with Kraal to wait while they filed in—the Master of Law, the Master of Taxation, the Master of Learning, the Master of Healing, the doddering old Master of Diplomacy and a handful of others picked for their intelligence and experience.

They solemnly took their places in a circle around Elkin's dais, while in the gallery above, ordinary griffiners came to watch the proceedings.

Once all were settled, Kraal screeched for silence, and Elkin could speak.

"My lords and ladies, griffins and griffiners," she said, the echo in the chamber helping to carry her voice to every ear. "We are gathered here in council to discuss the need to appoint one of our number as Master of War, to be the general we will need in this time of war and danger."

As she spoke, she watched the faces of the councillors, reading their expressions with practised ease. She could see their discomfort, mixed in many cases with doubt or suspicion. Few of them had even gone to watch Arenadd's execution, and Elkin knew perfectly well that many of them had been openly sceptical about the story, and the need to appoint a Master of War and build up an army again. Well, she had no reason to try to persuade them just yet. They trusted her enough to do as she commanded without question.

"I have spoken to the candidates," she continued, once the formalities were done, "and made a list of three who I believe would be best for the post. However, before I make my final decision I must consult the council."

"Who are your candidates, my lady?" asked the Master of Law.

Elkin took the list from her sleeve. "The first is Lady Malla, currently your assistant and in command of the city guard. I feel that her experience in the arts of command would be invaluable. What is your opinion?"

Shrae, the Master of Law's partner, spoke out. "I do not think that Malla would be a good Master of War."

"Why is this so?" Kraal rumbled.

She lowered her head toward him. "Ratch, her griffin, is too weak."

There was a stirring among the assembled griffins; calling another griffin weak was a deep insult.

Kraal showed no surprise or anger. "Why do you say this, Shrae?"

Shrae flicked her tail, dismissing the anger around her. "I have seen him. He has hidden it, but he is ill. I believe it is a problem in his lungs. Even if he recovers, he will not be able to use his magic again."

"Can any other griffin confirm this?" said Kraal.

"My human can," said Shrae.

Lady Lerran nodded. "Malla is my niece. I visited her recently, and her partner is indeed sick."

Elkin frowned. She had liked the young Master of Guards. If her griffin was as ill as that—and Lerran would be unlikely to tell a lie that would stop her own relative from being given such an important post—then Malla would probably lose even her current position. A weak griffin was almost as bad as a dead one.

"Then we'll move on to the next candidate," she interrupted.

"Yes, my lady."

Elkin consulted the piece of paper. "The next on the list is Lord Rhyl. He's young but an accomplished swordsman, and Kael, his griffin, is very powerful in magic. Both of them have studied warfare and are keen to be appointed."

There was a murmuring among the humans.

"What magic does Kael have?" a griffin asked.

"Her power is ice," said Kraal. "I have spoken with her and witnessed it myself."

"And how well does she control it?"

"She is well practised," Kraal said.

Nobody tried to argue with that.

"I can vouch for Lord Rhyl," said the Master of Learning. "I myself helped to provide him with books on battle strategy. He has been interested in the subject since he was a boy; he once told me his greatest dream was to lead an army into battle."

Elkin smiled slightly. "Maybe we can make that dream come true. I'll speak to him again, and tomorrow he will come before the council."

"And who is the final candidate?" asked Lady Lerran.

Elkin consulted her notes again. "The final candidate is Lord Dallin . . ."

As she read out the details for the candidate, a sudden flurry of movement from the councillors' seats made her look up. One of the griffins had made a quick half-turn, nearly upsetting the bench behind her, and an instant later Elkin saw why.

Lord Dahl, Master of Taxation, had collapsed, falling forward off his seat and onto the floor, where he was lying crumpled.

The Master of Healing was quick to react. She ran to her friend and turned him onto his side, shouting as the other councillors darted toward her, "Keep back! Give him room!"

Elkin stepped toward the edge of the dais while the healer checked Lord Dahl's pulse and breathing. No-one else dared do anything.

Finally, the Master of Healing looked up. "He's dead," she said quietly.

In that instant, Dahl's griffin lifted her head to the ceiling and screamed. Up in the gallery, the spectators began to shout and screech.

Elkin stepped off the dais. "Dead?" she exclaimed. "How?"

"I don't know, my lady."

There were shouts from behind, and Elkin turned sharply, in time to see the Master of Learning falter and then fall.

Lady Lerran stepped toward him. "He's—" She stopped, her face suddenly pale. She gasped and groaned, turning toward Shrae for support before she, too, collapsed.

The Master of Healing ran to her and her colleague, but an instant later the verdict came back. "Dead! Both dead!"

Elkin felt herself go hot, and then cold. She stumbled back onto the dais, instinctively pressing herself against Kraal. "What's happening?"

Kraal drew back, half-covering her with his wing. "I do not know."

Screams came from the humans in the gallery, and everything seemed to slow. Elkin stood, paralysed, unable to do anything but watch as three more councillors toppled. Two more quickly followed, one as he was running for the door in a panic. In the space of less than thirty heartbeats, more than half of her council died before her eyes, without a sound or a warning.

Only the Master of Healing, still untouched, managed to keep her head. She checked the bodies, one by one. "Poison," she said. "It's got to be poison. There's not a mark on any of them."

The surviving councillors had pulled away, hiding behind their griffins, keeping well back from the mourning griffins, some of whom began to attack each other in their fury and despair.

Kraal, seeing them, pushed Elkin aside and screeched. *"Enough!"*

When they paid no attention to him, he came down from the platform and ran at them, scattering them like a flock of chickens. Most fled; one or two actually tried to attack him, but all of them quickly gave up and flew away, through the portals in the roof.

In the silence that followed, Elkin stepped toward the cowering Master of Healing. "I don't understand," she said, trying to keep her voice calm. "How could it be poison?"

"It must be, my lady," came the reply. "There's no other explanation I can think of."

"Is there a poison that works that quickly?"

The Master of Healing sat silent for a few moments, rubbing nervously at her nose while she thought.

Her griffin interrupted. "Viper's Tears."

The healer's face lit up. "Yes! Yes, it has to be that."

The name was unfamiliar to Elkin. "Viper's Tears?"

"The fastest poison we know of, my lady," said the healer. "It must be taken through the mouth. The victim dies moments after it takes effect, just the way we saw—no noise, no struggle. There's almost nothing that kills as quietly as it does."

Elkin blanched. "But who could have done this? And how?"

"I don't know."

Kraal returned to the dais, stiff legged and bristling, seeming twice as big as before in his rage. "Come," he said harshly. "Elkin, come, now."

She went to him. "Kraal, something terrible has happened. I have to—"

"You are in danger!" he said. "Elkin, do you not see what this means? Half of your council has been poisoned. The Eyrie has been infiltrated, and you will be a target. We must not stay here."

Elkin nodded. "Yes, you're right as always. Karmain, I want you to alert the Eyrie. Tell Lady Malla and the guards. Have every tower searched high and low, question everybody who's come into contact with the food the councillors ate, and if there's a way of testing for Viper's Tears in food, use it."

The healer nodded. "Understood."

"Good. I am going back to my chamber. Send every piece of information you find to me as soon as you find it."

"Yes, my lady."

Elkin climbed onto Kraal's back as quickly as she could, and held on as he flew up and out of the chamber. He went straight back to their home, but refused to let Elkin enter until he had gone in and smelt every inch of it, searching for any sign of an intruder. Elkin waited outside, on the balcony, shivering slightly in the wind, until he returned.

"It is safe. Come."

They went to her room and from there into the audience chamber. Elkin, moving stiffly, went to the platform where she and her partner habitually sat. She slumped down on it, staring blankly into space.

Kraal did not sit. He paced back and forth, his claws clicking on the marble floor, his tail lashing violently and his wings twitching.

Elkin finally found her voice. "How?"

Kraal stopped. "I do not know," he said softly.

"But . . . how?" she repeated, not really hearing him. In her head, she saw the councillors fall, again and again, caught up in an endless loop. Her control—the agents of her power—dying in front of her while she looked on, utterly helpless. "How? Who could have done this? How did they get at them? Was it one of the servants? Was someone working for *him*? How could it have happened so quickly—he only escaped a few weeks ago, and he couldn't have even found his friends yet, and . . ."

Kraal resumed his pacing, his big muscles sliding and flexing under his skin, full of nearly tangible power, like a great coiled spring. "This is evil," he said. "This is magic. *Kraeai kran ae* has done this; this smells of him."

"But if he came back into the Eyrie, then someone must have seen him," said Elkin. "I don't understand. His face is too familiar. Someone would have recognised him, surely."

"I do not know the powers of *Kraeai kran ae*," said Kraal. "But the shadows are his friends."

Elkin began to feel afraid—more than she had done in a very long time. "Oh gods. This is too much. It's too soon. We're not *ready!*" She covered her face with her hands. "Half the council is dead—all my best advisors and officials. And they died in *public*. Everyone saw it happen; they saw us stand there and watch it happen. They saw us *fail*."

"Oh, but it gets worse."

Elkin looked up sharply. "What?"

Kraal stood. "Who is that?" he demanded. "Who spoke? Show yourself!"

They heard a laugh. It came from nowhere, from out of the air. "I see you," the voice whispered. "Do you see me?"

The giant griffin darted here and there, searching. Elkin, not daring to rise from her seat, turned this way and that, watching for the slightest sign of movement, but there was nothing. Nothing. Just an empty room.

"Where are you?" she called.

"I am the shadow that comes in the night," the voice replied, from behind Kraal. He swung around sharply, but found himself biting at the empty air.

"I am the fear that lurks in your heart," it said, this time right beside Elkin's ear. She cried out and lurched upward and away from it, while Kraal ran to protect her, but there was nothing there.

"I am the man without a heart," the voice called, this time from over by the door.

"Move this way," Kraal rasped to Elkin. "Stay back, close to the wall. Do not move."

There was another laugh, cold and sadistic. "I am the avatar of the Night God. I am the Dark Lord. I am the Master of Death."

Kraal herded his human into a corner by a drape and stood in front of her, guarding her.

"I killed your council," the voice taunted. "You couldn't

stop me, could you? And you can't stop me now. How can you stop . . . what you can't see?"

Kraal snarled and jerked toward the sound. "Show yourself! Come forth and fight! Coward!"

There was silence. The giant griffin began to tear at the drapes and the tapestries on the wall nearby, caught up in a frenzy. "Show yourself!" he bellowed.

In her corner, Elkin took a step toward him. "Kraal, please—"

He turned. "Elkin, I said—"

It all happened in less than a heartbeat. As Kraal moved toward her, angry and afraid, a pair of hands reached out of the shadow behind Elkin. Pale hands, clad in a pair of fingerless gloves. The fingers of one hand were long and elegant, and on the other they were twisted and maimed. Kraal opened his beak to shout a warning, but he was too late, too late. The hands seized Elkin by the shoulders and dragged her away, pulling her into the shadow.

Kraal charged, screeching, but there was nothing he could do. He tore through the drape and struck the wall on the other side. There was nothing there. Elkin had gone.

18

Evil Tactics

The Eyrie Mistress proved to be much lighter than Arenadd had expected, even in the shadows. He hastily stuffed a gag in her mouth and slung her over his shoulder before making his escape. He couldn't afford to stay in the shadows for too long; he was already risking taking too much of Skandar's magic as it was. Once he was well away from the audience chamber and the maddened griffin in it, he slid back into the world of the living, hiding in a storeroom. There he tied the gag more securely in place and put a bag over his prisoner's head before tying her hands behind her back. She put up a struggle, but only a weak one, and once he had rested and made sure she was restrained he dived back into the shadows with her and ran on, unseen and unheard.

It was more difficult than he had expected, even invisible as he was. He had long since plotted his escape route, but there were people everywhere, and he cursed himself for not having waited until nightfall. But he had spent too much time hiding in the Eyrie already, and the more he used his powers to stay hidden, the more he risked hurting Skandar. If the griffin was too weak to fly once they were reunited, his plan would end in disaster for both of them.

Feeling strangely calm even in the face of that knowledge, he dodged his way through a knot of shadowy people, whose voices he could hear as he passed. They were high-pitched and frightened, and he caught the words "all dead!" He grinned wolfishly to himself. Even if he failed now and was caught, he would have plenty of time to escape while they found a new Master of Law to try him. The last one had come to regret sentencing him to death.

He found the window whose latch he had broken the previous night, checked to make sure nobody was watching, and slipped out through it and away into the city.

Once he was well away from the Eyrie, he left the shadows and rested in an alley, laying Elkin down beside him. She was making a muffled whimpering sound, and he felt a brief pang of sympathy for her. She couldn't have any idea of what was happening to her. Still, she was safe enough for now. At the moment he should be more worried about himself.

Having caught his breath, he slung her over his other shoulder and left, this time darting from shadow to shadow to save magic. It worked fairly well, especially aided by the power of silent movement the Night God had given him. Even though his new boots were heavy things, they made no sound at all on the cobblestones. He walked like a cat.

The journey out of the city was a perilous one, as he'd expected, but easier than the one through the Eyrie. He moved from cover to cover, from alley to alley, avoiding people. However, he was unable to avoid every living creature he came across, and he became painfully aware of the effect his presence was having on them. Everywhere he went, horses reared and screamed, dogs howled and cats streaked away as fast as they could go. Even the pigeons and crows that lived on the city's rooftops flurried up into the sky as if they had seen a kestrel coming for them. *They know what I really am,* Arenadd thought grimly. *It's getting stronger. Once it was only intelligent animals. Soon . . .*

There was no time for introspection, however. He reached the slums on the edge of the city, and there he finally dared to stop. Behind an old warehouse he found a particularly squalid corner that even beggars apparently preferred to avoid, and went to ground there.

And there, he waited. He stayed for a long time, hiding under a heap of old cabbage leaves and other assorted garbage, ignoring the stench and waiting, with Elkin beside him. He dozed, woke, checked the sky and returned to his bolthole. Elkin, lying

helplessly beside him, struggled from time to time or tried to
speak through her gag. He ignored her other than to check her
bonds and make sure the bag wasn't suffocating her.

Time dragged by, while the sun ever so slowly sank in the
sky. Eventually Arenadd's nervousness turned to stultifying
boredom. He ate some food he'd stored in his pocket and went
over his plan in his head again to occupy himself. Elkin, meanwhile, tried to wriggle away from him, and he dragged her back
and held her down with a hand to her back. "Stay," he told her
quietly. "There's nowhere for you to go."

Naturally, she didn't reply. However, as the afternoon continued its slow advance toward evening, he began to have some
fellow feeling toward her. He might be unhappy with his situation, but it had to be far worse for her.

"Stay calm," he advised. "You're not going to be hurt. I'm
going to take you to a safe place."

Elkin wriggled again and made that muffled whimpering
sound that was probably a sob or a scream.

"Listen, my lady," Arenadd told her. "If I was going to kill
you, I'd have done it already, like I did to your council. I was
there when you were eating lunch, you know. I could have
poisoned your food the same way I poisoned theirs. I've been
watching you for a while, actually. I had a hundred opportuni-
ties to kill you. You're safe with me. If we get caught, *I'm* the
one who's in trouble, not you. So please, just relax and trust *me*."

He doubted that she had even heard half of what he'd said,
but he did notice that she seemed a little calmer afterward. Perhaps she had heard and believed him, or perhaps she was just
exhausted. He could understand it if she was.

The sound of griffins screeching echoed somewhere high
above him, and he tensed. They had been screeching for a long
time, calling to each other as they searched the city.

Too soon to move yet.

As he lay there, trying not to move more than he had to and
listening to the threatening sounds of hunting griffins, he felt a
strange numbness come over him. Images flashed through his
brain, and sounds with them, too. Pounding feet, the buildings
of a darkened city flashing past. He saw faces turn to stare at
him and ducked into a side street to avoid them. His neck hurt,
something was cutting it . . . he could feel cold blood on his skin.
But he was carrying something. No hand free to touch it. His

fingers were long and thin, and perfect in the moonlight. Unhurt. But overhead the griffins came screeching, and he ran, his boots thudding on the ground and his heart thudding in his chest.

He felt a sharp pain tear into his cheek and gasped involuntarily, reaching up to touch the scar. The motion woke him up, and the visions disappeared, leaving him feeling drained.

None of it had felt familiar. Had it happened to him? Was that one of the memories he had lost? He didn't know. *Maybe Skade knows. Maybe I told her before I forgot.*

He shook himself. It didn't matter now, if it mattered at all. "If it was a memory, it was Arren's, not mine," he muttered to himself. "Arren can dream if he wants to. Meanwhile *Arenadd* has a city to escape from."

He peered out at the sky again. The sun was sinking lower toward the horizon now. He touched the hilt of the sickle to reassure himself. The moment dusk set in, he could go.

The sun inched lower, and he watched it with an increasing sense of irritation bordering on anger. *Go away, Gryphus, and take your eye with you.*

He wondered, briefly, if the sun would stop rising once he had destroyed all of the Day God's temples.

No. That wouldn't do it.

Deep down, he was glad about that. The idea of a night that never ended bothered even him. The world needed sunlight.

At long last, the sun touched the horizon and began to dip below it. The griffin calls started to die away, and he knew they were returning to the Eyrie; no griffin liked to fly at night. Other than Skandar, of course.

As the sky darkened and the stars came out, he felt new strength come into him. He stood up, shaking away the garbage that had covered him, and stretched his arms and legs to limber them up before turning to pick up Elkin. She was limp and still—breathing, but apparently unconscious. To his disgust, he realised that there was a damp patch on her gown. Still, needs must. He lifted her onto his shoulder again and sprinted away into the gathering night.

M ost of the abduction from Malvern passed in a blur for Elkin—albeit a blur of sheer terror. She had always had weak hearing, and the bag over her head blotted out most sound. But she was aware of a presence near her—breathing but without warmth. Her captor carried her a long way; she could feel him running and dodging, and after that he dragged her through some opening, probably a window. She could feel his feet pounding on the ground and his thin arm wrapped around her waist, holding her in place over one bony shoulder, and yet . . . and yet there was something wrong about him and his touch, something she couldn't understand. Something not right. Later on, when they stopped and he put her down and lay beside her for a long time, she could feel his skin touching hers, and the feeling of wrongness increased.

It was a long time before she finally realised what it was.

He was breathing and moving, and once she heard his muffled voice speaking to her, but even though she was close enough, she couldn't feel his pulse. His skin was cool—not icy cold, but colder than it should have been—and there was no heartbeat moving beneath.

At first she tried to convince herself it was her imagination, but the longer he stayed close to her, the more she began to realise the truth. This was something she had never experienced or imagined in her life, something that put ice into her veins. A man without a heartbeat. Dead, but still walking.

If she screamed then, the gag killed it.

After that—she never knew how long after—she felt herself being lifted onto his shoulder again and carried away. Another uncomfortable journey followed, until she found herself being slung over the shoulders of a griffin—one who felt nearly as big as Kraal.

As the griffin took off, the Eyrie Mistress felt the first wave of a terrible, crushing despair go through her. It was too late. She had been taken out of the city and was being flown away to who-knew-where, and the gods alone knew what would happen then. How would Kraal find her now?

Moments after they had taken off, she felt a sudden burst of coldness all over her body—just as she had done before, when her captor had dragged her into the darkness. Now, though she couldn't see anything, she had a strange sense of *motion*—rushing and icy cold, as if through a torrent of water—carrying them forward.

The feeling stopped abruptly, and the griffin touched down with a thud, nearly throwing her onto the ground. But her captor held her in place, and she felt him climb down and then lift her off. After that there was a period of confused motion and jostling, until she finally heard the faint thud of a door closing and felt herself being set down on a solid floor. Her captor kindly lifted her into a sitting position, leaning against a wall, and then he removed the bag.

Light bit into her eyes, and she blinked, cringing away from it, though a moment later she realised it was only candlelight, and not very bright at that. As her vision readjusted, she looked up and screamed again, through the gag.

The face leaning over her was that of a wolf—reddish brown, with big, staring eyes that shone in the candlelight.

Elkin's heart thudded painfully, even after she realised it was only a mask—wooden, inlaid with copper fangs. As she calmed down, the scholar in her thought, *I've seen something like that before. In a book. It's ceremonial . . . the chief of the Wolf Tribe wears one.*

The man wearing the mask had crouched to look down at her, and now he straightened up, revealing himself to be very tall and clad in a black robe. "Hello, my lady," he said, his voice slightly muffled but courteous enough. "I hope the journey didn't hurt you at all. I did my best to be careful with you."

Elkin peered at him. He spoke Cymrian, his accent clipped and precise and decidedly Southern, though obviously not local.

The man tapped his mask. "I'm sorry for this, but we all agreed it would be best not to let you see our faces. The less you know, the better it is for us. I'm sure you'll understand. Now I'm going to take the gag off, but I'll tell you in advance not to bother screaming or calling out for help, because nobody who hears you is going to help. Nod if you understand me."

Elkin nodded resignedly.

The wolf-man knelt and untied the gag. "There. I'm sure that's much more comfortable for you," he said. "I'll untie your hands a little later, so you can relieve yourself and so forth. Would you like something to drink?"

Elkin's voice sounded faint and hoarse even to her. "Yes, please."

He brought her some water and put it to her mouth so she could drink it. It was cold and sweet and made her feel a little better.

"I'll give you some food later," he promised. "Now, how do you feel? Is there anything you need?"

"I am . . . not hurt," she managed. "But please . . . where am I? Who are you?"

He chuckled. "My lady, if I was going to tell you who I am, I wouldn't be wearing this mask."

"I know who you are," Elkin said more forcefully. "A Northerner with a Southern accent, who wears a black robe. You are Arenadd Taranisäii. The one they call the Shadow that Walks."

He was silent for a moment, and then he laughed again. "Very perceptive, I'm sure. Personally I've always thought 'the Dark Lord' sounded better. More dignified. A lord of darkmen couldn't ask for a better title."

"You're not a lord," Elkin said coldly. "You're nothing, Arenadd. Nothing but a cursed monster with blood on his hands. You don't even have a heartbeat. You don't know love or kindness; you're a twisted abomination, and one day you will be destroyed because of it."

He made a sudden motion, as if to hit her, but held himself back. "I'd watch that mouth if I were you," he said, with a dangerous edge to his voice. "I don't have to be this gentle."

"What are you planning to do with me?" she demanded, ignoring him.

He paused and then began to pace back and forth, his head bowed. The mask and the pacing made him look like a prowling wolf, following a scent. "Seven hundred oblong," he said abruptly. "Not many men know exactly how much they're worth, but I do. I know it to the last copper. Seven hundred oblong. That's how much they sold me for. A bag of money and a set of chains—that told me what I was. Property, bought and sold. Do you know what that's like, my lady? Can you imagine?"

"I'm sorry if bad things have happened to you," she said stiffly. "But—"

"Well," he interrupted, stopping in his tracks, "it doesn't matter if you can imagine what that would be like, because soon enough you're going to find out, my lady. Tell me, if a common blackrobe is worth seven hundred oblong, how much is an Eyrie Mistress worth? Eight hundred? Nine hundred? A thousand, maybe? They say you're clever for your age—what would your guess be, my lady?"

She stared blankly at him. "You're going to sell me as a slave?"

He rubbed his hands together; the action provoked a horrible cracking noise. "Come now, my lady. Surely you can understand what I'm getting at. The Eyrie has lost its Mistress. And most of its council as well. Invisibility and a bottle of Viper's Tears are the perfect tools for an assassination, or several. With them gone, and you, there'll be nobody left who can plan or take any important decisions. After all, you won't be there to appoint replacements for the officials I killed. Your partner will be desperate to get you back, along with everyone else in the Eyrie. Tell me, my lady, how much do you think they would be willing to pay for that privilege?"

. Elkin felt hot, sick relief fill her stomach. "You're holding me for *ransom*?"

"If you want to be direct about it."

She couldn't believe it. "Money! Is that all you want? You'll set me free for a bag of oblong?"

"No." He put his hands behind his back. "I'll set you free for several bags of oblong. Provided they're big bags."

Elkin's mind raced. "I don't understand," she said. "Why not kill me?"

He wagged a playful finger at her. "Don't be silly. A dead body isn't worth anything, is it?"

"Yes it is," she said. "If I was dead, Malvern would be leaderless and you would find it much easier to storm the city."

"True enough," he conceded. "But you seem to be labouring under the assumption that that's what I'm going to do. May I ask where you got it from?"

"We know about you, *Kraeai kran ae*," she said. "We all do. And we know how much you want power and how far you'll go to get it." She was inventing now, trying to scare him.

"Power!" he chuckled. "Well, power would be nice, I suppose. But I'm afraid you've misjudged me, my lady." He sighed. "You believe I'm evil, and therefore all my motivations are simple." Suddenly he was much closer. "Believe me, my lady," he said softly, "if there's one thing I know, it's that life is not simple. And neither am I. Now." He turned away. "I'm tired, and I'm going to leave you. Later on someone will bring food. If you do anything other than what you're told, there will be consequences."

He left the room, and Elkin was alone.

She tried to think, pushing away her fear to clear her mind. She had always prided herself on her ability to think clearly and to analyse any situation, and she had to do that now more urgently than ever before.

Nothing he had said made sense. He wanted to destroy Malvern and take the North for himself, that was certain—so why hold her to ransom? Why not just kill her? What did he need money for? For weapons, perhaps, but there has to be less dangerous ways of acquiring them than kidnapping an Eyrie Mistress.

And in any case, why had he told her about it? Wouldn't it be in his best interests if she *didn't* know what he was doing?

It had to be a lie, she decided.

Kraal's voice came to her, out of her memory. Kraeai kran ae *has a viper's tongue; he is deceptive. Nothing he says or does can be trusted.*

Quite unexpectedly, she found herself fighting back a sob. Kraal, her griffin, her best friend, who had saved her life so many times. What would he do without her? Did he even know she was alive?

And she thought of Erian, too. What would he do if he knew what had happened to her? Come rushing back pell-mell to look for her, no doubt.

Deep down, Elkin was glad he didn't know. She wanted him there so badly it hurt, but she forced herself to see that what he was doing was more important than her. But still . . .

Hurry back, Erian, she thought. *Please, hurry.*

Arenadd locked the door behind him and climbed up a flight of stairs and through the trapdoor at the top before he took off his mask and shook his hair out.

"Arenadd!" Skade darted over and flung her arms around him.

Arenadd returned the embrace. "Skade. You made it."

She held him tightly, her hands in his hair. "Thank the sea and the sky. I worried so much for you. If they had caught you . . ."

He pulled away from her, grinning. "They never even saw me. The plan was a complete success."

She grew solemn. "And now begins the most dangerous part."

Arenadd kissed her. She kissed him back, eagerly.

"So." Saeddryn rose from her seat in a corner.

Arenadd reluctantly let go of Skade. "Saeddryn. How are you?"

Saeddryn looked at him and Skade, hiding the resentment she was undoubtedly still feeling. "Well. The journey went well. I take it yer own was a success?"

"A complete success," said Arenadd. His companions had been sleeping when he'd arrived in the small hours of the morning, and he hadn't seen them yet.

A smile began to show on Saeddryn's face. "So ye did all ye set out to?"

Arenadd grinned wolfishly. "All that and more, cousin. And you?"

She nodded. "We got here in one piece. Davyn's been an' bought some supplies. How's Skandar?"

"Sleeping," said Arenadd. "He pushed himself very hard to get here and used a lot of magic. I'll go and take him some food in a moment."

"It'll be hard t'keep him hidden," Saeddryn observed.

"I know, but I can't force him to leave me," said Arenadd. "Wouldn't want to, either."

"And he knows the stakes," Skade cut in. "He will not betray us."

Arenadd nodded. "And speaking of steaks . . ."

"Sit down, sir," said Saeddryn. "I'll get ye some food."

Arenadd sat. "Thanks, Saeddryn."

There was no steak, but Saeddryn had cooked some stew. She heated it up and gave him a bowlful with some bread. Arenadd ate gratefully, suddenly aware of how hungry he was. "I want to talk to everyone once I've seen Skandar," he said between mouthfuls. "So make sure they're all here."

"Yes, sir," said Saeddryn. "What about the prisoner?"

"She's fine for now," said Arenadd. "I've left water for her. Once I've talked to the others we can do something more for her. Can't risk her getting sick or hurt."

"Yes, sir."

He washed the stew down with a cup of water and slipped out the back door and into the little stable that joined onto the house. His friends had done well: they'd purchased a good-sized town house with enough room for them all, even Skandar. And, best of all, it was flanked by the canal on one side and a warehouse on the other. No neighbours and plenty of ways to come and go without attracting attention.

Skandar had gathered the straw provided for him into a heap in the middle of the floor and curled up on top of it. He looked as if he was sleeping, but he lifted his head when he heard the door open.

"Human," he rasped.

Arenadd bowed to him. "How are you feeling?"

Skandar yawned widely by way of an answer, showing the grey, ribbed inside of his beak and the fleshy pinkness beyond.

Arenadd smiled. "It's only to be expected. You've finally started using magic."

"Use magic," Skandar repeated proudly. "Strong magic."

Arenadd nodded. "I *knew* you could do it. If I can use it, so can you."

"*My* magic," Skandar told him sharply.

Arenadd bowed again. "Yes. You're far better at using it than I am, and that only makes sense. You were born to it; I wasn't. After all, I'm only a human."

"Am griffin," said Skandar. "Hyrenna say we use magic."

"And now you believe her, don't you?" said Arenadd.

"Yes, believe." Skandar yawned again. "Hungry."

"I brought you this," said Arenadd.

It was a dead dog. Skandar sniffed at it suspiciously.

"Sorry it's not much," said Arenadd. "Saeddryn says she caught it in the street. Later on I'll send someone to buy you a nice fat horse."

Skandar hissed pleasurably to himself and bit into the dog.

Arenadd sat down by him, hugging his knees. "You and I did good work, Skandar. Everything is going to plan."

Skandar glanced up. "You kill?"

Arenadd nodded grimly. "I timed it all perfectly. The Master of Taxation, the Master of Law . . . all the most important officials. Half the council dropped dead, right in the middle of a meeting. I found out they were going to appoint a Master of War, so I poisoned most of the candidates as well. And before that I snuck into the prison and let the prisoners out. And, of course, we have the Mistress."

Skandar chirped. "Do good work!"

"Yes!" Arenadd had to force himself not to whoop at the top of his lungs. "You see, Skandar? With the council dead and the Mistress gone, they're as good as crippled! Once we've got our ransom and sent people south to buy those slaves, we can start doing some real damage. By the time they get here, we'll be ready to attack Malvern itself. And then you and I can fly into battle together, and those sun-worshipping scum will know what Northerners and wild griffins can really do."

Skandar's eyes gleamed. "And then I find Kraal," he said. "And I kill." And to emphasise those words, he ripped the dog's carcass clean in half with one blow.

19

The Sea and the Sky

When Erian Rannagonson saw the sea for the first time in his life, he could scarcely believe his eyes.

"It's so *big*," he breathed.

Beside him, Senneck ruffled her wings. "Yes." For once the brown griffin's usual cool confidence seemed to have failed her.

The two of them stood on the cliff top where Senneck had landed, looking out over a seemingly endless expanse of blue. It darkened toward the horizon, broken up by shifting patterns of white foam, until it joined with the sky and became a faint grey line.

"By the sea and the sky," Erian mumbled. Suddenly, the griffish exclamation seemed to make so much more sense. Even if griffins had no gods, something this awe-inspiring was as good as one.

He realised that Senneck was looking at him.

"All my life, I have wondered what the sea is truly like," she said softly. "Now I have seen it, and I am . . . humbled."

Erian squinted as he looked out to sea. The months of travelling had taken their toll on him. But for all that, there was a new strength and certainty in how he carried himself.

Nevertheless, his voice had all its old boyish uncertainty when he said, "This can't possibly be right. We must have come to the wrong place!"

Senneck flicked her tail. "We followed the path of the rising sun. This is where Kraal's advice brought us. There can be no mistake."

"But it's so huge!" said Erian. "How can you fly over it? There's nowhere to land! If you get tired, we'll drown!"

"It will be a challenge," Senneck admitted. But she acted as if she hadn't noticed Erian's agitation. She, too, had changed during the journey: she had become stronger, harder. Away from her old, easy life, she had taken on something of the ragged ferocity of a wild griffin. Her fur and feathers had grown thicker to protect her from the cold, and she looked to have grown physically larger as well, which was odd, considering the poor and sporadic food she had been living on.

"You really think you can fly over that?" Erian persisted.

"I believe I can try," Senneck said primly. "And I have come too far to give in without a fight."

Erian squared his shoulders. "Yes. You're right. But how are we going to do it?"

"We will rest here tonight," said Senneck. "In the morning, at sunrise, we shall set out. I shall fly until noon, and if by then I do not see the Island of the Sun I shall fly back and we will consider another plan."

"It sounds like a good plan to me."

They left the cliff for the beach below it, where it was a little more sheltered, and Senneck curled up on the sand while Erian built a fire. Once it was burning, he sat down and warmed his hands. He'd wrapped up some meat and stowed it in his tunic, and now he brought it out and staked some of it over the fire to cook. He gave the rest to Senneck, who gulped it down in one go.

"It's not much," said Erian.

"It will do for you," said Senneck.

"I mean for *you*," said Erian. "I don't know if there's any game around here."

"It does not matter," said Senneck. "I shall not hunt tonight."

"Why?" said Erian. "Aren't you hungry?"

"I am, but I shall not eat. Tomorrow I shall fly on an empty stomach. It will make me lighter in the air."

"Oh," said Erian. "That's clever. I suppose I should leave a few things behind, too, then."

"Yes," said Senneck.

"I haven't got much . . . I could take my boots off and my belt . . . and my . . ." He clutched instinctively at the hilt of his sword.

Senneck looked at the weapon and then at him. "Not your sword," she said. "I think it would be better to keep it with you. There is no telling what we may encounter on the island. And it would be a pity to lose it, after all we went through to retrieve it."

Erian wanted to hug her. "Thank you, Senneck."

She laid her head on her talons. "Eat and sleep now, little human. Tomorrow, we fly."

Erian let her rest and chewed on some dried berries from his pocket while he waited for the meat to cook. Once it was done and he'd eaten it, he sat and polished his sword, and thought.

It was odd, really. Gryphus had chosen him, Erian, but had merely commanded him to do the very thing he most wanted to do. Kill the murderer, save Malvern and be a hero. Gryphus had come to him and was helping him to find the way. Giving him what he wanted.

Erian felt a warm little glow in his chest, as he always did when he thought of that. Him, chosen by Gryphus! Not some arrogant noble, not some highborn lord, but him. From farm boy to warrior, to hero, to legend. It was so magnificent it made him want to cry.

"I'll do it," he promised the setting sun. "I'll do it, Gryphus. I won't lose faith in you or Senneck."

"I am sure the Day Eye is glad to hear it," Senneck mumbled and covered her head with her wing.

Erian slept soundly that night, curled up on the warm sand by the fire. His sleep had become much more restful over the last few weeks, most likely because he had been going to bed so exhausted every night. The dark dreams had more or less ceased, though from time to time he would wake up in the middle of the night, cold and sweating.

But not this night. This night his dreams were peaceful and happy.

He dreamt that he was back at Malvern, up on the top of the Council's Tower. There was a party taking place around him; he could see the long tables laden with delicious food and cups of sweet wine. Music was playing, and there were other people there, dancing, but they were an irrelevant detail—faceless and silent. All except for one of them.

She came out of the crowd to meet him, her sweet face smiling, green eyes alight with happiness. *Erian. Come, dance with me.* She held out a delicate hand.

Erian took it and kissed it. *What dance?*

The sacred dance, my sweet warrior, my Erian.

And they danced. He didn't know the steps, but that didn't matter. This was a special dance, and it didn't feel as if he was truly dancing at all, at least not in the usual way. This was a magical gliding, their bodies moving together in perfect harmony, as if they were flying without their feet leaving the ground. And all that mattered was Elkin and her soft flower scent and her eyes looking into his.

Erian groaned pleasurably in his sleep and curled in on himself, his fingers twisting themselves into the coarse cloth of his trousers and clutching at it.

In the dream, Elkin laughed. *Not now. There are other things to do. See, here?*

She led him toward the crowd, but the people seemed to fade away, and there were two griffins. Senneck, smoother and sleeker in his dream, her feathers shining with a golden sheen. Her eyes were like sapphires. Beside her was Kraal.

Erian knelt in front of the white griffin. *Mighty Kraal.*

Kraal looked down on him, his golden eyes peaceful. But there seemed to be something odd about him, as Erian looked up. The griffin's outline seemed to flicker, as if there was something inside him that had a different shape or size—the bones of some other creature in some other time.

I am old, Kraal said, his voice echoing. *I am so old, but I have seen much. Cross the skies like the Day Eye, always open, never closing or waning. Fight as your father would.*

I will, said Erian. *Wait for me.*

Look for the rising of the sun, said Kraal. *Do not fail us.*

I won't.

Then rest; rest and be ready.

After that the dream ended, or if it continued Erian didn't remember any more. He turned over onto his back, his hand brushing against Senneck's flank, and kept his face turned skyward until morning came and the sun brought light back to the world.

* * *

Senneck crouched low on the cliff top, her tail lashing. "Are you ready?"

Erian shifted in his seat. "I think so."

"Then let us begin," said Senneck.

Erian braced himself as the brown griffin launched herself into space. For a moment he could see the boiling foam below them, rushing upward, but Senneck quickly steadied herself. She climbed to soaring height and flew away, straight toward the rising sun at a steady pace.

For his part, Erian had to do more than stay put on her back. Riding a griffin was far more complex than most people thought; he had to stay alert and sensitive to her motion in the sky, leaning forward when she put her head down, or to the side when she leant on one wing. The rest of the time, he had to stay as still and steady as possible, lest he upset her balance. Perhaps it wasn't as physically demanding as walking or swimming, but it was mentally exhausting—as he had learnt over and over again on their journey. Only a few days ago he had let his concentration lapse and had leant to the wrong side, nearly overbalancing Senneck in the sky. He still had a deep gash in his arm that had yet to finish healing from where she had bitten him in return for that particular mistake. Most griffiners had plenty of similar scars, so he had all but forgotten it by now. Even so, it was a lesson.

Time dragged by. Erian saw the sea pass below them, frighteningly featureless and changing every second. It was impossible to tell how far they had gone. The sea might be awe-inspiring, but now he was beginning to see why it was also dangerous. There were no landmarks, nothing to remember. Nowhere to land. At one point he took the risk of looking back over his shoulder, and his stomach lurched when he saw how far away the cliff was now. It had faded to a black shape on the horizon; it would be all but invisible well before noon came. The thought made him feel panicky: what if Senneck couldn't find her way back?

There was no way of sharing that fear with her while they were flying. He breathed deeply, forcing himself to calm down. *Trust Senneck,* he reminded himself.

But as they flew on and the sun climbed slowly higher in the sky, he had to repeat it to himself again and again. He kept his eyes on the horizon, but he couldn't see any sign of an island. There was nothing but that same grey line he had been watching ever since they had first started out.

The sun moved closer to its zenith. Noon was approaching. Erian's backside ached unbearably. His fingers were numb from gripping Senneck's harness. He had left his boots behind, and his feet were freezing. The sun had scorched his face; he could feel it burning, as if in embarrassment. His stomach hurt with hunger. It was maddening.

But still Senneck flew on, and she was showing no sign of stopping. Her wings beat more slowly, and every so often her head drooped, and Erian knew she was as tired as he was.

The sun was directly overhead. Noon had come. And still there was no island in sight.

Why isn't she turning back? Erian thought desperately. *It's noon. We'll barely make it back even if she turns around now! Why is she still going?*

Finally, as the sun ever so slowly started to sink toward the land they had left behind, Erian lost his head. He tugged at Senneck's harness, yelling over the wind. "Turn back! Senneck, *turn back*! We'll be killed!"

Senneck bucked sharply in midair, nearly throwing him off her back. Then she recovered herself and gave a violent jerk of her head, tearing the harness out of Erian's grip. He threw himself forward in terror, this time nearly falling straight over her head to his death, but she lifted her head, shoving him back in place, and he managed to take hold of the harness again.

For a long moment after that, all he could do was sit very still. His heart pounded sickeningly; he felt as if he was going to faint. As he began to calm down, he suddenly realised just how close he had come to falling into the sea, and his stomach lurched.

But Senneck had not turned back.

Erian looked ahead, toward the horizon, and saw nothing. Not a sign.

"Oh Gryphus," he groaned aloud, partly in shock at his brush with death, and partly in horror. "What is she doing? She's mad!"

He was not stupid enough to try to get her attention by pulling on the harness again, and he kept quiet for a long while, terrified. But he couldn't keep his silence forever. Eventually, he started to shout at her again, pleading with her to turn back.

For a long time, Senneck completely ignored him. And then, abruptly, she sent a reply. She put her head down and screeched—a long, deafening screech that slammed into Erian's ears and made his head ring with it. In the same moment, she struck a great blow with her wings and shot forward. Erian, with great presence of mind, threw himself flat, and then they were flying—*really* flying, rushing through the air at an incredible speed. As Senneck beat her wings harder and harder, no longer soaring with the currents in the air but fighting them, she sped up. The wind tore at Erian, making his hair stream out behind him in a tangle of yellow. He shut his eyes and held on. It was all he could do.

It felt like a long time before Senneck finally slowed down again, and it was a little longer before Erian was finally able to sit up and open his eyes.

He took a moment to recover himself, and then looked ahead once more. Still nothing.

Erian blinked. Or . . . no. There was nothing there.

And still the terrible flight dragged on. When the grey smudge finally appeared on the horizon, Erian thought he was hallucinating.

But he wasn't.

Senneck was beginning to falter. She had never carried him for a full day. Even half a day without any breaks was a stretch. But it was far too late to turn back now.

Erian, clinging on, saw the smudge slowly begin to resolve itself into a definite shape, and felt cold despair plummet into his stomach. They had found the Island of the Sun, he had no doubt about that. And it was undoubtedly going to be the last thing they saw before they both died. Senneck could not possibly fly that far.

There was no way of knowing if Senneck was aware of this, but even if she was, she did not give in. She kept on going steadily, riding the wind whenever she could. But the air over the sea was cold, and there were no thermals to help her.

Erian kept his eyes on the island, hoping against hope. *Gryphus help us,* he thought.

But deep down, he knew that Gryphus could not help them. Slowly—painfully slowly—the island grew more defined.

Eventually, Erian could see the mountain that rose out of its centre. It looked jagged and unfriendly.

Senneck's wings were beating less and less frequently. She was beginning to struggle.

Erian knew it was going to happen, but when it did, it tore his stomach away from his gut and straight into his throat.

The island was straight ahead now. He could see the mountain, and the hills and the shore gathered around it, dark with trees beyond the sand. They were nearly there.

And then they were falling.

There was nothing Erian could do. He threw himself backward, clinging on for dear life, and shut his eyes.

Senneck's wings had collapsed, the feathers fluttering uselessly as she plunged headfirst toward the water. Erian dared to look, and saw the sea rushing toward him, sickeningly fast. He shut his eyes again, and braced himself for the impact.

But it never came. An instant before they hit, Senneck suddenly opened her wings and caught herself, gliding straight over the water. Erian, realising what had happened, opened his eyes and felt hot relief rush through him, mingled with joy.

Senneck, wings held out stiffly from her sides, opened her beak wide . . . and blew.

Green light came from her throat in a torrent, spreading out ahead of them. Where it touched the waves, they froze in place. Their colour changed from blue to grey, and Erian, thunderstruck, saw the greyness spread away toward the horizon. Senneck continued to send her magic forth, until a huge expanse of ocean had turned to stone.

The green light faded. Senneck flew on a few moments longer, and then she landed. Her paws and talons hit the stone waves, and cracks instantly spread over them.

"Off!" she screamed at Erian. "Get off!"

When he was too slow to obey, she threw him off. He landed hard, on his back, but pulled himself upright, staggering on his numb legs. "What?"

Behind them was open ocean, but ahead and to both sides there was the stone Senneck had made, shaped exactly as it had been before, when it was still water.

"Senneck!" Erian exclaimed. "You've saved us!"

Senneck did not reply; he turned to look at her, and saw her lying on her side.

His elation quickly turned to sick fear.

"Senneck! Are you all right?"

She did not reply. He could see her flanks heaving in and out like bellows.

Erian sat down beside her. "You've exhausted yourself," he said sympathetically. "But you can rest now."

"No." Senneck's voice was low and rasping, and she raised her head. "No . . . rest."

"Senneck, you—"

The brown griffin heaved herself to her feet. "We . . . walk," she said. "Come. The stone will not hold us forever. Do not stop moving."

Erian walked beside her, suddenly frightened again. "How long will it hold us?"

"Do not know," she said shortly. "Long enough. Stay alert. If I say, get back on, and I will fly."

Erian touched her on the shoulder. "I understand. There's no need to talk."

They made slow progress, hampered partly by the frozen waves but also by their own exhaustion, Senneck's in particular. Erian quickly found himself marvelling that she was still standing upright. Using magic took a lot out of a griffin, and she had already been flying for half a day when she had used hers.

Even so, he knew she was right. The stone couldn't hold them forever.

They had gone some way before it inevitably began to crack. Erian felt his blood freeze when he first heard a low, grinding, snapping sound, just below his feet. He looked down and saw hairline cracks unfurl from beneath his heel. They widened, and he saw water begin to seep through.

Panic bit into him. "Senneck—"

"I know," she said tersely. "Tread lightly."

Erian did his best, trying to imitate the soft padding of her hind paws. But the cracks continued to appear wherever he put his feet down, and he knew the stone was weakening by the moment. Water began to pool around his feet, deepening gradually. Soon it was up to his ankles. Ahead, the island loomed large. It was so close, but if the stone broke now . . .

An almighty crack made the false ground beneath them shudder.

"Run!" Senneck screeched, and charged. Erian broke into a run, trying to keep up with her, but even in her weakened state she was faster than him. She quickly outstripped him, leaving him floundering in water that was now up to his shins, while all around him the stone broke and fell apart, sinking into the depths. Erian struggled on desperately, mouthing a prayer to Gryphus to save him. But still the water continued to rise. Soon, there would be nothing left to stand on—and with the sword strapped to his back, he would sink like a stone.

Ahead, Senneck continued to slosh through the water. She raced forward and then launched herself into the sky. Moments later, a massive crack opened in front of Erian, and water came surging through. He stopped, looking frantically for an escape route, but the crack was directly in front of him and widening. He couldn't jump across. The water rose higher and higher, faster and faster. It reached his knees, then his waist and then his chest. He fumbled at the straps holding his sword in place, meaning to abandon the weapon, but he was far too slow. The water swirled around him, dragging him down. And then, at last, Senneck swooped down and grabbed him, wrapping her talons around his shoulders. She struggled to lift him, her wings beating hard, but as the stone finally crumbled away completely she plucked him out of the water and flew straight for the island, water dripping from her feathers.

Erian felt a greyness close over his eyes as Senneck flew that last, agonising distance. She landed inelegantly, in the shallow water just before the shore, dropping Erian as she did so. He landed face-down in a wash of water, and just barely managed to summon the strength to drag himself out and up onto the wet sand of the beach, where he flopped onto his stomach and promptly fainted.

When he woke up, some unknown length of time later, every bone and muscle in his body felt as if they were burning. He felt chilled and sick, and his mouth was full of sand.

Only the thought of Senneck made him try to get up. He managed to raise himself high enough to look back for her, and the cold, sick feeling in his stomach increased. She was lying in the surf, the water dragging at her wings and tail. Her head lay outstretched in front of her, beak open. She was unconscious . . . or dead.

20

Outwitted

In her prison, cut off from all light except that which came from a candle on the table, Elkin lay on the straw pallet her captors had given her, and shivered.

Down here, unable to see the sun, she had no way of telling how much time had passed—but she knew it must have been weeks.

Her bonds had been taken off, and she had been given fresh clothes and bedding. They had given her plenty to eat and drink, too, and water to wash herself with. She was well looked after, and they had not hurt or molested her. Every day her meals were brought in, but she never saw the faces of her gaolers. All of them wore masks; she had seen three different ones by now. Usually it was the crow face that came, but sometimes it was the deer or the bear. She hadn't seen the wolf again since the first day, and though she had not seen his face, she knew Arenadd hadn't visited her again. At least, not where she could see him.

She had tried to escape, of course. But it took her less than a day to see that it would be impossible. The door was thick wood, and they kept it locked even when they were inside with her. Even if she had had the means to dig her way out, she couldn't, as the room was lined with stone. A philosopher had once written that any room's weakest point was the door, but as far as Elkin could see, there was no way she could use this one. The people who brought her food and drink never came alone; there was always someone else waiting on the other side of the door, and whoever came inside didn't have an obvious weapon she could wrestle away from them. And she wouldn't be able to fight them, anyway, even if she was armed. She was thin and frail, utterly unsuited for combat, and she had no illusions about that.

The only weapon left to her was her mind. But even that was failing her.

Her captors never spoke in her presence. If she spoke to them, they acted as if they hadn't heard her at all. And they were Northerners; she could tell by their build and the black hair that hung down their necks, behind the masks. She was a Southerner—and not just one of the race they despised but one of their greatest leaders. There was nothing she could offer them that they would accept. Most likely they had been warned to expect her to try to bargain or plead her way to freedom— and who would dare to disobey *Kraeai kran ae*?

Despite herself, Elkin couldn't help but admire what her enemy had done. He had planned all of this down to the last detail. She was utterly at his mercy. Unless she was rescued, the Eyrie would have to accept his demands . . . whatever they were.

Elkin shivered again and curled up under her blankets. There was only one way for the Dark Lord's plan to fail. It wasn't a way she wanted, but now she was beginning to be afraid that it might happen against her will.

She could feel sweat prickling on her forehead. In her stomach, a sick churning had stopped her from eating the food they had brought her. Whatever she had eaten that day hadn't stayed down for long.

She knew the sickness was returning. And without Kraal's magic, this time it would kill her.

She slept for most of the rest of that day, aware of the pain in her lungs slowly increasing every time she woke up. The nausea increased as well, and she vomited again, bringing up nothing but mucus and bile. Her stomach had nothing left to give and contracted emptily as she retched, making her entire gut hurt. She slumped back, her head spinning.

If anyone visited her again that day, she never saw them.

The sickness advanced so quickly and so powerfully that it had fully taken hold of her by the time night came, and when she went to sleep again she slid into a hot, sickening fog of fever and despair.

But it was a fog that took her away from her prison, at least. Vividly coloured and bewildering dreams swarmed around her, flitting in and out of her mind. She thought she was back in her room at Malvern, lying on the floor in front of the fireplace. Kraal was there, trying to comfort her by pressing his great flank against her, but his fur and feathers were burning hot, and she couldn't breathe. She tried to ask him to stop, to move away, but her mouth was so dry her tongue stuck to the inside of her cheek and would not come free. But then a pair of hands wrapped themselves around her neck, and she was being dragged away, into a darkness and an icy cold that made her tremble violently, even though she was still burning hot.

Strange figures gathered around her as she drifted through the dark. They were robed, each one carrying a sickle. But their heads were the heads of beasts, not men, blank eyed, the muzzles wet with blood. She saw a stag's head rear above her, its massive antlers spiking into the blackness. It smelt of earth and damp and rotting leaves, and blood.

A voice, muffled and distorted, began to speak. *These are the chiefs of the tribes of Tara, armed with the moon's blade. These are the ones with snow in their blood, sun worshipper, come see, come run with us, see . . .*

Erian!

Elkin reached out for him. It was a mighty struggle just to lift her hand; she felt as if all her limbs were pinned down. Her hand wove slightly to and fro as it reached into the darkness. "Erian, help me," she whispered. "Erian, please."

And then someone took her hand; she could feel their own hand wrap around hers and hold it gently.

"My lady, please, calm down," a voice murmured. "Let me help you."

Elkin's face twitched, deep in her nightmare. "Erian . . ."

A hand touched her forehead. It was gentle and delicate, and cool . . . wonderfully, blessedly cool. Elkin sighed as the coolness spread through her body, soothing the fever.

"Is that better?" said the voice. It sounded sad.

Elkin's eyes slid open, and she cried out. It was not Erian.

It was not her beloved. It was one of the monsters from her nightmare, its wolf muzzle pointing straight down at her, fangs gleaming. She fought to get away from it, shaking violently and clawing at her blankets.

The wolf-man took his hand away. "Please, my lady, don't struggle," he said. "I'm not going to hurt you; I told you so."

Elkin slumped back, shivering. "Let me die," she moaned. "Please, let me die."

The wolf-man sighed. "Look," he said, and reached up to his face. He was clumsy; the fingers of one hand were bent and twisted, and the paralysed forefinger hampered the others. But he hooked them behind his ears, and pulled. The wolf face came away, and underneath was that of a man. He looked young, with his pale skin and long, curly hair, but there were bitter lines around his eyes and a long scar on his cheek that made him look older, and worn.

Even in the midst of her fever, Elkin knew she was looking at Lord Arenadd Taranisäii.

But he was looking down at her not with hatred or cruelty but with a kind of sadness, even concern. "My friends told me you were ill," he said. "I came to see if I could help you."

Elkin pulled away from him, her eyes burning with hatred as much as from fever. "Stay away from me," she gasped. "Monster!"

But he laid his hand on her forehead again, and kept it there, and she did not have the strength to knock it away. "Let me cool you down," he said softly.

Elkin's eyes fluttered shut. "No . . ."

"Don't give up," he told her. "Hold on. It isn't your time, my lady Elkin."

"Don't," she mumbled, but her voice was weak. She felt herself beginning to relax under his touch, wanting him to stay. "Don't," she said again.

"I am very cold," he murmured from above her. "Maybe it's because I'm dead. Or maybe the Night God made me that way. I hate the sun. It makes me feel so tired. But at night . . ."

At night comes the cold, Elkin thought, relishing the idea. *Cold like his hands.*

Lord Arenadd seemed to know that she didn't want him to leave any more. He murmured to her as he clumsily pulled her damp hair away from her face with his maimed hand and covered her with a blanket. "You need to drink something," he said. "Here."

She let him pour it into her mouth: cold water, tasting of herbs.

"Our healer made it," said Arenadd. "She says it's perfect for a fever. I don't get sick any more, myself. At least . . . not the way mortals do."

Elkin swallowed the last of it. "Want . . . I want . . ."

He leant closer. "What is it, Elkin? What do you want?"

She shuddered, and then tears began to flow down her face. "I want to go home."

He chuckled as he leant over her, his long hair brushing her face. "And you will, Elkin."

"No," she whispered. "The sickness will . . . kill me, before you . . . do."

"But you *are* going home, Elkin," Arenadd repeated. "That's why I came to see you, so I could give you the news myself."

Elkin stirred. "What?"

He pulled away abruptly. "Yesterday our messenger finally arrived with word from Malvern. The remnants of the council have given in to my demands. As soon as you're a little stronger, we'll take you out of here to the meeting place we've chosen, and there you'll be handed back to your friends. They'll take you home."

Elkin shivered. She wanted to believe him so badly, but part of her still held back. It had to be a lie, some kind of cruel joke. He was torturing her with false hope.

"Do you feel better now?" he asked.

"A little," she admitted.

Arenadd smiled. "Good. Can't afford to lose you now, can we?" He stood up. "I'll leave you to sleep. I'll bring you something to eat later. Maybe an apple or two. Or even a pear." He nodded to her and left.

Elkin rolled onto her back. She could still feel the touch of his hand on her forehead. The fever had abated for now, and she felt exhausted. But she was still alert enough to think.

Fruit, she thought. *Perfect for illness. But . . . how would he find . . .*

An instant later, the obvious reply came to her and she groaned—a low, hopeless groan. Of course. *Pears.*

There was only one place in the North where you could find pears without ordering them specially.

Fruitsheart.

They'd taken her to Fruitsheart. It was hundreds of miles away from Malvern—right in the middle of one of the richest regions in the North, and absolutely the last place anyone would expect them to be. The chances of her officials thinking to look there were close to none.

That cunning bastard, she thought. *He's outwitted us. He's outwitted* me.

But the memory of the sympathetic way he had looked at her kept coming back, and she wondered . . . couldn't help but wonder . . .

E rian never quite knew how he managed to move Senneck up the beach and away from the water, but he did. The brown griffin stirred as he was attempting to drag her out of the surf, and started to thrust weakly with her paws, but she was not strong enough to move without his help.

By the time they were above the waterline, Erian's legs were trembling. His back ached and his head was pounding.

He took a deep breath, renewed his grip on Senneck's forelegs and pulled. Senneck pushed with her hind legs, and after a few moments of painful struggling she slid a little further up the beach. Once she had come to rest, Erian slumped down beside her.

"I think . . . this is far enough . . . for now," he panted. "You can rest."

Senneck raised her head briefly, and then laid it down again. She was asleep in moments. Erian looked up at the sky. The sun was going down now, and it would be dark very soon. They were exhausted, they had nearly died, but they had made it. They were on the Island of the Sun. He had no doubts at all about that.

Part of him wanted to get up and leave Senneck to recover while he began his search of the island, but he knew he couldn't do it. Not just because he couldn't leave Senneck, especially in such a vulnerable state, but also because he knew he simply didn't have the strength for it.

He managed to get up and stagger over to where he had left his sword sticking out of the sand, and sat down by Senneck with it. His vision was grey; he felt dizzy and ill.

You need to rest, he told himself, stupidly. *Just for a moment.*

He lay down beside his partner with the sword clasped in his hands and was asleep in a moment.

Dawn the next day came in a blaze of red and gold. Erian woke up slowly and was bewildered to find himself half-buried in damp sand. His clothes were soaking wet, and he pulled himself free with a sucking noise. Fortunately the sword was still touching his hand, and he hauled it out and tried to wipe some of the sand off with his cloak. Beside him, Senneck whistled softly in her sleep. Her beak was half-covered, but her nostrils were still exposed, and Erian had an unpleasant moment of shock when he realised that this was probably all that had stopped her from suffocating during the night. She was fine.

Erian scraped the sand away from her beak and gently lifted her head onto her talons. She stirred but didn't wake, and he stroked her head as he sat and looked up at the mountain, while the sun rose from behind it like a great flaming eye.

The weeks that had followed Elkin's kidnapping had been little but pure misery for her partner.

Kraal flew slowly and wearily, hampered slightly by the pair of heavy bags slung over his shoulders but much more by the sheer and utter humiliation he had endured since Elkin had vanished—right in front of him, in their own home!

Arenadd's predictions had been absolutely correct.

At first, while he had made a frantic search for her, Kraal had pretended that nothing was wrong, believing he would find her soon enough. But he found nothing, not even a lingering scent. Before long the other griffins and their humans had realised that something was badly wrong and had finally found out the truth. After that the real search had begun. Kraal had circled endlessly over the Eyrie, calling for his human, while the city was scoured for any sign of her or her kidnapper.

Nothing. The Shadow that Walks had escaped.

After that . . . after that, Kraal had been lost. Without Elkin beside him, he felt as if his heart had been torn out. He had no ambassador to speak for him, no-one to confide in, no-one to protect. Without Elkin, he was more than alone; he was helpless. Diminished. A griffin without a human had no status, no command. He could not lead without her. And worse than that was the knowledge that he had lost her. He had been there when she had been taken, and he had failed to protect her. In the face of that, all his strength and his magic meant nothing. Other griffins, while they hid it, lost their respect for him.

He knew, bitterly, that they were mocking him behind his back. The Mighty Kraal, brought to his knees by a mere human—outwitted, stripped of his power in a heartbeat.

After two long, gruelling days, the message had *finally come*. A griffiner had flown to the Eyrie from a small outlying city to the east, saying that she had been visited one night in her private chamber by a man in a black robe who handed her a piece of paper and said it was for Kraal alone. Then the man vanished into thin air.

The city had been searched, of course; the griffiner had given the order within moments of the incident.

But nothing had been found.

As for the message, its contents had been stark and simple.

To the Mighty Kraal,

We have your human, the Lady Elkin. She has not been injured and we are treating her well. She will not be hurt, provided our demands are met.

Lady Elkin will be set free if Malvern pays us a ransom of nine hundred thousand gold oblong. If you accept, send a messenger to Wolf's Town and have them hang a black banner from the roof of the griffiners' tower. We will see it. At noon two days following, Lady Elkin will be brought to a clearing at the place where the River Snow splits into two, southward of Malvern. Come alone, and bring the ransom. If you attempt any sort of treachery, the prisoner will die instantly. We will come alone.

You cannot find us. You cannot trace us. We are shadows.

Lord Arenadd Taranisäii

The few surviving councillors had argued, they had tried to concoct plans to rescue Elkin without paying the ransom, they had tried to justify refusing or negotiating further—but in the end, they saw that they were beaten. They could not appoint a new Eyrie Master or Mistress while the current one still lived, and they could not afford to waste time. The longer they waited, the more likely it was that Elkin would die in captivity. Even if her kidnappers did not mistreat her, she was too weak to survive under stress. They had no choice but to buy back her freedom, even if it brought Malvern to the edge of bankruptcy.

Kraal knew the river perfectly, and he followed it now. Up ahead was the place where it split into two; the land around it had nearly all been farmed, but the fork itself was still forested. Supposedly, the Northerners believed that the place where two rivers met was sacred, but more likely the land was simply too rocky to bother with.

Whatever his current circumstances, Kraal had lost none of his strength, and he had always been a powerful flier. He flew slowly toward the fork, his great golden eyes watching out for any sign of another griffin.

The sky was empty except for a few circling crows.

We will come alone.

Kraal did not believe that was anything other than a lie, and he hoped that he was right. More than anything, he wanted an excuse to fight. He had not fought anyone for a long time; other griffins were far too frightened of him to do anything other than cower when he showed aggression. But now his pent-up anger was so great it made him long for combat—any combat, even if he was hopelessly outnumbered. He might have lived a peaceful life in Malvern for many years, but he was still a predator, and it was his nature to fight. And just now, he wanted to kill.

He found the clearing easily enough; close to the river, a large tree had fallen, taking several others with it. Kraal circled over it several times, moving lower each time, searching for any sign of danger. He saw nothing.

Hissing to himself, he landed on the trunk of the fallen tree and scanned the clearing. It looked deserted.

The white griffin lifted his head and screamed. The noise echoed over the treetops, making birds take off in fright. *"Come!"*

"You're late," said a quiet voice from out of the air.

Kraal turned sharply. *"You!"* he snarled. "Where are you? Show yourself! *Coward!"*

"Look to your left," said the voice, and Kraal turned in time to see a great dark griffin step into the open, from behind a tree far too small to hide him. Walking beside him with a hand on his shoulder was his human. Lord Arenadd.

Kraal leapt down from the fallen tree and stepped forward to confront them. "Do not try any of your wiles on me," he hissed. "I am more powerful than you can imagine."

Arenadd smiled confidently. "Are you sure, o Mighty Kraal? I have a very good imagination."

"Enough," said Kraal. "Give me back my human."

Arenadd lifted her down from his partner's back and held her upright, supporting her with an arm around her waist. For a moment Kraal thought she was dead, but then he saw her stir and put her own arm around her captor's shoulders, clinging on to him as if for comfort.

He moved closer. "Elkin. Are you hurt?"

Elkin blinked and stared at him. "Kraal," she said dully. "You came."

"Of course I came," he said. "I would never let them keep you from me. Have they hurt you?"

She coughed. "No. He . . . he looked after me himself."

Arenadd nodded. "That I did. I brought her food and medicine with my own hands. Now. There's only one step left, and it's the simplest. I see you've brought the money. Skandar will come and take it from you, and I'll check to make sure it's all there. After that, I'll let you take Elkin back. Understood?"

Kraal blinked resignedly. "Yes. It is understood. Come, dark griffin, relieve me of these."

Skandar stepped forward, tail lashing. He showed no sign of respect for the other griffin, but stood arrogantly tall. "You give now," he said harshly.

Kraal hissed to himself and unhooked the bags from his shoulders, placing them in front of him for Skandar to take. "It is all here," he said. "I watched the treasurer count it out myself."

Skandar did not take the bags immediately. He moved a little closer, scenting at him, his eyes narrow. "You are Kraal," he said. "Mighty Kraal."

"I am," Kraal rasped back. "And you . . ."

Skandar held his head high, wings slightly open. "Am Skandar. Am Darkheart."

Kraal suddenly felt very tired. "Skandar, do you remember your mother?"

Skandar stared at him. "Not remember," he said resentfully. "Mother die."

"Then no wonder you cannot speak griffish," said Kraal. "Skandar, I do not know what lies this human has told you to make you follow him this way, but there is something he cannot have told you."

Skandar bristled. "Human mine!" he said. "My human greatest, strongest, cleverest. I help him, and soon we take this territory, make it ours. None stop us. *None!*"

"I cannot allow you to do that," said Kraal.

Skandar flicked his tail. "You not stop!" he sneered.

Kraal did not know why he wanted to speak to the other griffin. He drew himself up, noting that Skandar's head reached to just below his own. He had never met a griffin so close to him in size. When he saw that, he lost the last of his doubts. "Skandar, I am your father."

Skandar started at him. "Father?"

"Yes. I was in the mountains where you were born, and I mated with your mother. That is why you are so large and why your magic is so powerful."

Skandar was silent for a moment. He seemed to be thinking. "Not need father," he said at last. "Wait in your nest. One day soon I come kill you."

"Then I will wait for you," Kraal said calmly.

Skandar ignored him. He picked up the bags in his beak and returned to his partner's side. Arenadd gently laid Elkin down and opened them, quickly checking to make sure both were full of gold oblong. "Good," he said, once he was satisfied. "You've kept your part of the bargain. Take your partner." He slung the bags over Skandar's back, and the two of them retreated, leaving Elkin alone. The moment she was out of danger, Kraal darted forward and lifted her in his talons, hissing angrily. "You have your gold, *Kraeai kran ae*," he said. "Now begone."

Arenadd bowed ironically. "It was a pleasure doing business with you."

In that moment, Kraal wanted to kill him. He wanted to charge at him and hit him in the chest so hard it would tear him in half. The hatred burned so powerfully inside him that it made him seem to double in size. "Go," he snarled. "Go, and do not let me see you again. And beware. Gryphus is not idle. You and your foul master can never defeat us, and you will never take the power you desire. I will see you dead, along with your followers. Know that."

Arenadd folded his arms behind his back. "I love threats. They're so . . . invigorating. The self-righteousness is quite tedious, though. You may want to work on that. Good luck." He climbed onto Skandar's shoulders, and the dark griffin began to walk away. He broke into a run and launched himself into the sky . . . and vanished into thin air.

Kraal stared for a long time at the spot where they had been, not quite able to believe what he had just seen, but then he turned his attention back to Elkin. "Dark magic—Elkin, can you get onto my back?"

Elkin stirred but didn't reply. She was burning hot. Kraal clicked his beak sharply several times in a griffish curse and took off, cradling her in his talons as gently as he could. He had to get her back to Malvern as soon as possible.

21

On the Island of
the Sun

The day after their arrival on the island, Erian and Senneck were strong enough to begin exploring it. They walked off the beach and entered the surprisingly thick forest beyond. It was cool and silent under the trees; the only sounds were the chirping of birds and the soft whirring of insects. They pressed on, making for the mountain, until the trees thinned out again and they found an open field. A few wild goats skipped away from them as they walked over thick, fragrant grass dotted with flowers. Erian went ahead, climbing the gentle slope until he reached the top. And beyond that . . . was a village.

Erian froze, open-mouthed in bewilderment. "What?"

Senneck joined him. *"Humans?"* she said. "Here?"

Erian paused a moment. "No. It's a ruin. Look."

They ventured in among the cluster of buildings. They were simple wooden huts, most of them falling down but a few surprisingly intact. Sand had blown up, half-burying some of them. Erian saw other things the former occupants had left behind: earthenware pots, most of them in pieces, and a couple of broken tools. There was even a boat, mostly buried with part of its hull still visible through the sand. He could see where there had been vegetable gardens: the descendants of the original plants grew wild all over the place.

"I didn't know people lived here," he said eventually.

"Neither did I," said Senneck. "It seems that your ancestors must have settled here for a time before they discovered Cymria itself. But it is astonishing that their homes have been preserved so well."

"Who knows how long they stayed here?" said Erian. "Maybe some stayed behind when the others left. People too old or young to cross the sea. They can't have known what they'd find on the other side, after all."

"True," said Senneck. "This is a lucky accident for us. Some of these huts look large enough for you to live in, and there is food."

"We won't be staying here long," said Erian. "It shouldn't take more than a day or so to find this weapon."

Senneck sighed. "Perhaps, but . . ."

"What?"

"I am sorry," she said at last. "But I should have told you earlier. I have managed to bring you to the island, but I cannot take you back."

Erian's blood ran cold. "Why? What's wrong?"

"I cannot travel again," said Senneck. "I scarcely made it here to begin with. It will be a long time before I am able to carry you back . . . unless you could make a boat and paddle it back."

"I won't leave without you," Erian said firmly. "I don't understand. Why can't you carry me? I know you're tired, but if you just take a few days to rest . . ."

She made a hacking griffish laugh. "Erian, you are still so naïve. Do not tell me you cannot see it."

"See what?"

"Look at me," said Senneck. "Have you never wondered why I have managed to grow so fat on so little food? Why I have been tired and irritable for the last few weeks?"

Erian gaped. "You're not—"

She inclined her head. "I will lay my eggs in a few days at most. When that happens, I will not be able to leave the island until my chicks are old enough to fly."

"But how long will that take?"

"Months," she sighed. "Assuming they all survive."

Erian groaned. "But . . . didn't you know?"

"No," she said sharply. "I did not know I was bearing eggs until long after we had left Malvern, and in any case there would have been nothing I could have done. We have reached the island, and we will be safe here."

"But while we're away—!"

"Yes. I am sorry."

To his surprise, he realised she was avoiding his eye. "It's all right, Senneck," he said more kindly. "You weren't to know. Anyway, you deserve a family of your own. I would love to have children myself," he added, half to himself.

"And with your new mate, I am certain you will," said Senneck.

Erian thought of Elkin, wondering once again if she was safe and well. Did she miss him as much as he missed her? He smiled sadly to himself. They would meet again; he knew it. And maybe one day, after the war was done, they could settle down and raise their children. A real family. He smiled. "I'd like that."

"Let us find a place to shelter, and we will gather food," said Senneck. "We have had a long journey, and we shall need time to recover."

Erian agreed, and they wandered among the huts until they found one that was sufficiently intact. The interior was full of sand and creeping vines, but Erain leant his sword against the wall and sat down gratefully. This was a far better shelter than he had had in a long time.

Senneck favoured it with a cursory glance. "It will suffice."

"Will you stay here with me?" said Erian.

"Of course. It is cold here; you will need to share my warmth."

"But what about when you lay your eggs?"

Senneck ruffled her feathers. "If I was a wild griffin, I would build a nest high on a mountain top or atop a cluster of the tallest trees. But I am not wild, and there cannot be any predators on this island large enough to threaten my young. I shall choose a place that is sheltered and comfortable, when the time comes."

Despite the situation, Erian felt a little thrill of excitement. "So, I'll get to see the eggs?"

To his shock, Senneck came close to him and rubbed her cheek against his. "Yes, Erian. You are my partner, and I trust you before all others. I would trust you with my life. To let you see my young would be nothing."

Erian smiled and stroked the sleek feathers on her neck. "Thank you, Senneck."

She chirped. "I am sorry that I have done this to you, Erian. But perhaps it was meant to be."

"Gryphus controls everything," Erian observed. "Maybe he wanted it to happen."

Senneck made a dismissive rasping sound in her throat. "Come. If you have the strength, let us seek out our food."

Erian followed her from the hut. "Shouldn't we start looking for the weapon?"

"There will be time enough for that later. For now, we shall eat."

Arenadd and Skandar returned from their meeting with Kraal a mere day after they had left. Now that he had finally uncovered his power, Skandar could travel astonishingly fast, and the black griffin glided silently through the shadows with so little effort it was as if he had been doing it all his life.

It was close to midnight when he landed in the little yard between the house and the stable, but the others were still awake to receive him.

As Arenadd dismounted, they came running.

"My lord!" Saeddryn was pale with excitement. "My lord, did ye get it?"

Arenadd grinned at her. "Yes, Saeddryn. I got it." He lifted the bags down from Skandar's back, grunting under the weight. "Help me get it inside."

The others were more than willing. Davyn and Rhodri lifted them and took them into the house. Arenadd saw Skandar into the stable. The griffin wasn't in the mood for talk; he stumped over to his makeshift nest and slumped into it without a word.

"Sleep well, Skandar," said Arenadd. "You did magnificently."

Skandar opened a sleepy eye. "Always do magnificently," he intoned, and closed it again.

"I can't argue with that," Arenadd murmured, and left, grinning.

The others were waiting for him inside the house, and to his surprise he found that they'd prepared a special meal, which Caedmon and Torc were helping to lay out on the table as he entered.

Skade and Saeddryn, meanwhile, were deep in the bags of money. Saeddryn buried her hand in one and pulled it out, clutching a fistful of oblong. They gleamed brightly in the candlelight as they clinked softly back into the bag. But there was danger about their shine as well as beauty, Arenadd thought. People had killed for far less gold than this.

Rhodri pulled a chair out for him. "Sit down, sir, everythin's been taken care of."

Arenadd sat down with a grateful sigh. "Thank you."

Skade came over and touched him on the shoulder. "My love," she said softly and kissed him on the cheek. "You look tired. Were there any problems?"

Arenadd reached up to touch her hand. "None," he said, for everyone's benefit. "The plan worked to the last detail. The Mistress is winging her way back home as we speak, and meanwhile . . . we're rich as lords."

"Ye mean *ye* are rich as a lord, sir," said Saeddryn, rising from her crouch and shaking out her hair. "After all, it was ye who kidnapped the Mistress an' ye who made the deal. This was all yer own plan, sir. So." She came closer, her eyes aglow. She almost looked lustful. "Tell us how it happened, sir. I want t'hear everything."

Arenadd smiled at her. "Sit down, everyone, and let's eat this food before it gets cold. But"—he grinned to himself—"I've started to like the idea of making deals. I'll tell you what happened, but only after someone's paid me the ransom of a good cup of wine."

Caedmon, chuckling, poured one and obligingly gave it to him. "Now that's enough of yer teasin', my lad," he said. "Tell us the story before we go mad."

Arenadd sniffed at the wine and tasted it. "Not bad," he said and tossed it back. Once he'd emptied the cup, he shuddered a little and dabbed at his mouth. "Fill this up again, would you?" he said and then began his tale. It didn't take long, and the others listened with interest, asking eager questions.

". . . and when we got there, we found him waiting for us, all alone, as agreed."

Saeddryn grinned. "Was he angry?"

"Unbelievably." Arenadd took another gulp of wine. "I swear I've never been more frightened of a griffin in my life. I had to put my hands behind my back so he wouldn't see them shaking."

"He could never have beaten you," Skade scoffed.

"He could never have *caught* us," said Arenadd. "As far as fighting is concerned, I'm not sure. But Skandar didn't seem frightened by him. *He* was more cocky than I was. It's an interesting thing, though . . ."

"What, sir?" said Rhodri.

"Pass me that jug would you, Caedmon? Well, Skandar and Kraal spoke a little; Kraal seemed very interested in him, in fact. He said something that surprised me."

"Why?" said Skade.

Arenadd kept his eyes on the jug as he refilled his cup for the second time. "He claimed to be Skandar's father."

The others murmured.

"Odd," said Caedmon. "But sir, didn't ye say Skandar was born in the Coppertops? That's on the other side of the world!"

"I know, but Kraal claimed to have travelled there. It's not impossible. I'll admit it makes a kind of sense, actually. There's some resemblance between them; Skandar's only a little smaller than he is. But I don't know why Kraal thought it was so important. Griffins don't care much about family ties."

"Little," Skade said quietly.

Arenadd glanced quickly at her. "It didn't make much of an impression on Skandar. He's vowed to kill that white griffin himself. I asked him why, and he said a strange griffin came to him in a dream and told him to do it."

Saeddryn raised her eyebrows. "The Night God?"

"That's what I thought." Arenadd nodded. "It's said she has a different shape sometimes. When she wants to. How could it possibly be outside her powers to make herself look like a griffin, considering everything else she's done?"

"Then Skandar must be chosen by her, too," Saeddryn said firmly. "It makes sense. The Night God sent him to help ye, sir."

Skade muttered sourly under her breath.

"She did," said Arenadd. "Anyway, let's eat, shall we?"

The food was good, and there was even an apple pie for dessert. Arenadd ate a little of everything and drank steadily. It had become a habit of his lately, but none of the others had commented on it, and if they had, he wouldn't have cared. Drink was the only thing that calmed him down nowadays, and the only thing that could stave off his dreams. Dreams of battlefields strewn with the dead, where he walked alone with his bloodied sickle in his hand, bones crunching under his boots, slick with gore. What he saw was bad enough, but not the worst part.

The worst part was how he looked on all this and laughed.

But tonight he was in a good mood and drank less than he might have done. Afterward, once the food was gone, Caedmon fell asleep in his chair while Torc, slightly drunk, made shy conversation with Saeddryn. Arenadd and Skade excused themselves and retreated to their own room.

Arenadd sat down on the bed and hiccupped. "Ooh, pardon me. So, how were things here while we were gone?"

Skade sat beside him. "Uneventful. I did not worry for you as much this time as before."

"That's good." Arenadd took her hand in both of his, his maimed fingers clumsy as they tried to grasp hers. He pulled away. "Gods. These fingers, these useless fingers . . . I should have this one cut off. It doesn't do anything except get in the way."

"If only the Night God had healed them for you," said Skade, with just a hint of sarcasm.

"Yes. Well." Arenadd sighed. "It's punishment. A reminder of my mistakes. Letting them get their hands on me cost me one of mine. If I'd only listened to her when she first came to me, if I hadn't tried to run away from my duty, I would have known how to use my magic—*Skandar's* magic—and I would have been able to rescue you without being captured."

"You were brave," Skade said softly.

"I was a damned fool," said Arenadd, without much emphasis. "Let's not talk about it any more. There's no point in torturing ourselves."

Skade nodded. "We have other things to talk of."

"Yes, that we do." He yawned again. "The first part of the plan is complete. Now we can begin the next part, and this is where you come in."

"Me?" said Skade.

"Yes, you." Arenadd took her hand again, this time ignoring his useless fingers. "The money I took from Malvern was for you, Skade. I'm going to entrust it to you."

"Why?" Skade asked sharply. "You said you would use it to—"

"Yes, exactly. Skade, I'm sending you south. Some of my best warriors will go with you, to protect you and the money. You'll take it with you and make the deal with the slavers."

Skade stood up. "No. I will not."

Arenadd stood, too. "Yes, you will. I'm not going to argue with you about this."

"I do not want to be away from you!"

"And neither do I!" Arenadd exclaimed. "D'you think I possibly could? No. Listen, Skade—I'm sending you because I have to. You're not a Northerner. You carry yourself like a noblewoman. With your help, my deal with the slavers would look far more legitimate. And more than that, I *trust* you. I trust you more than Saeddryn. I even trust you more than Skandar. I know you'd never give in or let yourself be cheated, and that you'd never surrender to greed and run away with the money. You don't trust anybody, and that's how you have to be with money. This deal can't go wrong. Everything hinges on it. That's why I'm sending you."

She softened, and stroked his face. "For a master of deception, you are utterly transparent to me, Arenadd. You are sending me because you do not want me to be here when the war truly begins."

He spread his hands in a gesture of defeat. "No, Skade. I don't."

"But you are selfish," she added, without accusation. "You do not realise that your death would be as terrible for me as mine would be for you. What would I do if I returned to the North to find you dead? I would lose you, and know that I had not even been with you in your last moments."

Arenadd laughed. "Dead! Skade, you saw what happened to me. I *can't* die. I can never die."

She looked into his eyes. "Can't you?" She asked it so softly he only just heard it.

Arenadd shook his head, as if hoping to dislodge that one nagging doubt. "Only *Aeai ran kai* can kill me," he admitted. "But he's not here. By the time he comes back from this made quest of his, I'll have conquered the North. You'll be back by then. And . . ."

"And?" she pressed.

He took her by the wrists, holding her hands to his face. "And I don't believe that *Aeai ran kai*—the Bastard—could kill me."

"Why not?"

"The Bastard is mortal," Arenadd said, smiling. "And I'm not. And I have the Night God to help me. That's why."

Skade looked away. "I fear you have too much faith in your god," she muttered. "In my life, I have seen faith do little but lead to betrayal and death."

"So have I," said Arenadd. "But I wonder: would that be *our* death, or *theirs*?"

22

Raising the Banner

Senneck laid her eggs in a hut close to Erian's, three days after they had arrived on the Island of the Sun. She had built a nest inside the abandoned building, dragging dead branches and clumps of grass inside and arranging them in a crude circle. She did this alone, ignoring Erian's offers of help. As her time drew near she had become less communicative, preferring to spend most of her time alone, generally sleeping in her nest.

Erian, realising he wasn't wanted, occupied himself with his own affairs. He gathered dry grass and made it into a semblance of a bed in his own hut—though the sand on the floor was already comfortably soft—and took planks from the other huts to try to shore up the roof and make it waterproof. He gathered fruit and vegetables from the wild gardens for food, but, quickly consumed by a desire for meat, he soon went after something more substantial. He hadn't hunted in a long time, but he was confident in his skills, and he spent the best part of a day trying to make a bow. That was something he hadn't done for an even longer amount of time. He found a vaguely suitable piece of wood and sat in the sun for ages, whittling it into the proper shape. He used a strip of leather from his pocket to make a string; it wasn't really strong enough, but he managed to make it hold. After that he made a few arrows, and this time he had a stroke of good luck. During his search of the village, he had found a good number of stone arrowheads, left behind buried in the sand. He used those to make the tips and fletched the crude arrows with leaves or feathers Senneck had shed.

Hunting with his makeshift new weapon proved to be hopelessly impractical, but the goats were unused to any sort of predation and were surprisingly placid. This was probably the only reason why he eventually managed to catch one, but catch one he did, and he spent a gruesome evening skinning and gutting the beast, ready to share it with Senneck. She accepted his offering with a brief chirp of gratitude, and he left her in her nest and went to enjoy his own helping.

When the day finally came for Senneck to lay her eggs, she came to wake him at dawn.

"My eggs will be laid today," she said briefly. "Do not enter my nest."

"I won't—"

"*Do not,*" she repeated. "Not for any reason at all, Erian. Laying is a matter of absolute privacy for a griffin, and not even my human may witness it. And if that does not convince you, be warned that the process will awaken my wild nature. If you disturb me, I will attack to kill."

Erian nodded dumbly.

"I will see you tomorrow, perhaps," Senneck said, almost breezily, and left without another word.

The day that followed was agonising for Erian. He did his best to keep busy, drying the leftover goat meat and gathering fuel for the fire, but his eyes and his thoughts kept straying toward Senneck's hut. He couldn't hear a single sound coming from inside, and the silence lasted for most of the day.

Erian took his bow and went hunting again. This time the goats were absent, and he returned empty-handed. Instead, he went looking for bird's eggs and found a few.

He returned to his hut, pausing for a long moment outside Senneck's nest before moving on. After that he sat down, enjoying the warm sunlight on his face. "Gryphus, please protect Senneck and her chicks," he murmured and then slipped into a doze.

He woke up again in the evening, and now there was a faint sound from Senneck's nest. It wasn't the screeching or any of the other vocal sounds he had been expecting. Instead there was a thumping sound, as of something heavy striking wood.

It came intermittently, and he sat and listened to it. Somehow, the noise was far more disturbing in its own way than what he had been anticipating.

It stopped as night fell, and Erian reluctantly retreated into his hut to sleep. He dreamt of an indistinct golden figure trying to speak to him, while Senneck lay on the ground, dying.

When he woke up it was dawn, and for a moment he couldn't remember anything. An instant later it came back, and he sprinted out of the hut. He went straight to Senneck's nest, ignoring his desperate need to empty his bladder, and only slowing when he was nearly at the door. Remembering Senneck's warning (or had it been a threat?), he crept to the doorway and peeked through, tensing himself to run.

Senneck was curled up in her nest, with her back to the door. The light was bad, but he could see her flank moving up and down in time to her rumbling breaths, and he sighed silently in relief. She was alive, at least. But he couldn't see her eggs. He retreated quietly and left her to rest.

She did not emerge from her nest that day, but when he ventured near again she heard him and called him inside.

Erian went in and found her looking at him, tired but bright-eyed. "It is safe," she said softly. "You may come in and see them."

Erian obeyed, walking around so he could see from the other side. The eggs were lying nestled against her belly, partly covered by her wing, but she raised it to let him see. There were three of them—brown and speckled, like oversized hen's eggs. Each one was the size of a melon, but one was a little smaller than the others.

Erian examined them, wonderstruck.

"What do you think?" Senneck asked, sounding almost shy.

"They're beautiful," Erian said simply.

She flicked her tail. "This is my first clutch," she said. "They were difficult to lay."

"Did it hurt?"

"Of course. All of the important things we do in life are painful in their way." She touched the smallest egg with her beak, tapping the hard shell. "I do not think this one will hatch. If it does, it will hatch into a runt. I have not eaten well enough during my pregnancy."

"I'm sorry—" Erian began.

"Do not be. This was my choice. Now I must rest."

Erian nodded. "How long before they hatch?"

"Three full moons, at least," said Senneck.

Erian groaned involuntarily.

"Do not complain," Senneck snapped. "You, at least, have the freedom of the island. I must stay here and keep my eggs warm until they hatch."

"I know," Erian said hastily. "I'm sorry." A thought occurred to him. "But if you have to stay with them all that time, how will you eat?"

"I will not eat, unless you bring food to me," said Senneck.

"I will," said Erian. "I can catch the goats here; it'll give me something to do."

"Thank you," she said gravely.

Erian bowed to her and left. In spite of his frustration and anxiety, he couldn't help but feel excited. He had never seen griffins hatch or watched them grow up, and he thrilled at the idea of Senneck—*his* Senneck!—as a mother. What would her chicks look like? What would she name them? Would they look like her, or Eekrae? Maybe he, Erian, could help raise them.

And maybe . . . his pace slowed. And maybe he shouldn't be so upset about this. They had made it to the island safely, after all, and they would be safe here together. Gryphus was master of new life; Senneck's eggs could never have quickened without his will.

Yes. Erian felt himself cheer up at the thought. He had to trust in Gryphus. Everything would be all right.

Two days after his return from the rendezvous with Kraal, Arenadd gathered his friends together in their hideout.

"It's time," he said simply. "The war begins now."

They had been planning this for weeks, and nobody raised a protest. Skade, Saeddryn, Rhodri and Davyn looked grimly at their leader.

"We're ready, sir," said Saeddryn, speaking for all of them.

"Good. Go to work." Arenadd thrust his sickle into his belt. "I'm going to go to Skandar now. Wait for our signal."

Skade hugged him briefly before he left. "Be careful."

"I will. Watch for me, Skade. When the moment comes, you'll know what to do." He gave her a quick smile and left.

In the stable, Skandar was awake and ready for him. "We go now?"

The black griffin's tail was lashing furiously.

Arenadd touched him on the side of the neck. "Yes. It's time, Skandar. From here on, we do things your way."

Skandar hissed, lowering his head and opening his beak wide to emit a harsh, rasping sound. "Now we *fight*," he snarled. "Fight for true, never fly away."

"Yes." Arenadd scratched his partner under the beak, the way he liked it. "From today, Fruitsheart will become *our* territory, not theirs. When they know where we are, people will start gathering to follow us. Our time has come."

Skandar did not want to listen to any more rhetoric. "Fly, now!" he said. "You, climb onto me and I go, *now*."

Arenadd hooked an arm over Skandar's shoulders and nimbly hauled himself up. He still preferred to fly without a harness, and he held on as well as he could. Once he was in place, Skandar tore at the ground, ripping huge furrows with his talons. He paused for a moment, leaning backward on his powerful legs to brace himself, and then lunged forward, straight into the shadows.

This was nothing like travelling through that dark realm on his own. Arenadd lay flat, his arms wrapped around Skandar's neck, as pure blackness rushed past around them. Skandar never seemed capable of becoming lost. He slid through the shadows without a sound, never seeming to change direction, until he opened his beak wide and let out a screech so horrible, so full of pent-up violence, that it made even Arenadd shudder.

In that instant, the darkness vanished and they were bursting back into the real world—into a large, richly decorated chamber where another griffin was turning to meet them, wings half-open in shock.

Arenadd was ready. He threw himself sideways, off Skandar's back, rolling when he hit the floor and using the momentum to land on his feet. As he rose he pulled his sickle free and charged.

Skandar had hit the other griffin head-on, full in the chest. Now the two were struggling together, Skandar's talons locked into his opponent's neck and shoulders while he tore at vulnerable flesh with his beak. The other griffin bit back, tearing a long gash down the side of Skandar's face, but could not dislodge the talons still stuck in his own body.

Arenadd had no time to waste watching his partner's struggle. The griffiner was there, already grasping the hilt of his sword, and Arenadd attacked him instantly, hoping to catch him before he could draw it.

The griffiner, a solidly built middle-aged man, proved to be faster than Arenadd had expected. He wrenched his sword out of its scabbard and raised it, protecting his face and chest. Arenadd's own weapon was far too small to knock it aside, and at the last instant he changed his tack, darting away to attack side-on. The griffiner struck, turning to face this new attack, but Arenadd was faster. The hooked point of the sickle pierced the skin, and he pulled it downward, tearing a deep wound in the unprotected flesh under the man's arm. The griffiner bellowed in pain, like a bull, and charged at him.

Arenadd did not panic. Combat never frightened him any more, and he grinned to himself and began his dance, moving this way and that to confuse his enemy and make himself nearly impossible to hit. The griffiner, bleeding badly from his wound, came after him, but Arenadd refused to let himself be cornered. He ducked under the wounded arm and struck again, this time with the sharpened edge of his sickle. It opened a long wound over the griffiner's back, and bright blood soaked into the man's tunic as Arenadd darted away.

"Gryphus . . . damn you!" the griffiner yelled, gasping in pain. "Hold still! Fight like a . . . like a man!"

Arenadd sniggered. "Why would I want to do that? Men die. I prefer"—he wove around the man and cut him again—"to fight like a shadow. Can you kill a shadow?"

The griffiner made a quick and powerful attack, aiming to flick the sickle out of Arenadd's hand. It missed, but only just; Arenadd, caught unawares, barely managed to avoid it, and the blade caught him a glancing blow on the arm. He snarled at the sudden pain and made a reckless attack, charging straight at his enemy. The griffiner protected himself with his blade, ready to swing it at Arenadd the instant he came close enough.

At the last moment, Arenadd dodged sideways. Utterly silent on the wooden floor, he ran past the griffiner and then behind him, and as he ran he struck. His aim was true, and the

inner edge of the sickle hit the man full in the throat. The edge
did most of the work, but the hook, following it, did the rest.
The griffiner made a sickening wet gagging sound and fell to
his knees.

Arenadd stood over him, panting, his eyes burning. "No," he
said. "I don't think you can."

The noise of the fight, short though it had been, had not gone
unnoticed. Even as the griffiner fell, dying before he hit the
floor, the door burst open and a dozen armed guards ran in.
Arenadd turned to face this new threat, holding his bloodied
sickle in one hand, and a grin spread over his face. It was not
fearful, or angry, or even hateful. It was full of a raw and terrible hunger.

Skandar raised his head from his kill, blood dripping from
the tip of his beak. He saw Arenadd attack, and his heart beat
fast, pumping hot blood through his own body, bringing him
strength to help his partner. *"Fight!"* he screamed, and charged.

The occupants of the Governor's Tower at Fruitsheart had
been warned of a possible attack and had prepared themselves
as well as they could. The five griffiners who lived there kept
their swords with them, and the griffins stayed alert at all times.
The number of guards in the tower was doubled.

But, truly, there was almost nothing they could have done.
Bewilderment only added to the panic that spread when Skandar and Arenadd entered the tower to begin their attack, and
man and griffin carved a bloody path through the building, killing every griffin or Southerner they encountered.

And even if their enemies had been prepared, what could
they have possibly done against a massive griffin who could
appear and disappear at will, and a man as silent as a shadow,
who seemed impervious to any form of attack?

It was not the first massacre that Skandar and Arenadd committed together. Nor would it be the last.

When the killing was more or less over and all five griffiners were dead, Arenadd climbed to the top of the tower. While
Skandar guarded him, he tore down the banner and threw it
from the edge, to float down over the city. He reached into his
robe and brought out a large folded cloth. Caedmon and Torc
had made it, with his help.

He tied it to the rope that had held the old banner, and hoisted it high. The wind soon caught it and unfurled it, showing it to the whole of Fruitsheart.

It was a black flag emblazoned with a running wolf, which seemed to dance as the cloth flapped in the wind. The wolf held a silver moon in its jaws.

That was the signal.

Down in the city, Saeddryn had climbed onto a rooftop with help from the others. She raised her arms and shouted in the Northern tongue, the ancient tongue. The forbidden tongue. "The time has come! The moon is rising! Your master's flag has been raised! Look! Look at the tower! *Look!*"

People walking past stopped to gape at her. Saeddryn continued to shout her message over the rooftops, while elsewhere in the city, Rhodri, Davyn and Torc did the same. Even Skade had been taught the words, and she shouted them out, too, calling her beloved's name with all her strength. Below, people began to look at the tower, and they saw the banner and began to shout their surprise.

This was Saeddryn's cue. She picked up the griffinbone horn. "Listen!" she cried. "And I will call!" She lifted the horn to her mouth and blew with all her might.

A sound like a griffin's screech echoed up into the sky.

Up on top of the tower by his partner's side, Skandar lifted his head and screamed.

Beside him, keeping well back from the edge, Arenadd saw the panic in the streets below and smiled grimly to himself. *The city is mine,* he thought. *And this time, I won't run away. The time for that has passed.*

He returned to the pole where his banner hung, and climbed it. Clinging to the top, ignoring the height, he drew his blood-stained sickle and held it high over his head so that the metal gleamed in the sunlight. They would see him in the city, and they would know who he was. They would see their true master and choose to ally with him or . . .

They will join my side, he thought. *They don't have any choice. The moon is their god, whether they remember it or not, and I am the moon's greatest servant. And why would they choose the Southerners? No. They are my people.*

Arenadd stayed at the top of the flagpole for a few moments longer and then slid down again.

"Come on," he said to Skandar. "We should go back inside. There could still be enemies to fight."

Skandar hissed and gladly followed his partner. This was what he wanted. This was what he had been waiting for. Not running and skulking around in the shadows, but true fighting. Arenadd had promised it to him, and now he had it. He felt the ache of his wounds and tasted blood in his mouth. It made him feel more alive than he had for months. He had bided his time for so long, and now his dreams were coming true at last.

He walked close to Arenadd, wanting to press himself against the human to show his gratitude. But this was no time for affection. They had work to do.

Arenadd rubbed the top of his head, just behind his beak, and Skandar closed his eyes briefly and crooned. It didn't matter. His human understood.

23

The Weapon

Three and a half months after his arrival on the Island of the Sun, Erian sat outside his hut and chewed at a piece of dried goat meat. He didn't have much left. Tomorrow, he would have to catch another goat. Or maybe he would go back to the shore to look for mussels. It would be less taxing but perhaps more time-consuming. And Senneck would probably want more meat, too.

The last few months had taken their toll on him. Later on, he would speculate that perhaps the first few weeks of life on the island had done more to change him than all his time travelling with Senneck.

His appearance had changed, certainly. His face was tanned and weather-beaten, and while he hadn't quite grown a beard his chin and cheeks were rough with yellow stubble. His hair had grown long, and he had tied it back with a leather thong. His hands, which had grown soft after so much time spent handling nothing but paper and quills, were rough and hard, the finger-nails broken.

There were no mirrors here, and no way for Erian to see his own face, and after so long living away from human contact he had ceased to think about his appearance, but anyone who saw him would have been hard-pressed to recognise him for the boy who had left Malvern long ago. Senneck had not left her nest once since laying her eggs, not even to eat or drink. He had brought her food every day and had hauled in water in a makeshift container fashioned from a broken pot he had found, and she had accepted it but still refused to leave her eggs for an instant. She preferred to be left alone, and her conversation was sparse to the point of virtual silence. Erian had finally realised that she did not want to talk and had left her alone, though his loneliness had been all but unbearable for the first few weeks.

"Well, she wants to be left alone," he mumbled. "This is her special time with her eggs. What would I know about it? It's her business. When they hatch, maybe she'll start coming out. She doesn't need me now. Maybe I'll go hunting today. Yes."

He was barely aware of talking to himself; it had been a habit for so long that he did it without thinking. When he *did* think of it, he forgot about it soon enough. What did it matter? He was alone. Nobody was here to see him. He could walk around naked if he wanted, and nobody would see that, either.

He finished his snack, and took his bow and arrows out to the field to hunt. By now he had got the process down to a fine art, and he chose a hiding place at random and lay in wait until a goat came within range of his bow. After that, it was just a matter of aiming.

Afterward, he hauled the carcass back to the village and cut off a leg for himself before taking the rest to Senneck.

He paused in the entrance to her nest, as always, to announce his presence. "Senneck? I've brought food."

There was a pause before she answered. "Erian. Come in."

He came, dragging the goat with him. "It's a good big one today. Where do you want it?"

Senneck, curled up in her nest as usual, said, "Leave it by the door."

"All right." Erian let go of the goat. "Do you need more water, or shall I leave?"

Senneck yawned briefly. "No. Come here."

Erian obeyed, full of curiosity. "Why? What is it, Senneck?"

She said nothing, but raised her wing. Erian saw what was underneath and stared in amazement.

When Senneck's wing moved, it revealed two tiny, shivering shapes. Griffin chicks, newly hatched, all downy and pathetic.

Erian came closer. "They've . . . they've *hatched*!"

Senneck's tail flicked. "You may look different now, but you still delight in stating the obvious. Look on my young, Erian."

Erian's face split into a grin. "They're so tiny! Have you given them names yet?"

"No griffin is *given* a name. We name ourselves when we are old enough." Senneck gently nudged one of the chicks closer to the warmth of her belly fur. "One is a male, and one female," she added more kindly. "The third egg did not hatch."

Erian watched the chicks. Their forequarters were covered in down instead of feathers, and their hindquarters were fluffy, like those of kittens. Their eyes were huge and bulging, but sealed shut. One was slightly larger than the other, but beyond that he couldn't see any difference between them. They both looked to be about the same colour—a sort of pale yellowish brown.

"When did they hatch?" he asked.

"Early this morning," said Senneck.

"How long will it be before they're old enough to fly?"

"At least two months, but I will be able to leave them in the nest far sooner than that."

Erian felt a strange sense of peace spread through his body. "So we can start looking for the weapon soon?"

"Yes, although I do not know why you have not sought it yourself before now."

"I couldn't do it on my own," Erian said simply. "You've been with me all this way; I can't end the journey without you."

"Well." Senneck sighed. "Soon I shall be able to help you end it. My chicks' eyes will open in less than a week, and when that happens I will leave them and come with you."

Erian sat down with his back to the wall. "Gods, it's been so long. I've wandered a fair way, but I never saw anything on this island except plants and rocks. Where would we start looking?"

"I have had plenty of time to think of that," said Senneck. "We shall try the mountain."

Erian rubbed his chin. "The mountain . . ."

"It is the most obvious landmark on the island, and the most likely place your ancestors would have chosen."

Erian began to get excited. "Of course! It makes perfect sense . . . I thought of trying to climb it before, but I didn't want to go too far or try and go up there by myself."

Senneck made a crooning sound in her throat and nosed at

her sleeping young. "You have been patient for a long time, Erian, and I am proud of that. Be patient a little longer, and when we are ready we shall go to the mountain."

Erian stood up and bowed to her. "I'll be ready."

Three and a half months had been a long time to wait, but after the first few weeks it had ceased to feel like waiting, and the weapon had faded to the back of Erian's mind while he concerned himself with other things.

But the week that followed the hatching changed all that. Suddenly, the search for the weapon wasn't a distant prospect any more but an immediate one. He found himself counting the days, unable to focus on what he was doing. He visited Senneck at every opportunity, and while he said he was only coming to see the chicks, he knew he was really checking to see if their eyes had opened yet, if perhaps the time would come early.

The chicks grew with astonishing speed; sometimes Erian became half-convinced that they were larger in the evening than they had been that morning. At first they were feeble, too weak to do anything except drag themselves very slowly toward their mother's beak to accept the food she offered them. But after a few days they were strong enough to begin trying to stand up, gathering their little limbs under their bellies and pushing to lever themselves upright. They became more vocal, too; when Erian came to bring them food he would hear their high, piping voices calling eagerly from inside the hut. It was an odd feeling for him; sometimes he almost started to think of himself as a father to them, though male griffins never took an active role in raising chicks.

One day toward the end of the week, the chicks, now strong enough to begin crawling, strayed out of the nest. Senneck hauled the female back, but the male was out of her reach. Erian was there, though, and he hesitantly reached toward the chick.

"Bring him back," said Senneck.

Erian smiled and gently lifted the chick into his arms, cradling him against his chest. The chick wriggled and squeaked, but he was used to the scent of this human and his squeaks were sounds of protest rather than fear. Erian stroked his head, marvelling at how soft the downy fluff felt against his fingers. The chick nibbled his hand.

"Aren't you brave?" Erian murmured. "You're not afraid of

anything, are you? Well, you're too young to know what danger is, aren't you?"

The chick raised his head and peered myopically at him. His eyes were filmy gold.

Erian gaped. "Senneck! Senneck, his eyes are open!"

Senneck peacefully clicked her beak. "What colour are they?"

"Gold." Erian stroked the chick again. "I wish I could give him a name. I know what I'd call him."

"What name would you give him, then?" said Senneck.

"I'd call him Rannagon," said Erian.

"Not a griffish name," said Senneck. "But a worthy name," she added.

"I'd call my own son that." Erian carried the chick back to the nest and put him down beside his sister. "So . . ." He gave Senneck an imploring look.

She yawned. "By tomorrow, the female's eyes will have opened as well. And I am tired of this tiny hut. Tomorrow, you and I shall begin our search. Be ready; have food to bring."

Erian straightened up, grinning broadly. "I will, Senneck. I certainly will."

She chirped her amusement. "Go, then."

Erian left the hut for his own, his heart pounding. After so long, he could barely comprehend that the wait was finally over. One sentence, and it was done. And even though he had had so much time, he hadn't stopped once to think of what he would do when they were ready to begin.

He had gathered some shellfish from the rocks down by the shore and had managed to dry the meat along with some goat and fish. He gathered up these emergency rations along with some nuts and a dried apple, and wrapped them in a makeshift bag he had made from a crudely tanned goatskin. His feet were tough now, but he had devoted a chunk of his spare time to trying to make a pair of boots. His experiments had been less than successful, but he had cut some strips of leather to wrap around his feet. They would have to do.

Other than that, he gathered his bow and arrows and his sword, and laid them out ready for the morning along with his cherished water bottle, which he had bought in the marketplace at Malvern. That should be enough.

He slept very little that night.

* * *

Erian rose at dawn and gathered his belongings. He ate a quick meal of melon and some fish left over from the previous night, and left his hut. Outside, he found Senneck already waiting for him in the grey light.

"How long have you been here?"

"A little time," she answered. "I could not sleep."

It was odd to see her standing up after such a long time. "What about the chicks?"

"I left them sleeping. They will be safe; I have taken precautions."

She had dragged a heavy log over to the hut's entrance to block it and had piled sand over the top of that. She had used more sand to cover the holes in the walls. The chicks would never be able to escape the hut, and predators . . . well, Erian had been over most of the island and had never seen any predators beyond a weasel or two. The chicks should be safe.

He straightened up and tried to contain himself. "Shall we go?"

She came closer and pushed against him with her head. "Climb onto my back, and we shall fly to the mountain."

Erian obeyed. It felt strange and clumsy to be on her back again, and though he still remembered how to balance properly, he had the nagging feeling that he was doing it wrongly. Senneck was obviously in the same situation; she stumbled a little as he shifted about, and for a moment she sagged downward. But she recovered herself and ruffled her wings. "It is a short flight," she said, in answer to his unspoken question. "I shall not have trouble. Hold on."

She took off, and Erian held on as she flew upward to the mountain. Closer up, it looked much taller and more craggy than he had thought, full of spurs and fissures that had been invisible from the ground. Senneck spiralled higher until she was close to the peak and then began her descent.

She landed on a rare level spot on the mountainside; it looked like a goat track and was so narrow that Senneck had to grip a nearby boulder with her talons to keep herself from sliding off it.

"Get off," she said tersely.

Erian half-fell off her back, landing awkwardly on the path, and instantly lost his balance. He teetered on the edge, and then Senneck's beak shot out, hooking the back of his tunic. She wrenched him toward her, and he fell hard against the rocks by the path, breathless and dizzy.

"Are you hurt?"

Erian got up, wobbling a little. "Ow. Gods, that was close." He rubbed his head; he had hit it on a rock, and there was a bruise already forming under his hair. "You saved my life, Senneck."

She clicked her beak. "As is expected of me. Can you walk?"

"Of course. Did you see something?"

"This path," said Senneck. "Perhaps it leads somewhere. Do you think you can follow it safely?"

Erian looked ahead. "Well . . . it's narrow, but there are plenty of handholds. I think I'll be safe."

"Good." Senneck shifted awkwardly, still half-on and half-off the path. "This perch is too narrow for me. I will take off again and follow you from the air. If you are in difficulty, I will help."

Erian didn't like the idea, but he nodded anyway. "I'll see where it leads."

Senneck thrust away from the mountainside, dislodging several large chunks of rock and a shower of dirt. She found her wings and soared over the mountain, and Erian took a deep breath and began to walk. He placed each foot carefully and kept one hand on the rocks heaped to the side, ready to grab on if he lost his balance again.

The path was indeed tiny, and far from well used; several times it vanished altogether, and he had to clamber over fallen rocks or dirt to find it again. At other times it became so narrow that he had to put one foot directly in front of the other, as if he was trying to walk on a tightrope. Before long he was breathless and sweating, his fingers bruised from the times when he had had to snatch at the rocks to stop himself from falling, and his shins covered in cuts and grazes. His feet hurt inside their makeshift wrappings.

But while the path may have been difficult to use, it never petered out altogether, even after he had thought he had lost it more than once. It always reappeared, gradually winding its way up the mountain toward the peak.

Every so often, Erian glanced up to see Senneck flying

overhead. She looked very far away, but he knew that if she
thought he needed help she could reach him in an instant. It
helped to comfort him and keep him going. But still the path
went on, and he had no idea when it would end and whether it
was leading to anything.

But this had to be where the weapon was. Senneck was
right: where else would his ancestors have hidden it? What else
on this island looked like a landmark? What else reached this
high into the sky—toward the sun, and Gryphus?

As if to encourage him, the sun rose as he climbed, growing
brighter and brighter from behind the mountain until it had set
its peak ablaze with pure red and golden light. Erian, struggling
on through a clump of spiny bushes, saw it and felt awe burn
in his chest.

"Gryphus, guide me," he prayed.

A distant call from Senneck reminded him of the task at
hand, and he forced himself to look down again. He was nearly
at the peak of the mountain now. The rocks here were a pale
golden colour, flecked with silver. Ahead, he saw the path
widen and sighed in relief.

Once he had gone some way further, the path suddenly took
a sharp upturn. Erian paused briefly to rest and then forged on
up it, gritting his teeth with the effort.

The path grew yet steeper. Before long he found himself
almost climbing it, hauling himself up on the rocks that pro-
truded from the mountainside. When he tried to put his foot
on the path itself, the sandy soil gave way and his leg thrust
straight downward, pulling him off balance. For a few heart-
stopping seconds he scrabbled for a foothold, before he mercifully found one and pulled himself to safety, where he held on
for a good long moment, gasping in shock.

A little while after that, he was ready to go on.

It seemed the path would never level out again. But, finally,
he thrust upward with a hand and found a clump of grass hanging over a ledge. He grabbed hold of it, paused to take a deep
breath and pulled. A quick and rough struggle hauled him up
and over, onto a flat spot at the base of a heap of rocks, just wide
enough for him to lie down on. He used it for just that purpose,
his nose ground into the dirt, and wheezed.

There was a sudden loud thud from above him, and he

started up, but it was only Senneck, preched on top of the rock heap and looking down at him.

"Erian, are you hurt?"

Erian sat with his back to the rocks, his head pounding. "Exhausted."

"I think this is as far as the path goes," said Senneck, her voice sounding rather distant through the thudding in his ears.

Erian grunted a response and wiped the sweat off his face with a grubby hand. "All . . . right," he mumbled a little while later, and reluctantly stood up.

Senneck was right, the path ended there. He climbed around the rock heap but found nothing. "Why in Gryphus' name would goats want to come up here?" he said aloud, in irritable tones, before deciding to try the other side of the heap. Might as well, after coming all this way.

And that was where he found the entrance.

It was small, just a gap in the rocks only large enough for his head to fit through. He clung to the edge and peered in, and the breeze coming from inside instantly told him that there was a space beyond it.

His heart beat fast. "Senneck, I've found something."

She climbed over to look, and was quick to see what he had seen. "There is a cave beyond these rocks," she declared.

Erian's excitement mounted again. "This must be it! I'll see if I can fit!"

He ignored Senneck's protest and pushed forward, thrusting himself into the gap. He managed to fit his head and shoulders in, wedging them between two rocks with difficulty, but the gap became much narrower beyond them, and he became stuck almost instantly. He managed to pull back out, after much swearing and a moment of panic, and leant against the rocks, red faced. "Godsdamnit!"

"Move away, Erian," Senneck snapped. "I will clear away the rocks, but you must not get in the way."

Erian hastily obeyed. Once she was satisfied that he was out of harm's way, Senneck climbed a little further down the heap and levered at one of the large rocks with her talons. It shifted, and she hissed and wrenched at it. A moment later it came free, and she sent it tumbling down the mountainside. A good number of other rocks went with it.

Erian coughed in the cloud of dust. "Is that it? Did you do it?"

Senneck flicked her tail to clear the air with her feathery fan. "The hole is larger. Try again, but with care. There may be loose rocks."

Erian didn't need any further prompting. He hurried back and found that the gap was indeed larger, more than large enough for him to fit. He climbed through it without a pause. Beyond, to his astonishment, there was . . . light.

The rock heap had been covering the entrance to a cave in the mountain. Erian went in, wonderstruck. There was light inside—daylight. There had to be another way out, and thank Gryphus, he wouldn't be needing a torch.

"Erian!" Senneck's voice came from outside. "What have you found?"

Erian turned back, "Senneck, it's a cave! Come and look!"

"I cannot fit through that hole." Her voice drifted back. "Wait, and I shall force a way through."

Erian took shelter just inside the entrance while she pushed the rocks away, and saw something that made his heart leap. A carving in the stone.

He reached out to touch it, brushing the dust and sand away. It was a simple symbol, at about eye height, and from how worn it was he could tell it had been there for centuries. Nevertheless, he recognised it, and his hand went to the amulet around his neck.

Outside, the sunlight was suddenly cut off with a crash. But it reappeared a moment later, and he saw a shower of rocks fall away to his left, in a landslide that exposed the cave entrance entirely.

Moments later Senneck appeared, coughing irritably. "Erian."

Erian grinned at her and backed further into the cave. "Senneck, look at this! See? There, cut into the rock! It's a sunwheel! Senneck, we've found the place!"

Senneck squeezed into the cave. Once she was inside she looked at the spot he was indicating and hissed softly in surprise. "The symbol of your people. Perhaps Kraal was right after all."

Erian ducked past her and touched it. "Of course he was. This *is* the Island of the Sun, and this cave must be where the weapon is. You were right."

"Let us explore the cave," said Senneck. "We shall find out soon enough."

"Yes, of course," said Erian. As he turned to go after her, his eye was caught by something else. There was another carving, on the opposite side of the entrance to the sunwheel. He examined it, puzzled. The symbol looked vaguely familiar.

Senneck was already pressing deeper into the cave. "Erian, come!" she called. "Do you want to search for this weapon, or do you not?"

Erian shook himself and went after her. It didn't matter what the symbol was; he had important things to do.

Behind him, the sun shone into the cave. It illuminated the sunwheel, filling its simple lines with shadow. The other symbol, though, stayed in darkness.

It was a triple spiral.

The cave didn't look like anything much, at least on the surface. It was small and low-ceilinged and vaguely round, lined with jagged rocks. Someone had painted images on the walls, but time had faded them to little more than shades of brown and grey.

There was a hole in the centre of the roof, and the risen sun shone through it. It seemed to glow with an otherwordly light, turning everything it touched to gold, and when Erian saw it he knew. This was where the sun touched the earth.

Without even knowing what he was doing, he took his sword from his back and laid it down in front of the heap of rocks where the sun glowed. Then he knelt before it, bowing his head.

"Gryphus," he murmured aloud. "I'm sorry I doubted you. I *know* this is your home. I *know* it is. This is where you wanted me to go. Gryphus, guide me. Help me. Show me the way to destroy the Cursed One. If I am *Aeai ran kai*, your chosen warrior, then give me the power I need to win this struggle. Give me the weapon, so that I can confront *Kraeai kran ae* and put a stop to his evil forever. Gryphus, I am yours. Please, help me. Give me the weapon and I swear I will use it to do your will. Gryphus, please answer me . . . *Help me.*"

He kept his head bowed once his prayer was complete, and waited. He knew he had already said everything he had to say, and done everything he had been asked to. Now all he could do was wait for Gryphus to answer him.

But no reply came.

Still, Erian waited.

After a long moment, he dared to look up. Nothing had changed, but the sunlight looked somehow brighter. Or perhaps he was only imagining it.

But nothing had happened. Gryphus had not answered his prayer.

Erian let out a low, miserable sigh. He opened his mouth to say something else, but in that moment he saw movement, and froze. Something was up on the rock heap, something alive.

"Gryphus?" he breathed.

The thing moved again; he could hear scrabbling at the rock. Then it appeared, rising over the top like the sun rising over the mountain, silhouetted in black against the light.

It was a rabbit.

Erian, seeing the little animal pause to comb its ears, groaned aloud.

The rabbit froze for an instant as it saw him, and then bolted. It leapt from the top of the rock heap and ran past Erian, toward the cave entrance, in a blind panic. Erian turned and saw it bound across the floor before Senneck rose up from beside the entrance and pounced. She flicked the rabbit upward with her talons and caught it in her beak, and then swallowed it in a single go.

Erian relaxed. "What in Gryphus' name was that thing doing in here? Oh, who cares? Senneck, I—"

Senneck didn't seem to hear him. She sat back and scratched her throat with her talon, gulping slightly as the rabbit went down. And then she stopped dead. Her eyes went wide with shock, and she sat there, one forepaw still raised.

"Senneck?" said Erian. "Are you all right?"

The brown griffin stood up abruptly, planting her paws well apart on the floor. There was a rigidity about her that looked strangely familiar to Erian, but her eyes had a fixed, staring quality about them. She opened her beak, and a horrible gagging noise came out.

Erian stepped toward her. "Senneck! Oh no! What's happening? Senneck, are you choking? What should I do? Senneck!"

Senneck looked straight through him. She took several jerky

steps forward, toward the rock pile, beak still wide open. She certainly looked as if she was choking; the sick sounds from her throat grew louder and harsher, until they had an almost metallic edge to them, and she kept her neck stiffly extended and her beak open, saliva dripping from its tip.

Erian was panicking. He wanted to help her, but he didn't know how, and he knew that if he came too close while she was distressed she could attack him. But he had to do something.

"Senneck! Senneck, please . . ."

Senneck stopped. She made another strangled rasping noise and then began to rock gently back and forth, tail lashing. A faint gold light appeared around her body and then grew brighter and brighter, unbearably, until it outshone the sunlight coming in through the roof.

Erian gaped and then wisely dived for cover as the light gathered itself in Senneck's throat.

He hit the floor and covered his head with his arms as the light shot from her beak, and a heartbeat later a blast of pure gold seared into his eyelids and he was consumed by heat.

The sound of it was indescribable. A rushing and roaring, like fire but a hundred times louder, mingled with a high sound like a voice singing a single note. A hot metal smell burned in Erian's nose, but behind that there was another scent—a sweet, wild, wonderful scent that made him think of Elkin and Senneck and a warm home full of love and children running about him.

The light grew more and more intense, covering him like a blanket of flames. He felt as if it was burning him alive, turning his entire body to ashes. But, strangely, it didn't hurt.

The roaring grew louder . . .

Erian was terrified, and yet, somehow, somehow he loved it. The light filled him with a hot passion, like lust or hate or joy—some powerful emotion that could change the world. He felt as if it was killing him, but he loved it, wanted it, *needed* it, and nothing else mattered, nothing . . .

When the light and the heat began to die, he wanted to scream or cry. It was over. It was gone. He was alone.

He came back to his senses to find himself lying on his face on the cave floor, shivering and sobbing. The light was gone, and so was the heat. Everything was as it should be.

He dragged himself to his feet and tried to see.

"Senneck?"

His voice sounded shaky and not like him.

He staggered forward.

"Senneck?"

She was lying in front of the rock heap, breathing slowly. Erian went to her side to see if she was hurt, but as he reached her, he stopped and looked stupidly around.

The cave floor was covered in flowers. They were everywhere, growing in all different colours, fresh leaves and bright blooms reaching up to his ankles.

"What?"

Erian decided to ignore them for the moment and crouched by Senneck, touching her neck. She was warm and alive, and her eyes were half-open.

"Senneck," he said. "Wake up. Please, wake up."

She opened an eye very slowly.

Erian rubbed her head with his knuckles. "Senneck. Can you talk to me? Are you all right?"

It took a lot of effort, but the brown griffin finally roused herself and got up. She shook herself vigorously and looked at him. "Erian," she said, and her voice sounded tired but wonderfully normal.

"Senneck." Erian sighed in relief. "What in Gryphus' name happened?"

She was looking around at the flowers. "Where did these come from?"

"I don't know. Senneck, what happened to you? What did you do?"

She shuddered. "I do not know. I know I used magic, but I do not understand why or how. I did not intend to use magic; I felt as if I was compelled to do it. But it was so powerful . . . a hundred times stronger than my own. I have never used such magic. Erian . . ." She looked at him. "I did not hurt you?"

"I don't think so. Senneck, do you know what that magic did?"

"I think it created these flowers," said Senneck. "But I do not think that is what it intended to do."

"Intended?"

"Yes." Senneck bit nervously at her flank. "I know that magic was not mine, and that it used me. But what for, I do not know."

Erian looked ahead of her, toward the rock heap. "You cast

it this way," he said, trying to keep his voice steady. "It must have gone here."

He walked forward, keeping himself in line with her body. Close to the rock heap, he nearly tripped over something buried in the flowers.

It was his sword. He lifted it out and clutched it tightly by the hilt. "Thank Gryphus; I completely forgot about it. Wait . . . Senneck!"

She came to see. "What is it?"

Erian turned the sword over to show her. The hilt looked the same, but the blade did not. It was covered in strange markings: odd rippling shapes, like water or wood grain.

"I don't remember them being there before," he said.

Senneck leant down and tapped the blade with her beak. "I know those markings. The sword was in the path of my magic," she said.

"What d'you mean?" said Erian.

"When an object is touched by magic, these marks appear upon it," said Senneck. "They show that magic has passed through it, infused it. Nature stores magic, but sometimes a griffin passes that magic on into something else, usually by accident."

Erian looked at the sword a moment longer. Then, without a word, he stepped forward and hugged Senneck tightly around the neck.

She nibbled at his back. "Erian? What are you doing?"

He let go and looked her in the eye. "Thank you, Senneck. You've done it."

"What have I done?" she asked blankly.

"You've created the weapon," said Erian. He touched the sword. "And it's this. My father's sword. You've made it magical, Senneck. Gryphus put his power into you, and you used it to do his will. This sword can destroy *Kraeai kran ae*."

Senneck blinked. "Are you certain?"

"Yes," Erian said immediately. "I've never been more certain in my life. This is why you came with me, Senneck. So you could make the weapon."

She thought about it for a moment. "I do not know if I have created anything. But that magic was outside of my control, and who can say what it may have done?"

"Look," said Erian. "*Kraeai kran ae* has magic, doesn't he?

That's what keeps him alive. This sword is full of magic now, Gryphus' magic. Good magic. It can destroy *his* power. Why else would Gryphus have given it to you? To us? So we can kill him! Don't you see?"

Senneck paused for a long moment. "Perhaps you are correct," she muttered. "It does not matter whether your god is real. The sword is infused with magic now." She broke off suddenly and then made a hacking, coughing sound that was probably a griffish laugh. "So you have your magical sword after all, Erian Rannagonson."

Erian's eyes were wide and fanatical. "Yes," he breathed. "And I can destroy him with it. And I will. Oh, I will. I'm coming, *Kraeai kran ae*. I'm coming, Shadow that Walks. And when I find you, you're dead."

24

Fatherhood

After the massacre of the griffiners in the Governor's Tower, it hadn't taken long for the rest of the city to fall under Arenadd's shadow. Goaded on and led by Saeddryn and the others, the local people who had already been secretly won over to Arenadd's side had risen up and attacked the city guard. Others had joined them—some of them brave men and women swayed by Arenadd's message, and others merely criminals with scores to settle. Arenadd didn't care which was which; followers of any sort were welcome. And followers were what he found in Fruitsheart . . . by the hundreds.

Once Saeddryn had led them to the tower and occupied it with their help, Arenadd went out into the city with Skandar and led the attack on the nearest guard stronghold. If Arenadd had been expecting anything when he and Skandar appeared down in the streets, it was not this.

People recognised them easily enough; he heard them shouting his name as he passed, and Skandar's, too. But when he reached the guard tower and the mob that surrounded it, what followed shocked him.

The people nearest the back of the mob saw him first. Some moved away to hide, but the others stayed where they were, staring at him as if they could hardly believe their eyes.

Arenadd inclined his head toward them, a little awkwardly.

"My name is Arenadd Taranisäii," he said, in Northern. "And this is Skandar. We've come to help."

There was silence, and then a man came forward. Arenadd touched his sickle, but the man did not attack. He stood for a moment, and then fell to his knees.

As if that was a signal, dozens of others threw themselves down at Arenadd's feet, abasing themselves as if he was an Eyrie Master, none of them saying a word.

"Get up," Arenadd said uncomfortably. "Please, get up. We have work to do."

The nearest of them obeyed, and the others followed. Then the man who had knelt first spoke.

"Lord Arenadd." He kept his head bowed, murmuring the words, but then he looked up at Arenadd's face and said it again. "Lord Arenadd. Master."

The others near at hand repeated it, and then the man suddenly turned to them, raising his fist into the air, and shouted.

"Lord Arenadd! Lord Arenadd!"

The shout was taken up by others, and others, and in an instant the mob surged forward, roaring Arenadd's name.

"Attack!" the man yelled, and now he was speaking Northern, shakily but with anger and determination. "Attack! Break down the doors! Kill the Southerners! Fight in the name of the dark griffin and the Shadow that Walks! *Fight!*"

Arenadd felt a hot, fierce triumph and confidence rush through his body like blood. He drew his sickle, still covered in griffiner blood, and pointed it at the tower. "Attack!" he echoed.

In an instant, Skandar obeyed. He screeched and surged forward, and people scattered out of his way. The dark griffin hit the doors head-on, and his beak impaled itself deep in the wood. He wrenched it free, taking a chunk the size of a man's head with it, and struck again and again, tearing at it. Blood oozed out of his wounds as he pulled back and then leapt, his huge muscles flexing. He hit the doors yet again, and they shattered into pieces. Wood scattered everywhere, but before the chunks had even hit the ground Skandar struggled over the remains of the barrier and into the tower. The mob charged after him.

Arenadd followed in the rear, but his sickle was not needed. The guards inside the tower were hopelessly outnumbered, and Skandar scattered them like chickens. Those who didn't die at his talons or break met their end at the hands of the rebels. None survived.

When the massacre was over, Arenadd directed his new followers to take weapons and armour and follow him back to the Governor's Tower.

They obeyed, forming themselves into a rough column behind him and Skandar. As they went up the main street of Fruitsheart, other people came to join them. Saeddryn opened the doors to the Governor's Tower, and Arenadd took them all inside with him.

"We have no enemies here," he told the astonished Saeddryn. "Only friends."

Later on, when things had calmed down somewhat and he had sent people to search through the tower for any survivors who might be hiding, he went looking for the man who had rallied the mob on his behalf and found him up on top of the walls. When he saw Arenadd coming, he stopped and knelt to him again.

"Please, get up," said Arenadd.

The man obeyed. "My lord Arenadd," he murmured reverentially.

Arenadd looked him up and down. He was strongly built but young—probably not much older than Torc—and quite well dressed.

"What's your name?" Arenadd asked.

"Iorwerth, master," said the man.

"You were a great help to me today," said Arenadd. "I wanted to say thank you."

Iorwerth bowed low. "It was nothing but my duty, master."

"You don't have to call me that. 'Sir' will be fine."

"Yes, sir."

"Good. Listen . . ." Arenadd paused. "You knew who I was when you saw me. How?"

Iorwerth's black eyes gleamed. "I knew before ye came here, sir, even before I heard one of yer friends talking about ye in a tavern and realised ye were in the city somewhere."

"Oh?" Arenadd was instantly curious. "How?"

"My father, sir," said Iorwerth. "He's a merchant. He was in Malvern, sir, on the day . . ." He looked at the ground. "On the day ye revealed yerself to us, m— sir. He saw what happened, when they tried to kill ye, sir. And he saw ye risen from the dead, sir. And he told me . . ."

"Yes?" said Arenadd.

Iorwerth looked up. "He said that ye were the one the Night God had sent and that when the time came we must all follow ye if we believed in her, sir."

Arenadd smiled. "You showed a lot of resolve and quick thinking today. And more than that, you showed loyalty."

"I am loyal to the Night God, sir," Iorwerth said fervently. "To follow ye is to follow her, and we all know that."

"It is, Iorwerth," said Arenadd. "And I know it, because I've seen her, and spoken to her."

Iorwerth's eyes widened. "Ye have, sir? Ye've seen her?"

"Yes. I've seen her." Arenadd fingered his beard. "She looks like a beautiful woman with black hair, and one of her eyes is the full moon. Iorwerth, I can see that you're a brave and resourceful man, and I need brave and resourceful men for what I have to do. If I'm going to destroy Malvern and drive the Southerners out, I'll need good followers, and men with the ability to help me lead them. Now that Fruitsheart has become my stronghold, it's time for me to start organising my followers, and I can't do that alone."

Iorwerth watched him keenly. "Yes, sir?"

"I've formed a council," said Arenadd. "As a reward for what you've done today, I want to offer you a place on that council."

Iorwerth gaped at him. "Ye want *me*?"

"I think you could do very well," Arenadd said mildly.

"But I'm just a—"

Arenadd chuckled. "Iorwerth, once upon a time I was the son of a boot maker and Skandar was killing criminals in an arena. If it comes to that, you're probably more highborn than I am. Now, will you accept a place on my council?"

Iorwerth bowed to him. "I'm yer own to command, sir."

"Thank you. Okay, let's go. We've got work to do."

Iorwerth fell into step beside him. "Sir?"

"Yes, Iorwerth?"

Iorwerth paused very briefly, as if to steel himself. "Sir, if I'm on yer council, then I can advise ye, can't I, sir?"

"You certainly can."

"Well then," Iorwerth said boldly. "I think ye should put archers on the walls, sir. If griffiners come, we need a way to defend ourselves."

Arenadd smiled. "Yes, I'd already thought of that."

"Of course, sir," said Iorwerth. "I thought ye had, but I wanted to be sure, sir."

Arenadd smiled again, internally. *I've made the right choice*, he thought. *Exactly the right choice.*

Later on, in the dining hall, he gathered together his new council. So far it included Skade, Saeddryn, Caedmon, Davyn, Rhodri and Iorwerth.

"Now then," he said. "Fruitsheart is ours. Iorwerth"—he glanced at him—"has sent men up to the walls to keep watch, but I doubt any griffiners will come here for a while. Even so, it's only prudent that we post some archers up there."

"I don't think there's many in the city, sir," said Saeddryn.

"I know, but there will be," said Arenadd. "We'll pick a few people who're interested and give them some training. It doesn't have to be much; all they'll have to do is frighten them away. The odds of a griffin being killed by an arrow aren't much. Anyway, the other thing we have to do is something Skandar and I can handle."

"What, sir?" said Saeddryn.

"Send a message to Nerth and the others, obviously," said Arenadd. "Skandar can take me to them quickly enough, and I'll tell them what happened."

"Good idea, sir," said Saeddryn. "Will ye be tellin' any of them to come here?"

"Not yet. We need to keep a few good men in hiding, away from us. If anything goes wrong, we can join them. And they can be a haven for anyone who can't fight. Anyway, moving on to another topic . . . I intend to stay here for a good while, as long as I can. The country needs to know where we are. If people know, they can come here to join us. We can build up an army here, and once we have enough numbers we'll be ready to move on. We'll conquer cities one by one, until the time comes for us to attack Malvern itself."

"It will work, sir," Iorwerth said resolutely. "There's not a man in Tara who won't fight for ye if he knows where ye are, sir."

"That's my hope, Iorwerth," said Arenadd. "But in the meantime . . . well, it's beyond obvious that Malvern will attack the instant they know we're here, and we have to be prepared for that. Now, Rhodri . . ."

They spent a good amount of time discussing defence tactics

and siege weapons before the coversation turned to Skade and
her mission.

"I can't say it's not a very big risk," said Arenadd. "Because
it is. But it's a risk we're going to take."

"Yes, sir," said Saeddryn. "I understand."

Arenadd looked at Iorwerth. "The others here already know
the plan, but I'll repeat it now for your sake. I kidnapped Lady
Elkin, and the Eyrie paid me a very hefty ransom to get her
back. I plan to use that ransom to buy our brothers in the South
back into freedom. I've asked Skade here to do it. But . . ." He
paused. "She hasn't agreed yet. Skade?"

Skade kept her eyes on his face for a long moment. Arenadd
wanted to say something, but he kept silent, waiting for her to
speak.

Finally, Skade spoke. "If you believe I am the one to do this,
then I will," she said.

Arenadd wanted to hug her. "Thank you, Skade. I know
you're the right one to do it."

"I agree," said Saeddryn.

She was probably very happy to know that Skade would be
leaving, Arenadd thought. He turned his attention to the rest of
the council. "What do you think?"

Rhodri frowned. "Why Skade, sir? Out of curiosity, why her?"

"Because the Southerners won't trade with our race, Rhodri,"
said Arenadd. "At least, not on equal terms. Skade looks like a
Southerner. More than that, she's beautiful and imposing. The slavers will probably fall over themselves to make a deal with her."

Skade gave her odd flat little laugh. "Men have always
thought with something other than their brains. Of course, I
will need protection."

"Yes, and that's what I want to discuss now," said Arenadd.

"I'll go with her, sir," said Rhodri.

"So will I, sir," said Iorwerth.

"Not you, Iorwerth," said Arenadd. "I need you here." *And
you haven't proven yourself yet.* "But you can go, Rhodri. I can
only afford to lose one of my council, and you're the best fighter
here—but we can't send just you. Who else would you suggest?"

Rhodri frowned. "Nerth would be a good choice, sir. He's
tough, an' he knows how t'handle a situation. There's a few
others with him in the Gorge who'd be good."

"He's right, sir," said Davyn.

"Yes . . ." Arenadd scratched his beard. "I can talk to Nerth when I get there and tell him to come here to meet up with Skade, along with a few others he thinks would be good. It'll be harder without them, but we have to send veterans, trusted men. But that will mean waiting longer than I wanted to."

"Can't be helped, sir," Rhodri said bluntly.

"I suspected as much. Well." Arenadd stood up. "The sooner the better. I'm going to go up and see if Skandar's rested enough. While I'm gone, you're in charge, Saeddryn. Here's what I want you to do . . ."

Saeddryn listened to his instructions and gave a curt nod when he was done. "Consider it done, sir."

"Good. Skade, stay by her. If anything happens, barricade yourself in the master bedroom and stay there. Rhodri, you and Davyn will protect her if there's danger. Caedmon, I want you to inspect the armoury and the pantries. Make a rough list of everything we've got. Torc, you're good at counting—have a look inside the treasury and estimate how much money is in there. Iorwerth, you can organise the defences with Davyn. Are there any questions?"

"No, sir," said Iorwerth.

"Excellent. Now." Arenadd nodded to them. "I shouldn't be gone long; I'll be back before moonrise at latest."

"Yes, sir." Saeddryn stood, too. "Give my greetings to the others at the Gorge, sir."

"I will."

Arenadd left for the griffin roost near the top of the tower. Skandar was there, tearing voraciously at the carcass of a dead griffin. His exertions that day had made him so hungry that he didn't pay the slightest attention to Arenadd's appearance and continued with his meal.

Arenadd sat down by the entrance and waited politely. Every so often the sound of tearing sinews made him wince.

The other griffin was more than half Skandar's size, but the dark griffin had already eaten well over half of it, and he utterly demolished the carcass before he finally had his fill and slumped down beside it, gagging a little.

Eventually, Arenadd had to break the silence. "Do you want to sleep now?"

Skandar opened one eye partway. "Tired," he said. As if to illustrate that, he opened his beak wide in a yawn.

Arenadd couldn't help himself; he yawned, too. "Aaaaah . . . ooh, that felt good. Well, I suppose you should rest before we do anything else. You did a lot today." He yawned again. "So did I. Get some rest, Skandar. I'll be right here."

Skandar said nothing. Arenadd smiled to himself and leant back against the wall. His partner had used a lot of magic today and fought for a long time.

I can wait for him, Arenadd thought. *There's nothing else I have to do just now . . .*

Moments later, he had slid into a doze.

And a dream.

The sky was the colour of a bruise, laced with blue lightning. Below, on the ground, it cast a ghastly dark light over the battlefield and the dead that lay there. He walked slowly through it, feeling no pain from his wounds. His heart was dead and silent in his chest, and he looked at the dead and felt nothing. They had joined him. They were at peace.

His sickle hung loosely from his hand, blood dripping slowly from its tip. It had killed many men today.

Above, Skandar circled, his mottled wings spread wide. As Arenadd looked up at him, the griffin let out a long, mournful cry.

Arenadd watched the crows begin to gather, and laughed until he cried.

The thump of Skandar's paws on the wooden floor woke him up. Arenadd sat up, blinking. "What . . . was I asleep?"

Skandar looked up from his grooming and clicked his beak in a businesslike way. "You sleep long," he said. "I sleep. Dream of war."

"You too, eh?" Arenadd got up and rubbed his back. "Ow. Damned thing. Do you feel better now?"

"Am strong," Skandar declared.

"Strong enough to travel again?"

Arenadd had already known that the griffin's pride wouldn't let him say anything other than what he said next.

"Am strong!" Skandar repeated. "But why leave? You say, this home now. Why go?"

"We'll be coming back. I just want to go to the mountains again, to talk to our friends there and tell them what happened. D'you want to go?"

Skandar appeared to think about it. "Mountain . . . where Hyrenna is."

"Yes, but I don't know if she'll be there."

"Go!" said Skandar. "We go, go now!"

"Are you sure?"

"Am sure!" Skandar snapped. "You come."

Arenadd climbed onto his partner's back and steadied himself. "Let's go, then."

Skandar braced himself and leapt into the shadows.

Even now, Arenadd was astonished by how fast Skandar could travel in the shadows. He held on and watched the darkness blur past them. They could have been flying at an almost leisurely pace but for the feeling of huge momentum. It made Arenadd feel a powerful sense of triumph and certainty, and pride and awe toward his partner. Skandar was far more powerful than he had seemed, and certainly more powerful than him. He should never forget that, he told himself.

The journey seemed to pass in no time at all. Skandar burst back into a night sky and immediately descended toward a spot of glowing fire. He was over Taranis Gorge, and he landed directly in the middle of the rebels' camp, sending them running in all directions. Nerth must have prepared them for a possible attack, because the initial panic didn't last long. In moments men were drawing their weapons, running to find easily defendable positions. Bows were appearing, too. Skandar, seeing them, screeched and lurched threateningly toward them.

Arenadd slid off his back and drew his sickle. "Peace!" he shouted, in Northern. "Peace, my friends! I am *Kraeai kran ae*, your master and friend! Peace!"

Most of them recognised his voice and sheathed their weapons. The rest looked uncertain and went back on their guard as Skandar rose up, beak wide open.

Arenadd ran to him. "Skandar, no! Don't attack. They're friends!"

Skandar dropped back onto his paws and glared at him. "Metal talons," he said. "Attack."

"They're just confused. Nerth!" Arenadd raised his voice as he dropped back into the Northern tongue. "Nerth, where are you? It's Arenadd and Skandar. Nerth!"

There was a moment of confusion among the men, and then a man came running to meet them.

"My lord!"

Arenadd relaxed. "Nerth, there you are."

Nerth turned to his followers. "Put up yer weapons, yer idiots! It's Lord Arenadd!"

They obeyed, and Nerth came to meet his master.

Arenadd put his sickle back into his belt. "Nerth."

Nerth bowed low. "My lord—my lord, I'm so sorry, they didn't realise who ye were. My lord, please don't blame them."

Arenadd realised the man was trembling. "Relax, Nerth!" he said. "If anything, I should be thanking you for having them all so well prepared. If I'd been an enemy, I'd be dead by now."

Nerth grinned in relief. "Thank ye, sir."

"Now." Arenadd looked at Skandar. "Skandar, calm down. We're safe. Nerth, can we sit down by the fire?"

"Of course, my lord!" Nerth quickly issued commands, and his friends hurried to obey. In moments Arenadd was sitting comfortably by the fire with Skandar, and food had been brought for both of them.

Nerth, however, didn't want to spend too much time on hospitality. "My lord," he said, sitting down beside Arenadd. "Why have ye come?"

"Just call me 'sir' if you really must," said Arenadd. "Skandar and I have come to bring news."

Nerth sat up straight. "Yes, sir. What is it, sir? What's happened?"

Arenadd paused. He could see Nerth's followers sitting or standing on the opposite side of the fire. Most of them were men who had joined at Warwick, and he even recognised one or two of them, including the man who had made the sickle for him. But all of them looked ragged now, toughened by their time in the wild. He smiled to himself. Nerth had done his work well. He had reminded them of who and what they truly were.

"Sir?" Nerth prompted.

Arenadd brought himself back to reality. "My news is good," he said.

Nerth grinned. "Sir?"

Arenadd gave a brief outline of the kidnap and ransom of Elkin, followed by the capture of Fruitsheart. The others listened intently, and he saw disbelieving grins spread over many faces.

Nerth's grin was widest of all. "So the war's begun, sir?" he said when Arenadd was done. "It's really begun, sir?"

"Malvern might not know it yet, but it's begun," said Arenadd. "The others are at Fruitsheart, preparing for a siege, but

Skandar and I came here to give you the news. Now it's your turn. Report, Nerth."

"I've a few things to report, sir," said Nerth. "Well . . . two things, mainly, sir. First, as ye can see, sir, we all made it here. I've been trainin' the men in fightin', an' teachin' 'em other things as well, sir. They're true darkmen again now, sir."

"That's wonderful to hear, Nerth," said Arenadd. "You've done everything I hoped for and more. Soon it'll be time for you to come back out of hiding and join the fight. Now, what else do you have to tell me?"

"Well, sir," Nerth grinned. "We've found Hyrenna."

Arenadd started. "What?"

"She was here, sir," said Nerth. "In the Gorge. She came here t'lay her eggs, sir. She's here now, sir."

"Where?" Arenadd said sharply.

"Not far away, sir. Shall I send someone t'get her, sir?"

"Yes. Immediately."

"Yes, sir." Nerth gestured at a woman near to him. "Difyr, ye know where t'find her. Be careful not t'startle her."

The woman bowed and dashed off.

Arenadd put his hands behind his head and leant back. "Hyrenna. By the Night God, I never thought I would see her again. Is she well?"

"Yes, sir. I don't speak much griffish, sir, but I could tell her a little." Nerth paused and sighed. "I told her Arddryn was dead, sir. I dunno if she understood, sir, but I tried."

"Did she react?"

"Not much, sir. I mean, I'm not really sure, sir."

Arenadd looked into the fire. "I think she probably knew she wasn't going to see Arddryn alive again. What about her eggs, though? Have they hatched?"

"Yes, sir. I've seen the chicks, sir. Three of them, sir. Very healthy,"

Arenadd glanced at Skandar. "You hear that, Skandar? You're a father."

Skandar looked blankly at him. "Father?"

"I'm sure Hyrenna will tell you when she gets here."

Arenadd chewed at the spit-roasted venison Nerth had given him, and settled down to wait.

A little while later, he heard a swish of wings from over-head and stood up. Beside him Skandar rose, too, spreading his wings in readiness to attack. The men around the fire moved hastily out of the way, and an instant later Hyrenna landed.

Skandar made a strangled snarling sound and ran at her. She reared up in response, talons extended and beak open.

"Skandar, don't!" Arenadd yelled.

The two griffins struck each other, hard. Hyrenna lurched backward and nearly fell, but she recovered herself and pushed toward Skandar, wrestling with him. The two griffins struggled, biting at each other's shoulders and shoving with their chests, making odd high chirping sounds all the while. For a while it looked like Skandar was winning, but then he suddenly backed off and the two griffins relaxed, chirping and grooming each other. Arenadd realised that they were speaking griffish as griffins did among themselves when no humans were part of the conversation—too quickly and primitively for any human to understand except on the most basic level.

Arenadd didn't need to understand anyway. They were only saying the same kind of things humans said when meeting each other, and it was none of his business.

He waited politely until they had calmed down and Hyrenna finally turned her attention to him.

He bowed low. "Hyrenna. I'm honoured to meet you again."

The grey and rust-brown griffin came closer. She looked older than he remembered, but fitter as well. She was much younger than Arddryn had been, only middle-aged by griffish standards.

She stood over him for a moment, taking in his sight and scent. "Arenadd Taranisäii. I did not think I would see you again at all."

Arenadd bowed again. "I can't say anything to make it better, Hyrenna. All I can say is that I'm sorry."

Hyrenna hissed. "Sorry! What does that mean to me, human? You abandoned us. Abandoned Arddryn, your protector and friend, your own blood relative! She believed you had fled because you did not want to fight, because you were either a coward or a traitor. She died believing that. Tell me, Arenadd: what can 'sorry' do to undo that?"

Arenadd stared at his boots. "Nothing, Hyrenna, and I know it."

"Well then." She sat back on her haunches, regarding him through her great orange eyes. The white markings around them and her beak made her face look like a mask. "If you know it, then what can you offer me?"

Arenadd clasped his hands together. "I have been punished for what I did to you and Arddryn, Hyrenna," he said hoarsely. "Over and over again. But I set Saeddryn free, and her friends. They're safe."

Hyrenna clicked her beak. "Saeddryn lives?"

"Yes. She's in Fruitsheart, with Skade."

Hyrenna stood up. "Why?" she said sharply. "What is she doing there? What have you done?"

"What Arddryn wanted me to do," said Arenadd. "Begun the war."

The brown griffin stared at him. "The war—how? What have you done to begin it?"

"Warwick fell to us," Arenadd said briefly. "Most of the men here joined us there. Skandar and I kidnapped the Eyrie Mistress and held her for ransom—successfully. Now we've conquered Fruitsheart, and I intend to make it my stronghold, at least to begin with. I'm gathering followers, and right now they're preparing for when the Eyrie sends griffiners to take the city back. If Malvern wants to keep control of this land, it'll have to go through me first."

Hyrenna looked at Skandar. "Is this true?" she said. "Skandar, is your human telling the truth?"

Skandar blinked lazily. "Human tell truth," he said. "We fight, many times. Kill many. See!" He raised his wings, showing the fresh scars on his flanks. "Have new territory," he added. "Good territory. Soon, will have even bigger territory. Will be greatest. Human promise it. We fight, together. Great warriors!"

Hyrenna looked at him, then at Arenadd, her tail flicking rapidly. "The war . . . you have already begun it, and I did not know . . . Arddryn would have . . ."

"I know she would have wanted to see this," said Arenadd. "And I'm sorry she didn't. But I'm sure her spirit knows, wherever it is now."

Hyrenna stood very still. For a moment Arenadd expected some sort of outburst from her, but in the end she only let out a great sigh and lay down on her belly. "Then Arddryn's faith in you was not misplaced," she said. "And nor was mine in Skandar. Skandar—" She stood up abruptly, looking at him. "Skandar, I have something to show you."

Skandar blinked. "Show?"

"I have taught you to speak griffish properly," Hyrenna said acidly. "You may be powerful, but you are also lazy. Now, come to me, and see."

Difyr, the woman sent to find Hyrenna, emerged into the circle of firelight, holding a large bundle in her arms—three griffin chicks, squirming and hissing angrily. When they saw their mother they broke free and scuttled over to her. She spread her wings over them, and they hid behind her legs, chirping.

Hyrenna nudged them toward Skandar. "See here, Skandar, what you have given me. These are your three sons. All of them are sturdy and strong, and all bear your colours."

Skandar looked at the three squalling chicks. "Son?" he said blankly.

"Hatched from the eggs we made," said Hyrenna.

Skandar lowered his head to look at them. One of the chicks boldly reared up and bit at his father's huge black beak, his own tiny beak tapping on its hard and pitted surface. Skandar peered at him as if he had no idea of what he was looking at.

Arenadd, watching, could easily tell that the chicks were Skandar's sons. Their downy feathers were silver, and all of them had black on them somewhere: one had the same night-coloured hindquarters as his father, another had the same black cap and ear tufts, and the third had black scattered through the feathers on his tiny chest.

Seeing them scurry around their father, Arenadd felt a deep and painful sadness grow inside his chest.

My best friend is a father, he thought. *Even if he never cares. And he'll never know how much he has compared to me. His life, his soul, his heart . . . his family.*

He looked away, shuddering. The bitter truth had been with him for a long time, but he had never properly acknowledged it until now.

The Night God gave me power and status and protection, but she took from me as well. She took my life and my heart . . . and she made me sterile. I know it. I'm the Master of Death, and what does the Master of Death know about making life? No, I'm the Night God's creature now. And the Night God can't give life—only take it away.

25

Skade's Quest

After he had seen his young, Skandar wanted to leave. But Arenadd had more to say to Hyrenna. The grey-and-orange griffin was more than eager to listen.

"I want to know everything," she told him. "Speak, Arenadd. Hold nothing back."

So Arenadd did. He outlined everything that had happened so far, in as much detail as he could. She took a lot of interest in the plans he had made, particularly with regards to Skade's quest to buy the slaves.

"It will be dangerous," she observed. "Are you certain you wish to take that risk? After all, it would not be your own life you would be putting in danger."

"I am," said Arenadd. "And so is Skade. If she has enough protection, she'll be fine."

"Very well, but how much protection can you provide?" said Hyrenna. "Too large an escort would draw too much attention."

Arenadd looked up at her. "Yes. But it's not size that counts; it's quality. Hyrenna . . ."

"Yes?"

"Hyrenna, finding you again changes a lot," said Arenadd. "You see, the biggest problem I can see is this: Skade will be carrying a lot of money. A *lot*. And people are going to wonder just how she came across it and just who she is. They'll ask questions, and I'm not sure Skade can answer all of them."

"How do you plan to guard against this, then?" said Hyrenna.

"Well . . ." Arenadd took a deep breath. "Something has occurred to me. You see, everyone gets asked questions. There's always someone willing to poke their nose where it's not wanted; there's always curiosity. But there's one kind of person who's immune to that. Someone no commoner would ever question. Someone everyone in Cymria respects as a matter of course."

Hyrenna clicked her beak. "You want Skade to pose as a griffiner," she said. "But you have no griffin to send with her."

"No," Arenadd said slowly, not looking away from her. "I don't . . . do I?"

Hyrenna met his gaze for a few moments and then looked away. "I will not go. I will not leave my young. They are not ready to care for themselves."

"No," said Arenadd. "But I can look after them."

Without any warning, Hyrenna started up. "You!" she hissed. "You, a human, care for my chicks?"

Arenadd forced himself not to back away. "Skandar could protect them, and I could bring them food. After all"—he was careful to keep any trace of sarcasm out of his voice—"I'm only a human, but everybody knows humans are very good at fetching and carrying."

Hyrenna sat still for a time, tail twitching. Finally, she said, "You do not need to do this now, surely. These slaves have been slaves all their lives—do you truly believe that they can fight for you? They would be nothing but a burden."

"But I have to set them free," said Arenadd.

"Then do so once the war is over!" said Hyrenna. "You will have time then."

"No," said Arenadd. "Do you want to know why, Hyrenna?"

"Tell me," she snapped.

"Once the South knows about what we're doing, what do you think they're going to do, Hyrenna? If darkmen are rebelling in the North, why not the South as well? You know how they think. In some places there are more slaves than free men— how do you think the Southerners will react? They'll kill them. Whether officially or unofficially, they'll find ways to stop them ever escaping or fighting back. I know what happens to slaves who've ceased to be useful. And I can't let that happen because of me."

"So you would send me south, away from the fighting, while Arddryn's followers face death here?" said Hyrenna. "Is that your plan?"

"No. My plan is for you to handle a very dangerous mission that will take all your strength and courage. And which, if it succeeds, will do the very thing Arddryn spent her whole life trying to achieve: set our people free."

Hyrenna glared at him, but he knew he had backed her into a corner. Now all he had to do was wait while she came to a decision.

A nervous protracted silence followed. A few people dared come back toward the fire. Even the chicks looked apprehensive.

Finally, Hyrenna raised her head and looked down on him. "You have made me an offer, and here is mine," she said. "I will go south with this female . . . this *Skade*. I will protect her and advise her. While she is with me, nothing shall ever hurt her. In return, you will fight this war. You will never surrender, never give way, never show mercy. And you will care for my young. You will protect them with your life. You will never let them be cold or hungry or frightened for an instant. If I return and find one of them injured or dead, I will tear you to pieces. Do you understand?"

Arenadd bowed to her. "Yes."

She rose up, frighteningly large. "I said, do you understand?"

"Yes," he said, more loudly. "I understand completely. You have my word."

"Good," she said. "And this is for Arddryn."

Her talons hit him in the chest, and an instant later everything rushed past him sideways and he slammed into a tree. Pain overwhelmed his senses, and he fainted.

He woke up some unknown time later and found himself lying on a heap of straw in Skandar's nest. His back was agony, and his head was a solid ball of pain.

He groaned and mumbled something, and a moment later Skandar was there, nudging at him in a well-meaning way. "Human hurt?"

Arenadd stirred. "Well, I can . . . still move my legs," he mumbled. "I think that's a good sign."

"Hyrenna hit you," Skandar said matter-of-factly.

"Oh . . . really?" Arenadd tried to raise his head. "You didn't attack her, did you?"

Skandar looked away. "Want to," he muttered resentfully. "Not strong enough. Hyrenna say take you and go; she come later."

"She's . . . coming? Ooh, what a lucky lad I am." Arenadd slumped back. "Skandar, could you find Skade? I need someone to help me up."

"Help!" Skandar snorted. "Not need that. *I* help."

Arenadd grasped the griffin's beak, and Skandar lifted him. He found his feet and managed to stay on them, though putting weight on them was extremely painful.

"Gods, what did she do to me?" he moaned. "I feel like I've been hit by an oxcart."

Skandar helped him toward the door, moving slowly. As they reached it, Skade appeared. She paused for an instant and then ran toward them.

"Arenadd! Skandar! What—Arenadd, are you hurt?"

Arenadd let go of Skandar's beak as she reached out for him, and he collapsed into her arms.

She held him up. "Oh, by the sky . . . what happened? Can you walk?"

Arenadd clung to her shoulder to try to hold himself up. His legs felt weak and useless. "My back," he said. "Can you help me to a bed?"

She did, carrying him into the next room and laying him down on the bed, where she tried her best to make him comfortable, asking questions all the while.

"How did this happen? Will you recover? Did you go to Nerth?"

Arenadd blinked; his eyelids felt heavy. "I've found you an escort," he mumbled.

"An escort? You mean Nerth agreed to come?"

"No. Hyrenna."

"Hyrenna? The griffin? What—"

"You're going as a griffiner," said Arenadd. "I'll . . . explain later."

"But how were you hurt?" said Skade. "Were you attacked?"

Arenadd was about to tell her that Hyrenna had attacked him, but at the last moment he realised that if she knew, it would make it very difficult for her to work with her new accomplice.

"No. Don't worry, Skade. It's not important. I fell over. Hit my back on a rock. I'll be fine."

Skade still looked concerned. "Rest, then. If there is nothing you must tell us immediately . . ."

"One thing," said Arenadd. "Hyrenna is coming. Tell the sentries. She's got orange-brown wings with white mottling. Tell them not to attack her."

"I will," said Skade. "Rest now, Arenadd. I will see to it."

He nodded vaguely and let her leave. After she had gone, he lay still and tried to rest. He worried for a little while that the pain in his back would stop him from sleeping, but his lingering exhaustion was strong enough to override it, and he slid into an uneasy sleep.

When he woke up early the next morning, the pain had gone. Or at least it seemed to have gone. It came back the instant he tried to move, only now moving was much more difficult. All his damaged joints and muscles had stiffened horribly, and for a few awful moments he thought he was paralysed. When he found out that he wasn't, the revelation did very little to cheer him up.

Skade had been asleep beside him but was up in a moment, urging him to stay in bed until he was better. Arenadd was tempted to give in to her, but he knew he couldn't afford to lose any time. Once she had realised he wouldn't be persuaded, Skade reluctantly found a stick for him and helped him out of the room.

Walking slowly and supporting himself with the stick, Arenadd went to find Saeddryn, who was busy training archers. She looked concerned when she saw him.

"Sir, what happened?"

Arenadd tried to straighten up, and cringed. "Aah! Oh gods, that was a bad idea . . . don't worry, I'll be fine in a day or so. Just a few torn muscles. How are things?"

"Not too bad," said Saeddryn. "We've done a search of the tower. Found a few Southerners hiding; they've been dealt with, don't worry. This lot are learnin' all right, an' Iorwerth already has a squad up on the walls. He's a good man, that Iorwerth. Ye picked him well, sir. Now, what's yer own news, sir? Did ye go t'the Gorge?"

"Yes. Nerth's there, and all the others he took with him. He's got them well trained and very loyal to him. I gave him the news, and he had some for me. Saeddryn, Hyrenna's alive. She's at the Gorge."

Saeddryn started. "Hyrenna! Sir, really? Did ye see her yerself?"

"Yes. Her, and her three chicks."

"Oh my gods—did ye see the chicks, sir? How do they look? Are they all well?"

Arenadd chuckled. "Yes, they're well. Skandar should be proud; he's got three strong sons out of Hyrenna. They're some of the biggest chicks I've ever seen. But don't take my word for it; you'll see them yourself soon enough."

"What? Why? Ye ain't sendin' me there are ye, sir?"

Arenadd explained.

"An' ye got her to agree t'that, sir?" Saeddryn asked when he was done.

"On condition that I care for her chicks, yes. She wants us to win this war as much as your mother did."

"I see, sir. So when is she comin' here?"

"Soon, I would think. Today or tomorrow. The moment she gets here, Skade can leave."

"Are ye still sendin' the others, sir?"

"No. I only wanted to send an escort for protection, but Hyrenna can protect Skade perfectly well on her own. You've seen what her magic can do. And it would look far less suspicious if Skade . . . *Lady* Skade doesn't travel with a group of free Northerners."

"Aye, an' we'll be better off keepin' 'em with us, sir."

"Quite. Now, you'll have to excuse me. I've got a lot to do today."

"Ye don't have t'worry too much, sir," Saeddryn said unexpectedly. "We've got time. Malvern won't know about this for a week at least, by my guess."

Arenadd looked back at her. "They'll come sooner than that, Saeddryn. We've got a day or so at most."

"What, sir?" said Saeddryn. "How d'ye know, sir?"

Pain had made him impatient. "Don't question me," he snapped. "I told you they'll be here in two or three days at most, and I expect you to prepare for that."

Saeddryn nodded curtly. "Yes, sir. I'll see to it the others know."

Arenadd left her, walking slowly and wincing with every step. He hoped that he would be recovered enough when the time came. If they were going to survive the assault, he had to be fighting fit.

And they would come soon. He knew it in the pit of his stomach. They would come in force, and they would come with rage. All too soon, Fruitsheart would be consumed by them. Griffins and griffiners, armoured for battle and thirsting for revenge. Skade had to be away by then, away from danger. She had to survive. He had wanted to tell her so many times, but he knew he couldn't. *When I rule this land, it will be with you beside me, Skade. You and Skandar and I—three rulers, three powers. All of us.*

That made him smile. *It* will *happen,* he told himself. *I have the power. I can do anything I want.*

The thought of the battle looming on the horizon did nothing to diminish his anticipation. Battle didn't frighten him, not any more. *They will come here and find death waiting,* he promised. *Now Skandar has his magic, let the world beware.*

E lkin was sick.

Kraal took her straight to her chambers when he brought her back, and summoned the Master of Healing with a furious screech to her griffin, who brought her up immediately.

Lady Karmain examined her patient quickly, aware of Kraal's rage-filled gold eyes fixed on her.

"Burning-Lung sickness," she said eventually. "Very bad. Fever, restricted breathing . . . very hot to the touch."

"Well?" Kraal interrupted.

"I don't know if she'll recover," said the healer, "But she needs to stay in bed for a long time. I have potions that can help with the fever, and a compress for her chest, and certain herbs we can burn in here to help her breathe."

"*Will* she recover?" said Kraal.

"I don't know, Mighty Kraal. I'll do everything in my power. It's touch and go."

"Do so," Kraal commanded. "I will leave you to your work. Do not fail me."

"I won't," said the healer.

"Good. Now I have my own work to do. May the Day Eye smile on you."

He didn't want to leave Elkin now, but he knew he had to; there were still important things for him to do, and far too little time to do them in.

Down in the councillors' chamber, most of the officials and the remnants of the council were waiting to receive him. He landed on his and Elkin's platform as usual, while they called out to him, demanding news.

Kraal rose up. "Silence!"

Silence came, but much more slowly than usual. Plently of griffins continued to screech, most asking questions. Others were complaining or even daring to mock him.

Kraal sat on his haunches with his tail wrapped around his talons, haughtily ignoring them.

"I have brought my human back to the Eyrie safe and unharmed," he said. "She is ill and exhausted from her ordeal and needs time to recover, but she is alive."

"Prove that is true!" a griffin called from the gallery.

Kraal stood up sharply and screeched. The noise filled the chamber, deafeningly, and the hecklers abruptly fell silent.

"My word is all you will need," Kraal growled, "We have important matters to discuss. Most important of all is the whereabouts of the Mistress' kidnappers and what they intend to do next."

"What do you believe they have planned?" one of the council griffins asked politely.

"They cannot fight us openly yet," said Kraal. "Not at Malvern. They are too few."

"You have seen their leader," the same griffin said. "And his human, of course. Did you learn anything from them, Mighty Kraal?"

Kraal stirred. "Yes, I have seen them. But I am not the only one."

The councillors stirred.

"Who else has seen them?" one of the humans asked. "Do you have information, Mighty Kraal?"

The giant griffin's eyes gleamed. He had been wanting to reveal this for a while now, but the time had never seemed right. "I do," he said. "I have a witness."

"What witness?" said the human. "Is he here?"

"A few days ago, a griffin returned to Malvern after some time away," said Kraal. "I already knew her a little; she and her human are newcomers here, and lowly in this Eyrie. Her name is Kraeya, and her human is Branton Redguard, who now serves with the Eyrie guard."

"Where had she been?" asked Shrae, whose dead partner had been Master of Law.

"In Warwick," said Kraal. "She told me she and her human had decided to travel the land for a little while, to visit each of the cities, since they have only come here recently. They had permission from my own human. Some time during their travels they flew to Warwick, and there . . . they were attacked."

The councillors, and all those in the gallery, muttered among themselves and began to pay close attention. None of them had known about this.

"By whom were they attacked?" said Shrae. "By the dark griffin?"

"Yes. They were lured into a roost, trapped and attacked by him and by his human. Kraeya escaped with her life, but her human was taken prisoner by rebels. They had overrun the city and murdered every Southerner and griffin within it. Kraeya hid herself in the wilds outside the city, while her human was held captive and interrogated. Fortunately, he escaped before they could torture him as they intended to do, and was reunited with his partner. They came back here at once, to tell us what had happened."

"Warwick," muttered grey-feathered Skark, whose dead human had been Master of Learning.

"Warwick must be the place where we will find them," said Kraal. "I have already sent many griffins there, to attack the Governor's Tower and destroy every darkman who dares fight back."

Shrae bristled. "Mightly Kraal, why did you not consult us before you gave this order?"

"You have no humans," Kraal snapped back. "I only keep you on this council because I have not had time to find *part-nered* griffins to advise me. And I have sent many griffins," he added, with less certainty. "Warwick will be made an example of, whether *Kraeai kran ae* is there or not. The moon worshippers must be reminded that we rule this land, not that heartless demon of the shadows."

The humans still left in the council looked deeply unhappy at this, but none of them dared to argue.

"Did you send partnered griffins or unpartnered?" one asked eventually.

"I sent nearly a hundred unpartnered griffins," said Kraal. "It was time such griffins ceased being a drain on this land and began to give back. I sent four griffiners to lead and organise them."

"When did they depart?" asked Skark.

"At dawn on the day after Kraeya returned," said Kraal. "And perhaps if you had not been so distracted, you would have seen them."

"I saw them," Shrae said coldly. "But I assumed they had merely decided to abandon this city after they saw you humiliated and defeated, Mighty Kraal."

Several of the humans breathed in sharply, and the griffins raised their wings.

Kraal stared at Shrae for a moment, unblinking, and then stepped down from his platform and struck her across the face. She was a large griffin, but the blow hurled her sideways into a bench with her wing crumpled beneath her.

Kraal stood over her, hissing softly. "I rule here," he said. "I am master of this territory. And I will not be brought low by humans, least of all dark humans, *least* of all the moon-sent monster who dares to defy the power of the Day Eye and bring his shadows here. And I am master of you, and I will not tolerate insolence or disobedience."

Shrae lay still for a moment, breathing heavily, before she pulled herself up. And then, without any warning, she attacked.

It was the last thing Kraal had been expecting. No griffin had dared to attack him in decades. He staggered backward, bright blood spreading over his magnificent white neck feathers. Shrae, taking advantage of his shock, sprang at him with her beak wide open.

The remnants of the council, human and griffin, ran to get out of the way.

Kraal took several more blows to the face and chest before he recovered himself. He reared up onto his hind legs and struck back. His paws and talons slammed into Shrae's head, first from the right and then from the left, each blow landing with an audible crunch. She fell, bleeding profusely, but Kraal

was not done. He leapt at her, his beak striking her in the neck
with the force of a falling tree. There was a dull thud, and suddenly she was thrashing wildly with her limbs jerking this way
and that. One wing unfolded and beat uselessly at the air. Her
beak opened wide but her eyes were unfocused, and after a
moment the wild motion stopped and she went limp.

Kraal didn't linger over her body. He climbed back onto his
platform, trembling with pent-up fury. "I will not tolerate insolence," he said again. "And let none forget it. Soon my human
will be recovered, and we will form a new council. When we
are together again, none will stop us. And let rebels and traitors
beware."

26

Traitors

Hyrenna arrived at Fruitsheart a day after Arenadd and Skandar, carrying two of her chicks in her talons and the third perched on her back. She flew straight to Skandar's roost, completely ignoring the few badly aimed arrows that came her way, and when she landed, Skandar and Arenadd were both there to meet her.

The grey-and-orange griffin put her chicks down and lay in the straw to let them snuggle with her for comfort. "I have come," she said brusquely in answer to Arenadd's polite welcome.

Arenadd gripped the head of his walking stick. "Thank you for coming, Hyrenna," he said.

"It is no more than what we agreed," she said, and turned her attention to Skandar, who nibbled affectionately at her head feathers before lying down beside her.

"I'm sorry my sentries attacked you," said Arenadd. "They haven't been very well trained yet. But I'm sure you could have dealt with it. Now, I'll send for Skade. It's best if you two meet and get to know each other before you leave."

Hyrenna clicked her beak. "I agree. But before then, I would speak with you."

Arenadd bowed. "Of course."

"Good. Now listen. Here are my chicks, and this is how you

must care for them. They must be fed well, but not overfed. Half their body size in meat for each chick every day will suffice, and they must have bones to peck at to strengthen their beaks . . ."

Arenadd listened dutifully as Hyrenna droned on, detailing every aspect of how the chicks were to be fed, watered, sheltered and taught.

"Teach them griffish," she said. "Speak with them every day to see that they learn. Teach them all the griffish lore they must know, tell them the stories, pass on all you know. I will teach them the rest when I return. Is that all understood?"

Arenadd bowed again. "I'll care for them as if they were my own, Hyrenna. You have my word."

"And you will protect them with your life," Hyrenna added.

"That's what I would do for my own children," said Arenadd. "So it's what I'll do for them. Don't worry; you can trust us."

"I will trust Skandar more than I trust you, human," Hyrenna said coldly. "Now bring me food and water. And send for this Skade. I assume she does not speak griffish?"

"She does," said Arenadd.

"Oh?" There was a note of surprise in Hyrenna's voice. "So she knows griffins?"

"More than most griffiners I've met," said Arenadd. "Trust me."

"I prefer to trust my own judgment," said Hyrenna. "Send her to me now."

Arenadd's expectations were gloomy when he sought out Skade and brought her to the nest: Hyrenna was in such a bad mood he doubted if Arddryn herself could have brought her out of it.

But, to his surprise, after a rather formal beginning the silver-haired woman and the griffin took to each other very well. Skade addressed her new partner with the utmost politeness, which pleased Hyrenna, and the two of them sat together and talked.

The chicks seemed to like Skade as well—one of them let her touch his head—and she helped Hyrenna to feed them chunks of raw mutton. Afterward, well fed and tired, they went to sleep, one of them snuggled down in Skade's lap.

Skade stroked his feathers and talked to Hyrenna, discussing the journey and their mission. Hyrenna questioned Skade about her background and how she knew Arenadd.

Skade was careful without being evasive: she told Hyrenna
that she was from Withypool and had grown up among griffins,
and briefly explained how she had been forced to leave after
killing a man—a Southern man, she lied—who had killed a
Northerner who had been her friend. Hyrenna, by now apparently very pleased with this well-mannered human, accepted
the story easily enough.

"So, I see you understand the arrogance and the unjust
nature of the humans from the South, though you are one yourself," she said. "I can see why Skandar and Arenadd accepted
you to their cause."

"Arenadd saved my life," said Skade. "I love him."

"And he loves you, and therefore trusts you," said Hyrenna.
"I see. Yes." She looked up at Arenadd, who had politely
watched the whole conversation from over by the door. "I am
willing to work with this one," she said. "You have chosen her
well, *Kraeai kran ae*."

Arenadd held back a sigh of relief. "Thank you, Hyrenna.
When will you be ready to go?"

She dipped her beak into the water trough. "Tomorrow, at
dawn, and no later."

"Skade, is that all right with you?" said Arenadd.

She nodded. "I will be prepared."

After the meeting was over, Kraal returned to his nest.
He was tired, but the anger still burned inside him. The
council was in tatters, and the griffins were beginning to
rebel. Unless Elkin recovered soon, he would lose control of
Malvern . . . and the North.

Still, he allowed himself another moment of pride for how
he had dealt with Warwick. The griffins he had sent had been
some of the worst troublemakers—the most vocal of those
mocking him behind his back, the slowest to dip their heads
when he came near. With them gone, the city was peaceful
again and several dangerous challengers to his power were far
away, where they could do no harm. And if some of them died
at the hands of *Kraeai kran ae*, then all the better.

Kraal landed in his nest and hissed triumphantly to himself.
Elkin would have nothing to worry about when she recovered;

he had done good work for her. With that thought, he passed through the archway into her room with his wings folded neatly over his back.

Lady Karmain the healer was still there, resting by the fire with her partner. They stood up when Kraal entered.

"How is she?" he asked brusquely.

"Better," said Lady Karmain. "The fever has gone down, and she's had some good rest."

Kraal's confidence rose even higher. "Excellent. I will see her now."

He went to her bedside and looked down at her. She looked pitifully small and frail, almost lost among the bedclothes. He could see her chest slowly rise and fall, every breath an audible rasp. She smelt of sickly sweet disease.

Kraal touched the side of her head with his beak, with a gentleness that would have astounded anyone who had seen him kill with it mere moments before. His breath touched her face, and she stirred and groaned.

"Elkin," Kraal said. "Elkin, do not be afraid. I am here and you are safe."

Her eyes crinkled but did not open, and she mouthed something barely audible.

"Elkin, I must know," said Kraal. "Where are they? Are they in Warwick? Only tell me this one thing, Elkin. They must be found."

Elkin's hand, resting on the blankets, clenched into a weak fist. "Fruit," she mumbled.

"I will tell them to bring you fruit later," said Kraal. "Elkin, where are they? Where did they keep you prisoner? Do you know?"

The fist clenched more tightly. "Fruit," she said again. "Fruit . . . place."

"Fruit place?" Kraal repeated. "Elkin?"

She sighed and slumped again, her face slackening as she drifted back into sleep. Her hand uncurled, and something small and green fell out. Kraal sniffed at it; it had a sweet scent that he thought he recognised. Fruit.

His tail began to lash. "Pear," he muttered aloud. "But where did you find that? Fruit . . . place?" A hissing, rasping snarl began to rumble in his throat as he realised.

Fruitsheart.

* * *

Saying goodbye to Skade was one of the hardest things Are-nadd remembered doing in his life.

He and Skandar were up on top of the tower at dawn, with Hyrenna standing by and waiting while the lovers said their farewells.

Arenadd held Skade tight, pressing her into his chest as if he were trying to take her into his body and make her part of him forever. "Please, stay safe," he said quietly. "Please, Skade, stay safe. Don't die. Never die. I don't care if you fail, I don't care if you lose the money or if you give in and come back, just come back to me alive. Please, Skade . . ."

To his shame, he couldn't stop tears leaking from under his eyelids. He held her even closer and swallowed a sob.

Skade seemed to understand. She caressed him, losing her hands in his hair the way he liked her to. "Hush," she said softly. "Please, Arenadd, do not cry. You will make this more difficult for me, and for you."

Arenadd couldn't help it. "I'm so scared," he whispered in her ear. "Gods, I'm so afraid."

She let go of him to look him in the face. "Do not be afraid!" she commanded, her voice clear and ringing. "You are the Shadow that Walks! The man without a heart! You do not know fear!" She touched his cheek, tracing the scar with her fingertip. "And most of all, you are my Arenadd," she added more gently. "I am no seer; I do not know the future or anything more than what ordinary mortals can know. But I do know that we shall not be parted forever. Before this war ends, you will be in my arms again."

"Skade, we don't know that," said Arenadd.

"But I know," said Skade. "Arenadd, this is not only a sorrow for you. And if you will command me to return, then here is my command for you."

"Anything, Skade. Anything."

"Protect yourself," said Skade. "You know you are not invulnerable, Arenadd, and you must not let your powers make you think otherwise. Mortal weapons may still injure you, and despair may still claim you. And if this man, this *Aeai ran kai* returns . . ."

"I'm not afraid of him, Skade."

"But you must not dismiss him!" said Skade. "If there is a

weapon that this Bastard has found, if he has been . . . chosen to fight you, then you may still be vulnerable. Do not be complacent. Be cautious. Overconfidence is your weakness, Arenadd. Do not allow it to become your downfall."

"I won't, Skade. I promise."

"Then see that you keep your promise," said Skade. "Now—" She stopped abruptly, turning to look. Arenadd turned, too, his hand already on his sickle.

But it was only Saeddryn. She emerged into the grey light, blinking and tired, but alert enough. "My lord," she said, bowing. "I'm sorry if I startled ye, but I thought I should come t'see off the Lady Skade."

She looked sharply at Skade, who looked back, unwavering. "Saeddryn. I am pleased that you have come."

Arenadd tucked his hands into his sleeves to keep them warm. "And so am I. How are things down below?"

"Quiet," said Saeddryn. "Most of the others are still in bed, sir. Now . . ." She walked past him, to Hyrenna.

The old griffin lowered her head to let Saeddryn stroke her feathers. "Good morning, Saeddryn. I am pleased to see you again."

"And I'm pleased to see ye, too," said Saeddryn, in fractured griffish. She paused a moment, and then hugged Hyrenna around the neck, pressing the side of her face into her feathers. "I'm so glad ye came back," she said softly. "I was so afraid ye were dead, Hyrenna. Now Mother is gone, ye're the closest thing I have to a family."

Hyrenna nudged her gently. "Saeddryn, you have much of your mother about you. Her strength, her will and her grace. It makes me glad to think that you carry something of her, and I know that she would be proud to see you now, as great as you have become . . . and due to become greater still."

"Thank you, Hyrenna. That means everything to me."

"And to me," said Hyrenna. "Care for yourself, Saeddryn, and help your master to care for my chicks. Stay close by him, little human. Honour and obey him in all things, for it will mean to honour and obey your mother as well."

Saeddryn folded her hands over her stomach and bowed her head. "I will, Hyrenna. I wish ye good luck on yer journey. Bring our brothers an' sisters back safe." Then, softly, she said the blessing over the griffin, murmuring the words in Northern.

Arenadd watched and then stepped closer, joining his voice to hers.

"Wisdom of Serpent be thine, wisdom of Crow be thine, wisdom of valiant Wolf. Swiftness of Deer be thine, strength of Bear be thine, courage of Man, magic of Griffin, protection of the Moon and the Stars."

The words rang in Arenadd's ears as Skade embraced him one last time and gave him a sweet, lingering kiss on the lips before she let go and climbed onto Hyrenna's back. She had the money bags slung in front of her and a long dagger in her belt, and she settled herself down among the griffin's feathers.

Hyrenna stepped toward Skandar and nibbled at his shoulders. "Good fortune go with you, Skandar Deathwings," she said. "I entrust our chicks to you; help your human protect them, and protect him. Trust in your strength and your magic, and your enemies will be destroyed."

"You teach," said Skandar. "Teach well. I remember, always."

"And I trust you to do that, Skandar," said Hyrenna, and with one last affectionate push at him with her beak she turned away and began the short, rough run that preceded flight.

In that moment, Arenadd had a strong urge to run after her, to shout at her to come back, to plead with Skade not to go.

He didn't move.

Hyrenna's wings opened and began to beat hard. Skade held on to the harness, steady and confident on the griffin's back. She braced herself, and then Hyrenna took off.

Arenadd went to Skandar's side and rested a hand on his shoulder as they watched the old griffin fly higher and higher, all power and control in the sky with her wings spread wide and her tail rigid for balance. She flew higher, spiralling, until she was tiny—a black outline against the endless blue. She turned southward and flew away.

Arenadd heard footsteps behind him, and Saeddryn came to join him. "I wonder if we'll ever see them again?" she said.

"We will," said Arenadd. "I trust Skade completely."

She looked at him. "An' I trust Hyrenna completely."

"Then it sounds like we have a good balance," said Arenadd, but there wasn't much emphasis to the sarcasm.

Saeddryn nudged him in the arm. "Don't fret, sir," she said unexpectedly. "Hyrenna's one of the strongest griffins ever born. She might be gettin' on now, but she ain't no pushover, sir."

Arenadd glanced at her and smiled. "I know. She defeated Skandar once, after all."

"Only before he found his magic, sir," said Saeddryn. "Now I doubt there's any griffin could challenge him."

"The Mighty Kraal, maybe," Arenadd muttered.

"Well, we'll see, won't we?" said Saeddryn. She yawned. "I'd better go below, sir. Got t'get everyone up an' workin'. I'll see ye later."

Arenadd rubbed his eyes. "All right. I'll see you then."

He knew he should go with her, but he didn't; he didn't feel like dealing with people just yet.

Skandar didn't seem in a hurry to go anywhere, either. He sat on his haunches, the wind ruffling his feathers, and peacefully groomed his wings.

Arenadd kept his eyes on the retreating dot that was Hyrenna and Skade, until it had long since vanished on the horizon. *Gods, I miss her already.*

The sun began its slow ascent, and Arenadd and Skandar, silent and comfortable in each other's company, watched it spread light over the sky.

And that was why they were the first to see the dark cloud approaching from the west.

Skandar saw it before Arenadd. He looked westward for a long moment and then said, "See something."

"What?" said Arenadd.

"Cloud," the dark griffin said simply. "See?"

Arenadd followed his gaze. "I don't see . . ." He trailed off.

There was a dark smudge on the horizon. It was difficult to tell how far away it was, but it looked big.

Arenadd squinted. "What *is* that? Is that a storm?"

Skandar clicked his beak. "Too fast," he opined.

"If it's not a cloud, then what is it?" said Arenadd, but a horrible possibility had already occurred to him. "Oh gods," he groaned. "It can't be. Not this soon!"

But as the cloud came closer, moving with great speed, the suspicion grew with it. Perhaps he should have acted at once—sounded the alarm or run to warn the others. But something kept him where he was, still unwilling to trust his own senses as he kept his eyes on the cloud, watching details emerge.

Now it was much closer, and it looked less dense. He could see it seething like a nest of ants.

When it was nearly over the city, it exploded. Dark shapes shot outward from it, dozens and dozens of them, pinwheeling in all directions. And that was when Arenadd's suspicion became awful certainty.

Beside him, Skandar reared up, screeching in rage.

"Griffins!" Arenadd shouted. "Skandar, sound the alarm! *Call!*"

Skandar wasn't listening. He ran to the edge of the tower, closest to the oncoming horde, and screeched again and again, calling his name in a demented challenge. *"Skandar! Skandar! Darkheart! Skandar! Darkheart!"*

A mad babble of swearwords streamed out of Arenadd's mouth as he ran for the trapdoor. *Griffins! Not now, not now, not now! It's too soon!*

He wrenched the trapdoor open and was about to jump through it, but he stopped and ran back to Skandar, shouting, "Skandar! Skandar, come here! *Skandar!*"

Skandar paid no attention. He continued to call his name, all his promises forgotten in the midst of what consumed him now: a male griffin's utter and most powerful need to protect his territory against all comers, no matter how large or numerous.

"Skandar, they'll tear you to pieces!" Arenadd yelled, and ignoring the danger, he reached out to grab his partner's flank.

Skandar turned on him instantly, snarling.

Arenadd backed off hastily. "Skandar!" he said. "Skandar, it's me!"

Skandar advanced on him, radiating aggression. But Arenadd was horribly aware of the griffins above, spreading out to circle over the city and the tower, and he stood his ground. Below, people had already seen them, and he could hear faint screams drifting up toward them.

"Skandar, we've got to go below," he said. "We can't fight them all on our own; there's too many of them."

"No!" Skandar rasped. "*My* territory! Mine! *Mine!*"

"You won't protect it by getting yourself killed!" said Arenadd. "We have to go below, we have to plan—"

"No! *You* plan, I fight! You go, I stay!"

"I'm not going anywhere," said Arenadd. "My place is with you, Skandar."

The griffins were no longer approaching. They were *there*,

just above them, flying over the tower in slow circles. Arenadd could see them—even hear the sound of their wings. They would attack at any moment.

"Then stay," said Skandar. "Fight." He was already tensing, preparing to fly to the attack.

"But Skandar—*look out!*"

A griffin had suddenly folded its wings and dropped toward the tower. Arenadd dived behind Skandar, who opened his wings and reared up to intercept the attacker.

The griffin, however, rolled out of the way. It landed neatly on the tower-top, close to the flagpole.

Arenadd picked himself up and wrenched his sickle out of his belt. Ahead of him, Skandar was already charging, feathers flying, ready to strike . . .

The griffin turned to face him. But it did not attack. It backed away a few steps and lowered its head, bending its forelegs and bowing low in a gesture of submission.

Skandar halted his charge at the very last moment and stood over the other griffin, hissing and confused.

The other griffin did not raise its head. It made several quick trills and clicks, sounds Arenadd vaguely recognised.

He moved forward, to Skandar's side, sickle in hand. "Who are you?" he demanded.

The other griffin raised its head partway. It was a good-sized male, thickset with powerful limbs and tawny brown feathers. "I do not wish to fight," he said. "Only to talk."

"Talk," Skandar snapped.

The griffin lifted his head all the way, though he still kept his forelegs bent. "Are you Skandar, the dark griffin?" he asked.

"Am Skandar," he said.

The brown griffin's eyes glinted as he looked at Arenadd. "And is this human your partner, *Kraeai kran ae*, the Shadow that Walks?"

"I am," said Arenadd.

"And you have conquered this city?" said the griffin.

"Our territory," said Skandar. "We fight, win, keep. Go now, or we kill."

"Does he speak the truth, *Kraeai kran ae*?" said the griffin.

"He does," said Arenadd. "Who are you? I warn you: if you are here to fight, then Skandar and I will fight back. And we don't lose easily."

The griffin drew himself up. "I am Kaanee, hatched at Malvern. Tell me, *Kraeai kran ae*, is it true that it is you who were behind the kidnapping of the Mighty Kraal's human?"

"Skandar and I," said Arenadd.

"We take human," said Skandar.

"And you killed the humans belonging to the councillors at Malvern?"

"Yes," said Arenadd.

"And it was you who killed the griffiner at Warwick?"

"We kill," said Skandar.

"What do you intend to do?" said Kaanee. "Is it your intention to attack Malvern and take this land from the Mighty Kraal?"

Arenadd's grip tightened on the sickle. "Yes. And we will kill anyone who tries to stop us."

Kaanee regarded him; his eyes were yellow, and they glittered with intelligence. "We have seen the Mighty Kraal," he said. "At Malvern. He is . . . angry, desperate. Without his human, he does not know what to do. For all his strength, he cannot lead alone. We griffins know this. A griffin is a fighter, not a thinker. Humans do this for us . . . for partnered griffins, at least. Without his human, the Mighty Kraal is no longer mighty. He failed to defend her; he failed to rescue her. He is diminished."

Arenadd felt a hint of cruel pleasure. "I know," he said. "That was my intention."

Kaanee bowed his head to him, and to Skandar. "We have seen this," he said. "We have seen your triumph and his defeat, and we have decided—"

"What decide?" Skandar interrupted. "My territory! You go, or fight!"

Kaanee clicked his beak. "We cannot follow a griffin who has been defeated," he said in a businesslike way. "Yet we must have a leader. And now we have found another." He turned to look at Skandar. "A griffin with great strength. A griffin of great renown. A griffin with a cunning and powerful human. A griffin who has defeated the Mighty Kraal, when no others ever have. We have decided what we must do." He lowered his head again and bowed low. "We have come to offer you our strength," he said. "Mighty Skandar."

Arenadd was dumbfounded. "You mean you've come to *join* us?"

Kaanee looked up. "We follow the most powerful griffin in the land," he said. "And the most powerful human. Once Kraal was that griffin and Elkin that human. But now you have proven yourself more powerful than they. Therefore, you are our masters now. Command us, and we will do your bidding. We will give this land to you."

Arenadd couldn't believe what he was hearing. He looked at Kaanee, then up at the cloud of griffins over Fruitsheart. "All of you?" he said.

"I am the strongest of the griffins that came here," said Kaanee. "I have been asked to speak for them. They are your followers now, Mighty Skandar."

Arenadd stared at him and the circling griffins a moment longer. Then he began to smile.

27

Plots

Arenadd's prediction had been right.

Two days after Kaanee's arrival, two days after Arenadd and Skandar had accepted the griffins' allegiance and begun to organise the defence of the city with their help, the first of the griffiners arrived from Malvern.

There were only ten, a small force sent to search the city and, with the governor's help, find the rebels hiding there. They were seen within moments by the new griffin sentinels, which attacked them at once.

Arenadd and Skandar never had to even leave their new quarters. Kaanee and the one hundred unpartnered griffins he led attacked their erstwhile friends in the air and tore them to pieces. By the time the short fight was over, there was very little left of them to identify. Down in the city, people gathered in the streets to watch, and some were even bold enough to climb onto rooftops for a better view. They yelled encouragement and jeered the dying griffiners and scrambled to pick up the feathers that drifted down.

Arenadd knew that wouldn't be the end of it—not by a long way. The instant Malvern realised that ten griffiners had vanished at Fruitsheart, they would know what was happening and the true assault would begin.

He called a meeting of the council very quickly after the attack and waited impatiently while the councillors gathered.

Saeddryn was the first to arrive. "Arenadd, I want a word with ye."

Arenadd groaned and rubbed his forehead; he was hung over and in no mood for another argument with his second-in-command. "Do tell," he mumbled.

Saeddryn sat down on his left-hand side, since Skandar had taken the right. "Sir, have ye really decided t'put that griffin on the council—Kannie, or whatever his name is?"

Arenadd yawned. "Saeddryn, let me put it like this: Kaanee and his friends killed four griffiners and came to look for us so they could offer their support. Skandar doesn't want to have to talk to these griffins, so Kaanee does it for him. He has to be here so he'll have something to tell them, don't you think?"

"Obviously, sir, but that wasn't what I meant," Saeddryn said stiffly. "Sir, I don't trust him. He turned on Kraal. Who's t'say he won't turn on us, too?"

Arenadd laughed softly. "You don't know griffins very well, do you?"

"I know—" Saeddryn began.

"Griffins don't care about patriotism," said Arenadd. "They don't plot or scheme, at least not without the help of a human. They're not *thinkers*. All they care about is strength. They follow the strongest, and Skandar is the strongest. As long as they never see him lose to another griffin, they'll stay on our side. We're fighting a very dangerous war against a very dangerous enemy. Frankly, we need all the help we can get."

"Yes, sir," said Saeddryn. "Ye make a good point. All I'm sayin' is we should keep watch on 'em. Just t'be on the safe side. Trust no-one, sir."

"I don't," said Arenadd. *I trust Skade and Skandar, and no-one else. Not even you, cousin.*

"That's wise, sir," said Saeddryn.

Arenadd watched her curiously. She was certainly being more agreeable today. Maybe she was just in a good mood over the deaths of the griffiners.

The rest of the council arrived shortly afterward. Kaanee came last, panting and a little bedraggled.

Arenadd stood and inclined his head to the griffin. "Kaanee, welcome. Take any place you want; Skandar and I are in your debt."

The tawny griffin looked pleased. He padded around the edge of the room and settled down by Skandar, taking the honoured seat to the right of his new master.

Arenadd smiled to himself. *I have Saeddryn, and Skandar has Kaanee. I'm not sure which of us got the better deal.*

He pulled himself back to the present. "Welcome, my friends," he said. "Relax and have something to drink; you've earnt it. Now . . ."

The humans around the table leant forward intently.

"We won a victory today," said Arenadd. "And an important one. Our new allies have shown us what they can do, and they won my trust. Kaanee, I want to thank you on behalf of all of us, but especially on my own. With your help, we can defeat the griffiners and take Malvern."

Kaanee dipped his head, obviously flattered. "We did only as we were asked," he said. "I am proud to have served such a powerful griffin and such a worthy human."

Arenadd translated his words for the benefit of the council, who looked duly impressed.

"Unfortunately," he went on, "we can't afford to rest on our laurels. This victory may have been important, but it was also minor. There are hundreds of griffiners still left at Malvern, and ordinary soldiers as well. We're outnumbered but not out-led—not yet. I don't know if Lady Elkin will recover, but we have to take advantage of the chaos we've created at Malvern as quickly as we can. Kraal is leading poorly without his human, so we have the upper hand. And he still doesn't know where we are. The faster we act, the better."

"I agree," said Saeddryn. "But what d'ye advise we do, sir? If we send people out t'attack other cities, we'll weaken ourselves too much here."

"I agree," said Arenadd. "But we still have to strike now, while they're unprepared."

"What about Nerth, sir?" said Caedmon. "What orders have ye given him?"

"That he's to come south immediately," said Arenadd. "I told him to leave some men behind but bring three-quarters of them down the river and take cover in a certain spot where the land is very wild. When they arrive, if Fruitsheart is still in our

hands, Skandar and I will go to them and order them to come
here. They'll give us the numbers we need."

"But it'll be months before they get here, sir," said Saeddryn. "Too long."

"I know," said Arenadd. "Until now I thought it would have
to do. But now it's different. Kaanee, I have orders for you."

Kaanee looked alert. "Speak, Lord Arenadd."

"We don't need all of your griffins here at once," said Arenadd. "Twenty would be enough to defend Fruitsheart if we
were attacked, at least for a while. In the meantime, I have a use
for the rest of them."

"You want them to attack other cities?" said Kaanee.

"Exactly." Arenadd unrolled a map on the table and pointed
to different marks on it. "I've been reading the records in the
library here—the governor's aides were kind enough to keep
them all nicely up-to-date. Now obviously none of these towns
have been used for military purposes for a long time, but they all
still have walls and defences and so on. We'll want to attack the
largest and most well placed of them, and I'll welcome suggestions once I've finished speaking. I've already marked out two
that I think should be the first. Caerleon, a little further north,
deals in cows and has at least twelve griffiners in permanent residence and a small garrison. Obviously they're still prepared in
case us nasty rebels decide to attack from the mountains again."
He grinned, and then became serious again. "Kaanee, I want
that city. Do you think you and your friends can overrun it?"

Kaanee curled his talons. "If the strongest and most magi-
cally powerful of us are chosen, then we shall defeat the griffiners there easily."

"Skandar, can you help him do that?" said Arenadd.

"Will help," Skandar said.

"Good. The other city we must attack is closer to us: Skenfrith. An important trade centre, very large and well populated
and, more importantly, two days' march away from Malvern.
If we own Skenfrith, we'll be in the perfect position to strike."

"That's a strong city, sir," Saeddryn said doubtfully, following his pointing finger. "I'm not sure we could send a force big
enough."

"I know," said Arenadd. "That's why I plan to use the strongest weapon we've got on that city."

Saeddryn raised an eyebrow. "Weapon, sir?"

Arenadd patted Skandar on the shoulder. "Us. Skandar and I will lead that assault ourselves."

"Sir, are ye sure we could hold on here without ye?" said Davyn. "What if we were attacked while ye were gone?"

"Don't worry," said Arenadd. "Skandar and I can be back here in a —"

"—Heartbeat," said Saeddryn.

"I suppose so. And as I've said before, I didn't agree to lead this rebellion so I could sit on my backside and do nothing while everybody else did the fighting for me."

"It's a good strategy, sir," Saeddryn soothed. "But if ye want t'hear, I've got some suggestions, sir."

"I'm all ears," said Arenadd.

They spent a good portion of the rest of that day in the hall discussing strategy. It was a long and slightly tedious process, but by the end it was agreed that they would attack Skenfrith first. Once it had been secured they could consider an assault on Caerleon, but for now Skenfrith was their priority. Half the griffish force would mount the assault with Arenadd and Skandar, and the other half would stay to guard Fruitsheart.

"Even if Malvern finds you here before we return, they'll have a hard fight on their hands—much harder than they could be expecting," Arenadd said confidently. "And Skandar and I will only be gone a few days. The instant we get the chance, we'll come back with news."

Saeddryn nodded. "Ye're right, sir. As ye've said, ye an' Skandar were given power so ye could use it."

Arenadd grinned wolfishly. "Are you ready to fight again, Skandar? Skenfrith will be a much bigger struggle than we've faced yet."

"Am ready!" said Skandar. "Always ready. *You* ready?"

"If you're ready, I am," said Arenadd. "It's time the Southerners know exactly who they're up against."

Kaanee stirred. "They are up against an enemy more powerful than they have ever faced before," he said. "An enemy that will destroy them."

Arenadd sat back in his chair, ignoring his lingering headache. *Are you happy yet, master?* he thought. *Have I pleased you yet?*

No. He knew the answer at once. No, not yet. But she would be pleased, she would be . . .

28

Skenfrith

Arenadd had been afraid when he went into battle at Fruits-heart, but as he and Skandar flew toward Skenfrith with fifty griffins following them, he felt nothing but hot, fierce confidence and determination. He could feel Skandar's huge muscles flex, and his ears were full of the sound of the wings of Kaanee and his followers. This was not a ragtag group of escaped slaves or a band of rioting civilians. This was a real army.

The records at Fruitsheart had said that there were fifteen griffiners in permanent residence at Skenfrith but that there were quarters for twenty.

Twenty griffiners against fifty griffins. Unpartnered griffins, faster and more agile in the air without humans to weigh them down. Griffins who had been organised into a true army. And they would strike without any warning.

Arenadd had to suppress a laugh. Skenfrith wouldn't stand a chance. He and Skandar would be walking over the corpses of their enemies before the day was out.

They had organised it well in advance. The moment Skenfrith's walls came into sight Skandar banked sharply upward. The griffins followed him higher and higher, until the air became icy cold. Few griffins could fly this high for long before the thin air began to suffocate them, but they would be almost impossible to see from the ground unless someone was actively looking for them—and why would anyone do that?

Arenadd clung on to Skandar's back, shivering. The height quickly made him dizzy, but he ignored the discomfort and focused on staying alert. He had to be ready when the moment came.

Skandar flew calmly, keeping his eyes on the ground. Skenfrith looked ridiculously small from here, but a griffin's eyes were made to pinpoint anything on the ground from a great distance, and this target wasn't even moving. Skandar knew exactly what he was doing.

When the city was directly below him, he wheeled around and flew in a tight circle. He screeched a command to the griffins, and then folded his wings and dropped.

Arenadd instantly lost his grip with his knees, and very nearly lost everything else, too. He had persuaded Skandar to wear a harness, and he had tied his own wrists to it before they left, and thank the Night God for that. As Skandar dived, Arenadd flapped helplessly in midair like a human flag, the straps around his wrists the only thing keeping him from tumbling out of the sky.

Skandar ignored his partner's troubles. All his attention had to be focused on what he was doing.

Skenfrith grew larger and larger below, as if it were hurling itself toward them. All around Skandar, griffins were falling out of the sky.

There were other griffins visible below them now, flying idly over the city. None of them seemed to have noticed the danger hurtling toward them from above.

Skandar chose his moment. He closed his eyes for an instant and burst into the shadows without slowing.

Blackness enveloped them. The wind seemed to vanish, and everything slowed. Arenadd finally managed to grab the straps and pull himself onto Skandar's shoulders, leaning back so far his head touched the griffin's wing.

The enemy griffins were silvery shadows moving below them like fish in a pool. Skandar chose the nearest of them and flicked a wing to roll sideways, directly above the enemy griffin. He opened his talons wide, folded his wings back as far as they would go and plummeted.

Arenadd closed his eyes and braced himself for the impact.

When it came, it felt as if they had flown into a stone wall. Arenadd lost his hold on the harness again and jerked backward so hard the straps cut into his wrists.

Skandar's dive ended in a clumsy sideways spin that nearly knocked him out of the sky. But he recovered and managed to right himself with a skilful flick of his wings.

The griffin he had struck fell toward the city, its own wings trailing uselessly behind it. It was probably dead already.

Arenadd dragged himself upright and slumped across Skandar's neck. He could feel blood on his hands, and though he wasn't in any pain he knew that the moment they left the shadows his spine would be sheer agony. No griffiner would ever be suicidal enough to actually be on his griffin's back during a manoeuvre like that. No mortal griffiner, anyway.

Skandar didn't pause to gloat over his victory. Around him the unpartnered griffins had begun their own attack. Some had hit their targets, others not. Skandar saw an enemy griffin that had escaped unscathed, and attacked it. He passed directly over it and lashed out with his beak on his way. The blow broke the other griffin's wing and sent it spiralling helplessly down into the city.

It was a short fight. The enemy griffins were caught completely unprepared, and few of them had a chance to fight. Kaanee's griffins—the unpartnered, as Arenadd had dubbed them—fought ruthlessly and did not let a single one escape. Perhaps the enemy could have put up more of a fight, but Skandar stopped that. The constant attacks from a griffin they could not see, a griffin who struck in complete silence, drove them into a panic. After that, the unpartnered made short work of them.

Once the last of them was dead, Skandar flitted back into the sunlit world, and Arenadd groaned as the pain finally hit him. But there was no time to worry about that. The black griffin gave another commanding screech and flew toward the two griffiner towers that loomed over the city. Many of the unpartnered had already begun to attack them. Arenadd had directed a group of griffins whose power was fire to fly to the nest entrances and hurl flames through them. The strategy must have worked: he could already see smoke beginning to plume out as the nesting material caught fire.

Some griffins who had been inside when the attack began emerged from the towers and were instantly set upon by the

unpartnered ones that Skandar had brought with him. The
black griffin himself flew between the towers, seeking out targets wherever he could. It quickly became clear that the griffins
in Skenfrith were all but defeated.

Arenadd fumbled with the straps around his wrists, and
managed to peel them away from the bruised and bleeding flesh
as Skandar came in to land on top of the larger of the towers.
Once they had touched down, Arenadd dismounted and limped
around to his partner's head.

"You did it, Skandar," he said. "You're a fine commander,
you know."

Skandar clicked his beak. "No talk!" he said. "Now, fight!"

Arenadd grinned and freed his sickle from his belt. "Yes.
Now it's my turn. Let's go."

They found the trapdoor set into the brickwork in a moment.
It was made from solid wood, but a few blows from Skandar
shattered it into pieces. Arenadd jumped through it and into
the tower, all his senses alert and ready. Somewhere deep in
his chest, where his heart had been, the dark thirst awoke
again.

Time to kill.

Grinning to himself, he darted down the corridor without
a sound.

The griffiners in the tower were in a panic, faced with the
twin threats of attacking griffins and a fire beginning to
spread through the building. Most of them were more interested
in escaping the flames than trying to fight, and when Arenadd
appeared in their midst they had no time or presence of mind to
organise themselves.

For Arenadd, it was almost a game. Whenever he saw an
enemy he would jump into the shadows before he struck. The
sickle was a perfect weapon; now he had had time to become
used to it, he found it easier and easier to use. The wickedly
sharp inner blade could open a throat with one blow, and the tip
finished the job. He struck from behind, unseen, and watched
blood spurt away from him like water.

As he worked his way down the tower, killing everyone
he met, he stopped using the shadows. Skandar needed his
strength, and besides, he could fight without their cover.

A woman appeared around a corner and stopped, open-mouthed in shock at the horrible blood-spattered apparition coming toward her. She had the presence of mind to draw her sword, but too late. Arenadd ducked under her arm and struck.

Moments later, she was dead.

As he stepped over her body, Arenadd wanted to laugh, and he did—a wild, crazed laugh that went on and on and sounded nothing like his usual self. Oh gods, he loved this so much. Why had he ever thought that there was anything wrong or horrifying about killing? Why had he ever doubted his master?

The Night God was in him now, whispering silently in his mind, pushing him onward. He didn't know what she was saying, but he could guess. *Yes, Arenadd, yes. Kill them. Kill them all.*

"Kill them all," Arenadd repeated, as he cut a man down where he stood. "Kill them all. Kill the sun worshippers. Kill them all, yes, yes." And he laughed.

There didn't seem to be anyone else on this level. He made a quick check of the rooms—very quick, since the flames were spreading. The air was full of smoke, enough to suffocate an ordinary man. But not him. No, not him.

He descended to the next level. The air was much clearer here, but there didn't seem to be any people about. Arenadd rounded a corner and went into a side chamber, where a man with a bandage wrapped around his face stepped out of the shadows and stabbed him in the chest.

Arenadd stopped dead, staring in astonishment. "What . . ."

The man lunged forward and stabbed him again. He left the knife embedded in Arenadd's body and drew another from his belt.

Arenadd looked down. There were two hilts protruding from his chest. He looked up again, with an almost shocked expression. "Where in the Night God's name did *you* come from?" he said. "What are you *doing*?"

The bandaged man stabbed him again. *"Die!"* he screamed. "Die, curse you! Why won't you die?"

The pain hit Arenadd out of nowhere, like an animal lunging at him. He staggered, and the man took advantage of this to stab him yet again. Arenadd made a weak swing at him with the sickle, but the man easily dodged it.

Arenadd reached up for one of the knives and tried to pull it

out. But all his strength seemed to have gone. His knees buck-
led, and he fell.

The man stepped toward him. He was trembling with pent-
up terror as he drew his last knife. "This is for my wife, you
son of a bitch," he snarled, and stabbed downward with all his
strength. The knife slid through Arenadd's ribs, directly into
his dead heart.

Arenadd jerked and coughed, bringing up blood, and then
he was still.

Arenadd could feel the knives embedded in his body, and he
could feel the sickle still clutched in his hand. His mind
screamed at him to move—to get up, to pull the knives out and
kill the one who had attacked him—but his body would not
obey. The knives would not let him heal. They were sapping his
energy, taking away his strength. Making him helpless.

He fought to stay awake for as long as he could, but there
was nothing he could do. *Take them out!* he pleaded. *Someone
take them out!*

But no-one came to help him. He could feel the heat around
him growing more and more intense, and he was dimly aware
that the tower was burning down. If he did not escape from it
soon, his body would be destroyed and he would have a fate
worse than death.

There was a crash and a thud, and something hit him hard
in the chest.

And after that everything vanished and he spiralled away
into absolute blackness.

He was not alone in the dark. As he lay there, he became
aware of a presence coming toward him. Soon it was hov-
ering over him, pure white and glowing, but somehow keeping
its light within and never dispelling the comforting darkness.
He knew her at once, even without seeing her face. Her beautiful face.

He tried to get up, but he could not. He had no body here; he
had left it behind.

"Master," he said.

Arenadd. Her voice was soft, but so powerful. *You have made a terrible mistake.*

"Master," he said again, struggling to reach out to her. "Master, please, don't leave me. I need you."

You were a fool, she said. *To think you could fight alone! Why did you go into battle without your griffin? I sent him to you to fight beside you! To protect you! You have gone without him before and suffered for it. Why did you think you could do it again?*

Arenadd coughed. "The building was on fire; I didn't want him to get hurt. Besides, they were only other humans. I can handle humans, I . . ."

Yes, that must be why you have found yourself disabled and trapped inside a burning tower, she said, and her voice was not accusing but icily matter-of-fact. *Your overconfidence has brought you to this.*

A spike of defiance rose in him. "Of course I was overconfident," he said. "You made me immortal. You gave me powers, you told me I was the Master of Death. All my victories were so easy because of you. Why shouldn't I have been confident?"

Your victories were easy because you were lucky! she said, and her voice was not loud or angry, but full of a rushing and roaring like water. *And because you planned them well! Do you not understand, Arenadd? I am too weak to interfere! All I can do in this world is through you! If you do not emerge victorious, I shall never be powerful again!*

Arenadd shrank back in the darkness. "I'm sorry, master. I'm sorry. I shouldn't have . . . I want to help you. I *want* to do your will, I do. I belong to you."

Her presence became softer and kinder. *I hear you, and I am pleased. You have done well thus far, and I begin to trust in you, as you have trusted in me. Arenadd—*

"Please," said Arenadd. "Can you help me? I want to get out of here so I can keep fighting for you, but I need help."

Arenadd, she repeated. *I cannot stay long. Tell me what you wish. Do you wish to become more powerful? Do you wish for your powers to increase?*

"I—" Arenadd stopped. He hadn't known that he could become more powerful. "How?"

Only tell me, she said. *Do you wish for your powers to become greater?*

"Yes," said Arenadd.

If you bind yourself to me utterly, your transformation will be complete, the Night God whispered. She said it seductively, almost like a lover. *If you give up what has made you mortal, there will be no more fear. No more doubt.*

Arenadd strained to reach her, almost *lusting* for her presence. "Tell me how!" he said. "I want to—I want to do that. How, master? How?"

It will be simple, she said. *Painless.*

Somewhere inside him, a flicker of doubt awoke. But he pushed it aside. "What is it? Tell me, and I'll do it."

You must give up the last of your mortality, said the Night God. *Shed the final traces of the man you were.*

"You mean my memories?" said Arenadd. "I've forgotten so much already . . . I didn't understand why."

Yes. Your memories. Give them to me, she breathed. *Give them up, give them all up. Discard them as if they were an old suit of clothes. Forget the mortal utterly, cast him aside. Become Arenadd Taranisäii, from mind to spirit.*

Arenadd was silent for a long time, trying to think. It was so difficult to think in her presence; he felt as if she filled his mind from end to end, drinking in his essence like water. *Forget.*

Could he do it? *Should* he do it?

Answer me, said the Night God, interrupting his thoughts. *Answer me quickly, Arenadd Taranisäii, Lord of Darkmen.*

"But my memories . . ."

What use are they to you? She sounded almost angry now. *What use have they ever been? Your life before you died was nothing but pain and misery! You have been rejected and persecuted since the day you were born, and nobody has ever loved you!*

"No—"

Shall I show you?

And she did show him, bombarding him with memories, dozens of memories—all real, all vivid, all terrible.

A small boy cowering as other children pelted him with mud and stones. *Blackrobe! Blackrobe!*

An older boy now, nearly ten, trying in vain to fight off a dozen much older boys before he fell, bleeding from the nose and mouth. *Blackrobe! Filthy blackrobe! Moon lover!*

And the boy grew older, but no matter where he went or who

he spoke to, the reaction was always the same. Stones thrown at him, insults and sneering that followed him wherever he went, every day. Nowhere to hide.

Blackrobe!

Now he was a man, and another man snarled hate at him. *Go back to the North, blackrobe!*

A blond-haired young man, one he recognised, watching him with open disdain. *Are all slaves this insolent?*

A brown griffin, hissing contempt as she leant down to tear his ear. *Not just a blackrobe, but an arrogant blackrobe.*

And still the memories came, more and more of them, suffocating him with hate and despair. He saw himself betrayed, beaten, tortured, tried and sentenced to death for a crime he had not committed. He saw himself fall from the edge of the city, the arrows that sent him there still embedded in his body as he hurtled to his death.

Arenadd screamed. "*Stop!* Stop it! Make it stop! I don't want to see any more!"

Finally, mercifully, the memories stopped coming. *You see now?* the Night God said. *See the misery you lived in before you came to me?*

Arenadd breathed hard; he felt as if he had been rescued from drowning. "But . . . but wasn't there . . . something?" He strained to remember, grasping at memories that stayed just out of his reach. "There were people . . . friends . . ."

False friends, and a lover who betrayed you for another man, said the Night God. *Only that.*

"But . . . I don't . . . don't remember . . ."

You do not wish to see it, said the Night God. *But you must, and soon. The only ones who have ever cared for you or accepted you were your own people.*

"And Skandar and Skade."

Yes.

Arenadd lay there, staring at nothing. "Then I had nothing at all. Back when I was . . . when I was . . ." He shuddered and made a sound that was almost a sob. "When I was Arren Cardockson."

Nothing, Arenadd. Truly nothing.

Arenadd tried to speak, and fell silent. The memories still hurt, like the knives stuck in his body. "I . . ."

What do you choose? said the Night God. *Choose, Arenadd.*

"Take them!" Arenadd shouted, the words so full of pain they were almost a scream. "I don't want them. Take them away, please! Let me forget. Let him die. Let Arren Cardockson die."

Her light increased. *You have chosen wisely.*

Arenadd lay still. "Take them," he said again. "Take them away from me forever. I don't want to remember it ever again."

You never shall, she soothed. *I promise. You will be under my protection. Rest now, and when you wake all shall be well.*

"It won't," Arenadd said bitterly. "Even if you let me forget and make me more powerful, I'm still done for. I'll never get out of this cursed tower, not like this."

She chuckled; it was an oddly human sound for her to make. *Do not fear, Arenadd. Your partner has not abandoned you. Even now he is dragging you out of the tower to safety. He will know what to do; trust in him.*

Arenadd let out a great sigh. "Oh, master, I'm so sorry. I should never have let this happen. I'm such an idiot."

Do not blame yourself. At least your mistake has allowed us to meet again. And you like to see me, don't you?

"I do," he said instantly.

Good . . . good, Arenadd. I am proud to have you serve me. Now rest. You have worked so hard. When you awaken, all will be well.

And Arenadd slept.

29

Consequences

Skandar emerged into the open air, carrying Arenadd's limp body in his talons. Smoke had invaded his lungs, and he paused in the street outside the tower, coughing and retching. Once he felt better he took off with a flick of his wings and flew back to the top of the tower, where he put Arenadd down and inspected him.

The human lay utterly still, like a dead thing. He smelt of blood, and that cold metal scent he usually had. Skandar tried nudging him to wake him up, and speaking to him, but nothing worked.

Skandar hissed to himself in dismay.

Other griffins were already gathering. One dared to come close and inspect Arenadd. He recoiled quickly. "The human is dead!" he said.

Others took up the cry. "Dead!"

Skandar rose up, screeching in rage. "Not dead!" he roared.

They backed away at once, intimidated.

"Mighty Skandar, the human has metal talons through his body," one ventured. "He cannot have survived."

Skandar pecked at one of the protruding knives, trying to pull it out, but could not grip it. He dismissed it with a scornful hiss. "My human Shadow That Walk," he declared. "Not die. He wake again soon, see."

The other griffins did not look convinced.

Skandar ignored them. He sniffed at Arenadd again, thinking. The human was hurt, and he needed help. But not from him. Other humans could help him. The female, Saeddryn—she knew how to heal. Arenadd had told him she had helped before.

A plan slowly formed in his mind, and he clicked his beak in satisfaction. Yes. He would take Arenadd to Saeddryn, and she would help him. There was nothing more to be done here, anyway. The battle was won and the enemies were dead.

He lifted his head. "I go back, to fruit-nest," he said. "Take human. You, griffin, stay here. All stay here. Protect this nest, fight if others come. I say do this."

Skree, the largest of the griffins who had come with them to Skenfrith, bowed her head. "I hear and obey, Mighty Skandar," she said. "We shall guard this city with our lives."

"Good," said Skandar. "I go now. Return soon, when my human is healed."

"Yes, Mighty Skandar. I will make sure all of us know it."

Skandar flicked his tail and lifted Arenadd back up with his talons. He heard a clattering sound as the sickle fell onto the stonework, and he stared at it for a moment before scooping it up in his free paw. That was Arenadd's talon; he needed it to fight and would be unhappy if it was lost.

"Go now," he said, and took off.

He was tired from the journey to Skenfrith and even more tired by the battle, but he shook off his tiredness and dived back into the shadows. He had grown used to them by now, and he liked them. They were cool and refreshing, and he could feel them giving him extra strength. This was his magic, and he loved it.

The flight back to Fruitsheart passed quickly, and he left the shadows when he was over the tower. But the moment he emerged he could tell that something bad had happened.

Smoke was rising from several places down in the city; he could smell burning wood and flesh. Huge areas of the city had been utterly destroyed, and the Governor's Tower looked as if it was barely standing. Chunks were torn out of the stonework, as if a giant griffin had attacked it with its beak.

When Skandar landed at the top, he saw several dead griffins lying scattered there. Moments later, he was attacked.

He heard the aggressive cries of griffins from above and the running paws of humans below. Skandar laid Arenadd down between his forepaws and reared up angrily to protect him.

But the griffins did not attack. They swooped at him, only to wheel away at the last moment. As they did so, the humans emerged. Northerners all, armed with steel talons.

Skandar dropped back onto his paws and hissed at them. Dark humans were usually friends, but these smelt of anger and fear.

One of them ran ahead of the others and gestured at them. "Stop! Stop, it's Skandar, ye idiots!"

The humans slowed and then halted, but kept their weapons at the ready. They were all afraid of him. Skandar did not care. He liked to be feared.

The human who had shouted came toward him. She moved unevenly and with pain, and there was blood on her, but Skandar recognised her when she stopped and bowed to him.

He stretched his beak out to scent her, and grunted to himself. Saeddryn.

Saeddryn bowed again. "Skandar," she said, and then, in broken griffish, "Where's Arenadd . . . ?"

Skandar regarded her for a moment and then gently lifted Arenadd in his talons and laid him at her feet.

Saeddryn dropped her sword and knelt by her cousin's side. "Oh no. Oh holy moon . . ."

Skandar wrapped his tail around his hindquarters. "Hurt," he said roughly. "You help."

Saeddryn swore as she feverishly ran her hands over Arenadd's chest, probing at the knives where they entered his body. "Oh, *shadows* help me, what happened to him?"

Skandar only watched her, waiting for her to do something. She would know what to do.

Saeddryn pulled herself together. "Come here," she said sharply to her companions. "We have t'take him below."

They advanced nervously, their eyes on Skandar. Instantly he reared up, hissing and rasping. "Stay away!" he warned. "You stay away!"

Saeddryn cringed, but did not run away. "Please, Skandar, we have t'take him away from here," she said. "Can . . . can ye understand Cymrian?"

Skandar didn't, but he grasped her meaning easily enough.

"Not take!" he hissed. "Leave here. He stay with me, I protect. You . . . heal, heal now. Help."

"Well . . ." Saeddryn touched one of the knives. "I could . . . I guess I could take the knives out; that'd help . . . try an' bandage the wounds . . ." She straightened up. "Ye an' ye! Come back here, ye damned cowards. I want ye t'go below. Get clean water, bandages an' that stuff we use on wounds. Run!"

The humans fled, and Saeddryn slumped down by Arenadd. She prudently avoided looking Skandar in the eye as she spoke to him. "They'll be back soon enough, an' I'll do what I can. But . . . Skandar . . ." She tried griffish, stumbling over the words. "I think . . . will not . . . heal."

Skandar clicked his beak. "My human Shadow That Walk," he said. "Magic human. See him die once, then wake. Never die and stay dead. My human walk in shadow."

Saeddryn did not understand. "Well . . . I've seen him recover from wounds almost as bad as these," she mumbled. "Though I dunno what he's gonna say if he wakes up again. Gods, it all happened so fast." She winced and touched her face, where there was blood.

Skandar said nothing. He waited patiently with her until the other darkmen returned. She dismissed them again and then set to work.

First she pulled the knives out, groaning softly when she saw how long they were, and how sharp. Arenadd did not react when she pulled them out. His eyes, which were open, had a glassy look about them, as if there was nobody behind them.

Once Saeddryn had laid the knives in a neat pile beside her, she pulled Arenadd's blood-soaked robe open and set about cleaning his skin. The wounds looked ghastly, but he hadn't bled much, and she finished swabbing them and put on some herbal paste that would fight infection. That done, she wrapped bandages around his torso until she had covered all the cuts.

"There," she said, sitting back and wiping her forehead. "I've done what I can. The rest is in the Night God's hands."

Skandar chirped his satisfaction. "Female do good work!" he said. "My human wake soon."

Saeddryn stood up, wiping her hands on her gown. "Listen, Skandar, we have to take him inside. We were attacked only a short time ago, an' the bastards could be back. If they come, ye'll be right where they can see ye."

Skandar only stared at her, uncomprehending. "You go now," he said eventually. "Bring meat."

Saeddryn paused. "Hungry?" she said, in griffish.

"Am hungry," Skandar agreed. "Bring meat."

Saeddryn nodded and left. Once she had gone, Skandar pulled Arenadd toward him and lay down, cradling him against his chest, where his feathers would keep him warm.

Saeddryn returned with meat, and Skandar gulped it down. Using so much magic had made him ravenously hungry, and when he was done he sent Saeddryn to bring more.

Sated, he yawned and laid his head down over Arenadd, covering him with his neck.

"Skandar," said Saeddryn. "Skandar, ye have t'come inside. Ye need shelter, an' so does he. Skandar, can ye understand me?"

Skandar didn't, and even if he had, he wouldn't have listened. No human could tell him what to do. No human could persuade him, either, except for Arenadd. Arenadd was the clever human who always knew what to do. Saeddryn was nobody. She could do useful things, but she was not for talking to or listening to.

Besides, Skandar didn't need to be told what to do. He knew what he was doing.

Saeddryn lingered nearby for a long time, apparently reluctant to give in, but she eventually saw reason and left.

Satisfied, Skandar settled down to sleep. He wanted to be near the moon. It reminded him of the beautiful griffin who had come to him and made him feel safe.

Night came while he slept. He woke up briefly as the moon rose, and felt Arenadd jerk and begin to breathe again as its light touched them. Skandar sighed contentedly and went back to sleep.

Erian gripped the sword more tightly and stared intently at the target hanging in front of him. It was swinging wildly back and forth, still juddering from the impact of his last blow. Moving targets were always more difficult to hit, but they were the most likely kind. And now he had been entrusted with Gryphus' weapon it was his duty to ensure he knew how to use it.

The target swung back toward him, turning sideways so he could see the vulnerable spot he had daubed on it with a handful of mud. He planted his feet well apart and struck.

His aim was true, and the sword hit it right in the centre. The target folded around the blade and then broke apart in a shower of dry grass and twigs.

Erian lowered his sword, panting and grinning. "That'll teach you to get in my way, you evil straw dummy," he said, and chuckled at his own joke.

Well, that was probably enough for one day. He stretched and rubbed his aching back before walking back toward the village.

Senneck was sunning herself outside her hut, watching her chicks fight over the remains of their most recent meal. She looked up when Erian approached and greeted him with a chirp.

Erian sat down beside her, holding the sword across his lap. "By Gryphus, they're getting big, aren't they?" he said.

Senneck yawned widely. "Perhaps they know how urgent our business is," she said.

"They're very clever chicks," said Erian, with as much pride as if they were his own offspring.

The chicks broke off from their play and waddled over to inspect him. Erian petted the male. He trilled, liking it, and pushed his head against the man's hand, asking for more.

Erian scratched him under the beak. "You're a handsome one aren't you, Rannagon?" he murmured. "Eh? I bet one day you'll be as big and strong as your mother."

The chick chirped. "Rannagon!"

Erian grinned. The chicks had been using basic words and phrases for a while now, and "Rannagon" was one of the first words the male had ever used. "My father's name," Erian said. "Rannagon."

"Rannagon!" the chick repeated. It would be a long time before he knew what it meant.

Erian sighed contentedly and leant back against the wall of the hut. He didn't mind that he had to wait before they could leave. In a way, he felt it was necessary; it was a time for him to train with the sword and learn to use it, a time for him to meditate and plan. And a time for him to be with Senneck and her chicks, and think about things other than war and death for a while.

Out here, in the sunlight and the peaceful silence, nothing seemed very urgent.

He ran his fingers over the sword blade. Other than the rippled marks, nothing had changed as far as he could tell. The

weapon was as heavy as it had been before, the hilt had the
same tarnish marks and ingrained dirt, and the blade was still
notched. It didn't feel any sharper or stronger. But Erian knew
in his bones that it was not the same sword it had been when he
had brought it to the island.

*You would be so proud, Father, to know your sword has
become Gryphus' weapon.*

Erian tried to imagine what Lord Rannagon would say if he
were there and knew what had happened. But his father's face
had faded in his memory by now. His eyes had been brown,
hadn't they? No, no. Blue. They were blue. *Just like mine. The
line of Baragher the Blessed carried his blue eyes for generations. And now—*

He stiffened as a chill suddenly bit into his bones. The sun
seemed to darken, and as the shadows around him lengthened
he felt a terrible sense of dread come over him.

The chicks whimpered and ran to their mother, who had
half-risen as the darkness came, beak opening.

Without thinking, Erian pressed himself against her. "Senneck, what's happening? Why is it so dark?"

The darkness passed as quickly as it had come, and the
warmth of the sun returned along with its light.

Erian relaxed, but cautiously. The day had gone back to normal, but the sense of dread stayed inside him. "What *was* that,
Senneck? Did you feel it?"

"Yes." She looked skyward as she kneaded gently at the
sand with her talons. "You felt it, then?"

"Yes. It was . . . I don't know. I felt so scared all of a sudden.
Senneck, what did you feel?"

"I had a sense of something," she said. "I do not understand
it, but perhaps because I am a griffin I could feel it more powerfully than you."

"Feel *what*?" said Erian. "Is there something here? Are we
about to be attacked?"

"The world has shuddered," Senneck said in distant tones.
"And so, as a part of it, did we."

"But why?" said Erian.

"Something terrible has happened," said Senneck. "Somewhere. I do not know what it may be."

Erian's fists clenched. "It's *him*," he said. "I know it is. He's
done something. Senneck, what if . . ." Paranoia swept through

him. "What if we're too late? What if he's already in Malvern? What if he's killing Elkin and the others right now? What if—"

"Be calm," said Senneck. "There is nothing to be gained from panic."

"But—"

"But nothing. We shall leave here the instant my chicks no longer need me."

Erian scratched the ragged beard that had slowly covered his chin. "Can't we just bring them with us?"

"I cannot carry them as well as you," said Senneck. "We shall barely be able to reach land again as it is."

"But I've been thinking," said Erian. "What if . . ." He hesitated, and then plunged ahead. "I thought may be I could make a boat. You could fly overhead to help me navigate, and I could get back to land that way. I could take the chicks with me."

Senneck started to say something and then stopped. She put her head on one side, thoughtfully. "You think you could make a boat?" she said eventually. "I did not know you knew anything about them."

"I don't, really, but—but there's already a boat here. In the village. I could dig it out and see if I could do anything with it. Maybe I could repair it! And even if I can't, I can look at how it's made and learn what I can. It's got to be worth a try."

Senneck thought it over. "I do not see why not. It would be better than doing nothing."

"I *can't* do nothing," said Erian. "Not now. Not if . . ."

They were silent for a moment, sharing the same thought. If *Kraeai kran ae*'s power had increased, if he had won some victory or committed some evil great enough to make the whole world shudder, then nothing mattered any more but to return to the North as quickly as possible. Not even the chicks were important enough any more.

The Dark Lord had to be stopped.

A renadd woke up and greeted the new day with a yawn. He sat up and rubbed his back. It ached, and no wonder: he'd been sleeping on hard stone. But he felt wonderfully refreshed and alert. *Godsdamnit, that was the best night's sleep I've had in months,* he thought.

As he looked around, he realised he was on top of the

Governor's Tower in Fruitsheart. Skandar was there, still sleeping.

Arenadd stood up as the memory of the previous day came back. Skenfrith, the attack . . .

The knives!

He clapped a hand over his chest, searching for them, but they were gone, and he sighed in relief.

"Skandar." He patted the griffin's shoulder. "Skandar? Wake up."

Skandar's eyes cracked open, and he peered at him.

"Good morning, Skandar," said Arenadd. "Are you hurt?"

Skandar yawned and got up. "Am not hurt. Human . . . hurt?"

"I don't think so. Skandar, why are we here? Why aren't we at Skenfrith?"

"You hurt," Skandar said. "I bring you here, to female. Tell her help you, she help."

"Saeddryn? You mean Saeddryn?"

"Yes. Female help."

"You brought me back here so she could take the knives out," Arenadd guessed. "I don't know how to thank you, Skandar. You did exactly the right thing. You're a clever griffin, aren't you?"

Skandar blinked modestly. "You clever. I fight, you think. But you heal now?"

Arenadd prodded his chest. There was no pain. "I feel fine. What happened at Skenfrith?"

"Leave griffin there, tell them guard nest," said Skandar. "Then come back here."

"So, all the enemy griffins at Skenfrith died?"

"Yes. Human run from tall nest, we kill. Some not come; they die."

Some of the humans ran out of the towers, and the griffins killed them, Arenadd translated. *The rest died in the fire. Good.* "Then we can probably leave them for a while and talk with . . ." He trailed off as he suddenly noticed the damage to the tower and the city, and the dead griffins scattered nearby. "What happened? Skandar, what . . . was there an attack?"

"Must be," Skandar said carelessly. "Not while we here."

Arenadd's gaze travelled over the city, noting the smoking craters. "Firebombs. Must have been. The griffiners must have . . ." He looked around quickly and found his sickle, which he scooped up and put back in his belt. "Come on. We have to talk to Saeddryn."

"Plan now," Skandar agreed.

"Yes," Arenadd said darkly.

In spite of what had happened, he felt a strange calm and certainty as he went into the tower with Skandar. He remembered the Night God visiting him in his dreams, and remembered her whispering advice and the comfort she gave him. She was with him, and she would not let him fail.

But he did have a moment's doubt. Just briefly, as he went down the ramp beyond the trapdoor that led into the tower, he had the nagging feeling that he had forgotten something. But he couldn't for the life of him decide what it was.

He shrugged it off. It probably wasn't important. If it was, he'd remember it eventually.

As he explored the tower, he quickly saw even more evidence of the attack that must have taken place in his absence. The upper levels were deserted; the defenders had gone, leaving behind signs of their fight in the form of bodies.

Arenadd stopped to look at one or two of them. All of them were Southerners, and from their clothing he could tell that they were griffiners. If any of his own people had died here, their friends must have taken their bodies away. At least that meant enough of them had survived . . .

Something else occurred to him at that moment, and he swore and ran away.

He found the governor's quarters and ducked inside, with Skandar on his heels. The bedchamber had been badly damaged; he could see sword cuts on the furniture, and blood had left a stain on one wall. There were no bodies here, at least.

Arenadd freed his sickle and padded into the griffin nest.

It was full of griffins, all asleep.

Arenadd stopped in the doorway, motioning to Skandar to be quiet. He stayed as still as he could, quickly taking in every griffin in the room. Four . . . five . . . six of them, all big and powerful looking. There was no sign of Hyrenna's chicks.

Skandar poked his head through the door, over Arenadd's shoulder, and sniffed, "Kaanee," he growled. *"Kaanee!"*

The griffin nearest the door started awake, rising in an

instant with his beak wide open. When he saw Skandar, he stopped abruptly. "Mighty Skandar!"

Arenadd returned his sickle to his belt. "Kaanee. Thank the Night God."

Kaanee came toward them. He was dragging one foreleg and there were chunks torn out of his feathers, but he looked strong enough. "I did not expect you here so soon," he said, hastily ducking his head while his fellow griffins stirred around him. "Mighty Skandar, I am pleased to see you are unhurt. May I ask how the attack on Skenfrith succeeded?"

"Have captured human nest," said Skandar. "Tall nest burn, enemy die. Leave friend griffin there to guard."

Kaanee eyed them. "Good. And your human . . ." He looked at Arenadd. "I am sorry, Lord Arenadd, but I had heard that you were . . ."

"I'm fine," said Arenadd. "Kaanee, where are the chicks? Hyrenna's chicks—they were in here."

Kaanee glanced over his shoulder. "They are well. We have guarded them and your commander ever since you left, master."

Arenadd looked past him and saw Saeddryn rising from a heap of dried reeds. "Kaanee? What's . . . *sir!*"

Arenadd smiled at her. "Good morning, Saeddryn. Are you . . ." He trailed off.

Saeddryn picked her way through the nesting material and stood in front of him, head bowed as if in shame. There was a bandage wrapped around her head.

Arenadd reached out and gently lifted her chin. "Your eye . . ."

Saeddryn grimaced. "I was lucky, sir. It was a glancing blow."

"You haven't lost it, have you?" said Arenadd.

"It's a wreck, sir," Saeddryn said resignedly. "But I'll live."

As she spoke, the chicks roused themselves and wandered over. Arenadd crouched to look at them. They appeared to be in perfect health, and he breathed out and silently offered up a prayer of thanks before he straightened up. "Tell me what happened, Saeddryn."

She was giving him a slightly apprehensive look through her remaining eye. "Sir, if ye don't mind me askin' . . . are ye all right?"

"What? Oh." Arenadd felt his chest and suddenly noticed

the bandages. "Well, I'm . . . uh . . . not in any pain. Thank you
for taking those blasted things out of me. Skandar says you
were a great help."

Saeddryn switched to the Northern tongue. "Sir, there were
five knives stuck in ye. One of 'em was straight through yer
heart."

"I know," said Arenadd. "*These* knives, I think." He touched
one of the weapons tucked into the back of his belt. "Good steel.
I think I'll keep them. Of course, if I meet the owner, I'll have
to give them back. It would only be good manners."

Saeddryn pulled herself together. "It's the power, isn't it,
sir?" she said. "Ye're healin' even faster now. Ye're gettin'
stronger, sir."

Arenadd nodded. "Yes. I can feel it."

"Ye're sure there's no pain, sir?"

"Only in my stomach," said Arenadd. "I'm hungry. Come
on, let's go and get some food. And while we're on our way, for
the love of the Night God, tell me what happened here."

"Yes, sir."

Skandar had been making halting conversation with Kaanee
but looked up as the two humans made for the door. "You go?"

"I need to get something to eat," said Arenadd. "D'you want
to come?"

"I come," said Skandar and followed them out of the chamber and down through the tower, stopping occasionally to eat
one of the bodies left lying in the corridors.

Saeddryn walked beside Arenadd and told him everything
in a low, terse voice.

"They came when ye'd barely even left. Dozens of 'em. They
can't have known Kaanee had joined us, or they'd have brought
more. Thank gods we outnumbered the bastards, but—"

"But they were better armed," Arenadd put in. "And you had
no good archers."

Saeddryn nodded. "We'd have been destroyed if it hadn't
been for Kaanee. Him an' his friends attacked the bastards in
the air. Nearly half of 'em died, but they fought the griffiner
scum off in the end. Not before they'd dropped firebombs an'
destroyed half the tower, mind."

"How many humans have we lost?" said Arenadd.

"Hundred," said Saeddryn. "Mostly in the city, but in the
tower as well. Davyn's dead, Rhodri close to it."

Arenadd swore. "What about the rest?"

"That Iorwerth," said Saeddryn. "Sir, ye've found a perfect commander. Sure, he's young an' he ain't fought before, but he's a clear thinker—knows what's best t'do an' does it quickly."

"Excellent." Arenadd nodded, pleased. "I knew he had potential."

"He saved my life, sir," said Saeddryn. "I got caught in one of the explosions when the firebombs hit. Cut up my arm somethin' bad. I was knocked silly an' would've burned t'death, but Iorwerth pulled me out of there. I lost the eye later, when some of the griffiners got into the tower t'fight us directly. But don't worry, I killed the bastard," she added grimly.

"Is everyone else safe, then?" said Arenadd, as they reached the kitchen.

"More or less, sir."

"More or less?" Arenadd tensed. "Oh gods, what about Torc?"

"Torc's fine, sir. Even joined in the fightin'. He's braver'n he looks." Saeddryn sounded almost fond.

"And Caedmon?"

Saeddryn closed her eye for a moment. "We did our best, sir. Ye have t'understand how fast it all happened. One moment everyone was gettin' food an' organisin' 'emselves for the day, the next we was bein' attacked."

"Yes, I understand, but did you get him to safety?"

"I sent Davyn t'get him an' Torc t'safety," said Saeddryn. "They was halfway down the tower when the firebombs started comin'. Davyn died shieldin' Caedmon. Caedmon was hurt. Torc stayed with him an' fought t'protect him when the griffiners came down the tower. Afterward he helped carry him t'infirmary. The boy's a hero, sir."

"And Caedmon? Is he all right?"

Saeddryn hesitated, then dared to touch his hand. "He's dyin', sir."

30

Lost Memories

Arenadd said very little while he and Saeddryn ate, both ignoring the complaints from the kitchen, where it seemed Skandar had decided to tear down a hanging side of beef. Saeddryn, realising her master was thinking, respected his silence, though she looked as if she wanted to talk.

Eventually Arenadd said, "I've made a terrible mistake."

"Ye weren't t'know, sir," said Saeddryn, who had obviously been expecting him to say this. "How were any of us t'know Malvern knew we were here?"

"But I shouldn't have left," said Arenadd. "I should have stayed long enough to make sure you were ready. I thought I could come back quickly. If I hadn't been stupid enough to let that bastard catch me unawares at Skenfrith . . ."

"But they shouldn't have come here that fast!" said Saeddryn. "None of the griffiners escaped when we took this place, an' we didn't spare any of the ones who came here later. So none could've got back to Malvern t'inform on us. An' that lot who came—all those griffiners—they came far too soon after the last lot. Too soon for Malvern t'have realised the first lot had gone missin'. How could they have known?"

Arenadd stared into his cup. "I don't know. Unless one of them did escape, and we didn't know about it. Or maybe . . ."

"What about the Eyrie Mistress?" said Saeddryn. "Could

she have figured it out? If she knew we were holdin' her at Fruitsheart, she could've told 'em. But she was blindfolded the whole time, wasn't she, sir? No-one said more than two words t'her, if that."

"I don't know," said Arenadd. "But she's a clever woman. I saw as much when I met her. Maybe she did realise. Either that or it was something else we haven't thought of yet."

"Well, we still won, sir," said Saeddryn. "We fought 'em off. The Night God protected us."

"Her and Kaanee," Arenadd muttered. "Maybe. But the cost . . ."

"No cost is too high for us to pay, sir!" Saeddryn exclaimed. "Don't ye see? I'm sad about what happened t'Rhodri an' Davyn, but they were willin' to die for Tara. An' so am I."

Arenadd though of the two Northerners. Honest men, and loyal. Losing them was a blow. "At least Skenfrith was a success. According to Skandar, none of the griffiners survived there, either. And we've destroyed the towers. It'll be nearly impossible for them to use it as a base. That's an important stronghold of theirs gone."

"Aye, sir," said Saeddryn. "Ye did us proud."

"*Skandar* did us proud." Arenadd stood up. "I have to go and visit Caedmon. If I don't do it now, I may not get another chance."

Saeddryn nodded. "Go t'him, sir. I'll take care of things while ye're gone."

Caedmon had been put in one of the griffiner bedchambers in the tower, away from the other injured people. Arenadd was surprised to find someone on guard by the door.

"My lord!" said the man, looking shocked.

Arenadd inclined his head. "Sorry to catch you unawares like this. Did Saeddryn tell you to stay here?"

"No, my lord. Iorwerth asked me. He said Caedmon deserved t'be left in peace, my lord."

Arenadd smiled internally. "Good. Just what should be done. Do you know if he's awake?"

"I think so, my lord. Torc's with him."

Arenadd saw the fear almost glowing in the man's face and suddenly felt depressed. "I'll go in, then. You stay out here and make sure we're not disturbed."

"Yes, my lord."

Arenadd entered silently. Caedmon was lying in the bed, almost lost amid the blankets. He wasn't moving, but he was obviously awake because Torc was sitting beside him with his back to the door, and the two were talking in low voices.

Arenadd closed the door behind him as quietly as he could and paused to listen.

". . . can't do it," Torc said. "I just can't, Father."

"Ye're a Taranisäii now, Torc." Caedmon's gravelly voice was weak but as resolute as always. "Not a slave. The . . . time's gone when . . . yer look t'others for what to do. If ye're certain, then do it."

"But what if she ain't . . . what if she says . . . I couldn't bear it, Father." Torc sounded almost tearful.

"Weaklings say 'what if,' Torc," Caedmon growled. "Warriors say 'I will.' Do it. I want t'know yer did it, before I go."

"I'll . . . I'll try," said Torc.

"That's my lad."

Arenadd hated to interrupt but realised at this point that it would be rude not to, so he coughed politely.

Torc turned, wide-eyed. "Sir!"

Arenadd walked toward him. "Hello, Torc. I'm sorry to interrupt. If you'd like me to leave . . ."

Torc stood up hastily. "No. No, sir, it's fine. I just didn't . . . Sir, Saeddryn said . . ."

"I'm fine." Arenadd smiled fondly at the boy. "Saeddryn told me you acted like a hero yesterday."

Torc blushed. "I didn't. I only . . . well, I couldn't leave Caedmon, sir. I had t'keep him safe, sir."

"Of course you did," said Arenadd. "But you were very brave. Saeddryn's very impressed with you. And so am I," he added.

Torc grinned shyly. "Did she say that, sir?"

"She certainly did," said Arenadd, watching closely for the response.

Torc looked even more embarrassed, but pleased. He put a hand in his pocket and glanced quickly at Caedmon, as if for approval.

Caedmon said nothing, but Arenadd saw him wink, and in that instant his suspicions were confirmed. "Well then," he said. "Maybe you should go and talk to her. I think she'll need some help while she organises everyone."

Torc nodded. "Yes, sir. I'll go, sir." He looked at Caedmon again and hurried out of the room.

Arenadd sat down by the bed, chuckling. "He's a good lad, isn't he?"

Caedmon's face crinkled in a smile. "Aye. I've known him a long time, I have. He was like a son t'me long before I took him into our family."

"You made a good decision," said Arenadd. "He's a brave boy, and good-hearted, too. And we Taranisäiis are all too rare nowadays, aren't we?" he added more quietly.

Caedmon sighed. "Ah, but we're comin' back. Bit by bit."

"Yes." Arenadd looked at him. The old man appeared frighteningly pale and almost shrunken. There were several painful cuts on his face, but it was obvious his injuries went far beyond that, even if they weren't visible.

Caedmon looked back resignedly. "There's not much t'see on the outside," he said. "It's all inside. I can feel it."

Arenadd touched his hand. "Are you in pain?"

"Not so much now," said Caedmon, wincing. "I can't feel anythin' much now. Can't move me legs. Can't move one arm. Half me gut's crushed, but it don't hurt. I ain't got long, though. I know that. I'll be with the Night God soon."

Arenadd rubbed a hand over his face. "Gods. Caedmon, I'm sorry. I should have been here."

"Stuff an' nonsense," Caedmon snapped. "Ye've our leader, sir, an' ye've got better things t'd than look after old men like me. But I'm glad to see yer back," he added more gently. "I wanted t'see yer again before I went."

"I came as soon as I knew," said Arenadd. "Caedmon, you're the oldest member of my family now. And more than that, you're a friend. You have been ever since we met in the slave-house at Herbstitt."

Caedmon smiled. "Same for me, sir. Same for me."

"Please don't call me that," said Arenadd.

"Of course, if that's what yer want. I wanted t'ask yer somethin' . . . Arenadd."

"Ask me, then," said Arenadd.

"No, no." Caedmon looked away. "No, it's not important, not now."

"Yes it is," Arenadd said firmly. "So tell me."

Caedmon coughed again, and shuddered. "It's nothing."

Arenadd had to smile. "Go on, tell me."

Caedmon was silent for a long moment. "They say . . . I mean, it's . . . everyone knows . . ."

"What?"

"Ye've met the Night God," Caedmon said at last. "We all know it."

Arenadd hadn't been expecting this. "Yes," he said. "I suppose I have."

"What is she like?" Caedmon asked. "What . . . I know I'll meet her soon. What is she like? Is she kind? Will she welcome me?"

Arenadd smiled sadly. "I could tell you what she's like."

"Please, do," said Caedmon. "I just want t'know. So I can . . . be ready."

Arenadd wondered where he should begin. "She's beautiful, in a way. Black hair." He smiled briefly. "Like Arddryn, a little, with one eye. The other eye is the moon, just like the stories say."

"Is she kind?" Caedmon persisted. "Is she?"

Arenadd thought of her pitiless eye. "She can be," he said. "She's . . . so powerful. She can be angry . . . terrible anger. But when she's happy, she makes you feel like . . ." He tried again: "She has the same emotions we do, but more powerful. A hundred times more powerful. When she's pleased, she can make you feel so happy and peaceful you think you're going to burst with it. When she's angry . . . but she wouldn't be angry with you, Caedmon."

Caedmon looked at him, his expression almost childlike. "Are yer sure, Arenadd? How d'yer know?"

Arenadd touched Caedmon's forehead. "Because you're a Taranisäii, Caedmon. You're from the greatest family the North ever bred. You kept faith in her even after all the suffering you went through while you were a slave. She won't forget that. She loves the people who stay by her. She loves *us*. We're her people, Caedmon. Her chosen people. She loves us when we're brave most of all. She sent me to help you. She guided me to you, so I could set you free. Because she cares about you."

"She cares?"

"Yes," said Arenadd, knowing it was what he needed to hear. "She cares, Caedmon. And She'll welcome you. When you get to her, she'll make your star one of the brightest."

Caedmon had begun to look sleepy. "Are ye sure?"

Arenadd leant close to him. "Yes, Caedmon. More than I've ever been. She'll be waiting for you. And so will I."

Caedmon's eyes drooped. "You?"

"Yes." Arenadd hesitated and then whispered in his ear. "The Night God already has my soul, Caedmon. She took it from me a long time before I met you, so she could put magic in its place. She took it and gave me power in return. My soul is already with her. Waiting. When you find her, you'll find me. I'll protect you. And so will she."

Caedmon's eyes had closed. "I'll see yer then," he mumbled. "One day . . ."

Arenadd sat back. "Sleep, Caedmon. You've earnt it. I'll win this war for you, and when I have, I will build a great temple to the Night God. The greatest temple the world has ever seen. And I'll carve your name on the altar. The North will know what you did for it. I promise."

Two days after the destruction of Skenfrith, Caedmon Tara-nisäii died. He spent his final day unconscious, while his adopted son kept up a vigil over him. That night, as the moon began to rise over the rooftops of Fruitsheart, he finally stopped breathing, one final, silent sigh marking the moment when his soul slid out of his body and away.

Arenadd himself conducted the funeral rites, which took place that very night under the moon—the best time for any Northerner to be laid to rest.

As the funeral pyre burned, the Lord of Darkmen stood by with Saeddryn to his right and Torc to his left—the two surviving members of his family—and said the rites while their friends looked on in silence.

"Of earth born and in fire forged, by magic blessed and by cool water soothed, then by a breeze in the night blown away to a land of silver and bright flowers. May . . ."

As he spoke on, Torc and Saeddryn sang a low humming song in the Northern tongue, invoking the spirits of the sky and the sacred animals. Deer, wolf, bear, crow, griffin.

Skandar had come to the ceremony, too, along with Kaanee and the chicks. The griffins stood by awkwardly, aware that they had no part in what was a human ritual.

When it was over and the pyre had burned itself out, the
mourners quietly dispersed, leaving the three Taranisäiis alone.

Arenadd watched the wind stir the ashes and blow them
away. "He was a good man," he murmured.

Torc wiped away his tears. "He was the only father I ever
had. If only I could've . . . if I could've done something . . ."

Saeddryn put a hand on his arm and shook her head. "No,
Torc. This isn't the time for that. And it wasn't yer fault. It was
never yer fault. Ye did yer best."

Torc stilled. "Saeddryn, I . . ."

"Yes?"

"I want to talk to you," said Torc. He paused to screw up his
courage. "Somewhere alone."

Saeddryn looked a little surprised. "Of course," she said.

Arenadd stood aside as Torc led her away. He was unable to
hold back a smile. "I'll see you two later, then," he said. "Take
care of yourselves."

Torc cast a nervous glance back at him as he left. Arenadd
gave him an encouraging wink.

Once they were gone, he leant against the wall, where a
bored Skandar had gone to sleep, and kept an eye on the chicks.
Poor old Torc. So used to being downtrodden and ordered about
that he was afraid to even think for himself. But he was learning.

Despite himself, Arenadd chuckled. True, not everything
had gone as well as he had hoped, but his plans were still working. The sun worshippers had suffered two crushing defeats.
They had lost more than two cities and dozens of lives. And
they had lost their credibility as well. There was no way, once
word of this had spread, that anybody would think of Arenadd
and his rebellious darkmen as easily defeated or as a minor
threat.

In fact, now that he thought about it seriously, he could most
likely be ready to attack Malvern well before Skade returned.

Skade.

Gods, he missed her already. Her absence felt like a weight
in his chest. There was so much he wanted to tell her.

"Lord Arenadd."

Arenadd looked up to see Kaanee limping toward him. "Oh.
Hello. Yes, what is it?"

The tawny griffin sat on his haunches, looking down at him.
"I am sorry to disturb you, Shadow that Walks."

"It's all right," said Arenadd. "What can I do for you?"

Kaanee yawned briefly and closed his beak with a snap. "My leg is badly damaged and unlikely to heal well," he said. "The unpartnered know this. Soon, I will be challenged as the strongest among them, and if I am defeated, then there is no telling what will happen."

Arenadd tensed. "If you want me to protect you . . ."

"No. I cannot accept that. A griffin who hides behind another's strength is weak. No."

"Then what are you going to do, Kaanee?" said Arenadd. "I can't afford any trouble."

"I have thought of a way," said Kaanee.

"Yes?" said Arenadd.

"It will be dangerous," Kaanee admitted. "But I believe it will be the best thing to do."

"Tell me, then," said Arenadd.

Kaanee scratched his head with his talons. "Iorwerth," he said.

"What about him?" said Arenadd.

"I have been watching him," the griffin muttered. "He is a strong human, a good fighter and a fine leader. Worthy. And he is one of your inner circle."

Arenadd blinked. "Oh. You don't mean . . . but Saeddryn is closer to me than Iorwerth is and . . ."

"The female is impressive, but not as strong," Kaanee said dismissively. "If I am to choose a human, he must be the strongest. Iorwerth has impressed me, and I wish to know him better."

Arenadd thought quickly. If Kaanee chose a human, his standing would improve immensely in the eyes of his fellow griffins. But if that human were a Northerner . . .

"I know I shall be looked down upon by some for choosing a Northerner," said Kaanee, apparently reading his thoughts. "Yet I have already accepted a leader who is partnered to one— what loyalty would there be in refusing the partnership of one of your race? No. I shall choose Iorwerth as my human and seal our alliance."

Arenadd smiled grimly. This was an unexpected turn of events but one he liked very much. If Kaanee chose a Northerner as his human, others would follow suit. Soon he could have followers who were more than ordinary people. He could have griffiners.

His mind filled with images, each one more pleasing than the last. His friends flying on griffinback. Northern griffiners loyal to him. Northern griffiners attacking Malvern. Saeddryn, Iorwerth and Nerth flying into battle with himself and Skandar. The Southerners at Malvern baffled and frightened in the face of the Northern onslaught, unable to believe that griffins born in *their* city would choose mere *darkmen* to ride them . . .

His smile widened. "Your plan is a good one, Kaanee. Very good. If Skandar agrees, then you can take Iorwerth as your human. I'm sure Iorwerth himself won't have any objections." *Although at first he may think he's been smoking too much whiteleaf.*

Kaanee made a rasping sound in the back of his throat. "I am pleased to hear it, Lord Arenadd."

Of course you are, Arenadd thought. *But you couldn't possibly be as pleased as I am.*

31

Endings and Beginnings

On the morning after Caedmon's funeral, Arenadd and Skandar returned to Skenfrith.

They found it utterly ravaged.

Arenadd, watching from Skandar's back, was shocked.

The fire had completely gutted the towers, destroying the wooden framework and causing the stones to crumble in many places. The ruins were festooned with griffins.

Skandar landed at the top of the largest tower, and the unpartnered were quick to come to him. They flocked around their leader, all calling at once in loud harsh voices.

Skandar reared up and screeched his name so loudly that every single person in the city must have heard him.

The unpartnered backed away, instantly cowed, and Arenadd dismounted.

"Where Skree?" Skandar called. "Skree, come!"

Skree, a big female who was the strongest of the unpartnered now in Skenfrith, appeared from among her fellows. She bowed her head to Skandar. "Mighty Skandar."

"Up," Skandar said.

She raised her head obediently. "We did not expect you back so soon, Mighty Skandar."

"Am back," said Skandar. "You stay . . . my human speak."

Arenadd obligingly stepped forward. "Hello, Skree."

The grey griffin stared at him. "The Shadow that Walks."

"The same," said Arenadd. "Skree, tell me what happened here after Skandar and I left."

She had not stopped staring. "Forgive me, but I had thought . . . it does not matter. I am pleased to see you back, and well."

Arenadd's mouth curled. "Yes, Skree, the stories are true. I am the Shadow that Walks—the Cursed One, as some griffins have called me. The Night God has made me immortal, and no human weapon can kill me."

Skree's tail flicked—the only sign of agitation she showed. "I had heard the tales but had not . . . I was not ready to witness the truth . . . master."

"Well, you've witnessed it now," Arenadd said shortly. "Now tell me, what happened after we left?"

"Little of note," said Skree. "We stayed in the city, as the Mighty Skandar had commanded, and killed any Southern humans who remained. We used our magic to ensure the towers were destroyed."

"Good." Arenadd nodded. "We won't need them. When we do come here in force, we'll only stay for a few days before we move on. And the sun worshippers won't be able to hold on to it for long if they come back."

"Your plan was a cunning one, master," Skree said politely.

"It couldn't have been done without your help," said Arenadd. "But now your work here is done, and we need you back at Fruitsheart."

She was instantly alert. "When shall we leave, master?"

"Soon," said Arenadd. "First Skandar and I are going into the city. If anyone there wants to follow us, we'll find them. When we leave, you'll follow us."

"Yes, master."

Arenadd nodded curtly to her and got back onto Skandar's back.

Their visit to the city proved to be a fruitful one. Its inhabitants, having witnessed the attack, were in no doubt at all about the extent of Arenadd's power, and while many of them hid when he and Skandar appeared in the town square, others gathered to see them.

Arenadd was tired and still deeply depressed over Skade's

absence, but he made a speech because he knew it was expected of him.

"My people," he said. "Men and women of great Tara, my brothers and sisters, chosen by the Night God. I, Arenadd Taranisäii, have come to you as a friend. I carry the tattoos of a chief, given to me by Arddryn Taranisäii herself. Beside me is Skandar, the Night Griffin, more powerful than the Mighty Kraal himself. We have come here to give you back your pride . . . and more than your pride. The Night God has chosen us. She has named me the Shadow that Walks, the Master of Death, the Lord of Darkmen, and sent me to free her land and her people. Join us, and we will lead you to Malvern, where we will crush the sun worshippers who have oppressed us for so long and take our land back!"

The people close enough to hear roared their approval. Others, spurred on by their enthusiasm, joined in.

"Unite under my banner!" Arenadd yelled. "Join with us, and you will see the same fate that befell the towers here befall the Eyrie at Malvern! That is my promise!"

"I will join ye, lord!" one woman shouted. "Command me, lord!"

Others joined their voices to hers, declaring their support.

"If you wish to join me, then here is my first order," said Arenadd. "Go to Fruitsheart. I will be waiting there with my followers. We will teach you to be warriors again. All of you come, men and women. I should warn you that if you stay here, you will be in danger when the griffiners return. They will suspect all of you because of the colour of your hair and eyes. Because you are darkmen. Warn your friends and your neighbours. Even if you choose not to join me, you must be ready when they come. The Southerners will show no mercy."

Over half the crowd pledged to follow him then and there, and once he had spoken to some of them and given them his advice on how to reach Fruitsheart quickly he got back onto Skandar's back and the dark griffin flew away.

The shadows brought them back to Fruitsheart as quickly as before but left Skandar tired and Arenadd nearly as much so. He left the dark griffin to sleep in his nest and went to find Saeddryn.

But she was already in his chamber, waiting for him.

Arenadd stopped in surprise. "Saeddryn. What are you doing here?"

She stepped toward him. "I'm sorry, sir. I wanted t'speak with ye. Are ye too tired? I can wait."

"No, it's fine," said Arenadd. "I wanted to speak with you anyway, to make sure nothing happened while I was away."

Saeddryn halted. "Everythin's fine, sir. We've got everythin' together. I've spent most of the day trainin' the archers. They ain't great, but they're gettin' better. The sooner Nerth gets here the better."

"Good," said Arenadd. "What was it you wanted to talk to me about?"

She looked uncomfortable. "Maybe we should sit, sir."

Arenadd began to feel suspicious, but he nodded anyway and sat down at the table. There was a bowl of fruit in front of him, and he picked up a pear and bit into it. Delicious.

Saeddryn sat opposite him and took an apple, which she toyed with rather than ate. "Sir, I wanted t'ask ye . . ."

Arenadd swallowed. "Yes? If it's important, then just say it."

She didn't look him in the eye; instead, she kept her gaze on the apple, which rolled back and forth across the table as she passed it from hand to hand. "Skade," she said eventually.

Arenadd tensed. "What about her?"

Saeddryn looked up. "I want t'know if ye love her, sir."

"What sort of question is that?" Arenadd snapped.

"A question I want answered," said Saeddryn, suddenly resolute. "Just tell me, sir. Do ye love her?"

"Yes, I do."

"Enough t'spend yer life with her, sir?" said Saeddryn. "Enough t'marry her?"

"Saeddryn, we've been through this," said Arenadd. "I don't have a stone any more. I can't marry her."

"As if that matters!" Saeddryn said, with sudden anger. "We're Northerners, Arenadd. We don't marry the same way; we've got our own rituals. Forgotten, maybe, but we can revive them. An' besides, ye ain't ordinary, sir. If ye commanded it, there's no-one would stop ye marryin' whatever woman ye chose. Sir."

Arenadd stopped to think about it. She was right. Who *would* try to stop him? If he won the war, he would be powerful enough to change whatever he liked. He could marry Skade . . .

"Ye see, sir?" said Saeddryn, impatiently.

"Yes, Saeddryn. I see."

She was looking at him very carefully. "So, ye see ye can marry, sir. An' if ye did—"

"Why does it matter?" said Arenadd. "Who I marry is my business."

"No, sir," said Saeddryn. "I'm sorry, sir, but it ain't just yer own business."

"Oh?" said Arenadd, hiding his annoyance.

"Ye are the head of our tribe," said Saeddryn. "An' the head of the Taranisäii family, too. Now Mother is dead, ye've inherited all her powers an' her position, too. Who ye marry is important to everyone in our tribe."

"So you think I should marry you because it would strengthen us," Arenadd concluded. "I know that's what you're thinking, Saeddryn, so there's no need to beat about the bush."

"Sir, I know what they're sayin'," said Saeddryn. "Nobody on our side trusts that Skade or likes her. They don't know who she is or where she came from, but they know ye an' her are sharin' a bed every night, an' they don't like it."

"Is that so," said Arenadd in his flattest, coldest voice.

"She's a Southerner, sir," said Saeddryn. "She's not one of us. How can the Lord of Darkmen bed a *Southerner*, one of his worst enemies? One of the cursed sun worshippers?"

"Skade is not a Southerner," Arenadd snapped.

"Well then, where did she come from?" said Saeddryn. "Her hair ain't black. Her eyes ain't black. Why does she look so odd? I never saw a woman with her colouring or heard one what spoke the way she does. Where did ye find her?"

"Skade is on our side, Saeddryn," said Arenadd, fighting to keep his temper. "She hates the Southerners as much as we do, and she wants to see us defeat them—that's all you need to know."

"Sir, it's not that I don't respect yer feelin's," said Saeddryn. "It ain't that. Ye're no fool, ye know what ye want, but . . ."

"But *what*?"

"But ye're a leader, sir," said Saeddryn. "Ye have more than yer own heart t'think of. A leader must think of his followers an' his cause before what he wants for himself, sir. An' that's why—"

"Why I should turn my back on Skade," said Arenadd. "Why I should marry a woman I don't love. Why I should betray myself. Is that it, Saeddryn? Is *that* what I should do, for the good of my followers and my cause? Well?"

"Yes, sir," Saeddryn said bluntly.

"I'm sorry to disappoint you, but the answer is no," said Arenadd. "Completely, utterly and finally, *no.*"

"But sir—"

"*No*, Saeddryn. You heard me, and that's my final word. Not now, not ever."

"But why, sir?"

Because my love for Skade is the only good thing left in me. Because if I lost that, I would be nothing.

"Because I am your lord, and that's my order to you, Saeddryn. I'll win this war and destroy our enemies, but I will not marry you. Not now, not ever."

Saeddryn stared at him as if he had just slapped her in the face. The apple she was holding fell onto the floor.

As if the thump had revived her, Saeddryn stood up. "Yes . . . sir," she said, and left the room with a slow, defeated tread.

The next day began quietly enough. After a quick breakfast, Arenadd had another meeting with the remnants of his council. Iorwerth had now become Kaanee's partner and had accepted it with a kind of awe. Arenadd would have to teach him griffish, but for now he had other things to deal with.

After the meeting, he returned to his chambers and spent some time with the chicks. They seemed lively enough and had taken to him quite well. That surprised him; for as long as he could remember, animals had been terrified of him. Even griffins seemed to feel the fear that drove lesser beasts away from him, but these chicks showed no sign of it.

Maybe it was Skandar's blood in them.

After that, Arenadd and Skandar paid a visit to Nerth. The darkman and his followers were still travelling away from the mountains and toward the hiding place Arenadd had chosen.

Arenadd had a brief conversation with Nerth. It seemed he had been doing well: they had avoided being seen by travelling mostly at night and were making good progress. Arenadd briefly shared with them everything that had happened, including the deaths of Rhodri and Davyn, and Caedmon.

Nerth accepted it all in impenetrable silence. "An' Skenfrith?"

"Destroyed," said Arenadd. "None of the griffiners there survived."

Nerth looked away. "Good."

Arenadd wanted to stay longer but knew he had to return quickly. He gave Nerth and his friends the supplies he'd brought for them and then got back onto Skandar's back.

"May the Night God bless you," he said, and the dark griffin took off.

When they reached Fruitsheart and landed on the tower as always, it was to find Torc waiting for them.

Arenadd dismounted. "Hello, Torc. What's going on?"

Torc shuffled his feet. "Sir . . ."

Arenadd looked closely at him. The boy had seemed uneasy and distracted lately, but now he looked downright ill.

"What is it?"

"Sir, something's happened," said Torc.

Arenadd tensed. "What?"

"Come with me, sir," said Torc.

Arenadd followed him into the tower, with Skandar trailing uninterestedly after them.

The boy took him to the room where Caedmon had died. "It's in here, sir," he said unnecessarily, pushing open the door.

Arenadd followed him, and stopped, staring in astonishment.

Saeddryn was there, rising to meet him. With her was a boy about Torc's age, clad in the ragged remains of a peasant's clothes. Limping toward him, leaning on a spear, was . . .

"Garnoc?"

The burly darkman bowed low to him. "Lord Arenadd Tara-nisäii," he rumbled. "It's an honour to see yer again."

Arenadd looked at him. Garnoc had shed the black slave's robe he had been wearing on their first meeting and now wore the clothes he had stolen from Guard's Post, but the scars of the collar were still livid and obvious on his neck.

"Garnoc," he repeated. "Good gods. I never thought I'd see you again."

Garnoc straightened up and grinned. "I didn't think t'see *you* again either, sir, but here we are. Seems yer've bin doin' pretty good since we last saw each other."

"How did you get here?" said Arenadd.

"Walked, sir," said Garnoc. "Slowly. Had some help from Yorath here, mind."

Arenadd looked at the boy. "Oh, hello. Yorath, is it? Where did you come from?"

Yorath gaped at him in silence.

Garnoc smacked the boy in the back of the head. "Bow to Lord Arenadd, boy. Ye're in the presence of a great man, so show some respect."

Yorath bowed hastily. "Y-yes, sir," he said, almost whispering.

Arenadd couldn't help but smile. "It's all right; I won't bite. Where did Garnoc find you?"

"He ran away from home t'follow me, sir," Garnoc growled when Yorath didn't answer at once. "He was a miller's son at Gwernyfed, a little peasant village way out east. I told him t'go home, but he wasn't listenin' to a word of it, sir."

"Y-yes, sir," Yorath stammered. "That's the truth, sir. I came 'ere t'help ye, sir, I wanted—"

"Shut up," said Garnoc. "Sir." He turned respectfully to Arenadd. "Sir, I've never stopped bein' yer follower after Guard's Post, sir. I've bin travellin' the land, spreadin' the word about yer, sir. Makin' all our people know what happened at Herbstitt an' afterward, sir. After what happened at Gwernyfed, I knew I had t'find yer, sir. So here I am."

"What happened at Gwernyfed?" said Arenadd.

Garnoc cast a glance at the bed. "It can wait till later, sir. But I came here from Warwick, sir. I've brought a good number of men with me, sir. They wanted t'come here t'join yer, sir."

Arenadd blinked at him. "You brought . . . Garnoc, how did you know where to find me?"

Garnoc looked at the bed again. "She told me, sir."

Arenadd looked past him and saw a hunched shape lying under the blankets. "Who?"

Garnoc stepped aside. "I'll leave yer with her, sir," he said softly. "I'm sorry. There was nothin' I could've done."

He left the room with Yorath. Saeddryn cast a sad look at Arenadd and left, taking Torc's hand on the way out.

Alone, Arenadd stepped toward the bed. He was full of apprehension. Who was this? What was going on?

The person in the bed was a middle-aged woman—or had been once.

Arenadd stood over her, just looking at her and wondering.

The woman had long curly black hair and had probably once had strong features. Now she looked withered and shrunken. Her hair had greyed, and her face was lined and scarred with pain.

Arenadd looked lower. Her hands, resting on the blankets, were a ruin. The fingers had been utterly destroyed, twisted and broken until the skin tore and bled.

"Tortured," Arenadd muttered.

At that, the woman opened her eyes. They were black and blank, like two empty pools. *"Arren."*

Arenadd, driven by some instinct he did not understand, touched her forehead with his good hand. "They tortured you, didn't they?" he said. "Like they tortured me."

The woman stared at him, unblinking. "Arren," she said again.

Arenadd frowned. "What are you saying? Are you trying to tell me something?"

The remains of her fingers twitched. "Arren. Arren. My little Arren."

"Who, me?" said Arenadd.

She looked at him, desperation showing through the pain and despair in her face. "Arren. My Arren. My little Arren."

Gods, what did they do to her? Arenadd thought. *She must have been driven insane.* "I'm sorry," he said softly. "I don't know who that is. Can you tell me your name?"

She didn't seem to hear. "Arren was my son," she intoned. "Arren is dead. The Dark Lord has gone to Fruitsheart, to kill his enemies. My son lies dead at Eagleholm."

Eagleholm . . . the name stirred something in Arenadd. "What's your name?" he said. "How did you know where I was? Can you tell me?"

"Our family is all dead," said the woman. "My husband died at Guard's Post; my son died at Eagleholm. I died at Warwick."

"You'll meet again in the stars," said Arenadd, wanting to comfort her. "I know you will."

Her eyelids drooped. "My son is dead," she said in a monotone. "He died at Eagleholm. His name was Arren. He died by falling. What came to our house was not my son. My son is dead. His name was Arren. He died the day after his birthday. His name was Arren. My son is dead."

Arenadd realised he wasn't going to get any sense out of

her. "I'm sorry," he said, and he meant it. Gods, what had they done to her?

The woman said nothing more, and Arenadd turned away. He wondered why the enemy had tortured her. How did she know he was going to Fruitsheart, and how had they guessed that she knew?

Garnoc and Saeddryn were waiting outside for him.

To his surprise, Saeddryn put a hand on his arm. "How was she, sir?"

Arenadd glanced at her and shook his head. "She's incoherent. Whatever they did to her must have broken her mind. I don't think she even knows how she knew we were here."

Saeddryn hugged him tightly. "I'm so sorry," she whispered in his ear.

Arenadd let go of her and gave her an odd look. "I'm sure I'll be fine, Saeddryn," he told her. "But thank you. Garnoc—"

"Yes, sir?" said Garnoc.

Arenadd thought of asking him if he knew who the woman was but pushed it aside. He could find out later. "I want to know more. What happened at Gwernyfed? How many men have you brought with you?"

Garnoc looked nonplussed. "I'm sorry, sir, but I thought yer'd want a moment—"

"I'm fine," said Arenadd, slightly annoyed and beginning to wonder why they were acting as if someone had just died. "Come on, we'll go to the dining hall and talk there. Saeddryn, can you go ahead and ask them to get some food ready for us? Thank you."

Garnoc followed him to the dining hall, still acting as if he was deeply shocked by something but sitting down readily enough when Arenadd indicated a chair.

"Now," said Arenadd, taking a seat opposite him. "Tell me everything."

"Sir," said Garnoc. "I met someone at Gwernyfed. Not Yorath—someone else. A griffiner."

"Oh?" said Arenadd. "Who?"

"Someone yer've met, sir," Garnoc said grimly. "Erian Rannagonson, the Bastard."

"Him!" Arenadd started; he hadn't thought of Erian in some time. "What was *he* doing there?"

"On his way somewhere, sir," said Garnoc. "I dunno where. He said—" He winced. "I talked t'him, sir. Din't want to, but that griffin of his had me pinned. They forced me t'tell them where I'd come from an' why. Afterward they gave me a message for yer, sir."

"What message?" said Arenadd.

"The Bastard said t'tell yer he was . . ." Garnoc rubbed his shaven head. "Somethin' . . . he said you was . . . I dunno, Kray kran something."

"Yes?" said Arenadd.

"He said t'tell yer that him—the Bastard—said t'tell yer *he* was Aee . . . somethin'. Ended with kay. Anyway, he said he was comin', sir. He said he was gonna kill yer. He said . . . said he knew what you was plannin', an' that . . . he said . . ." Garnoc's expression cleared suddenly. "He said, 'Remember my face, murderer, it's the last one you'll ever see.'"

Arenadd chuckled. "I see he thinks he's grown a sense of humour." He lost his smile to think. "Hmm. So he found you . . . but he didn't kill you?"

"Yes, sir," said Garnoc. "He said he wanted me t'give yer that message from him, sir."

Arenadd thought about it, and then snorted. "Hah. The Bastard still underestimates me. He's got no idea."

"Sir?" said Garnoc.

"I know what he is—or what he thinks he is," Arenadd said dismissively. "The Night God told me a long time ago. But I wonder what he was doing in Gwernyfed?"

Garnoc's eyes were wide. "The Night God, sir?"

"Of course," said Arenadd. "She talks to me every so often. She gave me my powers, after all; she gives me warnings and advice." *And she takes things in return.* "So you don't have any idea of where he was going?"

"No, sir," said Garnoc. "But he was on a journey, sir. Somewhere."

Arenadd scratched his beard. "Hmm. Well, I suppose it's not particularly important for the moment. So you went to Warwick?"

"Yes, sir," said Garnoc. "Me an' Yorath wandered around for a long time b'fore we found out yer were supposed t'be there. He's a good lad, Yorath," he added fondly. "Anyway, we went t'Warwick, got there one way or another, an' found all sorts of chaos when we did. All the griffiners was dead, an' people were just doin' whatever they wanted. But most of 'em was goin' on about *you*, sir. There was this group there—called 'emselves

Wolves. Spent their time goin' on about how yer were the Night God's avatar an' how yer were gonna drive the Southerners out of the North an' suchlike. Anyway, after I'd bin into the tower an' found . . . y'know, *her*"—he paused awkwardly, and went on—"I found 'em an' told 'em who I was an' so on. They din't believe me until I told 'em exactly what yer looked like an' what yer griffin was called an' so on. Then I told 'em I knew where yer were, an' they was all willin' t'come with me here. So here I am."

Arenadd listened. "You've done great work, Garnoc," he said solemnly when the big darkman had finished. "And proven yourself one of my most loyal friends."

Garnoc stared at the tabletop. "If it weren't for yer, sir, I'd still be in Herbstit with a collar around my neck, buildin' walls for the sun worshippers. It's my duty t'pay yer back, sir, an' don't think the others will've forgotten, sir. Dafydd an' that Prydwen—they won't have forgotten, f'sure, sir. They'll be out there somewhere, sir, just waitin' t'find yer again."

Arenadd smiled to himself. Dafydd and Prydwen—two Northerners who had been sold into slavery as punishment for trying to find Arddryn and join her. They had been good friends to him at Herbstitt and had begged to come with him and Skandar. He wondered where they were now and hoped he would meet them again.

"You'll be rewarded for this," he said.

Garnoc grinned. "Thank yer, sir."

"I can't do much now," Arenadd went on. "But to begin with you need fresh clothes and a good meal."

"I'd love that, sir," said Garnoc. "An' Yorath could do with the same, if yer don't mind. He was a great help on the way here."

"Of course," said Arenadd. "If that's all you have to tell me, I'll go and organise it."

"Yes, sir," said Garnoc. "Sir?"

"Yes?"

"There's one other thing I wanted t'know, sir," Garnoc said apologetically.

"Yes?"

The big darkman's look was eager, excited. "Are yer really gonna attack Malvern, sir? Are yer gonna set the North free?"

"Yes, Garnoc," said Arenadd. "That's exactly what I'm going to do. But not until after I've set every other slave in Cymria free."

Garnoc stared at him. "All of them, sir?"

"Yes," said Arenadd. "At Guard's Post, I found out that slaves could be warriors. One day, they'll help me destroy Malvern. And afterward I'll set them free, just as I did for you at Guard's Post. The greatest reward I can offer."

Garnoc's eyes shone. "Yes, sir!"

Arenadd smiled and left the dining hall.

Outside, he found Saeddryn. "Ah, hello," he said. "I was wondering, could you ask someone to find fresh clothes for our new friend? And for Yorath, too."

"Of course, sir," said Saeddryn. She paused. "What did he tell ye, sir?"

"That the slaves I freed at Guard's Post have been spreading the word," said Arenadd.

"That's good, sir."

"I would certainly say so. How many men did he bring with him from Warwick?"

"A good two hundred, sir," said Saeddryn. "They're undisciplined, but strong an' willin', sir."

"Excellent. Well, I need to go and get some rest, so if you could get on with that . . ."

"Yes, sir," said Saeddryn. "But sir . . ."

"Yes, Saeddryn?"

"I dunno if this is the right time, sir, but I've been wantin' t'tell ye . . ."

"What is it now?" said Arenadd, more sharply than he needed to.

She looked up. "Torc asked me to marry him, sir." She paused. "An' I've said yes."

32

The Siege

Erian stood back to admire his craft.

It hadn't been easy to make. He had dug out the remains of the boat from the sand, but although it had held its shape, it had proven far too weak to float again. Instead, he had had to use it as a template to try to build his own.

It had taken the best part of two months.

Erian had no axe. He had no carving tools. All he had were his hunting knife and his sword. He didn't know the proper names for the parts of a boat, beyond "hull" and "keel"—and he knew their names but not what they looked like—yet after weeks of trial and error, he had managed to re-create the part he thought of as the "spine," and then the "ribs." After that he had had to carve the planks that would fill the spaces between the ribs, and it had taken far longer than he had anticipated.

But his time on the island had taught him patience, and he worked away at his little project day after day, not particularly worried if it would work or not. During that time, Senneck's chicks had shed most of their baby fluff, and their wings—though not strong enough to support them yet—had grown the long feathers needed for flight. They were already testing them, and Senneck had said they would begin their first attempts at flight soon.

But they won't need to fly just yet, Erian thought, as he admired the little boat he had dubbed *The Pride of Gryphus*. It was crude, certainly, and unlovely, but it was his and he had worked very hard at it. He had tested it several times in the lagoon where he went for water every day. It leaked in a few places, but with a bit more work he hoped it would stay afloat long enough.

They could go back to the mainland soon.

To his surprise, the idea filled Erian with trepidation. He had grown so used to life on the island that he almost never contemplated the idea of going back to civilisation. Gods, it had been such a long time since he'd even spoken to another human being.

"But you have to go back," Erian told himself sternly. "It's your destiny to face *Kraeai kran ae*. And what about Elkin? She's waiting for you! Oh for the love of Gryphus, stop talking to yourself, you sound like a lunatic."

He fell silent, heaved *The Pride of Gryphus* back onto the sand and turned it over to inspect the places where it had been leaking. He'd stuffed palm fibres into the gaps he'd found; it worked well enough, though he had his doubts over how long they would last. Long enough, hopefully.

There was a soft thudding of paws on the sand behind him, and Rannagon came to join him.

Erian bent to scratch the chick's head. "Hello, Rannagon, how are you?"

The chick looked up at him, bright-eyed. "Am strong!" he boasted. As he grew toward adulthood, he had taken on some of the gawkiness of his father, Eekrae; so far, none of Senneck's grace was showing through in him. But his feathers were a rich shade of brown, mottled attractively with grey on the wings, and his fur was a pleasing sandy gold.

"Of course you are," Erian said fondly. "You're so big now!"

Rannagon, already bored, waddled over to inspect the boat. "Is big," he said. "We ride soon?"

"I think so," said Erian. "I've tested it, and it floats well enough. Do you think you're brave enough to sit in it with me?"

Instantly provoked, the chick drew himself up and puffed out his chest. "Am griffin! Griffin not know fear!" he declared. "I go with human!"

Erian chuckled. "I wouldn't dream of leaving you behind. Or your sister."

Rannagon snorted dismissively at the mention of his sister. "We go soon?"

"If your mother agrees," said Erian. "In fact, we should go to her now. Shall we?"

Rannagon darted away and rushed ahead of him by way of an answer, and Erian trudged after him, tired out from another day's work.

Back in the village, Senneck was sunning herself while the still unnamed female chick scampered about, chasing a butterfly.

Erian stopped to watch them, while Rannagon went ahead to his mother. Now he had been reminded of the trouble that had to be taking place in his absence, he found it hard to imagine that such an idyllic scene could exist while his home was being ravaged by war.

His resolve hardened, and he strode forward and sat beside his partner. "Senneck."

She looked up. "What news?"

"It's finished," said Erian, as he watched the chicks play fight each other. "I tested it again; it'll float well enough."

"Even when you are inside it?" Senneck asked, suspiciously.

"Yes," said Erian. "I paddled it around the lagoon without much trouble."

"You still have not told me how you plan to take it back to the coast," said Senneck. "I am not convinced that you could paddle that far."

"I can rest every so often," said Erian.

"But there are tides and currents in the open sea," Senneck pressed. "Could you fight back against those?"

"I . . ."

"As I suspected," said the brown griffin. "Erian, I am not willing to risk your life and the lives of my chicks by allowing you to do this."

Erian reddened. "Senneck, I spent *months* making that boat. I can do it!"

"You cannot paddle that far," said Senneck, with terrible finality.

"Well then—"

"However"—Senneck laid her head down on her talons—"I have a solution."

"You do?" said Erian.

"I cannot carry you that far," said Senneck. "But I believe that I can pull your boat with me as I fly."

"What?" said Erian "How?"

"With rope," said Senneck. "If you weave one long and thick enough, and tie it to the front of your boat, I shall grasp it in my talons and pull you with me."

Erian began to get excited. "You think you can do that?"

"It is a chance," said Senneck, reserved as always. "But we shall have to practise first, to see if it can be done."

"Of course," said Erian. "I'll start making the rope right now."

Senneck made a rasping sound. "Perhaps the length of your fur has changed, my human, but your impulsiveness has not. Weave your rope now if you must. And bring food for the chicks; they will be hungry after so much exercise."

"Of course!" said Erian.

He scurried off, heart pounding. After so long, they could finally leave. In a matter of days they could be back in Cymria, on their way to Malvern with the magical sword. He could be facing the Dark Lord before the next full moon. He could . . .

Erian's excitement darkened with fear, and he found some raw palm fibres and the carcass of a bird and took them back to Senneck without the trace of a smile.

Arenadd stood on the balcony outside Skandar's nest, watching the moon over the roofs of the city and trying to think.

He had lost half of his memories . . . including the memory of how he had lost them, if he had ever known why in the first place.

Why?

"Why have I forgotten?" he said aloud, his eyes on the moon. "What did I forget? Why did I need to forget? Did you make it happen, master? *Why?*"

There was no answer—not that he had been expecting one. Perhaps the Night God wasn't yet strong enough to speak to him while he was awake.

Maybe she had nothing to say.

He rubbed his broken fingers. Somehow, the loss of his memories didn't distress him. *And why should it? he thought. I don't know what I forgot. I don't have any attachment to it any more. For all I know, none of it was worth remembering.*

It wasn't that he'd forgotten *everything*. He remembered things he'd learnt, experiences, sensations, knowledge. It was the personal things that he'd forgotten. The names of his parents.

The place where he had grown up. The life he had lived before
Skandar found his shattered body and filled it with magic, and so
unwittingly fulfilled the purpose the Night God had given him.

"It doesn't matter who I was before then," Arenadd told the
moon. "That man is dead. I know who *I* am. What you made
me, master. What you made me. And at least you gave me
life . . . of a kind. And more than life."

More than life, oh yes. She had given him *power*.

Gods, how he loved it now. The ability to appear and disappear at will, and to kill his enemies without remorse, but most
of all the immortality—the sheer, perfect knowledge that no
matter what happened he could never be killed. He had seen the
looks of horror and dismay on the faces of his enemies when
they hit him and found it had no effect, when they realised that
nothing they did could save them. *I am the Shadow that Walks.*

Arenadd grinned to himself. He would have given up far more
than his memories and his heartbeat to become what he was now.

"Forgive me, master," he said. "I shouldn't be ungrateful.
Not after—"

He broke off mid-sentence, turning sharply as he heard a
noise behind him. Something big and dark moved: Skandar,
stirring in his nest.

"Human come," the griffin rasped.

Arenadd reached for his sickle, but it was only Saeddryn.

"Sir," she said. "I'm sorry . . ."

"What is it, Saeddryn?"

She sighed and looked him in the face. "Sir, yer mother has
just died."

Arenadd stared blankly at her. "What?"

"I'm sorry, sir," said Saeddryn. "We'd have called ye sooner,
but it happened so quickly. Yorath was with her; he says he
stepped out t'get a drink, an' when he got back she was dead."

Arenadd's blank expression did not change. "Saeddryn,
what are you talking about? What do you mean my mother
died? I don't . . ." He trailed off. *I don't have a mother, do I?*

Saeddryn looked sympathetic. "I can understand it's a shock
t'ye, sir."

"Well . . . uh, yes," said Arenadd. It was true enough. "I suppose I . . . I should go to her."

"Yes, sir," said Saeddryn.

Arenadd followed her back through the nest. Skandar looked

as if he was thinking of coming, too, but he changed his mind and lay back down in his nest with the chicks nestled between his front paws.

Saeddryn led the way down to a lower level of the tower, and as they approached a certain door, Arenadd had a sinking feeling in his stomach. This was the room . . .

Inside, Yorath and Torc were sitting by the bed and talking in low voices. They looked up when Arenadd came in, appearing as shocked and guilty as if they had just been caught stealing.

Arenadd nodded vaguely to them and walked over to the bed, but he already knew what he would find there.

The tortured woman from Warwick, grey faced in death, with her mouth slightly open. She looked as if she had died in great pain.

Arenadd, looking down at her, heard her voice again in his memory. *My son is Arren. My son is dead.*

Arenadd saw her hair, tangled on the pillow around her face. Curly. He reached up to touch his own curls, his expression far away. *Arren, my son is Arren.*

"Oh gods," he breathed. "Oh gods. She's . . . Saeddryn!"

He turned, only to find the room deserted. Saeddryn must have taken Torc and Yorath with her, thinking that her master needed to be alone.

Arenadd turned back to look at the body, his mind racing. *She looks like me. She said her son was Arren. She said he was dead . . . she looks like me.*

And yet, somehow, as he looked at her, he didn't feel as if he had any connection to her at all. Her face was completely unfamiliar. Her voice had been unfamiliar, too. No.

She's not my mother, he thought. *She can't be. I have no mother. I never had a mother. She's not my mother. She was mad . . . raving . . . thought I was her dead son. Yes. She's not my mother. Saeddryn was just confused.*

For some reason, the thought gave him a feeling of peace, as if some inner voice was whispering, *Yes, yes, that's right. You're right.*

Still, that didn't mean he shouldn't feel sorry for this woman. What the Southerners had done to her was unspeakable.

He reached down to touch her cold face. "I'm so sorry . . . Mother."

He wasn't sure why he called her that. Perhaps because she had wanted to believe he was her son.

"Saeddryn!"

Saeddryn must have been just outside, because she came almost instantly. "Yes, sir?"

Arenadd rubbed his eyes. "I want you to say the rites for her."

"Yes, sir. When, sir?"

"At once," said Arenadd. "A small ceremony—there shouldn't be any need to wake people up for this, especially when they've been training all day. And I don't think many of them would want to see the poor thing in this state."

Saeddryn looked taken aback. "Yes, sir. I can understand if ye'd want it t'be a private thing. We could hold it in one of the smaller courtyards if ye like, sir."

"We'll do that," said Arenadd. "I'm sure Yorath and Torc can carry her out there for you. As for me, I'm tired and I need to be alone. I'll be in my chamber, and I'd prefer not to be disturbed unless it's important."

Saeddryn stared at him. "Sir, I don't want t'press ye, but I think ye should come t'this."

"I've been to enough funerals lately, Saeddryn."

"But sir, she's yer own mother! Don't ye care enough t'at least come to the funeral?"

Arenadd glanced back at the frail shape in the bed. "She's not my mother, Saeddryn," he said. "I don't have a mother."

And he walked away without a backward glance.

Maybe he hadn't looked back, but that didn't stop him from feeling a strange sense of remorse as he locked himself away in his room. He did his best to push it out of his mind as he sat down in front of the fire and pulled off his boots. There was blood in the tread; he made a mental note to clean it off in the morning.

He'd put a jug of wine on the table close to his seat, and he put his feet up and poured himself a cupful. It was a good vintage—nice rich flavour, with a hint of raspberry.

He took a good swallow, and gasped as he felt it burn its way down inside him. Beautiful.

As the wine started to relax him, he sat back and thought

about Skade. She had been gone hardly any time, but it felt as if it had been a hundred years.

I need you here, Skade, he thought. *I need to touch you, kiss you . . . talk to you. I could talk to you about anything, couldn't I? Skade . . .*

He sighed and drained the cup before pouring himself another one, which he emptied even more quickly.

But despite his thoughts of Skade, and despite the alcohol beginning to dull his senses, the dead woman crept back into his mind.

Gods, what if she really was my mother?

He downed another cup of wine. No. It was impossible. How could he have a mother when he hadn't been born in the first place?

I was born . . . somewhere else, he thought. *Not in this world, but somewhere else. I was made to fill this body, which no-one needed any more. Yes.*

The conviction helped to soothe him.

But what about before then? What about before Arenadd Taranisäii was born? What if I was someone before that? Is there something left in me from that time?

He didn't know, and the realisation disturbed him.

Without thinking, he got up out of his chair and padded barefoot back out onto the balcony with his cup in his hand. Out in the cool night air, he looked up at the moon again.

"What have you taken from me?" he demanded. "*What?* Was that woman my mother? Did you make me forget her? Why would you make me do that? I don't understand! *Speak to me!*"

Nothing happened, and he breathed deeply to try to calm himself down. But his agitation did not die away, and he paced back and forth, sipping from his cup and muttering to himself.

". . . have to trust her. She's my master. She knows what to do; she's a god. If she made me forget, it was for a reason . . . a good reason . . ."

In the end he was driven back inside when he realised the cup was empty. He growled to himself and slipped past Skandar's sleeping form back to the fire and the wine jug.

He sat down again and tried to relax, but he couldn't. Angry with himself and his situation, and more than a little frightened, he refilled the cup again and again, gulping the wine down recklessly.

Eventually the strength went out of his limbs, and he slumped in his chair, staring fixedly at the fire.

He reached for the jug and nearly knocked it off the table. After a few attempts he managed to grip the handle. His cup had somehow ended up on the floor, so he tilted the jug to his mouth instead. Wine gushed into his mouth, and he managed to swallow most of it before the jug slipped out of his hand and bounced onto the floor.

"I feel better now," Arenadd mumbled, before sliding off his chair and landing on the hearthrug in a drunken stupor.

Something hit him, hard.

He stirred and tried to lift his head. Instantly a wave of unbearable nausea went through him, and his head dropped back onto the rug.

The thing hit him again. "Human! *Human!*"

Arenadd groaned. "Skandar?"

Skandar hit him a third time. "Human, wake!" he rasped. "Wake, now!"

Arenadd managed to open his eyes. The first thing he saw was Skandar's huge foreleg. He struggled to make himself wake up, but his head ached appallingly. Everything seemed to be spinning around him.

"Wake!" Skandar said yet again, and the urgent tone finally brought something resembling coherent thought back into Arenadd's mind.

He managed to lift his upper body off the rug, and rolled onto his back with a painful thud. He could see Skandar's enormous head looming over him. "What?" he said. "What's—"

"Enemy!" said Skandar. "Enemy come, human! Wake! We fight, now! *Fight!*"

All of Arenadd's sluggishness evaporated. "Oh, by the Night God's eye . . ."

He hauled himself to his feet, staggering slightly, but made it to the table, where he'd left his sickle. He stuffed it into his belt and, forgetting his boots, stumbled out to the balcony.

He saw them quickly enough. They were on the horizon—a massive dark cloud, coming closer all the while.

Mouthing Northern curses, he turned to run back inside. Skandar was there already, hissing with aggression.

"Quickly," Arenadd told him. "Go to the top of the tower and send out a call; wake the city, the way we planned! I have to get the chicks to safety and organise the other humans. The moment I'm ready, I'll come out onto one of the balconies and call for you, understand?"

They had already gone through his plan many times. Skandar clicked his beak. "Not wait long!" he warned, and hurled himself into the air.

Arenadd scooped up the chicks—no easy task—and ran out of the nest with them. He nearly fell over when he found the door to his room locked, but he managed to get in after some fumbling and ran down through the tower, shouting all the while.

"Attack! Attack! Griffins coming from the South! *Attack!*"

Everywhere people came running, as if his voice had called them into existence. Arenadd rapped out a few quick orders as he passed, still struggling to restrain the three wriggling chicks. In spite of the urgency of the situation, he still had room to feel like an idiot. The great Dark Lord Arenadd, staggering barefoot down the tower with a hangover and an armload of griffin chicks busy trying to claw his face off.

Iorwerth and Saeddryn came to him in what seemed no time.

"Sir, what's goin' on?"

Arenadd shoved one of the chicks into her hands. "Here, hold on to the little bastard, will you? We're being attacked. There's griffins coming from the South—Malvern, for sure. They're still a fair way away—Skandar saw them in time—but there's a lot of them, I know that much. And they're almost certainly carrying more firebombs—probably worse. Iorwerth, you and Kaanee must lead the attack in the air. Saeddryn, you'll organise the defenders on the ground, the way we discussed—is the water ready?"

"Yes, sir," said Saeddryn.

"Good. Iorwerth, go and get ready, and for the love of the Night God be quick about it. I want our griffins in the sky immediately. Go on, stop gawping at me and go!"

Iorwerth dashed away.

"Sir, what are ye going t'be doin'?" said Saeddryn.

"I have to take the chicks to the wine cellar, where they'll be safer," said Arenadd. "After that, Skandar and I will fly out together, the way we planned."

"Yes, sir," said Saeddryn. "I'll get to work. Good luck, sir."

"I don't need luck; I have the Night God on my side," said Arenadd. "But good luck to *you*, Saeddryn Taranisäii."

She smiled briefly, pleased to be called Taranisäii, and thrust the chick back at him before running away.

Arenadd, knowing how urgent the situation was, sprinted down the corridor. Fortunately his head seemed to be clearing; maybe it was panic, or some gift his powers had given him, but the hangover didn't feel so bad now.

Down in the wine cellar, he opened a trapdoor into a little chamber he had already fitted with straw bedding, food and water, and put the chicks into it.

"Stay here," he told them. "You'll be safe here, and I'll come back and let you out after it's over."

The chicks looked up at him with resentful eyes, but he shut the trapdoor on them and hastily weighted it down with a spare barrel or two just in case.

Someone had left a jug of cider on a nearby shelf. He paused to take a strengthening gulp from it, and ran out of the cellar.

The tower was a hive of activity. People were running in all directions, carrying weapons and armour, shouting orders, some pausing to take a few bites of breakfast. As Arenadd passed, many of them called out to him, asking him to bless them with the Night God's grace and protection. Some even reached out to touch his robe, as if that would give them some of the power he had. Arenadd stopped to bless every one of them, touching their heads and murmuring.

The moment he was at the griffiner quarters, he dashed through the nearest door and onto the balcony. There, he cupped his hands around his mouth and called.

"Arenadd! Arenadd!"

It wasn't long before Skandar responded. He called his own name and flew to his partner's side.

Arenadd patted the griffin's shoulder. "Don't worry, Skandar, your chicks are safe. Shall we go and kill some of those bastards?"

Skandar hissed and rasped, practically vibrating with anger. "Kill!" he said. "Kill now! Come, human! We fight!"

Arenadd climbed onto his back without another word. He had picked up a bow and a quiver of arrows on his way up; as the dark griffin took to the sky, he freed an arrow and nocked it onto the bowstring, balancing on his seat.

They weren't a moment too soon. The approaching enemy were huge on the horizon: there were a hundred griffins at least. When Arenadd saw them, he groaned aloud. Malvern must have sent nearly every griffiner they had to attack him. How were they going to hold this lot off?

Anger hardened in his chest. *I am the Master of Death! I cannot be defeated! If they want to kill my followers, they will die!*

Skandar knew what to do. He circled higher, following his fellow griffins. When griffins fought, height was the most important advantage. If they could be above their enemies, they could attack first and far more devastatingly, as they had already proved at Skenfrith.

Skandar, however, had other plans. As the attackers drew nearer, he broke away from the flock of unpartnered griffins flying over Fruitsheart and flew toward the enemy, screeching his name over and over again in a mocking challenge.

In the bright blue of a morning sky, the dark griffin was instantly visible and instantly recognisable. A perfect target for the griffiners from Malvern, who had come to Fruitsheart specifically to find the dark griffin and his human and destroy them both.

It worked. The bulk of the griffiners swept into the city, but at least twenty of them ignored their orders and broke away from their fellows to pursue the two rebel leaders.

Skandar waited until they were close and then flew away. Straight toward the rest of the flock now flying into the city. He folded his wings and slipped through a gap, leaving his pursuers to fly into their allies, scattering them. An instant later, the unpartnered attacked.

Skandar continued to drop until he was a hair's breadth away from the rooftops of Fruitsheart. His wings opened and he swooped up toward the attacking griffins. On his back, Arenadd loosed an arrow. It hit one of the griffins carrying a firebomb—a ceramic pot full of flammable oil, which was meant to be lit before being dropped onto the city. The griffin dropped out of the sky with his unlit burden, which smashed harmlessly on the roof of the Sun Temple.

The unpartnered were under strict instructions. They attacked the enemy griffins, aiming for the ones who carried firebombs, intent on killing them before their humans could light the deadly missiles. Meanwhile Skandar shot past directly below them, while Arenadd loosed arrow after arrow, frequently hitting his targets thanks to the fact that they were so tightly bunched together.

It was a cunning tactic and one that killed a good number of the firebombers, but some of them survived. Leaning over as far as they dared, they lit the cloth plugs of the firebombs with burning coals they carried in special fireproof pouches, and their griffins released them over the city. Some of them landed harmlessly in the street or failed to catch fire, but some of them hit their targets. When they did, they exploded.

Fire blossomed into the sky, yellow-orange and beautiful.

Fortunately the Governor's Tower had been built to resist this kind of attack, but Arenadd knew the city was suffering, and he cursed internally as Skandar angled his wings and banked sharply upward to attack the rest of the enemy flock.

After that, there was nothing but fighting.

Skandar attacked with all the mad ferocity that was his nature, rushing past enemy griffins with his talons spread to cause as much damage as he could, sometimes grappling with one of them in midair and tearing at them with his beak. Arenadd, for his part, did plenty to help. He loosed arrows at every griffin that came within range, and when they were fighting at closer quarters he drew his sickle and hacked at them and their riders.

Despite the success of these tactics, and despite the number of attackers who died during those first few moments, the defenders were still outnumbered. At least twenty enemy griffins broke away from their flock to attack the archers on the wall around the tower and on the balconies of the building itself. Arenadd's human followers did their best, but they had been hastily trained and organised, and few had ever fought in open combat before, least of all against fully trained griffiners.

Worse, the griffins did not take long to begin using their magic.

One of them swooped low over the ramparts, spitting fireballs at the hapless defenders and killing a good number of them. Another, small and fast, circled over the tower and breathed a column of blue light, which instantly froze a knot of archers solid. As if this was a signal, the griffins still in the sky—both enemy griffins and the unpartnered—began to unleash their own powers. Some, lacking powers that were useful in combat or perhaps simply wishing to conserve their energy, continued to rely on their beaks and talons.

A gust of wind nearly as powerful as a hurricane blasted into a group of unpartnered, sending them pinwheeling through the sky. Arenadd saw another griffin send out a wall of force that knocked away those who were snatching at his neck and wings, though whether it was an enemy or one of the unpartnered he couldn't tell.

The unpartnered fought back doggedly, using any and every power they possessed that could hurt their enemies. Arenadd saw griffins fall out of the sky with their wings consumed by fire. Others died more gruesomely.

He saw a large tawny-brown griffin with a human on his back fly past a bunched pack of enemy griffiners. As he passed the griffiners he released a thin line of silvery light from his beak, straight at them. Wherever it hit, it had a devastating effect.

Severed limbs fell away in all directions. In some cases, the light had cut through human and griffin in a single stroke. Dozens of griffins fell, horribly cut apart.

Arenadd looked quickly at the griffin that had killed them, and realisation hit him in an instant. *Kaanee.*

He had never realised just how powerful the leader of the unpartnered truly was.

The humans below were not faring so well.

Arenadd had kept most of his attention on balancing on Skandar's back and aiming his arrows, but during a brief moment of rest he glanced downward and felt his stomach lurch. There were huge gaps on the walls where the archers had been wiped out and not replaced. The tower itself was little better; he could see smoke billowing out of at least one of the openings and an alarming number of corpses scattered on the roof and elsewhere.

"Godsdamnit, they're being crushed," he muttered. "Skandar! *Skandar!*"

The dark griffin, caught up in the midst of battle, didn't seem to hear him. Arenadd tried yelling for a little longer, and when that didn't get a response he finally leant forward and yanked at a handful of feathers.

Skandar lurched slightly in midair, his head half-turning to glare back at him.

Arenadd waved urgently at him. "Skandar! Skandar, we've got to go down! *Down!* Skandar!"

At first it seemed that Skandar wasn't listening, but after Arenadd had repeated himself several times, he suddenly wheeled about and began his descent toward the tower. The enemy, seeing him, went in pursuit by the dozen. Arenadd could hear them screeching, and he fancied there was a note of vicious triumph in it: on the tower, he and Skandar would be sitting ducks.

Skandar touched down, a little too fast, making an audible thud. Arenadd was off his back almost the instant talon had hit stone, and they took up a fighting stance side by side, both looking up at their oncoming enemies.

Arenadd realised he had only a handful of arrows left, but that was more than enough. He loosed them as quickly as possible, not taking the time to aim them very precisely. Some of them hit their mark, and those that didn't managed to scatter the diving griffins. Once his quiver was empty, he hurled the bow aside and drew his sickle.

"Wait for it," he muttered. "Wait for it . . ."

Skandar knew. He crouched low like a wolf about to pounce, paws and talons spread wide in readiness. He kept his head turned upward, silver eyes narrow. Waiting.

The griffins came lower . . .

Arenadd could see the foremost of them now, talons open ready to strike, the human on his back holding on for dear life. It looked as if they were aiming for his throat, and they were coming so fast . . .

"Now!"

A mere instant before the griffin hit, Skandar and Arenadd both leapt.

The real world vanished in an eye blink, and cool, welcoming shadows embraced them both.

The oncoming griffin saw them vanish, but he had no time for more than a moment's terror. A heartbeat later, he hit solid stone.

The impact sent shock waves straight through the griffin's body. His outstretched forelegs took the full force. They shattered instantly, collapsing back into his chest. His beak struck the stone next, at an angle, snapping his head sideways and breaking his neck.

His human was thrown from his back and died almost instantly.

The rest of the attackers were only slightly luckier. Most of those at the front smacked into the tower like the first, some dying and others suffering crippling injuries.

Those who managed to save themselves were forced to land, angry and bewildered.

"Where have they gone?" one griffin screeched.

Above, the unpartnered were ready to carry out the next stage of the plan. They gathered together and attacked as one, driving the enemy down toward the tower-top, almost as if they were trying to herd them. A good number of them, thinking their comrades on the tower had cornered Arenadd and Skandar, went in the direction the unpartnered wanted for at least a short distance. The unpartnered continued to attack them from above for a few moments, but the enemy quickly began to drive upward again.

And then, inexplicably, the unpartnered fled. They broke off their attack and scattered, and the griffiners quickly spread out to chase them.

But only for an instant.

As they rose in a great untidy flock, now utterly disorganised, something huge and dark and horrible appeared directly above them.

Skandar hovered in place for a moment, his body strangely rigid. Then his beak opened, and light came forth. Black light.

It shot straight downward, spreading out in a great cloud when it hit the enemy griffins. It did not seem to do anything to them; in fact, it looked as if it was simply passing straight through them as it made its way down to the tower-top, touching every single one.

Skandar kept his beak wide open, belching his magic forth in an endless wave, apparently completely unaffected by all the energy he was expending. But on his back, Arenadd could feel the griffin trembling.

After a moment that felt as if it lasted an eternity, Skandar's beak snapped shut and the light vanished.

Moments later, they began to fall.

Every single griffin the light had touched dropped out of the sky, limp and unresisting. Dozens of them, all at once, falling like rain, not one of them trying to stop themselves. All of them stone dead.

Here and there the odd griffin who had escaped by pure luck
flew away from the tower at full speed, panic-stricken. The
unpartnered chased them and killed most of them, but one or
two managed to evade their talons and escaped from the city.

In the eerie silence that followed, Skandar descended slowly
back toward the tower. He was sluggish in the air, as if he was
drunk—or exhausted to the point of near-death. He landed
clumsily, stumbling a short distance before he collapsed in a
swoon.

Arenadd was thrown from his back, but landed on the body
of a dead griffin and picked himself up unharmed.

He paused to dust himself down, and hurried to Skandar's
side, checking for a pulse. It was there, though abnormally
slow, and Arenadd sighed in relief. He would be all right by the
time he woke up. And there would be plenty of meat ready for
him when he did.

Arenadd gently pulled his partner's limp wings onto his back,
folding them neatly, and smoothed down his feathers. "Rest
now," he murmured, as Skandar stirred. "You've earnt it."

He looked up, and felt a dull shock when he saw how empty
the sky looked.

There were no enemy griffins left—only the unpartnered,
circling slowly overhead. The battle was over, and they had survived. Just.

33

Waiting

The day when Erian finally left the Island of the Sun was an emotional one for him, and more painful than he had expected. It had taken him another two weeks, with Senneck's help, first to find a safe and easy way for her to tow *The Pride of Gryphus* from the air, and second to reinforce the entire craft and add even more plant fibres between the planks. He still had a suspicion that it might leak once they were out on the open water, but he had a pair of crude buckets he had made during his stay on the island.

He had also packed the tiny craft with food, the goatskin blanket he had made, and meat for Rannagon and his sister. Senneck was ready to leave. Everything was done.

Erian walked through the ruined village that had been his home for so long, suddenly unable to reconcile himself with the idea that he would, in all likelihood, never see it again.

It gave him a strange feeling: partly sadness, but also an odd sense of fear, as if in leaving the island he would also be leaving something else. *Home.*

No. More than home. Sanctuary. The Island of the Sun had been a haven for him ever since he and Senneck had nearly killed themselves to reach it. And even though he had thought he would go mad from loneliness and his longing to see Elkin again, he had finally accepted it as a new home.

He wandered into his old hut and ran his fingers over the walls, which he had carved with patterns and sunwheels during an idle moment. *I love this place,* he thought suddenly. *It feels more like home than my rooms at Malvern. How can I leave it?*

But he knew he had to. With a heavy heart, he turned and walked away, out of the village and back to the beach, where Senneck was waiting with the chicks.

"Are you ready?" the brown griffin asked tersely.

Erian nodded. "Let's go."

He lifted the chicks into the boat, and pushed it down the sand and into the waters of the lagoon before they could climb out. Once he was ankle-deep in water, he got in with them and sat down on the folded blanket.

Senneck, still on the beach, picked up the thick piece of wood Erian had tied to the end of the rope. "Are you certain that you are ready?" she asked. "Is there nothing more to be done . . . nothing you have forgotten?"

Erian grabbed Rannagon to stop him leaping over the side. "Yes, Senneck. Food, water, blanket, sword and chicks—everything. It's time to go."

She clicked her beak and took off, hampered a little by the rope trailing behind her. They had practised this many times, but Erian still braced himself nervously.

Once Senneck was well into the sky, the rope went taut, and a moment later they were off. Erian, still restraining the chicks, felt a sudden thrill as *The Pride of Gryphus* skimmed through the lagoon and then out into the open sea.

The chicks, too, seemed excited. Rannagon, escaping from his guardian's grasp, scampered to the front of the boat and looked out at the water, cooing to himself.

Erian, deciding it was safe to do so, let the female go and watched her explore the boat with her brother. The chicks were both the sizes of dogs by now, and difficult to restrain, and Erian hoped they wouldn't try to leap overboard. Fortunately, neither of them looked inclined to do so at the moment, and he relaxed and sat back while the boat sped on.

But he was out of luck if he expected the journey to be easy. The boat began to take on water when they were barely away from the island, and though he ignored it for as long as he could, it quickly rose until it was lapping around his feet. Sighing, he picked up a bucket and began to bail.

And that was what he spent most of the journey back to the mainland doing, in between keeping an eye on the chicks and making sure they didn't eat all the food.

Eventually, bored and irritated, he started to talk to himself again, a habit he would never lose for the rest of his life.

". . . cursed thing, useless boat, why didn't I take any extra palm fibres with me? Damn you, Senneck, why did you have to have chicks? I should have thought of this months ago, so we could go back to Malvern and Elkin . . . Gryphus curse it . . ."

The chicks were lively at first, running back and forth along the length of the boat, wrestling with each other and keeping up a high-pitched squabbling the entire time. Eventually, growing bored with that, they started to pick at the gaps in the planks, pulling out the waterproofing fibres. When Erian tried to put a stop to it, this instantly became their new favourite game. By midday he was wet, cut and bruised in several places, and utterly exhausted and frustrated.

Unfortunately, though this method of travel was safer than trying to ride on Senneck's back, it was also slower. The island had faded to a dot on the horizon, but there was no sign of the mainland ahead, and the boat's progress had slowed since they had set out, as Senneck began to pace herself.

Fortunately for the sake of Erian's sanity, the chicks eventually became bored of their new pastime and curled up in the prow to sleep. Erian, now thoroughly frazzled, chewed on a dried mushroom while he stuffed the fibres back into place, and then he resumed his bailing as quickly as he could. Fortunately, though the leakage was bad, it wasn't fast enough to overwhelm the boat.

Once it was as dry inside the little vessel as he could make it, he dared to sit back and rest. Gods, he was tired.

Above, Senneck continued to fly tirelessly westward. Not for the first time, Erian marvelled at her fortitude. He was tired, but Senneck probably was, too, and she would never complain.

He smiled to himself and slid into a doze.

Water touching his hand woke him up. He started and sat up, and was bailing again before his brain had even registered what was going on. The water had also woken up the chicks, who were huddled together in the prow and complaining loudly.

"It's all right!" Erian told them, as he tossed a bucketful of water over the side. "You're safe, just calm down . . . let me take care of this, and I'll give you some food once I've finished . . . would you like that?"

Rannagon stared accusingly at him. "Wet! Wet!"

"Yes, I know. I'm wet, too!" said Erian. "It won't kill you, all right? There." He scooped up a last bucketful and tossed it away. "That's better, isn't it?"

The chicks did not look comforted.

"Want nest," the female whined. "Want mother!"

"It's all right," Erian told her. "Look, up there! That's your mother, there! She's with us, see?"

The female did not look comforted. "Want home," she said again.

Erian unwrapped the meat he had brought. "Here," he said. "Eat. Your mother told me to make sure you didn't starve."

The chicks fell on the food the instant he gave it to them, tearing viciously at it. Erian, watching them, was suddenly struck by how savage they were when they ate and how easily their beaks cut through the crudely butchered goat meat. One day, they would be strong enough to cut through a human body just as easily.

Erian shivered.

Once the chicks had eaten, they came toward him, still demanding their mother. When Senneck failed to appear, Rannagon lay down with his head and foreclaws in Erian's lap and stared miserably at him.

Erian stroked his head. "It's all right, Rannagon. She hasn't gone. She'll be with you again by tonight, I'm sure."

The female nibbled at his ragged trousers. "Tired," she complained. "Wet. Want mother. Want home."

Erian felt sad for her, suddenly remembering that he wasn't the only one who had lost a home. "I'm sorry," he said. "But you'll find a new home. I'll show you Malvern. There's lots of other griffins there, and lots of nests to sleep in, and plenty of food . . ."

The female whimpered. She was smaller and slimmer than her brother, and unlike him she had something of Senneck's elegance.

One day she'll be as beautiful as her mother, Erian thought fondly and petted her, too. She recoiled and nipped his finger, hissing.

Erian withdrew. "Sorry," he said. "I'm sorry."

The female showed no sign that she was listening. She walked to the prow and perched with her forepaws resting on the side, looking intently ahead.

Erian, following her line of sight, felt his heart leap. *The mainland!*

It was barely visible—just a grey line on the horizon—but it was there. Unmistakeable.

"Look!" He touched Rannagon's head. "Look there, Rannagon. D'you see it?"

The chick turned to look but didn't register any surprise or interest; most likely he had no idea what the line actually was.

"That's land," Erian told him, wanting to share the excitement. "A new place. We'll be there by tonight."

Or so he hoped, anyway.

Inevitably, the boat began to leak again, and he resumed his bailing.

Despite his hardened muscles and the fortitude he had found on the island, the constant work finally began to wear him down. The sun beat down relentlessly, scorching his back; water soaked into his tunic and dried, leaving it crusted with salt. His hair stuck to his head, he was hungry and there were splinters in his fingers.

Erian's excitement drained away, little by little, leaving him numbed by the endless repetition. Scoop, lift, tip, scoop, lift, tip . . .

The leaks were getting worse.

Erian risked taking a moment to unwrap some dried meat and stuff it into his mouth, and he resumed his bailing yet again while he ate it. *Gryphus help me, my arms are going to drop off—if I don't drown first.*

Luckily, it wasn't all doom and gloom. Above, Senneck had found an air current and was riding it, barely needing to flap her wings and so conserving valuable energy. The boat sped forward with her; unfortunately, this was why it was leaking more copiously than before.

Still, Erian thought, at least they would get there sooner . . . if they ever did.

The journey dragged on, always with the sun at their backs as the distant coast of Cymria came closer and closer. Eventually, as the afternoon drew in, Erian could see colours begin

to emerge from out of the greyness. He leant forward eagerly
to look, and as they crested another wave he was convinced he
could see the shapes of cliffs and trees as well.

We're going to make it!

He wanted to whoop aloud, but he forced himself to stay
calm and keep on bailing. *Too early to celebrate . . .*

The land grew closer and closer, tantalisingly distinct now.
We're going to make it . . .

Erian weakened and ate the last of the meat and mushrooms
by way of celebration, giving some to the chicks, who were
becoming restless again.

As he sat back to allow himself a quick rest while he ate, he
felt a sudden coldness around his legs. Water.

He looked down and saw blue ocean swirling around his
ankles, then his calves, then up toward his knees . . . how could
it be getting in so fast?

For a few moments Erian stared blankly at it, unable to comprehend what was going on, and then a piece of wood bumped
innocently against his leg.

"What?" he said aloud, before realisation came crashing
down on him like a collapsing roof.

It's a piece of the boat!

A stream of griffish and human curses babbled out of his
mouth as he finally sprang into action. He thrust an arm into
the water, grabbing for the sword. His fingers closed around
the blade, and he hauled it out and tucked it under his arm. His
other hand caught the bucket as it floated away from him, and
he began to bail as fast as he could.

It worked—barely. He managed to reduce the level of water
in the boat with a mighty effort, but there was obviously a very
large hole, and deep down he knew he could never hope to keep
up his bailing.

In desperation, he snatched up the broken plank and tried
to find the place it had come from. He found it eventually—the
hole was nearly as big as his hand—and managed to wedge
the board back into place, but it didn't come close to plugging
the leak, and he knew it would work itself loose again in no
time at all.

Taking advantage of this brief respite, Erian slung his sword
on his back and found the other bucket. The chicks, sodden and
whimpering, clustered around him for comfort.

"It's all right," Erian told them, lying, while he continued to scoop water out of the boat, using both buckets at once this time.

It was only a temporary measure, and he knew it.

Senneck, oblivious, flew on. The land ahead grew closer, but it was too far away, too far . . .

Erian opened his mouth to call her, and heard an ominous splintering sound come from beneath him. An instant later, water gushed in. He bailed frantically, practically flailing at the water. It was a hopeless effort. The water came in torrents, swamping *The Pride of Gryphus* in no time at all. The chicks, panic-stricken, climbed on top of him to try to escape, clinging to his arms. Erian tried to shake them off, but they held on instinctively, weighing him down, hampering his efforts to save the boat. A wave, crashing over the bows, snatched one of the buckets and washed it away, and he lost the other one in a clumsy attempt to retrieve it.

The boat lurched alarmingly, juddering as the waves tore at it. And then, finally, it surrendered itself to the inevitable. Erian felt the planks begin to come apart beneath him, and did one of the most quick-witted and sensible things he ever did in his life.

He half-rose, supporting himself on the boat's hull even as it broke, and lurched toward the prow with the chicks still clinging to him.

An instant later, *The Pride of Gryphus* fell to pieces, consigning its three passengers to the water.

Weighed down by the sword and by the two chicks, Erian sank like a stone.

He struggled desperately, trying to hold on to the rope he had managed to grab at the last moment. It slid through his hands, escaping from him . . . but then the fragment of wood still attached to the end hit his hands, giving him a place to grip. He held on with all his might, and the rope pulled him upward, along with the chicks, dragging them along just at the surface. Safe.

Erian, coughing and spluttering, took one hand away from the rope and looped his arm around the terrified chicks, pulling them up to keep their heads out of the water. Rannagon prudently decided to climb onto his surrogate father's shoulder, which was above water, while his weaker sister simply dug her talons into Erian's arm and relied on that to keep her safe.

Erian wrapped his other arm around the rope, putting all his effort into not losing his hold on it. He looked up at Senneck—she didn't seem to have noticed what had happened—probably exhausted, and putting all her effort into flight.

Erian cursed himself for not calling to her sooner; he couldn't do it now, not properly. He opened his mouth to try, and was rewarded with a throatful of salt water for his trouble. Spitting it out, he held on and hoped Senneck would notice his predicament before he and the chicks all drowned.

This horrible continuation to his journey back seemed to last forever. His arm, already sore from half a day of near-constant bailing, throbbed in protest. He couldn't tell if the chicks were well. Rannagon seemed fine, more or less, but his sister barely moved, and Erian had the constant paranoid conviction that her head was underwater or that he was holding on to her too tightly and strangling her. He had no idea how close they were to land by now; he was too low in the water to see anything ahead but more waves.

But it did not last forever. Eventually, Senneck did indeed look down and see what had happened; Erian saw her head move. A moment later she began to beat her wings hard, flying higher. The rope went taut as she pulled it with her, and Erian clung on as it dragged him out of the water, chicks and all.

Senneck was not done yet. She flew still higher, lifting her passengers until they were well above the waves, and then she moved on toward land as fast as she could.

Erian found himself dangling in midair, his feet just above the water, with the chicks still holding on to him. Rannagon quickly lost his grip but managed to catch hold of Erian's arm, and Erian scooped him up with his sister.

In a way, this new state of affairs was worse than before: without the water to support him, it was much harder to hold on to the rope. But at least they wouldn't drown now.

Erian managed to turn his head to look in the direction Senneck was going.

The mainland is there! Right there!

It was barely any distance away; he could see the sand, the cliffs, the trees, everything!

The realisation gave Erian strength, and he redoubled his grip and waited, determined to make it.

When they were close—so close Erian could see the waves lapping at the shore—the rope suddenly went slack.

He fell back into the water, hitting it with a loud splash. Frantic, he let go of the rope and tried to swim. But he'd never make it: the sword was too heavy, and he couldn't swim and keep the chicks above water at the same time.

He churned forward as quickly as he could, barely able to keep his head above water. The chicks let go of him and began to swim, propelled by instinct. But they would never make it, Erian thought. They could never . . .

And then his feet hit sand. He struggled on, not quite believing it, but as the next wave let him go, he found it again. Before long he could walk along the bottom, and relief surged through him.

He forged his way toward the land, occasionally knocked down by a wave but managing to find his feet again. The chicks swam ahead, surprisingly powerful and certain in the water. Erian followed them on through the surf, until they reached the beach and climbed up it; he went after them, staggering through the wet sand until he was away from the water, then he collapsed.

The chicks flopped down beside him, panting, and Erian managed to reach out and pet them reassuringly. "Well done. Well done."

While he lay there recovering from his ordeal, Senneck appeared. She was limping and her wings dragged on the ground, but she stumbled over to her chicks and nudged them urgently, cooing to them. They stirred and looked up pathetically at her, and she lay down on her belly, inviting them to shelter under her wings. They went to her and huddled against her flanks, shivering. But safe.

Senneck touched Erian with the point of her beak. "Erian. Erian, look at me."

Erian raised his head and managed a watery grin. "Let's not do that again."

She hooted. "I am glad to see you are safe. I am sorry I did not realise you were in trouble sooner than I did, but I was tired and had let my mind wander."

"It's all right," Erian mumbled, knowing this was the most emotional apology he could expect from her. "We survived."

"I would not have dropped the rope," Senneck added. "But

the stick broke, and I could not catch it in time—we were lucky you were so close to shore. Thank you for protecting my chicks."

Erian rolled onto his back, ignoring the sword beneath him. "You're welcome."

Neither of them had the energy to say anything more after that. Erian thought of trying to get up and find a sheltered spot above the high-tide line, but he didn't have the will. Instead, he fell asleep. He was wet and coated in sand, he had lost most of his possessions, he was trembling with fatigue . . . but he had come home at last.

Hundreds of miles away, Lord Arenadd Taranisäii stood at the top of Fruitsheart's tower with Skandar and looked down on his city.

It had been nearly six months since Skade had left on her quest. Six months since the war had begun. Six months that had taken their toll.

Arenadd stroked his beard. He had become thinner, and his face had taken on a slightly hollow, tired look. But his black eyes were utterly calm, as if nothing could ever frighten or trouble him. Despite the protests of his friends and followers, he still wore the black robe of a slave, and it, like his hair and beard, was obsessively clean and neat.

Beside him, Skandar glanced at him and then looked away to watch the sky. The dark griffin was scarred from combat, but if anything, he looked even bigger and more powerful for it. He had finally shed the last of his tendency to be unsettled and nervy like the wild beast he had once been, and now his stance was full of self-confidence.

After the first battle with the griffiners, it hadn't been long before Malvern sent more to attack. But this time the troops they sent were ordinary men with conventional weapons—a large number of them. None of them, of course, were Northerners. Even now the griffiners were unable to forget the old laws and let their vassals use weapons.

With the unpartnered, and the help of all those who had joined them since the taking of the city, Arenadd's followers fought back against the attackers and did it surprisingly well. The troops on the ground were adequately led, but they fought half-heartedly, and many of them chose to run rather than stand their ground when the unpartnered attacked. It hadn't taken Arenadd long to understand why: they were demoralised. And who could blame them? Every one of them had to know that the unpartnered and their leader had effectively destroyed the majority of Malvern's most powerful griffins. What chance would ordinary soldiers have?

Very little, though the siege lasted for a good week. Then a simultaneous attack from the ground, led by Saeddryn, and from the air, led by Skandar and Arenadd, forced the army to break ranks and finally wiped them out.

Many of the soldiers had surrendered. All of them were killed. Arenadd had no use for prisoners.

Skandar stirred and hissed. "We win," he said. "Win war."

"Yes," Arenadd murmured. "I think we may have."

Less than three months after the victory over Malvern's troops, after sporadic attacks by griffiners, which had not succeeded, something had happened that had nearly made Arenadd evacuate the entire city.

A huge flock of griffins—nearly seventeen hundred of them of various ages—had come flying from the South. From Malvern. While Arenadd and Skandar gathered the unpartnered ready for a fight they knew they had no hope of winning, a small group of griffins had broken away from the Southern flock and come to the tower with a message.

The message was stark and simple.

"We are unpartnered griffins," one of them had said. "The last of those from Malvern. We know that a griffin called Kaanee has decided to abandon his home and ally himself with you, Mighty Skandar, and you, the cunning Lord Arenadd."

Arenadd had told her it was true.

"We have come to join with you," the griffin told him. "Some of us do not like it, but you have destroyed many of the Mighty Kraal's greatest allies, and we choose to make you our leader rather than fight you. We will not follow a griffin who cannot fight."

And that was that. In the course of a single day, the unpartnered went from a battered and somewhat demoralised group of less than seventy to a huge army powerful enough to destroy any city.

That was when Arenadd knew the war was won. His plan

had succeeded, far more effectively than he had ever imagined. With the griffins of Malvern on his side, there was no enemy who could hope to defeat him. Unless . . .

Saeddryn had been quick to point it out.

"If Malvern calls to its friends in the South, we'll be destroyed," she told him baldly. "Ye know that, sir. We would've won the war last time, with my mother . . . we were winnin', sir," she added defensively. "But when the other Eyries got talked into helpin' their friends up here, they sent their best griffiners. They destroyed us once. They could do it again, sir. Even to ye."

And yet, in spite of his cousin's objections, it hadn't happened. Arenadd doubted that it would. A lot had changed in the world since the dark days of Arddryn's rebellion. And Eagleholm, Malvern's greatest ally, no longer existed. Without even realising it, Arenadd had struck the first blow for the rebellion the night he killed Lord Rannagon and set fire to the Eyrie.

Now Arenadd stood with Skandar and looked down on the city he had transformed into a garrison for his army. Griffins were everywhere, festooning the outer walls or flying overhead in huge circles. They had made nests all over the place, even outside the walls, and despite Arenadd's complaints, they were eating every animal they could find in the city.

"My lord?"

Arenadd looked over his shoulder and saw Iorwerth—Lord Iorwerth, as people called him now. Kaanee was with him, as always.

"Hello, Iorwerth," said Arenadd, speaking griffish. "And you, Kaanee."

"My lord, I wanted a word with ye if ye don't mind," said Iorwerth, reverting to Cymrian.

"Of course I don't mind," said Arenadd. "Please, come and join me."

Iorwerth came to his side, while the two griffins sniffed companionably at each other. "I wanted t'ask ye something, lord."

Arenadd glanced at him. Becoming a griffiner and discovering the level of respect it had brought him from other people had changed Iorwerth. He wore fine clothes taken from the griffiners' rooms in the tower and on his back even carried one of their swords, which he had proved very talented with. But more than that was the way he carried himself. He had shed the instinctive half-crouch and submissive hunched shoulders most city-dwelling Northerners had. He had stopped looking for approval every time he spoke. Now he carried himself like a lord.

"Yes?" said Arenadd, his voice warm with appreciation.

"My lord, we can't stay here long," said Iorwerth. "I've talked with Saeddryn an' Nerth; they agree, an' so does Kaanee."

"Yes, I know," said Arenadd. "I've been thinking about it, too."

"It's just that we're runnin' out of supplies, my lord," said Iorwerth. "Especially for the griffins."

Arenadd nodded. Rather than burn or bury them, he had instructed the unpartnered to eat the bodies of the dead men and griffins. The corpses had sustained them for a long time but wouldn't last forever.

"An' besides that—"

Kaanee butted in. "The unpartnered grow restless, Lord Arenadd," he said. "They are asking me when we shall finally attack Malvern."

"I understand," said Arenadd.

"Then we must go!" said Kaanee. "The time is ripe! The unpartnered constantly ask me when we shall go, and they are at their strongest and most eager now, and Malvern at its most demoralised."

"An' the sooner we attack, the less likely it'll be for Malvern to call in reinforcements from the South," Iorwerth added. "We've got the upper hand, my lord, but if we don't act soon we'll lose it."

"I know," said Arenadd.

"Then when shall we go?" said Kaanee.

"Not yet."

"When?" said Kaanee. "Why do we wait, Lord Arenadd? If you agree that this is the time—"

"It isn't," said Arenadd. "But it will be soon."

"Why?" said Iorwerth. "When?"

"When Skade returns," Arenadd said finally. "When the slaves come home. *Then* it will be the time."

"Slaves?" said Kaanee. He sounded nonplussed. "Why are they so important? They cannot fight; we do not need them to destroy Malvern."

"I promised I would wait," said Arenadd. "And I know they'll come soon. All we have to do is wait a little longer."

"I want go," Skandar cut in unexpectedly. "Want to fly, go to Malvern. *Kill!*"

"Not now," said Arenadd.

"Maybe I go without you," said Skandar.

Arenadd gave him a challenging stare. "You wouldn't dare."

Skandar met his gaze for a moment, and then relaxed. *"Kreeee,"* he trilled. "No, not go without you. Always bring you."

"Yes, and you'll need me to command the humans on the ground when we attack," said Arenadd.

"My lord, why should we wait for the slaves?" said Iorwerth. "We do not know when they will come, or if they will come, at all."

"Because when I destroy Malvern, I want the world to know why," said Arenadd. "I want this victory to be symbolic, not just physical. If I attack Malvern with a thousand slaves behind me, it will show all of Cymria that the darkmen have taken their spirit back. *All* darkmen, even the slaves. And they will come. I know it."

"How?" said Kaanee.

Arenadd stared at him icily. "I know it," he said again. "Trust me."

In the Eyrie at Malvern, the Mighty Kraal sat in the weak sunlight with Elkin beside him. The last few months had taken a toll on him, too. He looked thinner and smaller. Everybody knew he was supposed to be old, but now his age was finally beginning to show. His white and gold feathers were dull and patchy, and there was a dim look to his eyes, as if he was ill or tired.

He looked down at Elkin. He knew he wasn't as strong as he had been, but she was far weaker. The sickness had made her even frailer than before, and deep down the white griffin knew she would never be as strong as she had been.

"Do you feel better now?" he asked softly.

She coughed. "A little."

He wrapped a wing around her, sheltering her from the wind. "That is good."

Elkin leant against him, snuggling into his warm feathers.

"Will he come back, Kraal?" she asked plaintively. "Will he come?"

"He is *Aeai ran kai*," said Kraal. "He must come. It is how the future must be."

Elkin didn't seem to hear him. "I still don't know," she said. "I still don't understand."

Kraal—nobody had called him mighty in a long time—leant down close to her. "What do you not understand?" he asked.

"How can this be real?" said Elkin. "This . . . prophecy, people call it."

"It is real," said Kraal. "I have always known it."

"But there's good in him, Kraal," said Elkin. "I know. I've seen it."

Kraal looked away. "There is no humanity left in *Kraeai kran ae*," he said in a flat, final tone. "He has long since given up his soul, and his heart with it. Only blackness remains. His hatred will destroy us all if Erian does not succeed."

"But he looked as if he cared," said Elkin. "He was kind to me. He nursed me himself when I was ill, as if I were his own family. He was kind," she repeated.

"Perhaps he wished to fool you," said Kraal. "He is cunning. But he cannot feel love or compassion, Elkin. *Cannot.* Those are emotions only a living creature with an intact soul can feel. He is no longer human, Elkin. You know it."

Elkin looked away and said nothing.

Kraal, feeling tired and depressed, lay down beside her and rested his head on his talons. *Sea and sky help me, how can this have happened? How could they have betrayed us like this? How could . . .*

He had lost his anger a long time ago. Now only misery was left.

Of all the terrible things that had happened since *Kraeai kran ae* had begun his vile campaign, the betrayal by the unpartnered had shocked Kraal the most. That he, the Mighty Kraal, could have his glory stolen from him so easily, that his fellow griffins could choose to follow that most evil of humans and his twisted, dark-furred partner . . .

Some of his anger returned at the thought, and disgust as well. *Your arrogance and your cowardice have made you slaves of the Night God,* he thought. *You fools. Do you think*

*Kraeai kran ae will let you share in his power if you help him
seize this land from me? He will betray you, and you will die
along with us.*

He breathed deeply, trying to calm himself down. It was too
early to despair. Malvern was under the protection of the Day
God; he would never let darkness triumph. He would find a
solution . . . *had* found a solution. It would stop *Kraeai kran ae.*
The champion of the light would triumph.

Kraal looked down on Elkin, who had slipped into an uneasy
doze. *For a long time I believed you were the one,* he thought.
My poor, frail little human. But you could never be Aeai ran
kai. *Not now I know the other signs. And if you were, your body
is too weak and your mind too full of doubts. No . . .*

A little while later, he, too, slept.

In his dreams, *he* came.

The mighty male griffin, huge and powerful, his golden
feathers shining with light. Flames burned at the end of his tail,
and his head was haloed in sunlight that glowed in his eyes.

Kraal bent his forelegs and bowed low. "Master."

Peace, Kraal, said the griffin. *You must remain steadfast.
You must not surrender.*

"I never shall, master," said Kraal.

*That is what you said when we first met, Mighty Kraal, do
you remember?*

"I forget nothing," said Kraal.

You were a youngster then, Gryphus whispered. *When you
fought me and I gave you your powers, along with my blessing.*

"I have always tried to do your will, master," said Kraal.
"Ever since the day I knew you were real."

*In particular when you chose Baragher the Blessed as your
partner and whispered your secrets to him,* said Gryphus. *And
when you led his descendant to invade the North and destroy
the Night God's people.*

"Yes," said Kraal. "Gryphus—"

Peace, Gryphus said again. *You and I have always known
she would strike back one day, and we have prepared for it.*
Aeai ran kai *shall come.*

Kraal raised his head. "But when, master? When? We are so
weakened. We have lost more in half a year than we did in the
whole of Arddryn's rebellion."

Once you thought she was the Night God's avatar, Gryphus

remarked. *You have become short-sighted over time, Mighty Kraal. But do not despair. There is always hope, and I shall never abandon you or my people. Now listen, for I have more to tell you . . .*

Kraal listened, as the Day God spoke on.

You must tell him, the god finished.

"I shall," said Kraal. "I swear, master."

Rest, then, said Gryphus. *The boy shall return soon.*

Far away, in his comfortable bed in Fruitsheart, Arenadd stirred in his sleep and knocked over the jug of wine he had left lying beside him. In his head, the Night God whispered.

The boy shall return soon, she said. *Soon the Day God's champion will be ready. But you must wait. When the collared ones return, so shall Erian Rannagonson. On that day, you will be ready.*

Arenadd's lips moved in his sleep, mounthing the words he said in his dream. "I will be ready, master. I swear."

And so shall I, my dear warrior. So shall I.

34

Homecoming

Erian had often tried to imagine what it would be like when he returned to Malvern, and he thought of it more and more during the slow journey back.

In the end, like so many other things in his life, it was far less glorious than he had thought it would be.

Senneck flew over the city's outer wall and toward the Eyrie, her wings beating slowly and wearily. She had pushed herself very hard over the last few weeks, and for her there was very little emotion in their return except dull relief.

Erian, looking at the city from her back, felt shock thud into his chest.

The city looked almost deserted—where had all the people gone? Worse, the griffins he remembered circling constantly overhead were also gone. The banners that hung from the Eyrie's walls were dirty and tattered. Strangely, though, he could see a handful of others down in the city, but they had designs on them he didn't recognise. They looked like animals of some sort.

Malvern, once a bustling metropolis, looked like a ghost town.

For a few horrible moments, Erian thought he was too late. What if the Dark Lord had already come? What if they were all dead?

But then he saw a handful of griffins flying around the towers of the Eyrie and almost groaned in relief. He wasn't too late.

Senneck glanced back briefly at Rannagon and his sister, flying behind her, and began to fly toward the Council's Tower, where she had taken off all those months ago.

As she got closer, she saw the two figures waiting for them.

Elkin, wrapped in a heavy woollen cloak, watched the three griffins flying toward the tower. The foremost one was brown—could it possibly be Senneck? But she was puzzled by the other two. They were small, obviously young, and flew a little unsteadily. Who were they? If this was Senneck, why did she have other griffins with her?

Beside her, Kraal flicked his tail rapidly. "It is him," he said. "It must be."

"I'm not sure," said Elkin, rather weakly. She already knew he wasn't listening to her.

Kraal rose up and screeched. Perhaps he looked weak and depressed now, but his voice had lost none of its power. *"Kraal! Kraaaal! Kraaaaaal!"*

There was a pause, and then the other griffin called back. *"Senneck! Senneck!"*

Elkin felt her heart leap into her mouth. "Senneck!" she gasped. "It's *Senneck*!"

Kraal drew her close. "It is them," he said, suddenly calm. "We were right not to despair. They have returned at last."

Senneck angled herself downward and came in to land, more neatly than she had done before. Her flanks were heaving, but she bent her forelegs to let her rider dismount. He extricated himself and stepped toward Kraal and Elkin.

Elkin stared at him, dumbstruck. This wasn't Erian. This wasn't him. This was . . .

A ragged, filthy middle-aged man, his long, tangled hair the colour of dirty straw, his face almost lost amid a scruffy beard. His clothes were rags barely clinging to his undernourished body, and he wasn't wearing boots—just a few scraps of leather wrapped around his filthy bare feet.

Instinctively, Elkin put a hand to her mouth. *"Who?"*

The man came closer, holding out his own big cracked hand. "Elkin," he croaked.

It was the eyes, still bright blue and untouched in his grubby face, that gave him away. *"Erian,"* she breathed. "It's . . . is that you?"

Erian grinned, and the illusion of age disappeared from his face. "Elkin. Elkin."

Elkin looked hesitated, not knowing what to do. "Erian you're . . . you're alive. You came back. I didn't think . . ."

Erian looked as if he wanted to go to her, but he stayed where he was. Incongruously, he shuffled his feet. "I, uh . . . I . . . uh . . ."

Kraal interrupted. *"Aeai ran kai!"* he exclaimed. "You have returned at last, and my waiting has not been in vain. Have you found it? *Have you found the weapon?"*

Erian blinked. "Er . . . er . . . yes. Yes. I think. Er . . ."

"Show it to me," Kraal demanded.

He pulled the sword from his back and held it out, somewhat nervously. Kraal stepped forward and examined it, sniffing it and peering at it as if it were a piece of food.

Finally, he sighed. It was a deep sigh, one that sounded as if he had been keeping it inside him somewhere for hundreds of years. *"Yeeeesss . . ."*

"Er . . . Kraal?" said Erian. "Mighty . . . Kraal?"

Kraal looked him in the eye. "Erian Rannagonson—*Aeai ran kai*—you have found Gryphus' weapon and fulfilled your promise. Thank you."

Erian managed another hesitant grin. "I . . . er . . . came back . . . came as soon as I could."

Kraal looked at Senneck. "Senneck Earthwings, what is wrong with your human?"

She rustled her wings diffidently. "I am sorry, Mighty Kraal," she said. "But he has not spoken to another living creature besides myself for a very long time."

"Ah," said Kraal. "Then that is to be forgiven. Who are these small ones you have brought?"

Senneck glanced briefly at the chicks. They had grown during the journey, and she had begun to lose interest in them. "My chicks," she said. "The male has chosen the name of Rannagon, and the female is Seerae. They were born on the Island of the Sun, and that is why we did not return for so long."

Kraal eyed them disdainfully. "So, you are what kept the

Day God's champion away all this time. You do not look as if
you are anything special."

Seerae looked away, but Rannagon met the giant griffin's
gaze boldly. "You are the Mighty Kraal? You do not look so
mighty to me. Where are the great griffiners Erian told me you
commanded?"

Kraal snapped at him, and Rannagon retreated to hide
behind his mother. But Kraal was too relieved to pay much
attention to one insolent youngster. "Erian Rannagonson, *Aeai
ran kai*," he said. "You are tired from your journey, and you
must rest and groom. When you are recovered, Elkin shall tell
you what has happened in your absence. But there is little time
left—you must know this. *Kraeai kran ae*'s power has grown a
hundred times. Soon he will come to Malvern. I marvel that he
has not done so already. You must prepare, and quickly."

Erian nodded. "I know, Mighty Kraal," he said, in griffish.
"I'm ready."

His room looked much smaller than he remembered, and it
was musty as well. It was exactly how he had left it, except
for the dust and cobwebs over everything.

By now, Erian was long past caring about dirt. He left Senneck and her chicks to sleep in her nest, and set to doing something he hadn't done in a very long time: having a bath.

There didn't seem to be any servants about, so he dragged
out the tin bath from the cupboard himself and filled it with
water heated over the fire (he certainly remembered how to
light one of those). Once it was full, he stripped off the remains
of his clothes and climbed in.

He sighed beatifically. *Oh Gryphus, how could I have forgotten how wonderful a bath feels?*

And soap, too. He scrubbed himself vigorously, taking away
so many layers of dirt that by the time he was done, the water
had turned an unpleasant murky brown. He still spent quite a
long time relaxing in it, not caring about the colour and simply
relishing the warmth.

It went cold all too soon, and he reluctantly climbed out
and dried himself down. After that, completely unembarrassed
about his nakedness, he filled a smaller basin and began to wash

his hair. *That* wasn't so enjoyable. His hair had grown so long it nearly covered his shoulders, and most of it was so tangled it was less like hair and more like a kind of mat. Eventually, realising he would never manage to clean all of it, he picked up a knife and cut off the long ponytail at the point where he'd tied it.

His head felt very light without it.

He washed and combed what was left of his hair, which took a long time. When he was done he went in search of a razor but couldn't find one, and settled for cleaning his beard as well as he could. It would do.

After that, he stumbled over to his bed and promptly collapsed on it. Oh gods, a real bed. He couldn't even remember what it felt like to sleep on a bed. Now he couldn't believe he had ever failed to notice how soft and wonderful it felt. Surely it hadn't been like this. He couldn't possibly have spent most of his life sleeping on beds like this.

It was the deepest and most wonderful sleep he had ever had.

When he woke up, he opened his old wardrobe and was pleased to find his clothes still in there.

He put on his favourite blue velvet tunic, a pair of woollen trousers and a pair of boots. Oh, to wear boots again! The sword was still on the table where he'd left it, and he picked it up and slung it on his back with a spare scabbard he found in the bottom of the wardrobe. He felt much better to have it with him. Somehow complete.

Senneck was still asleep in her nest, with her chicks curled up beside her. Erian thought of waking her but shook his head silently as he decided against it. She had done so much and come such a long way; she deserved to sleep.

Alone, he walked out of his room and up the tower toward Elkin's chambers, marvelling at how he still remembered the way there, and marvelling, too, at how he didn't need to stop and rest any more. The ramps that led him there felt like nothing at all.

Elkin was in her audience chamber with Kraal. Erian, seeing them again, suddenly realised how bad they looked. Kraal looked smaller, and Elkin pale and fragile. Had she been like that before? He couldn't remember.

Kraal stood up to meet him. "Come," he said. "Sit with us and eat."

Elkin was seated at a small table. Erian sat opposite her and eyed the food in front of him, suddenly aware of how hungry he was. He was used to ignoring his hunger pains, but here was bread, meat, fruit, cheese, wine—things he hadn't tasted in months.

He looked at Elkin, wanting to talk to her. "Elkin. You . . ."

All the Cymrian words he knew seemed to have fallen out of his head.

"Elkin," he said, in griffish. "Elkin, I'm so glad to be home. You can't imagine how glad I am. Are you all right? You look . . ."

She smiled sadly at him. "Erian. I thought you were dead, you know. I thought I'd never see you again."

Erian smiled shyly. "I missed you so badly, Elkin. I never thought I'd see you again, either. But how are you? Are you well? What happened while I was gone?"

She nodded toward the food. "Eat, and I'll tell you. There's so much to tell."

Erian needed no further encouragement. He grabbed everything that looked tantalising—in other words, everything—and ate ravenously.

While he ate, Elkin talked.

A moment later, Erian choked on his bread. "*What?* He *kidnapped* you?"

"Yes," said Elkin. "After he poisoned the council, he snatched me out of this very chamber. He pulled me into the shadows with him and took me away."

Erian groaned softly. "Oh gods. Oh Gryphus. I should have been here. If I'd known—"

"No," Elkin said sharply. "Finding the weapon was more important than anything else. Even me. And even if you'd been here, you wouldn't have been able to do anything."

Erian put down his food and reached out to touch her hand. "What did he do to you, Elkin? Oh Gryphus . . . what did he do? If he hurt you . . ."

She reached out with her other hand and clasped his. "No, Erian. Don't worry. He never touched me. None of his followers did."

Erian stared at her. "They didn't?"

"No," said Elkin, for some reason glancing at Kraal. "They gave me a comfortable room to live in, and brought me good food and water. Arenadd—*Kraeai kran ae*—came and saw me himself. I got sick after a while, and he came to me and—"

Erian tensed. "What? What did he do?"

She paused, suddenly and inexplicably ashamed. "He cared for me. Brought me water and medicine, comforted me with words. He even held on to me while I was feverish. He was . . . kind."

Erian just stared at her as if she had grown a second head. *"Kind?"*

"Yes," said Elkin. "He acted as if he cared about me. He wasn't . . . he didn't act as if he was evil. He seemed . . . sad and lonely."

Erian continued to stare blankly, but inside he was thinking. Kraal had said that the Dark Lord was being controlled, that he was the Night God's slave. What if that was true? What if, underneath—

"Do not be fooled," Kraal snapped. "Elkin, tell him what this *kind* man did next."

"Of course. After he set me free in return for the ransom, he destroyed Fruitsheart. Killed every griffiner in it. After that . . ."

Erian listened in silence as she talked on, telling him everything *Kraeai kran ae* had done over the last months. Every murder, every conquest, every burning and slaughter.

"Why didn't you do something?" he demanded at last, unable to keep his silence any longer. "Why didn't you send the griffiners against him?"

"I was ill," said Elkin, suddenly angry. "Do you understand, Erian? I was so ill I barely survived. I couldn't govern Malvern in that condition. I was so feverish I couldn't tell waking from sleeping."

"Then why . . ." Erian turned to Kraal.

The white griffin looked away. "I did what I could," he said stiffly. "The decisions I made were . . . were not the best I could have made. I sent a hundred of our finest warriors to Fruitsheart the instant I knew *Kraeai kran ae* was there."

"And what happened?" said Erian.

Kraal looked at him again. "They were destroyed," he said. "Utterly destroyed. The dark griffin's magic killed all but a handful, who fled back here to tell the tale."

Erian gaped at him. "A *hundred*?"

"Yes," Kraal said harshly. "Our strongest warriors have

gone. The few we have left . . . we have placed them under the command of our new Master of War, but there is little he will be able to do when *Kraeai kran ae* attacks Malvern. The unpartnered griffins have betrayed us to him, and now he commands more than twice our strength."

Erian sat back in his chair. He was flabbergasted. "Warwick, Skenfrith, Fruitsheart . . . the griffins working for *him*? How could they? What . . . how could he have . . ."

"The Night God gave him powers," Kraal reminded him. "And he has used them well. Erian, you are our last hope. If you defeat *Kraeai kran ae* when he comes here, his rebellion will be finished. The unpartnered ones will come back to us when they see their leader dead, and we will crush these upstart darkmen who have the arrogance to believe they can govern *themselves*, let alone a nation."

Erian put his hands over his face. "Oh gods. How can I do this? How can I kill *him*? He's . . . Oh Gryphus help me, I can't do this. How could I win against him? I'm not a warrior, I don't have any followers—"

"You can do this," Kraal hissed. "Erian, look at me."

Erian obeyed.

"You can do this," Kraal said again. "You are *Aeai ran kai*. There is no doubt left. You have come this far—how can you lose hope now?"

Erian couldn't look away. "But how can I do it?" he asked piteously. "How?"

"You have the weapon," said Kraal. "When *Kraeai kran ae* comes, you must go to the Sun Temple and wait for him there. He will come to you. When he enters the temple, he will lose his powers, and you will fight him as an equal."

Erian felt a stirring of hope return. "He'll come to me?"

"He will, for he knows what a threat you are to him, and he will stop at nothing to kill you before you destroy him," said Kraal. "In his arrogance, he will believe he can defeat you without his powers."

"I think I could fight him," said Erian. "If we fought like that . . . as equals."

"You can, and you shall," said Kraal. "Erian, listen. It is time for you to know the last part of what you must do."

"What?" said Erian.

"*Aeai ran kai* shall find *Kraeai kran ae*, driven to him by a power stronger than his own will," said Kraal, almost reciting the words. "The two shall meet, and they shall know each other. The avatar of the Night God shall be destroyed when the sun's champion finds his heart."

Erian listened closely. "His heart. I have to . . ."

"Yes!" Kraal hissed. "Find his heart, Erian. That is his weakness. Find his black, dead heart and plunge the sacred weapon into it. Do it, and he will die. *You must kill him.*"

Erian's own heart beat fast. "I will," he said. "I swear I will."

Perhaps Arenadd was confident that Skade would return soon, but Saeddryn wasn't.

"Sir, with respect, we can't afford to wait," she told him, having requested an audience and been reluctantly granted it by Arenadd, who had already suspected why she wanted it. Now she faced him determinedly, upon the tower-top, which had become his favourite haunt.

Arenadd looked at her and sighed. "Is that so?"

"It is, an' ye know it, sir," said Saeddryn.

Arenadd watched her thoughtfully. She, too, carried herself more proudly these days, despite her missing eye. Behind her, a young griffin clicked his beak and moved closer to her protectively. It was Aenae, one of Skandar's sons, who had inherited his father's silver eyes but his mother's ash-grey hindquarters and rusty-orange wing feathers.

"Well?" Saeddryn pressed.

Arenadd pulled himself back to reality. "Saeddryn, I know you're impatient. So am I. All we need is a few more days, I swear."

"How can ye be so sure?" she demanded.

Aenae nudged at her shoulder. "My father's human is the Shadow that Walks," he said. "I trust him to know what is best, and so should you."

Arenadd grinned. "Besides," he said, "there's something important we have to do first."

"What, sir?" said Saeddryn.

"Have you talked to your intended lately?" said Arenadd.

"A little," Saeddryn said stiffly. "What does that have t'do with—"

Arenadd yawned. "It's a half-moon tonight. The Deer Moon.

Perfect for a little celebration up at the Throne, wouldn't you say? Perhaps even a wedding?"

Saeddryn looked surprised. *"A wedding?"*

"Of course. I think you and Torc have waited long enough, and wouldn't you rather marry now than risk one of you dying at Malvern and losing the chance forever? I'm sure Skandar will take us there without any trouble. We can leave Iorwerth and Kaanee in charge. What d'you say?"

"I'm not sure . . ." Saeddryn began.

"If you're not, why not ask Torc?" said Arenadd. "I'm sure he can help you. He loves you, you know. He'd been watching you and secretly pining for you for months before he gave you his stone."

Saeddryn looked at her feet, suddenly shamefaced. "I understand, sir. I'll go an' find him now."

Arenadd nodded in satisfaction as she walked away, followed by Aenae.

Not for the first time, he thought of how cunning his cousin was. She had taken an active role in caring for Hyrenna's chicks, until one of them, Aenae, had taken to following her around. She had begun to favour him and give him the best food along with all of her affections, until he began sleeping curled up on her bed at night like a cat. When he reached physical maturity, there was no doubt left as to whether he would choose a human—or which human it would be.

The bond with the griffin had given Saeddryn all the respect she had wanted and had blamed Arenadd for denying her when he refused to marry her. And no doubt it had taken away some of her humiliation at having to marry Torc, a mere ex-slave half her age.

"Perhaps they can be happy together," Arenadd murmured and turned away to keep watching the sky. Around him, the banners of the four tribes fluttered from the poles that had once flown the sunwheel. The wolf with the full moon, the bear carrying the crescent, the deer with the half-moon and the crow with a star.

He smiled to himself, rather sadly. Perhaps Saeddryn could come to love her husband in time.

As always, Skade intruded on his thoughts yet again. His smile faded. *Gods, Skade. I miss you so much I want to die. Please, come back. Come back to me, Skade. Soon.*

Saeddryn didn't return, and he eventually gave up and went

below to find something to eat, his mind full of a vision of Skade smiling so sweetly at him. *I love you, Arenadd.*

In his memory, he reached out to touch her, his eyes lost in hers. Those beautiful eyes, so blue . . . *I love you too, Flell.*

Arenadd jerked in surprise. "What?" he said aloud.

Skade, he thought. *Skade, you idiot! You love Skade, no-one else. You've never loved anyone but her.*

In his head, the memory warped and shifted. And there was Skade, amber-eyed and silver-haired. *I love you, Arenadd.*

I love you too, Skade.

He sighed wistfully and wandered into the dining hall, where Yorath, who had taken to working in the kitchen, brought him some food.

While he was eating it, he heard a polite cough from the doorway.

"Come in, Torc," he said, without turning around.

There was a pause, and Torc stepped into his line of vision. He was neatly dressed, in a tunic with a high collar that hid the scars on his neck, and had a look of barely suppressed excitement on his face. "Saeddryn said you want us t'get married tonight."

Arenadd put down his cup. "I certainly do. The Deer Moon is tonight—a time for destiny, and for your tribe, Torc. Perfect."

Torc's eyes shone. "Who'll conduct the ceremony, sir?"

"I will, of course," said Arenadd. "If you and Saeddryn are ready."

"We are, sir," said Torc. "Oh gods, I can't believe it . . . I've waited so long, an' now . . ." He coughed. "Sorry. Yes, I'm ready, sir. So's Saeddryn."

"Good," said Arenadd. "We'll leave this afternoon, to make sure we get to the Throne in time for moonrise. We'll spend the night in Taranis Gorge and fly back in the morning."

"Yes, sir," said Torc. "I'll tell Saeddryn, sir."

That afternoon, having instructed Iorwerth and Kaanee to supervise during their absence, Arenadd and Skandar prepared to leave. Two of the unpartnered, wanting to see the mountains, agreed to carry Torc and Saeddryn. Aenae and his brother Iekee came too.

Nerth, Garnoc, Yorath and Iorwerth had gathered to see them off.

"Don't worry," Torc told them proudly. "I'll take good care of my wife, I will, and Lord Arenadd and the Mighty Skandar will take care of both of us."

"And in the meantime, Iorwerth, you and Kaanee will take care of Fruitsheart," Arenadd said sternly.

"There's no need to fear, my lord," said Iorwerth. "Ye can trust us."

Arenadd nodded, from Skandar's back. "I know I can. I'll see you all tomorrow."

Skandar rasped impatiently and took off, and his two sons followed.

The flight to Taranis' Throne took a long time, but Arenadd enjoyed it. It had been a long while since he and Skandar had flown any great distance, without relying on the shadows to take them there, and he suddenly realised how much he had missed the feel of wind—*real* wind—and the touch of the sun on his face.

Skandar, too, seemed to be enjoying it, though he had to fly more slowly than he preferred so that the youngsters could keep up.

They reached the mountains by late evening, and Skandar landed first, in the middle of the stone circle where Arenadd had first encountered the Night God such a long time ago.

Arenadd dismounted and scratched his partner under the beak. "Ah . . . it's good to be back, isn't it?"

Skandar shook himself. "Is good," he agreed. "Like this place."

"So do I." Arenadd walked slowly around the circle, touching each of the stones. He could almost feel the Night God's presence here, in her last surviving holy place.

He wondered, briefly, if *Aeai ran kai* would feel the same agony in this circle that he himself felt if he stepped inside one of Gryphus' temples.

The others landed a moment later. Saeddryn looked around rather uncertainly at the sacred stones, but Torc stepped toward her and took her hand. She started, but didn't pull away.

To Arenadd's surprise, she smiled.

Arenadd spread his hands. "Welcome to Taranis' Throne, Torc Taranisäii. This is where King Taranis was crowned, centuries ago when our people were all true warriors. And this is where I came to be initiated, and where I met the Night God for the first time."

Saeddryn looked up. "Ye saw her here, sir?"

"Yes," said Arenadd. "On the night of the Blood Moon, I met her in the circle. That was when she told me who I really was."

"An' after that ye ran away," Saeddryn murmured.

"Yes," said Arenadd. "Out of fear. But I came back." He looked up at the sky, where the first stars were coming out. "I realised I couldn't run away from my real self, or my god, or my people."

Torc was watching him with an awestruck expression. "What do we do next, sir?"

"We wait until moonrise," said Arenadd. "When the moon is highest in the sky, we'll begin."

A long time later, when night had closed in and the half-moon was directly overhead, Arenadd conducted the wedding ceremony while the griffins slept outside the circle.

He, Saeddryn and Torc had stripped to their waists, and wore nothing but simple fur kilts. Each of them had put on a mask. Saeddryn wore a wolf mask, and Torc a deer. Arenadd wore the griffin mask Arddryn had worn on the night she had initiated him into the Wolf Tribe.

Torc and Saeddryn stood on either side of the stone altar in the middle of the circle, and Arenadd, standing in front of them, began the ritual he had learnt from Arddryn, which he had never thought he would have any reason to use.

"May the moon and the stars and the night witness the union of two souls, who have chosen to unite in love and harmony before the bright eye of the Night God. The moon has turned and turned again since the beginning of the world, and now, with the coming of the Deer Moon—the moon of destiny—we have come before you, god of the shadows and the dark. May you bear witness to these two souls—Torc Taranisäii of the Deer Tribe, and Saeddryn Taranisäii of the Wolf Tribe—and give them your blessing."

Torc turned to look at Saeddryn's masked face, his own mask hiding the smile he was probably wearing. "Saeddryn Taranisäii of the Wolf Tribe," he declared. "I have chosen your heart an' declared my love, and I wish to spend my life with you." He drew a copper knife from his waistband and held it up. "Witness my sacrifice to you," he said and pulled it over the palm of his hand. Blood trickled out, and he handed the knife to Saeddryn.

She accepted it. "Torc Taranisäii of the Deer Tribe, I accept yer heart an' yer love for me, an' know I love ye in return an' always shall. I take yer sacrifice, an' offer mine." And she cut her own hand and took his so that their blood mingled.

Arenadd reached out and touched their clasped hands. "As the master of all tribes, and the one blessed and chosen by the Night God, I approve your marriage and seal it now. Saeddryn, come to me."

Saeddryn let go of her husband's hand and turned to face Arenadd. "My lord," she murmured.

Arenadd picked up another mask from the ground beside him. "Give up the wolf," he told her.

Saeddryn removed the wolf mask and held it out. As Arenadd took it, he caught a glimpse of her uncovered face, and saw the tears shining in her eye.

He put down the wolf mask and replaced it with the other, that of a doe.

Saeddryn accepted it.

"From this day on," said Arenadd, "you are a member of the Deer Tribe, Saeddryn Taranisäii. May your husband teach you the ways of his people, and may they welcome you."

Saeddryn turned away from him, and Torc took both her hands in his and held them silently.

Arenadd looked up at the moon, then back at them. "I now pronounce this marriage sealed," he intoned.

They spent the rest of the night after the wedding in Taranis Gorge, in the shelters they had built while they waited for moonrise. Arenadd had made his a good distance away from the one Torc and Saeddryn would share; he had no wish to disturb them or for them to disturb him.

He lay on his back on the crude heap of brush he had used to make a bed and stared at the ceiling, his ears full of Skandar's deep, rumbling breaths from just outside.

Gods, I wish I had something to drink, he thought, and eventually went to sleep.

Morning came, and he staggered out of his shelter, yawning and a little irritable. His dreams had been full of fighting, against a foe he recognised: the sneering, blond-haired boy and his arrogant, vicious griffin, always with the sun shining from behind them and into his eyes, blinding him.

It was a vision that had been troubling him for some time now.

The griffins were wide awake and complaining of hunger, but Torc and Saeddryn were slower to rise. They emerged eventually, both looking slightly embarrassed. Arenadd, watching them, wondered if they had consummated their marriage that night. If so, then they had probably both lost their virginity: Saeddryn had always been forbidden to involve herself with a man other than the fellow Taranisäii her mother insisted on, and Torc had been a slave since birth.

Well, it was none of Arenadd's business. "Let's go home," he said.

The journey back to Fruitsheart passed uneventfully enough, and Arenadd was very glad when its walls came into sight.

As they passed over it, he noticed some kind of disturbance in the streets, which puzzled him.

When Skandar landed on the tower-top, Iorwerth and Kaanee were already there, running to meet them.

"My lord!" Iorwerth exclaimed. "My lord, thank gods ye're back! Ye've got t'do somethin'!"

Arenadd almost vaulted off Skandar's back. "What's going on?"

Iorwerth paused to wipe his forehead. "They're everywhere, my lord. I don't know what t'do."

"*Who* are everywhere?" said Arenadd.

"Blackrobes," Kaanee interrupted. "Thousands of them. They came into the city somehow. They are everywhere, swarming like ants."

"Black—you mean slaves?"

"Yes, my lord," said Iorwerth. "Garnoc and Nerth are tryin' to get things under control, but—"

Arenadd's eyes had gone wide. "Slaves? Then—"

There was thump behind him, and he turned.

It was Hyrenna. "Arenadd Taranisäii, what have you done with my chicks?" she rasped.

Arenadd gasped. "*Hyrenna!* You're back—where's Skade? For the love of gods, *where's Skade?*"

Hyrenna ignored him. "Where are my chicks?"

"Two of them are up there," said Arenadd, pointing at Aenae and Iekee, who were still flying into the city. "Eerak should be around here somewhere. Hyrenna, where's—"

"Here, you blind fool," said a voice, and *she* emerged, from behind Hyrenna's wing.

Arenadd stared at her. "Skade . . ."

Skade came toward him, smiling. "Arenadd."

"Skade," he said again, and then she was there in his arms, and he was kissing her fiercely, holding on to her so tightly it was as if he were trying to make her a part of him.

She held him in return, just as fiercely, her sharp nails digging into his back and giving him exquisite pain. "My love," she breathed, and her voice was like music in his ears.

He didn't let her go for a long time, and when he did all he could do was look at her face. "Skade," he said, and laughed. "Oh gods, Skade. You're back. Skade . . . my sweet Skade, I missed you so much."

She laughed, too. "Oh, Arenadd. My Arenadd. I have wanted to die since we have been apart. But you are safe, and we are together again, and that is all that matters."

He kissed her again. "Yes. That's all that matters, Skade."

Hyrenna, meanwhile, had been reunited with her chicks, or two of them at least. Aenae and Iekee looked at her with a kind of awe while she inspected them, sniffing their feathers and apparently searching for any signs of sickness or injury.

Finally, she straightened up. "You are fine, strong youngsters," she announced. "You have been well fed and cared for. But where is your brother?"

"I shall find him," said Iekee, and flew off.

"Where have you been?" Skade asked Arenadd. "Hyrenna and I came directly to the city with the slaves, but you were not here and we did not know what to do."

"I'm sorry," said Arenadd. "I was at the Throne, with Saeddryn."

"Why?" she asked sharply.

"Conducting a wedding," said Arenadd, missing her angry paranoia in his joy.

Skade stared at him in utter shock. "What? A *wedding*? Whose wedding?"

"Saeddryn's, of course," said Arenadd. He nodded at Saeddryn, who was looking at Skade with veiled but intense dislike. "While you were gone, she finally found a husband for herself."

Skade's shock and hurt began to twist into pure fury, but at that moment Torc nervously approached. "Hello, my lady," he said. "I don't know if you remember me, but I'm Torc. Uh . . . and . . ." He pulled himself together and took Saeddryn's hand. "An' this is my wife, Saeddryn," he added proudly.

Skade looked blank. "You and Saeddryn were married?"

"Yes, just last night," said Arenadd. "I conducted the ceremony myself."

Skade stared at him, and then burst out laughing. "Oh! Arenadd, forgive me! I thought when . . . when you said Saeddryn had married, I thought *you* . . ."

"What?" said Arenadd. "No! Skade, how could you?"

She hugged him again. "I am sorry I doubted you. You have my congratulations, Saeddryn. And you, Torc." She looked at Saeddryn with just a hint of triumph in her yellow eyes as she slid an arm around Arenadd's waist.

Arenadd could see this was turning nasty. "Look, let's go below," he said. "We've got so much to talk about."

"Yes," said Skade. "We have."

35

Preparation

"We were lucky," said Skade, down in the dining hall with Nerth, Garnoc, Iorwerth, Saeddryn, Torc and the rest of the council there to listen. "If we had chosen any other time to buy those slaves, we would never have succeeded. But the whole of the South is afraid because of what is happening in the North."

"We kept expectin' them t'send help t'Malvern," said Saeddryn. "Like they did last time."

"They have not, and I doubt that they will," said Skade. "There is civil war in the South. The other Eyries fought each other for Eagleholm's lands, and now the situation has devolved into outright war. What was once Eagleholm's territory is now burning as those fools slaughter each other for the right to own what they are destroying in the process. They have utterly forgotten their cousins in the North."

There was a pause, and then Saeddryn laughed. "An' all because Lord Arenadd burned the Eyrie at Eagleholm! Hah! Sir, ye crippled the whole of the South with one burning tower."

Arenadd allowed himself a smile. "Who would have thought it?"

"Not I," said Skade. "Yet that is how it has happened. But the Southerners now expect to see strange griffiners flying everywhere, and they no longer want or trust their slaves. They were more than willing to sell them to me, at any price, for fear they would rise up and rebel as you have here. I doubt there is a single one left in Cymria who has not come with me to Fruitsheart."

Arenadd chuckled. "And that's that. The final step. We have our brothers and sisters back."

"And next . . ." said Iorwerth. "Malvern."

Arenadd looked around at the others, one by one. "Yes," he said softly. "Malvern. The time has come. Our time."

Saeddryn grinned horribly. "We'll see that cursed city burn at last, sir," she said. "In my mother's name."

"And I will meet *Aeai ran kai* and kill him at last," said Arenadd. "The time has come. Now I'm ready."

That same evening, Erian and Elkin sat together on the balcony outside her chamber, sharing a cup of wine in companionable silence.

Erian couldn't keep his eyes off her. *Gods, you're so beautiful.* He wanted to say it out loud, but he was too shy to break the silence. And besides, there was no need to say it. She knew how he felt.

He took in her pale green eyes and her fine hair, so blonde it was nearly white. Her features were so delicate he could imagine she were a wood sprite or a fairy rather than a human. Just looking at her made his heart ache magnificently inside him. *Oh, how I love you, Elkin.*

She caught his eye, and smiled. "You don't know how much I missed you, Erian."

Erian smiled back at her. "You can't have missed me as much as I missed you, Elkin."

"Oh, I don't know," she said softly. "I don't know."

He finally fought down his nervousness and reached for her hand. She didn't pull away, and he clasped it, marvelling at how small her hand was. It made his look big and rough.

"Elkin," he said. "I wish . . ."

"Yes, Erian?"

"I wish I could have been here. If only . . . if I could have come back sooner, if . . . if I could have been here to fight for you . . ."

"No. There was nothing you could have done without the sword," said Elkin. "And if Gryphus wanted you to be gone so long, who are we to argue? Our god knows best. He always has, and he always will."

"But what if I fail?" said Erian. "What if I can't do it? What if . . ."

She reached out and touched his chest with her delicate hand. "You won't fail," she told him. "Because you have what the Dark Lord doesn't: a heart."

Erian smiled. "No I don't. Not any more. I gave it to you a long time ago, Elkin."

She smiled back at him. "You're such a silly man sometimes, you know."

"I—" Erian was suddenly embarrassed.

"Perhaps that's why I love you," she said, and kissed him.

The kiss seemed to last for a long time.

Erian withdrew gently, his blue eyes bright with love. "Marry me, Elkin," he said.

That caught her off guard. "What?"

Erian took her hand and gently pressed something into her palm. "Take it," he said. "I want you to have it. Marry me, Lady Elkin."

It was a stone, uncut but beautifully smooth and round. It was blue. Blue as the sky, blue as his eyes. "Erian . . ."

"Please," he said. "Take it. I want you to be my wife, Elkin. I want to marry you now, before it's too late—while we still have the chance. Before the Dark Lord comes."

She stared at him a moment longer, and then her fingers closed around the stone. "Yes, Erian," she said. "You're right. I will marry you."

He leant toward her, eager. "When?"

"Tomorrow, at dawn."

Erian wanted to laugh aloud, but he didn't. He kissed her again instead.

And, in Fruitsheart, Arenadd and Skade were alone by the fire.

Arenadd held Skade's hand in his maimed one, and she held on to his twisted fingers without flinching. "Don't you wish we could get married?" he asked.

She laughed dryly. "No. Why should I? What would it mean to either of us? I am a griffin, and you . . ."

"I know," he said. "Dead men don't marry."

Skade stared at him, a little uncertainly, but then he laughed and squeezed her hand as well as he could.

"I know," he said. "You're right. It was just an idle question."

She watched him pick up his cup and take a swallow of wine. "Torc said you have been drinking heavily since I left. The whole tower seems to know it."

Arenadd put the cup down. "I know," he said calmly. "They're calling me a drunkard. Not that it matters. I only drank because I was lonely, Skade. Now you're back I can give it up."

"What of the nightmares?" she asked. "Do they still trouble you?"

In fact the dream of the battlefield still came to him every now and then, but he shook his head. "No, no. I'm fine now. I'm . . . more peaceful now."

"I am happy to hear it," she said. "You deserve to sleep peacefully."

Arenadd grinned wickedly. "With your help, I'm sure I will."

"Oh?" She raised her eyebrows archly. "Is that a suggestion?"

"If you'd like it to be, Skade. If you'd like it to be."

She made a show of considering it, and finally clicked her teeth. "I am not one for words like you are. Actions have always served me just as well."

"I noticed," said Arenadd.

Skade grinned in a predatory way and pounced on him. To anyone else it would have looked like a fight, as he pushed back at her to get out of his chair and she wrestled with him as if trying to pin him to the ground, but as they grabbed and shoved at each other their heads darted inward and they kissed each other again and again, more and more violently, their struggle half an embrace. Skade slashed at Arenadd with her claws, and he moaned softly in pleasure and kissed her again, hard, almost as if he was trying to hurt her.

The struggle finally ended when Skade made a sudden lunge that caught Arenadd off guard and knocked him onto the floor. He tried to get up, but she pinned him down.

They stared at each other for a moment, their eyes burning as if in hatred.

"No-one else could ever make me surrender," Arenadd said softly. "No-one, Skade. Never."

"Then surrender to me now," she said, and tore his clothes open.

"Oh, I will," he said, and smothered the rest of her words with a kiss.

Skade held him tightly, snarling with lust. But despite her outer savagery, inside her heart was full of a tenderness that no-one would ever see. She needed him now as she had never needed him before.

But in a way she was glad to have been away from him for so long. It had been long enough that he would never have to know the truth. She would never tell him about what had happened in the South, or ever mention the hideous creature she had given birth to. He would never see it, or know about it, and she would be free of the shame. She would make other young with him, better young, and they would take away the memory of the deformed thing she had left to die.

She would make him proud. Soon.

Erian and Elkin were married the day after his return, in the Sun Temple. Senneck and Kraal were there as witnesses, along with Senneck's chicks and every one of the surviving griffiners from the city. Erian, standing at the altar with Elkin, felt a terrible shock thud into his stomach when he realised how few of them there were. Elkin and Kraal were right: the Dark Lord and the dark griffin had decimated them.

The old priest who was the sole master of the temple, along with his crippled griffin, conducted the ceremony, waiting until the moment when the rising sun shone through the temple window and touched the altar, haloing it in gold.

"Mighty Gryphus, giver of life, master of the day, who makes the flowers bloom and the fruit ripen, ruler of the fair people of the South and master of this land, I bid you witness and bless the union of Lord Erian Rannagonson, your chosen warrior, and Eyrie Mistress Elkin the Fair. May they declare their love now, in the sight of you, Gryphus, who are lord over our hearts, and in the sight of these witnesses, who are their friends and family."

Erian listened as the old man droned on, but he kept his eyes on Elkin. Like him, she was wearing her ceremonial outfit—the

same one she had worn on the night of the dance where he had
fallen in love with her—and she had decorated her hair with a
gold clip studded with gems in the shape of a flower. Erian had
had his beard trimmed and neatened by a barber, along with
his hair, which was tied back in a little ponytail. He had the
sacred sword—now polished to a beautiful shine—strapped to
his back, unwilling to be separated from it.

Finally, the priest reached the pivotal moment in the ceremony. "Now may they declare their love and faith to each other
in the sight of their friends, the great griffins, and Gryphus'
blazing eye."

Erian picked up a flower from the altar and held it out. "Like
this flower, my love has grown and blossomed under Gryphus'
benevolent light. I ask that you nurture it and bring it to bear its
seeds in a future we shall share."

Elkin wrapped her hand around the stem, and his hand. "I
accept this flower," she said in her light, soft voice. "And with it
your love. May it never wither or fade."

The priest reached out and clasped his own hands around
both of theirs, linking them together around the flower. "As a
priest chosen by Gryphus to be his voice in the world, I declare
this marriage sealed," he said.

Behind him, his griffin lifted her head to the ceiling and
screeched—but she did not call her own name. *"Gryphus! Gryphus! Gryphus!"*

The other griffins took up the cry—Senneck, Kraal, the
chicks, every griffin in the temple—calling with all their might.
Creatures of the sun, blessed by the Day God and sent to guide
and protect his people, calling to the sky and therefore to him.

As the calls filled the temple, Erian leant forward to kiss
Elkin. She pressed herself against his chest, accepting his
warmth and his love, and the people in the temple cheered.

Afterward Erian and Elkin walked out of the temple hand in
hand, Elkin holding the flower.

Erian felt as if his heart were swelling with love when he
looked at her. *My wife,* he thought. *My beloved Elkin. Mine
forever.*

That same morning, Arenadd went into the streets of Fruitsheart to talk to the slaves. They had been prepared for it,

and they gathered in the square out the front of the Governor's
Tower, filling it from edge to edge. More than half of them
couldn't fit, but they climbed onto nearby rooftops, perching
there like an enormous flock of sparrows. None of them wanted
to miss what their new master was going to say.

Arenadd, a tall and imposing figure in a new robe decorated with silver spirals, stood on the platform that had once
been used for public executions. He wore a heavy silver band
around his neck, an ornate parody of a slave collar. Skandar
stood beside him, his feathers glossy with health, his forelegs
decorated with dozens of rings taken from the treasury, which
he had adopted with pride.

Arenadd looked down at the endless rows of faces, nearly all
of them turned upward to look at him.

Some ordinary Northerners had decided to come, but most
of them were slaves. He could see the weak early morning sun
gleaming on hundreds of collars, and the sea of black robes
that filled the square. Slaves tough and hardened from lifetimes
spent toiling in mines and fields and building sites. Slaves
scarred by whips and chains and the lifelong knowledge that
they would never be free or see their homeland again. Northern
slaves back in the North at last.

Arenadd knew he couldn't speak for long.

"Brothers!" he called, using Cymrian. "My brothers, my
sisters! My blackrobes!" He grinned as he said it. "Blackrobes, they called you, and they made you wear those robes as
a humiliation, like the collars around your necks! I am Lord
Arenadd Taranisäii, the Shadow that Walks, sent by the Night
God to save you and save this land! I wear a black robe! I wear
a collar! I have lash marks on my back and a brand burned into
the back of my hand, but I am a free man! And I have come to
tell you that the robes you wear are not a mark of shame but of
pride! I tell you, the black robe is not the clothing of a slave but
of a king. King Taranis, master of the tribes, the last ruler of the
North—of *Tara*, as it was known when it was still ours. Like
you, he wore a black robe. Like you, he wore a collar around
his neck. But he was a great king, a man who drove his enemies
away like rats, a man no-one could defeat. I say, you are men
and women of the North! Men of Tara! *My* people, Taranis'
people! I say, it is your right to stand up and say 'I will be free,
and no man may say otherwise!' *I* say, as this land was given to

us by the Night God, as she blessed us with her beautiful black
hair and eyes, her grace and cunning—*I* say we shall take it
back. I say the people of the South, the cursed usurpers who
worship the arrogant sun and the glaring day, shall be driven
away by *you*. You are not slaves now, and you never shall be
again. I, Arenadd Taranisäii, who have brought you home, shall
remove your collars and your bondage if you will fight for me!"
He took a deep breath. *"Brothers and sisters, men and women
of the North, will you fight to be free?"*

The crowd didn't shout. They didn't scream or bellow. They
roared.

Arenadd drew his sickle and raised it over his head. *"Will
you fight?"*

And the slaves roared their approval, stamping on the ground
and shouting, again and again. Chanting a name. *"Arenadd!
Arenadd! Lord Arenadd! Lord of Darkmen! Lord Arenadd!"*

Arenadd grinned his wolfish grin. "Then we shall go to
Malvern!" he shouted. "And we shall go today! We shall march
on that accursed city, and we shall find our enemies there and
smash them. We shall *break* them and drive them away like the
vermin they are."

And the slaves shouted back, howling their approval.

"If," said Arenadd, once they had calmed down. "If you
do not want to fight, then you do not have to. Stay here if
you choose. But if you choose to stay, I command you to find
another warrior and give him your robe to wear. Every man or
woman who charges into battle with me today shall wear a black
robe. From today, it will never be shameful to wear a slave's
robe—a king's robe. Those who choose to fight, come to the
tower and my friends will give you each a weapon. We march
at noon."

His piece said, he fell silent and watched the crowd surge
toward the tower. He had left orders for the gate to be opened,
and the slaves passed through them in a torrent. In the bay
where supplies were usually unloaded, Garnoc, Yorath, Torc
and Nerth would be waiting with a cart full of weapons to dis-
tribute. There wouldn't be enough for everyone, though Arenadd had emptied every armoury they had captured, down to
the last dagger. Those who didn't get a weapon would be given
a tool instead: a wood axe, a kitchen knife, a pickaxe . . . even

just a sharpened piece of wood. How they were armed didn't matter. They could fight, and they would.

As Erian was leaving the temple with Elkin, a voice called to him from behind.

He turned, grinning. "Yes? *What the—?*"

It was a thickset young man with a coppery beard. "Erian. Ye gods . . ."

Erian stared at him. "Branton Redguard. I didn't know . . ."

Bran stared back, unreadable. "We din't think yeh were comin' back."

"Well, I have," said Erian, suddenly feeling resentful. "How's my sister?"

"She's . . . good," said Bran. "We left yer quarters a while ago, after I got hold of somethin' a bit bigger. More room for us, an' it suited my status better anyway."

Erian blinked. *"Status?"*

"Oh, yeh din't know?" said Bran. "I'm the new Master of War."

"You? Master of *War*?"

Bran snorted. "I'm the only one out of these useless snivellin' drips 'ere what actually knows how t'fight an' lead. There wasn't much choice anyway after half the damn griffiners in Malvern got themselves killed."

"Congratulations," Erian said sourly and turned away to follow his new wife.

"Yeah, same t'you," Bran said to his retreating back.

"Bran." Flell appeared at his side and caught his arm. "We should get back. I don't want to leave Laela alone any longer."

Bran turned his head. "Of course. Let's go, love."

They waded through the crowd and were joined by Kraeya. "There you are," she said. "I thought I had lost you. Come, let us go home."

They got onto her back, and the red griffin flew back to the Eyrie and alighted on her new personal balcony. Once inside, Bran and Flell dismounted and went through the nest and into their own chamber.

Laela was there, asleep in her crib and watched over by Thrain. The grey griffin was an adolescent by now, though she was still small and thin.

"Flell," she said, coming to her and rubbing her head against the woman's hand.

Flell scratched her cheek feathers. "Hello, Thrain. How's my little girl?"

"Well enough," said Thrain. "I stayed close to her as you asked me to."

"Good." Flell went to the crib, anxious despite herself. Laela was a sturdy child, but Flell and Bran had conspired to keep her a secret from everyone else in the Eyrie, knowing that if anyone saw her they would instantly realise she was a half-breed. Not even Elkin knew; her eyesight was poor, and though she had seen the child once, she had apparently failed to notice her black hair.

Flell reached down to touch her daughter's cheek. "You poor little thing," she murmured.

"Her father's comin' 'ere," Bran said bluntly, from behind her. "He's comin' soon."

"I know," said Flell, without looking around.

"We shouldn't still be here," Bran added.

"We don't have anywhere else to go," said Flell. "And perhaps . . . perhaps Erian . . ."

Bran gave a hollow laugh. "If this plays out the way people're sayin', ye're gonna lose either yer brother or the father of yer child. Which one's better?"

Flell turned. "Don't say that, Bran. Please."

"There's no choice," said Bran. "Is there? Sooner or later, yeh've gotta face it. We both do. Arren's not gonna let anythin' stand in his way, an' certainly not that halfwit brother of yours. An' after that, what then? What if he comes up here? What if he finds us?"

"He wouldn't do it," Flell said flatly. "I don't believe it. Arren would never hurt me, and he would *never* hurt his own child."

"I'd have said that once," said Bran. "But now . . . now I ain't so sure, an' neither are you. Admit that."

"No," said Flell. "Because I *am* sure, Bran. My Arren is a good man. He wouldn't kill a child. Not his own child."

Bran came closer and put a gentle hand on her arm. "But what if he doesn't remember about you an' him?"

Flell stilled. "Not even then. And he will remember. I trust him."

"Perhaps you do, but I do not," said Thrain. "I have not forgotten how he was when he returned that night. He put fear into my heart even then."

Flell said nothing. Bran, watching her, could feel her fear and despair, and he wanted to take her in his arms and comfort her. He wanted, too, to tell her the secret he had been keeping for so many months. *Arren remembered me. He had me, but he didn't kill me. He let me go. He remembered me.*

But deep down Bran knew the last traces of the man who had spared him were gone now. Arren was gone, utterly gone, and only the Dark Lord Arenadd remained.

The march to Malvern took more than two weeks. Iorwerth had organised the carts of supplies that would follow the army, and Saeddryn and Nerth kept the troops in formation while Arenadd and Skandar kept control of the unpartnered flying above them, scouting ahead every so often to check for danger. But nothing happened. If any enemy troops were left in the area, they fled almost instantly at the sight of Arenadd's army—thousands strong, their faces hard with determination, every single one gripping a weapon they looked ready to use at any moment.

When they reached the spot where they had to cross the river, a team of a hundred slaves, well trained and used to working as a group, gathered wood and rocks and built a crude dam in a matter of a day. The army had to cross it in a single column, but they managed it well enough, and when some of them lost their balance and fell in, the unpartnered flew down and plucked them out of the water.

By noon the next day, the walls of Malvern were within sight.

That evening a huge camp sprawled over the landscape, patrolled by the unpartnered. At the centre, Arenadd and his friends had their own fire.

Skade sat close to her beloved, holding his hand. It went without saying that she had refused to stay behind in Fruitsheart.

"I suppose you'll be coming into Malvern with us," Arenadd murmured to her.

"Of course," she said. "You will be fighting for your life, Arenadd. I must be there to witness it . . . so that I will know if you are safe."

He hugged her. "Of course I'll be safe."

"Then I shall witness your victory," she said grimly.

Not far away, Skandar, Hyrenna and Kaanee sat together.

"Tomorrow, I fight," Skandar remarked. "Tomorrow, Malvern."

"Yes," said Hyrenna. "You and I, fighting side by side at last."

"And I," said Kaanee. "I shall be beside you, with my human. I will be proud to fight alongside two such great griffins."

Hyrenna dipped her head to him, flattered. "Tomorrow you shall see the great Hyrenna fight as she did long ago, when Arddryn's rebellion was at its height and the powerful griffiners trembled. I am old, but my power has not diminished. I shall make our enemies suffer once more."

"Tomorrow, I will unleash death," said Skandar, with unexpected eloquence. "Will show you what I can do! Am ready for this, have been ready a long time. My human"—he added proudly—"my human and I fight together, and we *win*. No human, no griffin stop us."

Kaanee trilled politely. "With your power on our side, victory is certain, Mighty Skandar. However—"

Skandar looked sharply at him. "What however?"

"Kraal," said Kaanee. "'Mighty' Kraal, now no longer mighty. Shall you fight him, master?"

"Will find," Skandar hissed. "Will find, fight, *kill*."

"You must, master," said Kaanee. "Already you have taken so much from him to prove your power over him. All you must do now is kill him. If you face him in combat and defeat him, it will silence the doubters among us, and we shall be yours forever."

Skandar drew himself up. "Will kill. Will kill him. Swear it."

"And we trust you to do it, Mighty Skandar," Kaanee intoned.

Skandar looked up at the darkening sky, full of equally dark excitement. He had no doubt that he would defeat Kraal; doubt wasn't something Skandar experienced very often, particularly when it came to a fight. But he hadn't fully realised until now just what it would mean when he did the moon-griffin's bidding and killed the Mighty Kraal.

Of course, it only made sense. This territory was Kraal's. Therefore if he, Skandar, killed Kraal, he would win it from him.

Soon, it will be mine, he thought. *This big land, full of prey and females. I want it. I will have it. Soon . . .*

36

Sun and Moon

The next day dawned bright and cold, and the army broke camp and resumed its march toward Malvern. As they neared it, they could see the men up on the walls, a good number of them and well armed.

But Arenadd had already planned for this, and the word had been put out among the army. They halted when they were just out of arrow range, and the plan went into action.

Kaanee and Iorwerth rose into the sky together, with Saeddryn, and the unpartnered went with them. They flew over the walls, far too high to be hit, and launched themselves straight at the Eyrie.

On the ground, Arenadd climbed onto Skandar's back and nodded to Nerth. Nerth reached out nervously and took hold of Skandar's tail. The griffin hissed irritably but didn't move, and behind him the army formed into a long line, each man clasping the hand of the man behind him. Arenadd had told them in no uncertain terms that they had to hold on with all their strength and not let go for any reason. He hoped they would obey.

When they were ready, the signal was passed along the line until it reached Nerth, who tugged at Skandar's tail.

The griffin's response was instantaneous. He braced himself and leapt into the shadows. For a few moments they were rushing through cold blackness, and then Skandar hit the shadow wall head on. His beak shattered the stones like matchwood, and he charged on through the wall and into the city, dragging the line of people until he leapt back into the light, bringing them with him.

The dark griffin exploded into the real world, followed by a stream of armed darkmen. They stumbled here and there, frightened and disoriented, but Nerth and Garnoc were there to bring them back into line.

"Attack!" Nerth yelled. "Go where ye will, attack any Southerner ye find, spare none of them!"

"Do it!" Arenadd echoed. "Attack! Kill the Southerners!"

And the slaves obeyed.

Arenadd watched them spread out through the city, some of them baying like wolves, every one of them ready to fight. Ready to kill.

"Nerth," he said. "Garnoc. Keep them together. Don't let them destroy too much of the city or attack anyone from our race. Skandar and I are going to the temple to find the Bastard."

"Yes, sir," said Nerth. "Sir . . ."

"Yes, Nerth?"

"Be careful, sir. We can't lose ye now."

Arenadd smiled down at him. "Don't worry, Nerth. The Night God will protect me. But . . ."

"Yes, sir?"

"But if I don't come back, Saeddryn is in charge. It'll be up to her to rule. Tell her that. If she doesn't survive, you, Iorwerth and Garnoc will decide what to do. I trust you."

"Yes, sir. Good luck, sir." Nerth bowed low and dashed away.

Now . . .

Arenadd looked down and found Skade standing by Skandar's side, waiting as calmly as always. He grinned and offered her his arm; she took it, and he pulled her onto Skandar's back and settled her down in front of him.

Skade held on as the black griffin took off, flying toward the temple. "You are certain the Bastard will be waiting for you?"

"Yes," Arenadd said in her ear. "He knows. We both know where the gods have decided we should fight."

Skandar flew powerfully, avoiding the other griffins flying over the city. He made straight for the temple and landed on the ground in front of it.

There, in the entrance . . . a massive white griffin was sitting and calmly waiting for him.

Arenadd got off Skandar's back and helped Skade down after him. "Be careful," he muttered to her. "It's him."

Kraal stood up. "Welcome, *Kraeai kran ae*," he said. "Welcome back to your city. And welcome to you . . . my son."

Skandar crouched low, hissing. "I kill you," he said. "Today I kill you."

"One of us shall die today," Kraal agreed. "*Kraeai kran ae*"—he glanced at Arenadd—"I know I cannot fight you. Go into the temple and face your destiny; I shall not stop you. But you must leave my son to me."

Arenadd nodded courteously. "I'm sure Skandar can deal with you. Skandar." He turned and touched the hissing griffin on the shoulder. "Good luck. Fight with all your power. I know you can win this. I have faith in you. I always have." And he hugged him.

Skandar nibbled Arenadd's upper back. "Will kill him," he promised. "Will kill him for you. You go fight now, human. Fight sun-human. Kill him."

"I will," said Arenadd, and let go. Almost instantly, he grabbed Skade and hustled her out of the way. And not a moment too soon.

Skandar screamed and rushed forward, charging so powerfully he was less like a griffin and more like a force of nature.

Kraal tensed and then leapt.

The two griffins met with an almighty thud, so loud it sounded as if it must have broken both their necks. But they recovered themselves, and an instant later they were locked in combat, tearing at each other with beak and talon. For a while it looked as if Kraal had the upper hand, but then he suddenly broke away and ran. His wings opened, and he lurched clumsily into the sky. Skandar went after him without a moment's pause, and Arenadd and Skade were alone.

"Come," Arenadd said quietly. "Let's go."

They stepped toward the open door of the Sun Temple, hand in hand.

As they passed over the threshold, Arenadd winced, and his hand tightened its grip on Skade's.

With every step, his pain increased. He could feel it inside him, in his chest, *burning* at him. He groaned softly, fighting the urge to run, to hide . . . to escape the pain.

By the time he had reached the end of the corridor leading to the great domed chamber, he was shuffling, his head and shoulders bowed, moving like an old, old man.

He stopped at last and turned to Skade. "Skade," he rasped. "You have to stay here."

Skade, looking at him, felt her heart cringe inside her. His face was grey, his eyes dull.

She clasped his hand. "No."

"Stay," he repeated. "Whatever happens . . . don't try to interfere. This is between him . . . and me. No-one else."

"Arenadd, he'll kill you!" she said. "You cannot fight him here!"

The ghost of a grin appeared on his face. "I can," he said. "The Night God is still with me. I trust her."

He gently took his hand from hers, kissed her on the cheek and stepped forward into the temple. Where Erian Rannagon-son, the sun's champion, was waiting.

From his place in front of the altar, Erian watched the Dark Lord approach. He came slowly, weakly, his face wearing an open grimace of pain. He looked as if he was at the end of his strength already.

Erian, seeing it, felt the last thing he had expected to feel: pity.

"My gods," he said. "Look at you. How can you stand to be in here?"

Arenadd came on determinedly. "I've passed through the gates of death and returned, Erian," he said. "Nothing scares me much any more."

Erian. He had used his name. Not "Bastard" or "Brat," but "Erian." A sign of respect?

"I'm surprised you came here," said Erian. "I didn't think you had the courage."

Arenadd coughed painfully. "It's easy . . . to be brave . . . when you have a god behind you."

Erian watched him. "Yes," he said softly. "I suppose it is."

Arenadd's eyes still had their old sly glitter. "So I see you returned from your journey. Tell me, do you think it was worth it? Did you find the magical weapon you were after?"

Erian started—how did *he* know about that? He drew the sword. "My father's sword," he said. "Stolen by you but returned to me. Now Gryphus has blessed it."

Arenadd eyed it. "Is *that* it?" he said. "A notched, rusty old sword? That's your magical weapon? *That's* the thing you think can kill me?" And he laughed unpleasantly.

"It can," said Erian. "But . . ."

But now he saw his enemy again, in this state, he felt like a coward for thinking of attacking him.

"Look," he said softly, taking a step toward him, "I . . . I know what's happened to you. I know what the Night God did to you."

Arenadd looked sharply at him. "Do you, now?"

"I know she's controlling you," said Erian. "I know you didn't want to do what she made you do."

Arenadd laughed again. "Oh. You're wrong, Erian. Wrong."

"How?" said Erian. "How am I wrong, *Kraeai kran ae*?"

Arenadd drew his sickle. "The Night God sent me, and the Night God gave me my orders," he said. "I had my doubts for a while, but since then I've found I'm rather inclined to obey them. Even if the Night God hadn't promised me everything I wanted in return, I'd still want to do her bidding. After all, she asked me to fight and kill my worst enemies; she asked me to take the revenge I already wanted. She helped me do it. And tell me, Erian Rannagonson, Erian the Bastard, what are you fighting for if not your *own* god?"

Erian drew himself up. "I am fighting for the sun, and light, and life," he said. "I am fighting for my god, and for my people, and for the woman I love."

Arenadd chuckled. "I am fighting for *freedom*, Erian. Freedom for my people. Don't you understand? I am fighting to give them their home back and their right to live the way they choose. I'm fighting for *them*, not myself. As for the woman I love—"

"You aren't fighting for *that*," Erian spat, suddenly angry at the man's calm, mocking tone of voice. "You don't love anyone, *Kraeai kran ae*. You don't have a heart."

Arenadd chuckled again. "You're right. I'm not fighting for the woman I love. I don't have to. She's quite capable of fighting for herself. Now." He straightened up. "Erian Rannagonson, are you ready to die?"

Erian went into a fighting stance. "Are *you*?" he said.

"Oh, but I already have," Arenadd said softly, and in that instant, darkness fell.

Erian stopped, fear squeezing his throat. He looked at the floor and saw that the column of light shining down through the domed window above had begun to fade.

Outside in the city, the people paused their fighting and looked up, dumbstruck.

In the sky, a shadow began to cover the sun.

Down in the temple, Arenadd felt all his strength come rushing back. He stood tall, his fingers strong on the handle of his sickle, and laughed a terrible laugh that had an edge of madness in it. "You poor fool," he said. "Did you think the Night God would let me fight in that condition? Show me what you can do, *Aeai ran kai*."

And he attacked.

Erian, terror burning in his heart, unable to look away from the dying sun, was utterly unprepared. Arenadd darted forward like a lick of black flame, silent and deadly. His sickle flashed, and Erian gasped and jerked back into reality as blood started to gush from his chest.

"What—?" he shouted.

Arenadd, dancing tauntingly around him, grinned. "Come on," he said. "Aren't you even going to fight? Don't disappoint me."

Erian felt pure hatred rush through his body, hot and energising and terrible. *"Curse you!"* he screamed, and then he finally attacked.

He knew how to use the sword. His exile had given him more than enough time to practise with it, and now he used it as it was meant to be used.

Arenadd darted here and there, still grinning, dodging every blow that came his way. "Come on!" he said again. "You're not even trying! Aren't you even going to *try*?"

Erian let out a scream of pure fury and charged straight at him. The sword caught Arenadd on the arm, leaving a deep gash.

Arenadd's grin disappeared. He staggered backward, swearing violently.

Erian laughed and swung at him again. "Is that better?" he

shouted. "Is *that* what you wanted? Is it? Answer me, you murdering son of a bitch! *Answer me!*"

Arenadd backed away, trying to find his footing again. The sickle couldn't block Erian's big, heavy sword, and the blows he didn't manage to avoid hit him, painfully.

These wounds did not heal. Every single one of them left a line of burning agony behind it, and the sudden, horrible realisation came to him: this weapon could hurt him. This weapon was a real threat.

Arenadd ran forward without any warning, ducking under Erian's arm. As he ran past, he struck again with the sickle. The blow cut deep into Erian's sword arm where it joined his body, spattering blood over Arenadd's robe.

Erian screamed.

The pain was unbelievable. His sword arm sagged, suddenly weak. He staggered sideways, feeling the blood soaking into his tunic; he tried desperately to lift the sword, but he couldn't. His arm was damaged beyond redemption.

Arenadd, panting and bleeding, stopped to watch him. "I cut the tendon," he said. "You'll never use that arm again."

Erian lurched toward him, holding the sword with both hands. "You . . ." he gasped.

"You what?" said Arenadd, confident mockery returning. "You evil bastard? You murdering piece of filth? You revolting blackrobe? Which one do you want? I've got more."

Erian said nothing. He collapsed against the altar, trembling with pain and blood loss.

Arenadd, advancing on him, became serious. "And now it ends," he said, and raised the sickle one last time.

Erian looked up and saw his enemy's face—not angry, not hateful, but full of distant calm. And behind him . . . he saw the light from the window suddenly brighten again.

The sun had returned.

Arenadd gasped, staggering as if he had been hit in the stomach, trying to shield his face from the awful burning light. "Oh no . . ."

But the light brightened, horribly brightened, filling the temple, bringing back Gryphus' protection.

Erian felt new strength flow through his body. "Arenadd," he said, and as the Dark Lord turned to face him, he thrust forward, pushing himself away from the altar. He held the sword in front of him with both hands.

It found its mark in the centre of Arenadd's chest.

Erian drove forward, putting all his strength and all his weight into that single thrust. The sword went deep, until the point had come out on the other side. Straight through the Dark Lord's dead heart.

A horrible scream rent the air.

Arenadd landed on his back, his good hand clutching at the sword, unable to pull it free. Blood bubbled up around it, and more leaked from the corner of his mouth, but he did not die. He convulsed sickeningly on the floor, screaming and screaming, his limbs jerking and twitching like those of a dying rabbit.

Erian slumped where he stood, holding his wounded arm, and watched in silence.

Arenadd's struggle did not last for long. He gave one last jerk and then became still, and what sounded like a long, slow sigh escaped from his bloodied lips. His eyes, wide open and staring at the ceiling, dulled and faded.

Erian dared to take a step closer, and then stopped with a jerk and let out an involuntary yell.

Black energy had begun to creep up the sword blade like blood soaking through cloth. More and more of it, until the shining metal had turned utterly black. Then, silently, it crumbled. The sword disintegrated, leaving nothing but black dust that flew away in a light breeze.

Then it was over. Arenadd Tanarisäii, the Dark Lord, the man without a heart, once the Shadow that Walks, lay dead on the floor.

Erian sighed. "Goodbye," he murmured, and began to walk away.

As he stepped over the body, a scream made him look up. *"No!"*

Erian stepped aside, half-lifting his good arm to defend himself, as someone ran toward him. But she ran past, straight to Arenadd's body, and he saw her fling herself down by it, lifting it into her arms. A strange silver-haired woman . . . a woman with yellow eyes . . . a woman he vaguely recognised from somewhere. She was clutching Arenadd's body, hugging it against her chest, kissing its cold face and calling his name.

Arenadd did not stir.

The woman sobbed—awful deep, racking sobs—and she held his body close, rocking back and forth and crying as though her heart would break.

Erian, looking on, felt his stomach lurch. "Oh Gryphus," he mumbled. "He was telling the truth."

He couldn't bear to look any longer. He turned away, leaving Skade to mourn for her dead lover, and walked slowly toward the door, back toward life.

He had expected to laugh, to feel that something wonderful had happened, to feel . . .

But as Erian limped out of the temple, frightened and in pain, he felt no triumph at all. Nothing but a heavy pain in his chest; it felt almost like grief.

Grief? he thought. *Grief? How can I be feeling grief for him? He was my enemy! He murdered my father, he murdered . . . he was the Dark Lord.*

But as he stopped and leant against the temple door, all he could think of was the woman crying over his body. Just as Elkin would have cried if Erian had died.

"Gods," he said aloud. "There really is no triumph, is there? There's no glory. I killed him, but I can't be proud of it. There's no . . ."

His words died in his mouth. He gaped silently, wide-eyed in shock; all the breath seemed to have gone from his body.

What? he thought. *What?*

There was wetness on the back of his tunic. He reached around to touch it, and found . . .

It was a knife. There was a knife in his back.

A hand closed on his shoulder, and he felt cold breath on the side of his face.

"I think I found something wrong with your plan," a voice whispered. "The appointed time, the chosen weapon . . . but not the chosen warrior. Just a bastard with a sword and the wrong idea."

Erian felt a sharp pain slice across his throat, and an instant later all the strength went out of him.

The hand let go of his shoulder, and he fell, sliding gently onto the floor.

Erian looked up. Everything was dark . . . faded . . . but

there was a face there, looking down at him . . . a face that
shouldn't . . . couldn't . . .

Arenadd Taranisäii gazed down at his dying enemy. "I knew
you weren't the one," he said softly. "I knew you couldn't be.
Deep down, I knew I was right. Goodbye, Erian Rannagonson."

Erian looked up at those black eyes, the sensation slowly
draining out of his body. He felt cold now . . . he couldn't hear
anything . . . the world was going dark . . . even his mind felt as
if it was emptying.

But he found the strength for one last thought, one last question, one last piece of knowledge.

I'm not the one. I'm not Aeai ran kai. *Kraal was wrong. But
who . . . who . . . ?*

Alone, mourned by no-one, watched by the bright sun above
and the Dark Lord below that, Erian Rannagonson died.

37

Arenadd's Triumph

The sickle dropped out of Arenadd's hand, and he turned and collapsed into Skade's arms.

"It's done," he gasped. "It's done."

She held him tightly, tears still running down her face. "Arenadd. Arenadd. You are alive."

"No." He managed to gasp at the irony. "No, not . . . not quite . . . Skade. But it's done. It's . . . over."

Skade sat down, lowering him into her lap. "Rest," she said. "Please, rest."

Arenadd didn't want to, but he didn't have any choice. The agony from his wound rose up once again, dulling his senses, and he slid into black unconsciousness.

But he was not alone. He was never alone.

The Night God stepped silently out of the dark, her pale face beautiful and smiling. *Arenadd,* she said. *Arenadd, my child. You have done so well. You have done magnificently!*

Arenadd smiled weakly. "Thanks, master."

You are one step closer, Arenadd, she said. *One very big step closer. You have destroyed Gryphus' champion, the most powerful of the three descendants of Baragher the Blessed.*

"But he wasn't," said Arenadd. "He wasn't *Aeai ran kai*. He couldn't kill me."

Because I protected you, said the Night God. *He was*

Gryphus' avatar, but you defeated him. You and I. You have given me great strength, Arenadd, and you have pleased me.

"It was nothing, really . . ."

Now, she said. *Now you must hurry. You are so close! Only two of them remain, both in the Eyrie and waiting for you. There will be no effort in killing them.*

"Yes," Arenadd said distractedly. "Master . . ."

Yes, Arenadd? Speak quickly; there is not much time.

"Master, why did you take my memories?"

She paused. *You gave them up willingly to me.*

"Why did I do that?"

Your memories were full of nothing but bitterness. They were the memories of a short and pointless life, a life that achieved nothing and never felt true love or joy. You had no use for such memories, and you wished to become your true self utterly and so attain your true potential.

"Oh. Did I?"

Most assuredly, she said, and smiled. *Now arise,* Kraeai kran ae. *Take this new strength I give you, and go to the Eyrie. Find them! Kill them! Finish it!*

When Arenadd woke up, he felt a new and miraculous strength flower inside him.

He sat up, groping for his sickle. "Where is it? Where is the damn thing?"

Skade started. "Arenadd, please—"

Arenadd stood. "I'm fine. Ah, there it is!" He strode over to his sickle and picked it up, feeling no pain from his wound. "Come," he said. "Let's go, Skade. You and I still have work to do."

As Arenadd and Erian fought, Skandar and Kraal had their own battle.

The two giant griffins circled each other, darting in to strike. Occasionally one of them tried to use magic, but the other would choose that moment to attack, and neither one found the room for it.

Skandar beat his powerful wings, climbing higher and higher, with Kraal in pursuit. When he was at his highest, he folded his wings and dropped, straight toward him. Kraal had been expecting this trick. He pulled one wing in tight against

his body and flipped easily out of the way. Skandar changed
direction in midair, losing speed as he did so, and by the time
he struck, Kraal had had plenty of time to protect himself, covering his vulnerable chest with his talons.

The two griffins plummeted from the sky, locked together
and ripping at skin and flesh with vicious hooked beaks, each
intent on crippling the other. Skandar attacked Kraal's chest,
tearing through the feathers and into the powerful flight muscles beneath. But doing so exposed the back of his neck to his
enemy. It was an opportunity, and Kraal took it. He struck, so
hard it made Skandar's entire body judder.

The dark griffin let go and flew upward, blood soaking into
his feathers. The blow had badly disoriented him, and he flew
in a slow, wide circle, listing to one side.

Kraal, too, was in trouble. He fell, bleeding badly from his
chest. Skandar had indeed managed to damage the muscle, and
the giant griffin's wings flailed weakly as he tried to pull himself out of the dive.

At the last moment, a hair's breadth away from a high rooftop, his left wing suddenly crumpled. He extended his talons,
and an instant later he struck the building.

The impact made the tiles shatter. Kraal's talons punched
straight through them, breaking the wooden frame beneath. He
scrabbled desperately, trying to extricate himself, but the roof
simply could not bear his weight, and the more he struggled,
the worse his situation became. If one more of the beams hidden under the tiles broke, he would fall through.

Above, Skandar had recovered his senses. He circled lower,
closing in on his enemy.

His blood ran hot with triumph. Kraal was finished, utterly
helpless. He had no hope of freeing himself from the human
nest in time, no hope of protecting his vulnerable wings and
spine.

Skandar folded his wings and dived straight at him.

But Kraal was not finished. Not yet. Not by any means.

He heard the rush of Skandar's wings overhead and looked
up to see the dark griffin coming, faster and faster, talons
spread and ready for a fatal below.

Kraal felt his heart still. *Gryphus,* he thought. *Grant me this
last victory.*

He opened his beak wide and reached into the store of magic

that rushed through his veins, fuelling his body. He took only a few moments to prepare himself . . . and unleashed it.

Skandar saw it coming, and he opened his wings, slowing his descent. Some instinct told him what to do, and as a beam of pure white light rushed toward him he opened his beak and sent his own strength forth, all of it.

The two beams met in midair—one black, one white. Magic more powerful than the city had seen in many long centuries. Magic of the sun and the moon.

Where it met, huge streams of grey light coiled away into the air, white and black embracing to create something else, neither light nor dark. But neither griffin could triumph.

Kraal put all his will into his magic, until his senses faded and his wounds ceased to hurt. He didn't care if he died, not now. All that mattered was to kill the dark griffin, to destroy him utterly—as he deserved to be destroyed, as he *had* to be.

Skandar didn't think. Not even in the vaguest terms. He had never been inclined to thought, and all he knew now was the power, the command—the fighting rage that had always been in his heart, which commanded him now. He hovered—almost hanging in the air—his entire body rigid with magic. He had never unleashed it this powerfully—not in Fruitsheart, not even before then at Eagleholm.

But he had already used his magic today. He had already drained his energy. And Kraal had not.

The black light from Skandar's beak began to falter and fade, and Kraal's white energy drove it back toward him, slowly but ruthlessly forcing it to spread out and weaken.

At that moment, the sun darkened.

Kraal, taking his eyes off his enemy, saw the flaming orb that was the Day God's eye suddenly dim. A shadow was moving across it, blotting it out.

Down in the city, people screamed.

And still the shadow moved. Bit by bit the sun vanished, in a ghastly parody of the waning moon. The Day Eye was closing. Gryphus' power was fading. And with it, Kraal's.

The white light faded. Kraal fought, putting all his strength into keeping it alive, but all his power seemed to have gone. He resumed his struggle to free himself from the rooftop, trying to get out before it was too late. He freed one foreleg, then the other, and as his magic finally died he threw himself sideways.

Skandar's magic touched him as he moved. Kraal felt a terrible numbness spread over his flank and hind leg, and he rolled helplessly down the shattered roof, trying to save himself with his three remaining legs.

He reached the edge and fell off it, straight down and onto the street.

The impact slammed pain into his belly and up through his body. He slumped onto his side with his wing crumpled beneath him, gasping in shock.

His numb hind leg refused to move. He struggled to get up, reaching back to touch it with his beak. There was no sensation left. His leg was completely paralysed.

Worse, the numbness was spreading.

Kraal shuddered, his eyes suddenly wide. He could feel a terrible coldness creeping over his skin, needling down into his flesh and bones. It was coming for his heart, and he knew that when it reached there, he would die.

As he lay on the ground, despair consuming him with the cold, the brightness of the sun returned.

He looked up through dull eyes and saw the shadow creeping away. The light was coming back. The Day Eye was opening.

And, as the warmth of the reborn sun touched his fur and feathers, he felt the deathly coldness ease.

With one last, mighty effort, Kraal heaved himself upright. His paralysed leg dragged uselessly, but the others were still sound, and so were his wings. He made a clumsy run forward, beating them with all his might, and—miraculously—gained the air.

He flew upward, fighting back against the coldness slowly taking his life, straight toward Skandar.

The dark griffin was ready for him. He circled about and rushed in for another attack, screeching his own name. *"Skandar!"*

Kraal ducked under him, turning on his back as he passed to strike upward, straight at Skandar's vulnerable underside. His talons found their mark, tearing a deep wound.

Skandar lurched and screeched again, this time in pain. As Skandar turned to meet his dying father, Kraal turned, too, striking the air in a massive, powerful blow. *"Die!"* he screamed.

But Skandar was ready. He angled his wings and flew sideways at the last instant, and as the great white griffin came within range, he hit him with his beak, directly in the head.

There was a thud and a crack, a tearing of talons, and the Mighty Kraal fell from the sky.

He was dead before he hit the ground.

Skandar didn't pause to watch him fall. He flew away, barely strong enough to beat his wings, not caring about the battle still going on around him.

All he wanted to do now was find a place to sleep, a safe place where Arenadd could find him and look after him, as he always did.

Confused by blood loss and exhaustion, he turned toward the Eyrie.

Senneck, too, was searching.

She had seen the sun darken—had seen, too, the death of Kraal. Both had frightened her, but she had something far, far more important to worry about. *Erian*.

She had wanted to stay with him in the temple, but he had asked her not to, and besides, she wanted to fight. But she hadn't strayed far from the temple, and now she flew back toward it, her heart pounding with sickening fear. She had seen the dark griffin, and he was riderless. The Dark Lord was not with him, had not rejoined him. Surely that meant he was dead.

The great dome of the Sun Temple loomed ahead. Senneck easily avoided the unpartnered; without Erian on her back, she was just another one of them.

She descended toward the temple, toward the open space outside its doors, and as she moved lower she saw the solitary human shape lying just inside the temple.

Senneck landed and stepped toward it, her tail swishing from side to side.

It was Erian.

Senneck broke into a run. "Erian! *Erian!*"

Erian lay on his back, utterly still. Senneck slowed, her blue eyes taking in his deathly white face and the blood that had soaked into his clothes.

"Erian . . ."

She crouched low beside him, touching his face and chest with her beak, nudging at him in an attempt to make him wake up.

Inside, she already knew it was futile. She could smell it. Smell the scent of death on him.

Senneck did not know what to do. She lay down, dragging him toward her, and covered him with her wings, sheltering him as if he were her chick.

"Erian," she said softly. "Erian."

Curse the sky. Curse everything. Curse the world. It is over. All over. We have lost.

If Senneck had been human she would have cried, but she did not. She laid her head over her partner's body and closed her eyes, outwardly expressionless but inwardly filled with utter horror and despair.

Erian had not won. He had *lost*. He had fought the Dark Lord, and the Dark Lord had killed him. It was over. Everything they had fought and struggled for was over. Malvern was lost, like the war. The night, the dark and the shadows had won.

But the battle for Malvern was not over.

In the streets not too far away from where Senneck mourned, Skade and Arenadd ran, hand in hand.

Arenadd could feel a hot and wonderful triumph burning inside him, a feeling of euphoria a hundred times more powerful than he had ever had from wine or whiteleaf. It was over. He had won. Won the war, won the struggle with *Aeai ran kai*, won everything. The North was his; the Night God had been served. All would be well, and he had nothing more to fear.

By the time they reached the Eyrie, it had already been partly overrun. The unpartnered had broken down the walls on Kaanee's orders, and their human counterparts had swarmed over them and into the towers themselves, smashing through the doors with axes.

Arenadd glanced at Skade and grinned. "I know where to go," he said. "Shall we?"

She grinned back. "I have dreamt of this day, Arenadd. I have dreamt of it for many long months."

Arenadd paused to kiss her cheek. "Some dreams come true. Let's finish this, beloved."

They entered the largest tower together, and the final fight of the war began.

Inside the tower, there was chaos. People ran everywhere, mostly Northerners, and a few fleeing Southerners. Arenadd saw some of them, cornered, try to surrender. They were killed instantly.

He walked past it all, sickle in hand. They didn't need his help.

Skade had brought a light sword of her own, and she gripped it with a new certainty. "Who are we seeking?" she asked.

"The last two people I have to kill," said Arenadd.

"The Eyrie Mistress?" said Skade.

Arenadd hesitated briefly; he had completely forgotten about Elkin. "Yes," he said. "We should find her. She'll be in this tower somewhere if she hasn't fled. I doubt she could have gone far."

They climbed the Council's Tower, meeting little resistance along the way. Most of the defenders left in it had already gone, either running to escape or to attack the enemy coming in from below. Here and there, the unpartnered had broken in, some of them wounded and looking for shelter. More than once Arenadd and Skade had to climb over a dead griffin lying huddled in a corridor.

When they were halfway up, Arenadd stopped by a shattered window. "Look," he said, and pointed.

Skade came to join him. She was in time to see Kraal fall. "My gods," she breathed, unconsciously using the human exclamation. "Skandar . . ."

"Skandar has won," Arenadd said proudly. "He's killed the Mighty Kraal, as he promised he would. I knew he could do it."

"Now the unpartnered shall never follow another griffin," said Skade. "Unless Skandar himself is defeated some day."

"I doubt it," said Arenadd. "There's no griffin left in Cymria who could beat Skandar. Not now."

Skade laughed as they walked on. "And you once tried to drive him away."

Arenadd smiled. "He's not easy to get on with, is Skandar. Neither are you, come to that."

She pushed him. "And you think *you* are more charming?"

Arenadd flexed his right arm. "I'm not as evil as I look."

"You are not evil at all," she said softly. "Not to me."

They had climbed higher while they talked, and now Arenadd stopped. "I haven't told you this . . . I should have."

"What?" said Skade.

He smiled into her eyes. "When this is done and the

Southerners are gone, I'll rule the North. My people will demand it."

"Of course," said Skade. "Why are you telling me this?"

"Because." Arenadd touched her awkwardly with his good hand. "Because no-one can rule alone. If I become king, I'll need a queen. You, Skade. You."

She stared at him. "Me?"

"Of course! Who else could possibly do it?" said Arenadd. "Stay with me, Skade, after the war is over. Be my queen; rule by my side. Please."

She looked uncertain for a moment longer, but then she smiled. "Oh, Arenadd. Of course I shall. I would not leave you."

"Then it's settled," said Arenadd, with his old mischievous grin. "Now." He turned to look at the wall, where there was a huge pair of doors. "This is the way."

"Where do they lead?" asked Skade, while Arenadd kicked the doors open.

"The councillors' chamber," said Arenadd. "I've been here before."

They went in.

The councillors' chamber looked far less glorious than Arenadd remembered. The colourful banners and other decorations were gone. Even the mural on the ceiling looked faded, but it was clear that no fighting had taken place here yet. The openings in the roof where the councillors had once flown out were sealed, and all the other doors were shut.

The room was utterly deserted . . . or looked as though it was, for a moment.

Arenadd stalked forward, like a cat, straight toward the platform in the middle of the councillors' seats.

Lady Elkin, Eyrie Mistress, rose to meet him. "Lord Arenadd," she intoned.

Arenadd stopped, and Skade did likewise, a few paces behind him. "Hello, my lady."

Elkin looked even paler than usual but completely unafraid. "I only want to know one thing," she said.

"Ask me, my lady," said Arenadd.

She looked him in the eye. "Where is my husband? Where is Erian?"

Arenadd paused for a moment and then reached up and opened his robe, exposing the awful wound in his chest. It was blackened, grey around the edges, so deep and wide it had cut through his breastbone.

"He did this to me," he said softly. "He had more courage than any man I've ever met. He believed in what he was fighting for. Just as much as I did."

Elkin looked steadily at him, and the wound. "What happened to him?"

Arenadd pulled his robe closed and silently held up the bloodied sickle. "I gave him a clean death," he said. "Painless. I swear."

Her expression did not change, but something died in her eyes. "And Kraal? My partner?"

"Skandar killed him," Skade interrupted. "Moments ago. We saw it."

Elkin looked at her, then at Arenadd. "You love this woman?"

"With all my heart, yes," said Arenadd.

Incredibly, Elkin smiled. "I knew I was right about you. You're not a monster. You still know how to love, and that makes you a human being." She reached into the pocket of her dress. "I'm finished, my lord," she said. "There's nothing left for me. Not without Erian and Kraal." Her hand emerged, holding a small bottle. "So I'm leaving it up to you now," she said. "If your people came this far to be free, then who am I to say they don't deserve it? They followed you here, Arenadd. Don't betray them."

"Never," said Arenadd.

Elkin smiled again, with infinite sadness. "Care for this land, my lord," she said. "And remember me." She took the cork out of the bottle and swallowed the contents in one mouthful.

Arenadd reached out to touch Skade on the shoulder as Elkin, still smiling sadly and with her eyes looking into his, crumpled onto the platform where she and Kraal had once faced the council and told the North and its people how to live.

The bottle rolled out of her hand and came to rest by Arenadd's boot.

He nudged it. "Viper's Tears. A quick death. Come." He tugged at Skade's hand. "Let's go. There's nothing more for us here."

Skade followed him out of the chamber. "Why did she do that?"

"Lady Elkin was a brave woman," Arenadd said solemnly.

"And an intelligent one. She knew what she was doing. Right up until the end. And if she loved Erian . . . well."

Skade shook her head. "I am glad we did not have to kill her."

"I wouldn't have killed her anyway," said Arenadd. "I'm a murderer, not a coward."

They went downward again, following an odd and seemingly random pathway down stairs and ramps and along corridors, occasionally pausing before Arenadd decided on a new direction.

"Where are we going?" Skade said eventually. "Are we lost?"

"No," Arenadd muttered. "No . . . not lost . . . I know where we're going."

The word "how?" formed in Skade's mouth, but died away. Her beloved had a strange, intent look about him, one that looked vaguely familiar. He walked in a deliberate way, sometimes slowing to a half-crouching stalk, sometimes darting ahead, pausing every so often with his head on one side, as if he was listening for something.

Skade, following him, eventually realised why it looked familiar. He was imitating how a hunting animal moved—a wolf, perhaps—probably without even realising it.

Finally, Arenadd stopped by a door. He ran his fingers over it, sniffing, his eyes narrow.

Then he stilled. "This is it," he said. "It's on the other side of this door."

Skade drew her sword. "Is it dangerous?"

"What? No. No. The Night God told me it wouldn't be." Arenadd tried the handle of the door. It was locked. He muttered irritably to himself and wandered away, returning a few moments later with a brick taken from a spot where an ill-timed magical attack had made a hole in the wall.

He squared himself in front of the door and then hit it with the brick as hard as he could. The door shuddered, and Arenadd hit it again and again, harder and harder, apparently feeling no pain in his hand. The door was thick wood, and another man would have given in before he made much impact on it, but Arenadd still had his unnatural strength. He continued to bash at it, until it made a splintering sound and caved inward a little. Arenadd tossed the brick aside and kicked the door square in the centre.

It gave way to his boot and swung open.

Arenadd gave a little hiss of triumph and drew his sickle before he stepped through.

As he entered the room, he glanced quickly at its walls and corners, checking for any sign of hidden enemies.

Nothing.

He looked again at what lay directly in front of him. A young woman, her fine brown hair hanging loose around her face and her blue eyes fixed on him, wide in terror.

Arenadd looked at her and stopped. "Oh *no*," he said.

Flell saw him. At last, after so long, she saw him.

And, most terribly of all, she recognised him. Just barely, but she recognised him.

The solemn boy she had once known was a man now, and she could see how awful his journey to manhood had been. He was tall and thin. Too thin. The face that had once been lean was now hollow and red-eyed with pain and fatigue, marred by the scar under his eye. He had a neat, pointed chin beard, and his hair was long and thick, but matted with blood, like the ragged black robe that all but hung from his body.

She could see the broken, twisted fingers on his left hand, hanging by his side. Could see the maze of scars just visible through the tears in his robe.

Her heart swelled, partly with fear but partly with love. *Oh gods, I still love him,* she thought. *I still love him.*

She wanted to step toward him, but she didn't. "Arren," she said. *"Arren."*

Arenadd wiped his forehead with his free arm. "Oh holy Night God," he said.

"Arren," Flell called again. "Arren, it's me! It's Flell! Don't you remember me?"

Skade appeared by her beloved's side. "Is this her?" she asked. "Is this the one you were told to kill? The Bastard's sister?"

Arenadd didn't look away from Flell. "Yes. Can't you see it? Look at her eyes. *His* eyes. Their father's eyes."

Flell's hand shook as she lifted her sword, not quite pointing it at him. "Please, Arren. *Please.* You have to remember me. It's Flell. Don't you remember? Remember Eagleholm? Remember Bran, and Gern, and Eluna?"

Arenadd's expression did not change. "I'm not Arren," he said. "I don't know who you're talking about."

"Remember!" Flell cried. "Please, remember! Remember your father; remember your mother. *Remember!*"

Arenadd's eyes turned cold. "My mother is the Night God," he said. "And my father is death." But a hint of uncertainty showed in him. Just a hint.

Flell saw it. "What happened to Erian?" she asked.

Skade had begun to grow impatient. "Your brother is dead," she said. "He died in the Sun Temple. Arenadd, why are you waiting? Why have you not killed her?"

Flell finally lifted her sword all the way, ready to defend herself. Behind her, she could hear Laela whimpering. "Please," she said. "You don't have to do this, Arren. You have a choice. Please, don't kill me. I don't want to die. I have to keep my child safe, please . . ."

Skade snarled, but Arenadd turned his head away. "Oh gods," he said. "Oh please gods, no. I can't do this. Please, master, don't make me do it. Don't make me kill her."

Skade touched his arm. "Arenadd, why do you hesitate? This woman is nothing to you; she is a Southerner, daughter to the man who betrayed you. They must all die, you have said so yourself."

Arenadd lowered the sickle and forced himself to look at Flell. "Skade, look at her. She's just a girl. She's trying to defend her baby. How could I . . . *no*." He said it sharply, almost angrily, as if he was arguing with an unheard voice. "No. I'm not a monster. I won't do it."

Flell's eyes lit up. "Yes!" she said. "Arren, yes! *Remember!* You're not a monster! You're not—*no!*"

Skade looked sharply to her right. "Arenadd!" she yelled, and pushed him aside as a grey griffin burst in from the nest, hissing and hostile.

Arenadd stumbled sideways, turning to face this new threat, while Flell screamed.

"Thrain! No!"

Skade managed to evade the enraged creature's talons as it ran to attack Arenadd. She turned, and there was Flell, sword raised and shouting.

"You filth!" Skade snarled. "You laid this trap to try and kill us!"

Flell did not hear her. In front of her, Arenadd ducked Thrain's talons and struck at her throat, trying to defend himself.

Skade's eyes narrowed, and she gripped her sword more tightly than ever. "You—"

There was a scream and a thump, and Thrain fell, blood pumping from her throat. Arenadd freed himself from her body, stumbling slightly.

"Arenadd, are you hurt?" said Skade.

"No, Skade, I—"

She turned her back on him, trembling with rage. "Well, if *you* will not kill this Southern scum, I will," she said and rushed at Flell.

Flell turned, caught by surprise. She dodged Skade's first, reckless blow, and the short sword, slicing past her arm, hit the cradle and embedded itself in the wood, the point an inch away from the infant's face.

"Not my baby!" Flell swung her own weapon, as hard as she could. Skade howled and staggered away, bleeding from a deep cut in her back.

"Skade!" Arenadd screamed.

Flell, half-mad with fear, drew her sword back and thrust. Arenadd's scream had not stopped. Flell turned, raising her arm to protect herself, but too late, too late. Arenadd's sickle found her throat, tearing it open so powerfully her head snapped back. Blood splattered over the cradle, as Flell took a step back and then slid down it onto the floor, her blue eyes still open and staring.

Arenadd did not even see her body fall. He knelt by Skade's side, reaching down to touch her face. "Skade. Skade. *Skade*."

She stirred, ever so slightly. Her silver hair was wet with blood.

Arenadd touched her chest, pulling her gown aside to see the wound. The sword had gone deep.

"Skade," he said again. "Skade, please, look at me. Please, just look at me!"

For a moment she didn't respond, but then her eyes flickered open. She turned them toward his face, just staring in silence.

Arenadd let out a hoarse sob. "Skade. Skade, can you hear me? Keep your eyes open."

Skade's eyes stayed on his face for a long moment. And, even as he looked, he saw the life drain away from behind them.

After that, everything seemed to become unreal for Arenadd.

He stood up, as if in a dream, with his sickle still clasped loosely in his hand. As if in a dream, he stepped toward the cradle where the child lay. As if in a dream, he stepped over Flell's motionless body and stood over the cradle. Inside, the child stared up at him. It had been wrapped in warm clothes, with a hood that covered the head. But the face peered through, and he could see the eyes. Blue eyes, blue as the daylight sky. The eyes of Rannagon.

Very slowly, Arenadd lowered the sickle into the cradle. He brought it down until the point was touching the soft flesh of the infant's throat. One blow and it would be done.

"Arren!"

Arenadd snapped out of the dream and looked up as two figures came rushing in—a man and a griffin.

The man stopped in the entrance, breathing harshly as he took in the bloody scene. He saw Flell. "Oh Gryphus save me," he moaned. "Flell."

Arenadd looked at him. *I knew you,* he thought.

Bran stepped closer to him. "Arren," he said. "Arren Cardockson. What have you done?"

Arenadd found his voice. "Stay back, Southerner," he said harshly. "I have the Night God's work to do."

Bran stopped. "Arren," he said. "Please. Please, don't do it. Yeh can't do it. *Don't do it.*"

Arenadd looked away from him, fixing his gaze on the child. His hand trembled. *Do it,* a voice whispered in his head. His own, or the Night God's.

"Don't do it," said Bran. "Please, don't."

Do it. Do it! *Finish it!*

"I have nothing left," Arenadd intoned in a voice that seemed to come from far away. "I have nothing but this. I must do the Night God's will. I must . . ."

Do it. Kill it.

"Arren, yeh can't," said Bran, his voice quiet and almost fatherly. "Yeh ain't no monster, Arren. Yeh never have been. The Arren I know wouldn't do this."

Arren Cardockson is dead. Do it.

"The Arren I know is a good man," said Bran. "The Arren I know wouldn't ever dream of doin' something like that."

What does it matter? Arenadd thought. *Why should I care? I'm not that man any more.*

"Arren Cardockson ain't dead," said Bran, breaking into his thoughts. "I told yeh. Arren Cardockson ain't dead, even if yeh've tried t'bury him. He's alive. He's *you*. You, Arenadd. Yeh can't make him go away, not ever. He'll always be there."

Arren Cardockson is dead, the Night God whispered.

"No!"

The word tore itself from Arenadd's throat. He lifted his arm and swung the sickle with all his might.

It flew out of his hand, spinning in the air, and hit the wall, embedding itself point first in the wood, where it stayed, quivering.

Arenadd pointed at Bran. "You," he rasped. "Southerner. I have an order for you."

Bran glanced toward the cradle. "Yes . . . my lord?"

Arenadd closed his eyes. "Take him," he muttered. "Take the child. Take him away from here. Keep him safe. Never, ever let me find him."

Bran stepped over to the cradle and lifted the child into his arms. "I will. I swear."

Arenadd walked away, toward Skade's body. "Now go," he said.

Bran hesitated. "Arren," he said. "Thank you."

Arenadd turned. *"Go!"* he screamed. "Get out of here, you Southern filth, before I kill you! Get out of my city, get out of my land, and never come back! *Go!"*

Bran, clutching the child to his chest, ran to Kraeya's side and got on her back. The red griffin lingered an instant, watching as Arenadd slumped down by Skade's side and lifted her into his arms, holding her close. Then she turned and ran away, out through the nest and onto the balcony, where she launched herself into the air and flew away.

The unpartnered tried to stop her. Some came close to catching her. But none of them succeeded, and none of them chased her far. It was almost as if there was a power protecting her and her precious burden, as she fled from Malvern as fast as her wings could take her and never looked back.

In the tower, Arenadd held Skade close. He could already feel her becoming cold and stiff in his arms. And the Dark Lord of the North, the Shadow that Walks, the man without a heart, cried.

He cried as he had not cried in years—as he had not cried even when he was alive, when there had still been a heart in his chest and he had known love and safety and friendship.

Inside, he felt the place where that heart had been become a gaping hole full of darkness and pain. It was all, all he had left now. All he was. All he had become.

Arenadd, the Night God whispered in his head. *Arenadd.*

He didn't answer her. Not now. Not any more.

Arenadd.

He reached into his robe, into the secret pocket where he kept things he might need. Inside, his fingers closed around a stone bottle, and he brought it out into the light. Inside it was all he wanted now.

He pulled the cork out and swallowed the entire contents. They burned inside him, but he welcomed the pain.

Arenadd, said the Night God.

Arenadd lifted a hand and made an obscene gesture at the empty air. "Here's to you, bitch," he snarled, and collapsed over Skade's body.

Later, when the battle was over and his friends and followers came searching, they found Lord Arenadd Taranisäii limp and cold on the floor. His skin was grey, his eyes unfocused, and there was no trace of a pulse in his neck or on his chest, where a ghastly blackened wound had cut straight through him.

Beside him, so close his outstretched hand touched its face, was the body of a large female griffin. She was slim and elegant, and her feathers were pure silver.

38

King of the North

The days that followed were joyous ones for the people of
the North.

Saeddryn, wounded but fit, took command of the undisciplined rabble now filling the city and set them to work. The
slaves, accustomed to doing as they were told, systematically
searched through the city, uncovering every surviving Southerner still left. They searched the Eyrie as well and found a
handful of griffiners who had attempted to hide rather than
fight.

They weren't killed, not yet. Saeddryn had them taken to
the old councillors' chamber, and once they had been secured
around the Mistress' platform, the slaves entered, too. They
flocked into the gallery, and when that was full they filled the
space down on the floor as well and had to be kept away from
the griffiners by a line of guards.

Many of them tried to push past the barrier, screaming
insults and threats at the humiliated griffiners. Most of the
griffiners stood arrogantly tall, pretending not to hear their
bloodthirsty voices. The griffins hissed through the ropes holding their beaks shut.

Saeddryn, with Aenae beside her, looked grimly at them.
With her were Iorwerth and Kaanee, both injured, Torc, Iekee,

Hyrenna, Nerth, Garnoc, Cai, Hafwen and Yorath. Skandar's other son, Eerak, had been killed in the fighting.

Saeddryn didn't wait for silence; she knew she wouldn't get it.

She turned to face the griffiners. "Ye've been beaten," she told them, her voice strong enough for them all to hear. She was speaking griffish, and the griffiners started in outrage at the sound of it. "Aye, I speak griffish," said Saeddryn. "Taught t'me by my mother, Arddryn Taranisäii. She fought for the freedom of the North an' failed only because of the cowardice of yer ancestors. In a fair fight, a true warrior always wins, an' ye are no warriors. But the North has always bred warriors, an' ye could never make us forget it. That's why ye've lost."

"You won by your own evil," one griffiner said coldly. "And the evil of the Dark Lord."

There were angry shouts from the Northerners within earshot.

"Be quiet," said Saeddryn. "Say whatever bitter, arrogant things ye like after this is over."

"Well, kill us then," said the griffiner. "Kill us like the cowards you are."

Saeddryn laughed. "Why? Why would we want t'do that when ye're so much more useful alive? Nerth." She nodded to him, and he came toward her, holding a large sack.

Saeddryn accepted it and reached inside. "We've devised a punishment," she said. "For ye. As a reminder. As a sign to those who see ye. Garnoc?"

Garnoc nodded grimly and turned to look at the brazier burning beside him. "It's ready."

"Good. Iorwerth?"

Iorwerth stepped up and took a griffiner from the group, hauling him forward by the shoulder. He came readily enough, obviously realising it was futile to resist.

"Ye can do it now, Garnoc," said Saeddryn.

Garnoc grinned nastily. As the griffiner was brought to the brazier, he took the man by the wrist. With his other hand, he pulled a long metal rod out of the coals. On the end was a small symbol, glowing red hot. The griffiner's eyes widened at the sight of it, and he tried to break free, but Iorwerth grabbed his other arm and twisted it behind his back.

"Don't worry," said Garnoc. "It won't hurt forever. Just a whole lot, for a long time."

He pressed the brand into the back of the man's hand and held it there.

The victim screamed, long before the smell of burning flesh had begun to rise. The people nearby grimaced in disgust, some rubbing their noses.

Finally, Garnoc withdrew the brand and put it back into the brazier. "Collar's next," he said, and the man was hauled away to stand in front of Saeddryn again.

She reached into the sack and pulled out a heavy metal ring. A slave collar, still hanging open, the spikes inside it sharp but crudely made, so that they were rough and serrated at the edges.

Saeddryn smiled coldly. "I'm sure ye'll be able to live with it," she said. "An' if it gets infected . . . what's one less slave?"

The man screamed. "No! Don't!"

His pleading was in vain. Saeddryn stepped forward and snapped the collar shut around his neck. The spikes went deep, and stayed there.

"Take him away," she said, waving a dismissive hand, and the man was led, shaking with pain and shock, back to his place, while the crowd jeered.

"Next!" said Saeddryn.

And so, despite their screams and threats, the griffiners who had survived the sack of Malvern were brought forward one by one to receive Saeddryn's punishment. A brand and a collar each.

When it was done, Saeddryn confronted the row of bleeding, shivering griffiners, some of them openly sobbing.

"Now ye've suffered the pain yer kind inflicted on generations of our people," she told them. "Now ye've felt our humiliation. Now listen."

They listened, most of them pale with fear.

"I'd keep ye," said Saeddryn. "An' see what work I could get out of ye, but everyone knows griffiners don't know the meanin' of hard work. Without yer precious power, without slaves t'care for ye, ye're useless."

One of them broke down. "Please don't kill us," he sobbed. "*Please!* For pity's sake!"

Saeddryn stroked Aenae's sleek shoulder. "Why bother?" she said. "No. My friends an' I have decided. Ye—all of ye—are banished. Get back on yer griffins an' fly out of here, an' don't stop flyin' until the Northgates are behind ye. An' never come back." She leant closer, her face twitching with passion. "Go back to the South, sun worshippers."

L ater, once the griffiners had fled, Saeddryn turned to the crowd of baying slaves.

"Now!" she yelled. "I bid ye come t'us. One by one, come an' be given yer reward for what ye have done. In the name of great Lord Arenadd and the Mighty Skandar, come!"

And the slaves came. One by one, they came.

Garnoc was ready for them. Iorwerth and Torc would hold each slave by the shoulders to steady him, while the big Northerner struck, just once, with a heavy metal hammer. And one by one the collars broke and fell away. One by one, the slaves were set free.

A nd, somewhere, lost and utterly alone, Arenadd spun through the darkness.

But no. Not alone. Never alone. Never.

The Night God hovered above him, whispering his name. *Arenadd. Arenadd. Sweet Arenadd.*

Arenadd said nothing. He turned away from her in the void, crying for his Skade, not knowing or caring about the Night God or the North or even Skandar.

Arenadd. Arenadd, you have done so well. I am so happy. Arenadd, listen . . .

"*Go away!*" Arenadd screamed. "Leave me alone! I never want to see you again, understand?"

But she would not leave. *Arenadd,* she said.

Arenadd sobbed harder. "Skade is dead. My heart is dead. I have nothing left."

You have me, said the Night God. *And you always shall.*

"Why should I care?"

Because you have done my will, and you have fulfilled all your promises. She laughed—a light, joyful laugh. *My strength returns, Arenadd! My people are rising! Their souls have awakened once more; their pride has come back! The North is free! And you have done this, Arenadd, my sweet Arenadd. You have done this for me, and for them. I am so grateful to you.*

He turned on her, his eyes burning with insanity. "Then kill me," he said. "If you're grateful to me, *kill me*! Let me die! *Please*, kill me."

Arenadd, I cannot do that.

"Of course you can't," he snarled. "I'm already dead. Leave me, then."

I shall not, she said. *Arenadd, why do you rage?*

"Skade is dead! Don't you understand, you heartless witch? She's *dead*. The only woman I ever loved is dead. You should have protected her! Why didn't you do something?"

I cannot give life, she said. *You know that. I can only take it away.*

"Then you wanted her to die?" said Arenadd. "Then you *willed* it?" But his rage couldn't last. He wanted to scream at the Night God, to vent all the horror inside him and free himself from it forever. But he didn't have the will. As he shouted at her, his voice broke and he collapsed, sobbing again.

Come, the Night God whispered. *Let me comfort you.*

Arenadd no longer had the strength to resist. He pressed himself against her, and she held him, embracing him as Skade might have done. Her touch was icy cold, but it soothed him.

My poor, sweet child, she said. *My Arenadd, my love. You have fought so bravely, so long. You have given all you have.*

Arenadd relaxed into her as he cried. "Skade. Oh, Skade. Why?"

Death is a mystery, said the Night God. *Like life.*

"Where is she?" said Arenadd. "Where did she go?"

Skade was a woman, but she had the spirit of a griffin, said the Night God. *Like all griffins, she will become a part of the land and its magic forever.*

"No," said Arenadd. He sobbed harder. "No. Not that. Don't let her fade away. Please. I want to see her again. I want—"

Aaahhh . . . the Night God sighed, her breath a cold night breeze. *Arenadd, in return for what you have done and as a favour to Skade, who helped you so faithfully, I shall grant that wish. I shall gather her soul to me and take it into the heavens as a star. When you look upward at night, she will be there by my eye, looking down upon you.*

Arenadd shuddered. "Thank you . . . master."

The Night God was still for a long time. Finally, she stirred. *And now I think it is time for you to awaken, Arenadd.*

Arenadd tensed. "No. I don't want to go back."

You have left your body helpless, said the Night God. *Your friends think you are dead. If you do not hurry, they shall burn or bury you.*

"Good," Arenadd said flatly. "Let them do it. Let me stay dead, forever."

She laughed softly. *Oh, Arenadd.*

Hope rose inside him. "I can stay? As a reward—you'll let me stay here? You'll let me sleep forever? You'll give me peace?"

The Night God rose. *You still have work to do, Arenadd,* she said, and pushed him away from her.

And Arenadd fell. The void rushed past him, and he saw the Night God above, her light still bright but growing further and further away.

"Curse you!" he screamed.

His fall ended in a sickening thud.

A renadd tried to move, and when he did he felt as if there was a terrible weight dragging him down.

He knew it was his body. His cursed body.

It jerked into a sitting position, driven by his will and by the Night God's magic. The eyes opened.

Arenadd awoke.

He lifted a hand and rubbed it over his face; it felt cold and stiff. But it was becoming more supple already. He took his hand away and looked around, wondering where he was.

He was sitting on a stone slab in a darkened room, and though it was too dark to see much, he could sense other slabs around him. Each one had an occupant.

Arenadd slid off his slab and onto the floor, and stretched. His back ached, and the wound Erian's sword had left was full of dull, burning pain.

Arenadd rubbed it and started to look for a way out of the room.

There was a door not far away. He pushed it open and went through.

Beyond was a corridor; it looked vaguely familiar, and Arenadd followed it. He wasn't aware of it, but he still moved like a predator.

The corridor took him upward, into what he eventually realised was the Council's Tower. It was still standing, then.

There didn't seem to be anyone around. When he reached the entrance to the councillors' chamber, he could hear noise coming from the other side. He stopped and pressed his ear against the door and heard voices. Hundreds of voices, *thousands* of voices. Human, and griffin as well.

He was about to straighten up and open the door when he heard one voice in particular, rising above the crowd. Eventually the crowd went quiet, listening.

". . . shall take axes and fire to this cursed place."

Saeddryn.

Arenadd listened more closely.

"As the great Arenadd would have wished, we shall tear this city apart," Saeddryn declared. "And when we are done, we shall make true Northern homes on this spot."

Arenadd straightened up. "As the great Arenadd would have wished?" he repeated to himself. "Nice, Saeddryn. Very nice. But perhaps I can help you there."

He checked himself to make sure he looked presentable: fortunately, someone had washed him and put a clean robe on him. He smiled slightly in satisfaction, pushed the door open and went in.

They didn't see him at first, but he saw Saeddryn, standing on the platform with Aenae and still speaking to the crowd. ". . . shall make this land ours again!" she said. "Once Malvern has been levelled—"

Arenadd strode toward her. "Excuse me, cousin," he said. "But I don't think that *is* what I said I wanted."

Saeddryn stopped dead, and turned. Her eye widened in horror. *"Arenadd!"*

Screams and shouts came from the gallery. Around the platform, Garnoc, Iorwerth, Torc and the others gaped at Arenadd as if they were seeing a ghost.

Arenadd pushed past them and climbed onto the platform. "Hello, Saeddryn. I was wondering if you could tell me—"

She pulled away from him, openly frightened. "Arenadd. How . . . how . . ."

Arenadd sighed. "The Night God has sent me back, Saeddryn. It would seem she still has more for me to do. Where's Skandar?"

"Wh—" Saeddryn, pale faced, managed to pull herself together. "He's alive, but unconscious. We don't know if he'll wake."

Arenadd nodded. "He will." He glanced down and saw his sickle hanging from her belt. He reached down and took it. "Ah, there it is. Thank you for looking after it. Now." He turned to face the crowd, which had begun to shout his name. "I'm sorry I haven't been here for a while," he told them. "But I'm back, and I feel much better now."

The crowd had risen to its feet. *"Arenadd! Arenadd! Lord Arenadd!"*

Arenadd glanced at Saeddryn, then looked at the crowd again.

Then he knelt. "My friends," he told them. "My followers . . . you have won this war for me, and won your own freedom. I, Arenadd Taranisäii, have done everything in my power to help you. Now I have come back, to give you my thanks. And to offer you my service again." Silence had fallen, and he raised his head. "My people. Men and women of the North . . . I am yours. What would you have me do? What do you want from me? I am your servant now. Give me my orders."

Silence. Deep, dark silence.

Then a voice came. Not from the crowd.

"King Arenadd!" it shouted.

Iorwerth. He stepped forward, his fist raised. "King Arenadd!" he said again. "King of the North! King of Darkmen!"

The crowd heard him, and they took up the cry—more and more of them, louder and louder, until the chamber rang with it.

"King Arenadd! King Arenadd. Taranisäii! King of the North! King of Tara!"

Arenadd felt a shudder of misery inside him. He stood up. "Then so be it!" he called back, raising his sickle in the air. "If you would have me be your king, then I shall be."

Saeddryn paused for a moment, obviously taken aback. But then she came to Arenadd's side and took hold of his other hand, raising it into the air along with her own. "King Arenadd!" she shouted. "We shall make him king!"

Outwardly, Arenadd's face was full of triumph and pride. Inside, his dead heart shrivelled with despair. *Gods save me,* he thought.

When the crowd had begun to quieten, Arenadd looked

quickly at them. He knew that whatever he said in the next few moments would be remembered forever. Later on there would be arguments and debates, but for this brief time they would do whatever he said.

"My cousin Saeddryn said we would destroy this city," he said. "I heard her as I came in, saying we would raze Malvern to the ground."

"Aye," said Saeddryn, her eye shining. "Malvern will be destroyed, along with every one of the cities the Southerners built, an' we shall live the way darkmen were meant to live, among the trees an' the mountains."

Arenadd laughed. "Destroy it?" he said. "Destroy Malvern, after we fought so hard to win it? No!"

Saeddryn paused. "What, sir?"

"I'm not going to destroy Malvern!" said Arenadd. "I'm going to *live* in it!"

The crowd had gone quiet.

"We will not destroy Malvern," Arenadd called. "We will make it our own. This is a good city, strong and well built. I will make this the seat of my government, along with all the cities the griffiners built. Tara will be a great land under our rule, and we will show the world that we can be as wealthy and powerful as any one of the griffiner states in the South. *That* is what we will do!"

In the cheering that followed, Arenadd turned to look at his councillors. Iorwerth, Garnoc and Torc both looked excited. But Saeddryn, Cai and Nerth looked utterly dismayed.

Arenadd ignored them. He had known some of them wouldn't like it, but they would have to put up with it. Tara would never survive unless it adopted the ways of its neighbours and learnt how to defend itself. The old ways were dead. This was the way of the future. The griffiners had been right about that, at least.

Afterward, when he had finished making his proclamations, Arenadd slipped into the shadows and escaped from the councillors' chamber. Unseen, he darted away through the corridors until he had found Skandar.

The dark griffin had flown to the top of the Council's Tower, into the massive nest that had once belonged to his father. Even though he could not have known that this was where the Mighty Kraal had lived, some part of him must have sensed that this, the highest and best of the griffin roosts in the Eyrie, was now his by rights.

Arenadd walked through the marble-lined audience chamber, admiring its design. Yes, this would be a good place to live. The Eyrie Mistress' old bedroom beyond it looked comfortable enough. But he would have to replace most of the furniture. No matter.

He passed through the archway and into the nest, and there was Skandar, curled up in the straw as though asleep.

Arenadd went to him. "Skandar. Dear old Skandar."

Skandar's massive flanks rose and fell with each breath. There were deep wounds on the back of his neck and on his belly, but Arenadd knew he would survive them. After all, few griffins were as tough as a wild griffin, and Skandar had been blessed by the moon.

Arenadd sat down beside him and patted his shoulder. "You fought so well, Skandar. You're already a legend." He made a bitter half-laughing sound. "And so am I."

He waited by him for a long time, unspeaking.

At last, Skandar stirred, and his eye slid open and focused. "Human," he croaked.

Arenadd touched his head. "It's over, Skandar," he said. "We've won."

Skandar blinked. "Win?"

"Yes. The war is over, and the North is ours. Skandar, listen. They've made me king. Your human is a king. And you, Skandar . . . you own this land now. It's your territory, forever."

The dark griffin sighed. "Home," he said. "Home."

Arenadd felt tears burning in his eyes. "Yes," he said. "We're home now, Skandar."

Home.

King Arenadd Taranisäii the First was crowned two days later in the councillors' chamber, at night, when the moon shone through the openings in the ceiling.

He stood on the Eyrie Mistress' platform with Skandar

beside him and the council standing in a ring around them, while Saeddryn began the ceremony, speaking the ancient Northern words that had been passed down through generations but had not been used in hundreds of years.

Up in the gallery, the witnesses had gathered. Former slaves, former renegades, former vassals, with the unpartnered sitting among them wherever they chose. Now all of them were free citizens of Tara's new kingdom.

Skandar looked up at the griffins with pride. His fur and feathers were neat and shining with health, and his stance was regal and proud. Gold, silver and copper rings gleamed on his powerful forelegs. He looked like the most magnificent Eyrie Master who had ever lived.

Beside him, Arenadd, too, stood tall. His hair was glossy from a morning of patient grooming, and his beard had been trimmed to a perfect point. He wore a brand new robe, embroidered with gold and silver spirals. A golden collar hid the scars on his neck. Perhaps he had been a filthy rebel once or a fugitive criminal, but now he looked like a lord. More than that.

Saeddryn spoke the last of the ceremonial words as she stepped up onto the platform, holding a silver circlet in her hands.

"May ye be judge and warlord, master and protector; may ye care for yer people above all else; may ye live long and shield us from misfortune." Arenadd bowed his head, and she placed the circlet there, so that it rested on his forehead. "Rise, King Arenadd Taranisäii the First, ruler of Tara," she intoned.

Arenadd stood.

"Hail King Arenadd!" Iorwerth shouted. *"Hail!"*

The crowd roared.

Arenadd looked up at them, at his subjects bellowing his name, their faces alight with joy mixed with awe. He saw men and women swearing their undying loyalty and devotion, giving him all the power the Night God had ever promised. Among them the griffins screeched Skandar's name, and he screeched back. This was everything Skandar had always wanted, everything his partnership with Arenadd had earnt him.

But Arenadd couldn't look any more. He bowed his head and stared at the floor, so that none of them would see the tears in his eyes.

"Skade," he whispered. "Skade . . ."

* * *

Far away, beyond the Northgate Mountains, in a moulder-
ing barn, Branton Redguard huddled into a corner to try to
shelter from the rain. Kraeya stood nearby, keeping watch, her
tail twitching.

"It's all right," Bran mumbled, again and again. "It's all
right."

But the child in his arms would not stop crying.

Bran felt the tears aching in his own throat, but he didn't
let them out. "It's all right, Laela." He held her close. "Laela,
yer safe. I swear. I'll keep yeh safe. He can't find yeh here,
never . . ."

But the child cried on.

About the Author

> "A lot of fantasy authors take their
> inspiration from Tolkien. I take mine from
> G. R. R. Martin and Finnish metal."

Born in Canberra, Australia, in 1986, Katie J. Taylor attended
Radford College, where she wrote her first novel, *The Land
of Bad Fantasy*, which was published in 2006. She studied
for a bachelor's degree in communications at the University
of Canberra and graduated in 2007 before going on to do a
graduate certificate in editing in 2008. K. J. Taylor writes at
midnight and likes to wear black.

For news and author contact, visit
www.kjtaylor.com.

**Don't miss
the first book in the Fallen Moon series**

K. J. TAYLOR

The Dark Griffin

THE FALLEN MOON, BOOK ONE

Despite his Northerner slave origins, Arren Cardockson
has managed to become a griffiner. With his griffin,
Eluna, he oversees trade in the city of Eagleholm, but
he knows his Northern appearance means he will never
be fully respected. When Arren and Eluna are sent to
capture a rogue griffin, Arren sees a chance to earn
some money and some respect, but his meeting with
the mysterious black griffin begins a dangerous chain
of events . . .

Available now from Ace Books

M774T0910